THE LAST TRAIN OUT OF HELL

A NOVEL

JULIE PRICE CARPENTER

HIGH FREQUENCY PRESS

PRAISE FOR *THE LAST TRAIN OUT OF HELL*

"Julie Carpenter's *The Last Train Out of Hell* holds a cracked mirror to the bleak landscape of 21st century America and the lost souls damned to exist here. Carpenter's Hell, like our Earth, has bad food, bad beer, bad TV, cranky bureaucrats, and a host of beautifully drawn characters who light up the novel, but alongside whom you would not want to spend eternity. Still, impossibly, for Brian, an affable demon in high-end management, and Liz, a mousy librarian whose last act on earth was an absent-minded step in front of a bus, there is also a chance at love. Unfortunately, all bad things must finally end, and, bringing Hell's continued existence into question, is an ancient mystery. Just why are there train tracks going both into and out of Hell and what might that mean for all the souls and demons in danger of oblivion along with the underworld they call home? Carpenter, the brilliant satirist behind the short story collection, *Things Get Weird in Whistlestop*, of a few years back, writes like an angel and proves her mastery of long-form fiction with her debut novel. One hopes that, Satan willing, there will be more to come."

—Jeff Weddle, author of *When Giraffes Flew*

"Julie Carpenter's outlandish rendering of hell is somehow uncannily believable, with relatable characters trying to solve an enthralling mystery.

—Bill Ectric, author of *Tamper*, and *Tamper Illustrated*

"*The Last Train Out of Hell* is sweet, sharp and subversively silly: come for the codependent cat demon, stay for the send-up of reductive dogma that would have us divide people into 'good' and 'bad.' Julie Price Carpenter's characters are just ordinary folks, gathered here to get through this thing called the afterlife. Fans of Terry Pratchett and Douglas Adams, this book is for you!"

—M.B. Valente, author of *"Four Words" Pithead Chapel*

"*The Last Train Out of Hell* is a delight from start to finish. Equal parts whimsy, sass, and sacrilege, it's a novel you won't soon forget. It's the book you want to talk about at work. It's the novel you wanted to read in school. But most of all, it's the novel you absolutely will not be able to put down. A fast-paced story that utilizes every single page to its advantage, the characters and the maps of Hell are a little bit what you expect, a lot what you don't, and usually hit way too close to home. It's 'The Office' meets Dante's *Inferno*. It's 'Parks and Recreation' meets *Needful Things*. It's everything the critics love about HBO and everything the fans love about Netflix, all mixed into one bonkers tale of the foreclosure of the least happy possibility after we bite the dust.

Fans of Stephen King, Joe Hill, and Chuck Palahniuk will love this adventure. The topics covered are both timely and timeless, giving us some much-needed light in these very dark times. The protagonist compels us to want more. The work is sharp and hip, the social commentary thought-provoking and laugh-out-loud funny, and the characters will stick with you for days after you finish you reading. Especially Dennis, the dragon/cat/pet/pest. In a world where work seems to be endless and the leaders seem to all be incompetent, look no further than Hell itself for the root of all silliness. I never knew I needed a love story set in the worst possible place until I read this book. Julie Carpenter has truly delivered a terrific story that will simultaneously bring you to tears of laughter and inspire you to rise up and lead and lead a little bit of a rebellion, consequences, and our souls, be damned."

—Jeff Hill, author of *Dead Socials*

"You think YOUR commute is bad? Demons, monsters, and bureaucracy collide with comedic chaos in *The Last Train Out of Hell* when newly-dead Liz arrives in Hell. Certain she doesn't belong there, Liz does her best to fit in and even finds a potential love interest in manager Brian, but her arrival heralds a much bigger problem—Hell is crumbling under the weight of its denizens, and if they don't figure out how to stop it, everyone will cease to exist entirely.

Equal parts charming and absurd, *The Last Train Out of Hell* proves that even in the depths of the underworld, there's always room for redemption and courage. Fans of 'The Good Place' will find their hearts hearts warmed (by the fires of the inferno).

—Lindz McLeod, author of *Sunbathers*

For my husband, Blake, who got dragged into Hell more times than anyone should have to while I was writing this book.

And for the kids—Evangeline, Essie, Josh, and Jarad—whom I pestered mercilessly with requests for feedback and weird discussions about the afterlife.

And for Crow and Willard, the cats who helped supervise this trip to the Underworld while sitting on my shoulder and whispering advice.

Of all the novels I've read in the past few years, I can't think of another that is so *of its time*, so pertinent to the moment, as Julie Price Carpenter's *The Last Train Out of Hell*. My old teaching colleague and fellow writer, William John Watkins, used to tell me "Irony is the engine of the world." And it is the engine of Carpenter's Hell, the setting of this book. Why 'irony?' Because it is the only antidote to deep cynicism. There is an analytical element to it, a comparison, that reveals the hypocrisy and immorality of a narcissist like Satan. The only thing that disarms them is an innate humor that comes with an ironic approach. They can't tolerate being laughed at. At the same time, *Last Train* pits self-sacrifice, the greater good and the friendship of individuals against an immense bureaucracy of neglect, cruelty, and selfishness. For our times, this novel seems almost radical in its outlook.

But forget about that and follow the story for the enjoyment of Liz Martin's adventure in the underworld, as a new intake in Hell. This imagined landscape—Perdition City and its environs, the overcrowded train station with its hordes of new conscripts for punishment arriving like clockwork on engine #13, teeming streets, the abandoned ticket booths and oozing bathrooms. Let's not forget the other worldly yet familiar demons. The description of place and character is what first ensnared me in the novel. Carpenter's wonderful imagination gives the reader succinct detail and a smooth style that so rivets you in the story, you might have daydreams that you were once actually there. In reading, I could feel the vastness of the layout of the city. And the enormity of the ubiquitously mentioned Admin Building—sort of like Kafka's novel, *The Castle*—where everything important happens, but the line to get there is years long.

The story is wonderfully entertaining and surprising. I was never certain where it was going to take me. Once the characters were introduced, though, and introduced so completely through those powers of description I mention above, I had no trouble following them through the madness of Hell and all its permutations. As I've noted, humor is at work here in a very integral way, but the novel is not a comedy, per se. The finality of death and the impossibility of escaping the grim punishments and torment of Hell always linger in the background and create a tension against the ironic laughs. Carpenter knows how to deal out the weird and unsettling, but in a strange sense it never reaches a point where it doesn't remind us in some way of our current lives. I was on hold on the phone with Medicare the other day, and for a few moments could have sworn I was trying to get through to the Admin Building in Perdition City.

All Aboard!

—Jeffrey Ford

Author of *Big Dark Hole* and
Ahab's Return: Or, The Last Voyage

ONE

The Train Station

THE TRAIN JERKED INTO THE STATION. THE DOORS opened and belched out a payload of souls. A gaggle of demons stood next to the defunct ticket counter, smoking, completely disregarding the incoming hordes, while nearby a thick, green liquid oozed out of the men's room.

Brian, who had just walked into the station that morning, frowned. "Hogshead?" he asked a demon who'd just tossed his cigarette and was grinding it into the pavement with his hoof. "Has anyone checked the restrooms today? Do I see slime bubbling out of the men's?"

The stocky, blue demon scratched a bump next to his right horn and shrugged. Then he thumbed the loin cloth out of his nether regions.

"For Satan's sake," Brian hissed at Hogshead. "Get Georgie and have him check. Great Lucifer only knows what's down there. If a bog eel took a wrong turn in the sewer system again, half of Perdition City will be backed up by the end of the day."

Hogshead shrugged and readjusted his loincloth. And shuffled off indifferently.

"Get to work, guys!" Brian called to the rest of the infernal workers.

Demons dawdled sullenly, crushing cigarettes under cloven hooves, but each eventually picked up pitchfork or pike and shuffled towards disembarking souls. Brian sighed, noted that the racks of photocopied maps needed to be refilled, sighed again. He scribbled *Maps* in his notebook, although he'd just lost his umpteenth assistant. Who could he send back with maps and brochures? The line at the help desk, a year long, was growing again, winding out of the Admin Building and around several city blocks where demons had set up food carts with chewy burnt hot dogs, flat sodas, and soggy chips, and tacky gift shops with cheap mugs and t-shirts for sale.

Demons were terrible at paperwork; they didn't have the necessary patience and attention to detail. They constantly effed-up or walked off jobs. Brian thought a soul might be better, but ever since he'd been created for his job, he'd never seen one working in Admin. He supposed he could ask Satan. That was more trouble than it was worth and would imply his own incompetence. Besides, he had been formed to carry out regulations, not to ask questions, even though infernal guidelines were in such knots from being bent to Satan's will that untangling them was almost impossible and often required groveling to the big guy. Breathe, he told himself. Worry about personnel changes later. He wondered why—since he'd been specially created to manage Hell—he was so badly behind.

The Train Station was on the eastern outskirts of Hell. There was only one train: Old Number 13, always coming in, leaving multitudes of souls. And eternally returning from whence it came—empty. Hell was a one-way destination. Pulled by an ancient steam engine, no match for the rest of the Hellscape, the train daily belched out its payload of souls onto the dilapidated platform.

The tracks ran into Perdition City station through two steep, red, rocky banks, bubbling with blood-red lava that seemed to come from nowhere and go nowhere, upon which swarms of small crimson demons clambered and scurried, switching their forked tails and brandishing pitchforks. They spat out poisonous green clouds, mostly for show, and their razor-sharp teeth kept the hillsides littered with bones. They were tasked with keeping the recently deceased from running back into the tunnels or climbing up the banks to escape.

This was Hell as marketed in the Upper World. What the residents considered *true* Hell, a region of indescribable, ineffable torment, was farther in and deeper down. If you could a get birds-eye view of the whole land, maybe from a helicopter or something—*not* as a passenger on the Hellicopter rides advertised at the Train Station, a mistake that could ruin your entire afterlife—you would see a sinkhole: a yawning, black cavity in the space/time/infinity continuum.

From the edge of this vast hole in the belly of Hell, a soul would see sharp-edged rocks, shaped like teeth, shallow pools carved out from the walls by acid. From one side, the gushing crimson Lava Fall from the Lake of Fire tumbled down the dark hole, eventually swallowed up by the gaping maw. On the opposite side, the invisible River Nepenthe poured chill torrents into the abyss. Once a soul fell in, it would be burned, frozen, then doused with the waters of forgetfulness. No one could say with absolute certainty what, if anything, was left of a soul afterwards, because no soul had ever returned from the bottom. It was assumed that what waited at the bottom was—nothing. Nonexistence.

A few souls arrived in Hell with the goal of annihilation, a pressing need to become nothing. They disembarked the train, felt the magnetic pull of the cold dead heart of nonbeing, and flung themselves over the edge—no hesitation. However, most of the damned and even the demons avoided the Abyss at all costs. Though the rules of Hell were byzantine, and constantly bent or broken to suit Satan's whims, one rule that remained constant was that no soul or demon, no matter what infraction was committed, could be thrown into the Abyss against their will.

Nevertheless, the great nothing was a constant backdrop to life in the infernal lands. No one questioned anymore why Hell had been built on this plot in the Netherworld. Only Satan and three executive members of the board—Mammon, Beelzebub, and Lucifer—knew exactly how Hell Incorporated had been founded: real estate deals, grant money, and charters were lost within the mists of eternity. If it had occurred to anyone in the infernal lands to wonder whether Satan had thought every cunning plan all the way through, they were unlikely to voice the concern. Like other rules in Hell, administration and staff rarely understood why and it made everyone's life easier to avoid questions. Questioning Satan, Lord of Darkness, King of Hell himself, was a one-way ticket to a job in the Western Wilds or Bogs of Despair.

As manager of Hell, Brian had unspoken questions, drowning as he was in too much work, not enough budget. Regardless, he did his best to follow the rules and take care of the inhabitants of his dark, sad corner of the Netherworld. He always wore a cardigan with elbow patches and a bow tie that matched the patches, with boring brown lace-up oxfords, neither athletic nor dressy. He felt the outfit put souls at their ease and distinguished him from the demons, goblins, and the other beings who were in his charge. Compared to the rest of the staff, he was a normal, albeit slightly geeky guy. No horns, no hooves. His only distinctive feature was that he was almost seven feet tall, and a little stooped. Sandy blond hair, and tortoise shell glasses completed the picture. He'd been created for this position and for whatever reason, Satan thought it best to have him appear human.

One of Brian's many jobs was supervising the influx of souls. Today he was making a scheduled inspection of the Perdition City Train Station; inspections were required twice a decade to make sure the blue Baalzephon demons, in charge of security and intake, were carrying out their duties to some bare minimum standard. They never were.

Each time he visited the station and saw souls pouring off the train in an inexorable, swelling river, Brian's anxiety grew. Every century the population of Hell increased. The budget never did. Over the last few trainloads, he'd noticed even more of an uptick. He always told himself that somehow things would work out. The sentiment was beginning to feel less reassuring.

During his last teleconference with Satan, he'd dared to express stress over the budget. Satan lectured him. "Any anxiety you feel is simply an unwanted byproduct of your creation. To create a good manager, you have to throw in a little angst, otherwise you don't get someone who cares about the work. Your feelings, though necessary, are meaningless to me. Get back to work."

Satan told him the budget didn't need to expand—his theory being that, eventually, greater numbers meant more misery. The more miserable the souls were, the more of them would decide that becoming nothing was preferable to the mere thread of existence they maintained in Hell. If souls were miserable enough to toss themselves over the edge of the Abyss, Satan argued, Brian's problem would be solved.

The problem was that few souls chose nonexistence—perhaps half a percentage point as population density rose—not enough to make a meaningful difference. Brian shipped souls without housing to the Western Wilds every day with no solid plan as to how they were to be housed or adequately punished.

Satan hadn't created him to *think*, Brian reminded himself. He'd been rendered existent to carry out a specific set of duties. He was made for Hell. He took out his black leather notebook and glanced at the checklist:

1. Garbage
2. Lost luggage collection
3. Repairs
4. Greet group of new citizens
5. Mingle
6. Maps

He added #7. Check restrooms. Then crossed it off. He often added completed tasks to his list to cross them off simply because it was so satisfying.

The rusted black sides and crooked smokestack of Old Number 13 had seen better days, but the train still huffed its way from the Valley of the Shadow of Life and Death every day, laden with the damned. Today, yet another throng of souls poured from the train doors. The wraith engineer tipped its cap and gave Brian a wave. He waved back and noted that one of the benches on the platform was rotten. He put it on his list, even though the budget wouldn't cover new benches.

With sudden decisiveness, he made a note to have Georgie remove them entirely. He wasn't even sure why they were there in the first place; passengers arrived at the station and were immediately herded into the city to await their eternal destinations. The benches, like the ticket counter, were holdovers from when Hell first opened.

The disintegrating welcome sign, rusting fences, rotten benches all made his anxiety spike. He didn't know how to stop the decay without more funding. Something needed to give. He just hoped it wasn't him.

TWO

Liz Makes a Mistake

WHILE BRIAN WAS CHECKING OFF HIS LIST, A WHOLE NEW group of souls was starting eternity. Some had led fascinating lives in the Upper World before disembodiment—but many, if not most, had led quiet, plain, boring lives. In the Upper World, it was often assumed that the more fascinating a life you'd led, the more likely your train ticket to the afterlife would be stamped with glowing red flames instead of a golden harp. Therefore, whole factions of people up top had devoted themselves to living the most boring lives possible, eschewing vulgar language, alcohol, parties, the more creative expressions of human sexual urges—in other words, fun. Many of these people were now disembarking the train as well. Shortly after stepping onto the platform, they were going to feel wildly cheated.

Elizabeth Rose Martin, twenty-seven years old at the time of her disembodiment, was among those riding Old Number 13. She hadn't been especially religious. Neither had she been especially rebellious or wicked. She'd been a librarian in the Upper World, in the Midwestern city of Chicago, the place of her birth. A soft-spoken introvert, her father's pet name for her was "Mouse"—partly because of her small stature, dark brown hair, and eyes, and partly because as a child instead of being able to articulate distressed thoughts, she often made a squeaking sound, a habit that sadly followed her into her adult years.

If you asked any number of friends and acquaintances for a list of the most interesting people they knew, Liz wouldn't have cracked the top one hundred for any of them. To top it all off, her life hadn't even ended in some sort of romantic tragedy that might have made up for the tedium which preceded it; she'd been hit by a bus. She had no famous last words, or indeed any last words. Having been upset with her boyfriend, Rob, the previous night, she had not woken him to say goodbye on the morning of her death. She'd spent the last few seconds of existence on a hot street corner, waiting to cross, trying frantically to remember if she'd put on deodorant and digging through her purse for a band-aid because her left pinky toe had a blister from her new sandals.

On the day of Brian's inspection, Liz exited Old Number 13 with everyone else. Her senses were immediately assaulted by pungent smells: burnt matches, weeks-old garbage, something dead and distinctly fishy. The multitude of exiting passengers pushed forward from the door as if squeezed out of a tube of toothpaste, thrusting Liz before them. Her memories of the train ride itself were very vague. She remembered another station, a crush of strangers, and staring at a ticket in her hand—then a dim green light and the rushing of wheels. Now the overpowering smell of trash roused her to her new existence.

The first thing passengers saw upon reaching the platform was a wooden sign that hung in two pieces from a rusted steel wall. It loomed over an abandoned, dilapidated ticket counter building, blocking any view beyond it. The slogan was hard to make out as the middle of the sign was burnt. Grimy ash-covered wooden letters spelled out WELC on one side. ELL, said the other. Wire waste cans spewed tickets, gum, train schedules, cans, and bottles onto grimy concrete.

Liz stepped into the chaos, trying to get her bearings. Who were all these people—was that gigantic man wearing a loincloth? Were her eyes deceiving her, or was he blue? Was he even a man? Someone pushed her from behind. She noticed belatedly that, like everyone else, her hand was wrapped around the handle of a rolling suitcase. A tag bearing her name fluttered against her wrist. She didn't remember packing. Everything up to the moment she disembarked the train was fuzzy.

"Holy fuck! Quit pushing!" someone screamed.

The crowd continued surging off the train, pushing her forward on a wave of panic.

"For Christ's sake," a man spat into her ear, "faster! They'll crush us."

Liz tripped and nearly fell on a splintered, ash-coated bench. She managed to regain her balance. Another push wrenched the suitcase handle out of her grasp. Her luggage was gone before she even had a chance to see what she'd packed.

There was no use trying to get it back. One of the large blue creatures was fighting over the case with a passenger, a well-dressed woman in a suit with luggage of her own, expensively yet conservatively dressed, like a bank manager or an accountant. They had already pulled it open and were fighting over the contents. A pair of Liz's underpants fluttered down the tracks. The demon grabbed a shoe with its teeth. The woman was tugging on a floral skirt and a Kate Spade evening bag. With a sinking feeling, Liz knew for certain. She was in Hell.

Her fellow passengers were making the same connection. A tiny, elderly woman turned and darted right back onto the train. A second later, a ghoul in a red felt cap and conductor's uniform emerged, holding the woman in skeletal, pincer fingers as though she were a three-day old fish, and deposited her in a heap on the platform. The terrified soul wailed for a moment, before a blue demon holding a rusty pitchfork herded her into the agitated crowd, away from the long black train.

A group of demons maneuvered from behind, cutting the crowd off from the train. Damned souls scattered like a flock of chickens fleeing a fox. There was nowhere to run. Demons lined all sides of the station. Apathetically, yet effectively, they herded passengers away from the train toward a damp brick tunnel with a crooked neon EXIT sign blinking in hiccup mode. Panicked souls running, sobbing, or screaming were singled out with sharp implements and slaps to the head. One man pushed past a phalanx of blue demons and sprinted back towards the tall rocky embankment surrounding the tunnel. Too late, the poor soul recognized the swarms of crimson demons. One bit off the man's hand and went running across rocks and lava with the appendage, trying to clean flesh off its prize even as other demons gave chase, howling and squealing.

Liz stayed in the middle of the herd and moved carefully. All around her, souls fought and scrapped over luggage—theirs, and anyone else's. Some souls seemed sad and confused. Some souls tried to read signs and wondered aloud what to do next. There were even souls shouting out orders to anyone who would listen. A small number of souls were gamely ignoring the wailing, howling, and pitchforks and steadfastly trying to get a cell signal as they bumped through, loudly complaining about the lack of service.

Any theft by the souls caught the immediate attention of a demon, and they were relieved of their prizes at once. The demons never returned property to the original owners; they went through anything they confiscated, simply taking what they wanted. The Erattus—upright, hairless rats about four to five feet tall—scurried through the crowd, gathering empty suitcases and other discarded items, placing the refuse on large carts. They were supposed to move the cases to warehouses, where they were meant for redistribution, but most sat moldering for centuries while requisition forms meandered through the system.

An older man in an expensive black suit yelled, "I was a preacher for thirty years. I demand to be taken to Heaven!" A demon promptly hit him in the head with a shovel.

Surprisingly, especially to herself, Liz wasn't trying to figure out how she ended up in Hell or weeping at the injustice of it all. She'd never been one to make a fuss. She handled anxiety by tamping down emotions, making herself small. Her mantra had always been, *figure out the rules, keep your head down.* She moved along with the crowd towards the Exit Tunnel.

Even with such a calming mantra, extreme panic would certainly have set in for Liz, except for one stroke of fortune—if anything that happened to a soul in that terrible place could be thusly designated. Liz was part of the group that Brian chose that day for his meet-and-greet. Brian was trying to set a good example for the demons. He'd spoken with them about how important it was to provide information to arrivals and keep them calm—unsuccessfully so far.

"Nergal," he summoned a large, blue demon with an odd, single cowlick of black hair curling over one eye, and a four-prong, bent pitchfork with more than a little blood on the points. "Could you herd a group of future citizens over here? I'd like to speak with them."

"Sure, boss." Nergal rounded up a group of damned that included Liz at its center. A short man in the back made yipping noises as the pitchfork found its target. The demon didn't stop until the group stood in front of Brian.

"Hello future citizens of Perdition City, or Lake of Fire, or Ashy Plains, or wherever you end up," he said, "if you could stand still for a moment, I'd love to become acquainted and answer a few questions." He waited for some confused shuffling to stop. "My name is Brian." He nodded at Nergal and another demon who'd helped wrangle the souls into position. "Gentlemen," he said, "you may go help others now. I'll show this group to the exit and off to their various destinations."

Nergal and the other demon wandered off. Nergal glanced over his shoulder. Seeing Brian occupied, he lit a cigarette and walked back towards the restrooms with his companion.

"Are we, you know, in the bad place?" a man asked, clutching a small carry-on sized suitcase tightly against his chest.

"Any place is only as bad as you make it!" Brian said cheerfully. "Of course, it takes some getting used to. We'll get you sorted. We do our best to meet your punishment needs. You'll receive temporary housing until your permanent assignment is built or vacated, so don't worry!"

Liz tried to wrap her head around both the suggestion that she *needed* punishment and the suggestion *not to worry*. These statements seemed diametrically opposed. A strong smell of sulfur wafted from the exit tunnel; she heard screaming from beyond the fence, and pointy ends of pitchforks surrounded her. She decided that, despite the polite suggestion, she would continue to worry.

"What happens now?" a tall woman in an elegant dress asked. She looked as though she'd died attending an opera or a gala.

"You all go to Admin," Brian reached into his bag and pulled out some folded photocopied maps. "My goodness, there are a lot of you today. If you are with someone you know, please consider sharing."

The man next to Liz handed her his map. She unfolded the paper while he and his friends gathered around. Out of the corner of her eye, Liz saw a demon chasing a tall blond kid, of maybe nineteen or twenty.

"I did way too many mushrooms!" the boy yelled.

"You don't know the half of it, kid," the demon said as he collared the young man and dragged him away.

Brian cleared his throat and waited for the hubbub to die down before he began again. "These maps should help you find your way around. Also, please be ready to hand in the customs forms the ghoul conductors gave you on the train, then get in line for a housing voucher. Feel free to treat yourself to a stay in the Brimstone Inn or another hotel here in Perdition City while you await your designation! Your Infernal account will be charged. You can be reimbursed for up to 25% of your expenses if you fill out form 1087-X-A7 within the first forty days of your stay. Read the fine print. The voucher doesn't cover the mini bar. For questions or complaints, get in line at the Help Desk, located on the first floor inside the Admin Building. If you *don't* have questions or complaints, go directly to the line for the DCB—the damnation compatibility battery—to receive a punishment and housing assignment. Requests will be considered, but there are no guarantees. There *are* brochures detailing our different punishment options, but for now—hmm?"

A short blocky man in a green and purple Hawaiian shirt pushed his way to the front of Brian's little group, shouting at top volume. "Do I need to hang onto my ticket? Where do I go now? Why will nobody around this dump answer my questions?"

Brian bent over, folding his lofty frame in two, and answered loudly, as though the man was deaf and not simply being rude. "Name's Brian," he said, "just Brian. No sir, no need for tickets anymore. You're here for the duration. Get your form to customs over in Admin. Yep. Right on your map. What's that? No, no cell coverage. We're a little behind the technology curve here." He scooted the angry man off towards the exit with a sturdy thump. "Go straight through that tunnel, turn left and out into Perdition City, and follow Broad Street to the Administration Building."

Liz didn't feel better, exactly, nor did she feel calm. She was a smidgen more composed knowing that at least someone was in charge. Brian started to speak again when a woman dressed in a low-cut silk shirt and expensive shoes wandered past the little group. "Fuck this!" she said. "Fuck you all! I don't belong here."

A sturdy man was following her. He whirled her around and gave her a solid gut punch. "Shut up, bitch! I told you this would happen. You never listen to me."

Brian sighed and waited politely until they had wandered past.

A slight, older woman standing next to Liz shook her head. "I don't understand what in the world I'm doing *here* with these dreadful people. I do *not* approve of vulgar language. Straight to the complaint line for me." The woman folded her arms across her chest.

"I was hoping when you died, that was it. You know, lights out," said a man in an AC/DC t-shirt and torn jeans. "This kinda sucks, honestly."

"Well," Brian said. "If you're seeking total annihilation, and please folks, let's think about it. It is, after all, permanent; the Abyss is in the center of your map. If you *are* headed for the Abysbs, no need to worry about paperwork, however, I can't imagine Hell without any one of you."

"No paperwork?" the man who'd given Liz the map said. "I might have to consider it." He dragged his finger along to the center, where it landed on a large dark blot labeled with a blood-red "A." He stared at it for a second, then sighed. "I guess I'll see how things go, first."

"You mean we can just quit existing?" the elegant woman asked, "Why have eternal punishment at all, then?"

"This is not the time and place to go into the theology," Brian said. "But yes, you can just quit existing. We don't recommend it, but it's a possibility."

"Can we do it later if we decide we don't want to exist after a couple of weeks or something?" the man who didn't like paperwork asked.

Liz glanced towards the tunnel. A knot of demons had gathered around one soul and were jabbing it with their pitchforks. The soul was cowering, covering its head. She turned her attention back towards Brian.

"Certainly," Brian said, "that's the spirit! Give Hell a chance. Remember the DCB is on the fifth floor of the Administration building, located on the corner of Broad and Gehenna." He cleared his throat and pushed up his tortoiseshell glasses. "Unfortunately, the elevator isn't working. You'll see the stairs as you enter the lobby. Get in line immediately; you'll be given hotel accommodations and an appointment time. Remember the custom forms! If you don't get those forms in, a demon will have to stop by to . . . um . . . assist you later this evening.

Trust me, you don't want to be on the streets at night—unless that's the punishment you're into." He cleared his throat again. "The Abyss will seem like nothing compared to these blue guys here once they get tanked up."

He pointed at the demon who'd been fighting over Liz's suitcase, who now had a suited arm dangling from his mouth; the demon gave a little nod of acknowledgement and a small wave. The woman who'd been fighting with the demon was shrieking that she couldn't fill out her form because she was missing an arm. Brian sighed.

"Medical requisitions are in the Admin Building. Go through the Help Line," he shouted in the direction of the bawling woman. He waved the people in Liz's little group toward the exit tunnel. "Restrooms here are experiencing some . . . technical problems. In the meantime, if anyone needs to go, you *might* want to hold it until you get to Admin."

Most of Liz's group had friends or acquaintances. Several were friends who'd taken a flight that had crashed into a mountain. The elegant woman had a husband; they'd died together in a car crash. As they drifted away together, Liz was left standing alone, loathe to begin the horrors of eternity companionless.

As Brian turned to go, she squeaked out, "Excuse me? Could you help me? Do we have to declare anything that's already been eaten by a demon?"

He answered perfunctorily, "Something stolen, eh? Complaints and questions are answered at the Admin Building. I'm going there now. I strongly suggest you get in line for the DCB first. The Help Line at this moment is . . . rather long."

He turned to go, then paused. "You can tag along if you want to."

Liz did want to. She scurried behind Brian, keeping his blue elbow patches in sight, ignoring shrieks and moans, loud laughter, metallic banging, and something that sounded suspiciously like howler monkeys. She didn't waste energy trying to see who or what was making all the noise. Liz's therapist had always shaken his head at her ability to ignore reality. He'd called it denialism. Here, it came in handy.

Brian walked in long, determined strides. Liz jogged to keep up. Streets threaded narrowly around dull-colored buildings, which blocked out indifferent gray light. Throngs of incoming souls pushed against variously colored demons, fallen angels, small dragons, and even a few faerie folk who'd probably ventured into Hell for purposes known only to themselves. A demon lunged for Liz; she darted behind an overflowing garbage can filled with bones, several dead bats, and a steaming, acidic liquid that was burning a hole through the thick, black metal. By the time she reached the office, still on Brian's heels, she'd been spat on by three ghouls, had a hole burned through her skirt, and was missing a sandal.

A tiny monkey with a skull for a head had darted out from under a dilapidated bench and snatched the sandal from her foot just as they reached a huge concrete box of a building with the words "Administrative Offices, Main Division, Perdition City" in black block letters on top. It would have made a Brutalist building seem frivolous by comparison. Liz's eyes were glued to Brian's gray sweater—focused on the navy elbow patches. She managed to stay inside the high-speed revolving doors until they spat her out in the reception area, all her limbs miraculously—if one could use that word in relation to Hell—intact.

Unfortunately for Liz, she was so intent on following Brian that she bypassed the stair well with a large sign that said DAMNATION COMPATIBILITY BATTERY. In fact, she also bypassed the long line of souls waiting in the Help Line, ignoring the now-expected catcalls and globs of phlegm, still solely focused on Brian.

She followed him straight into his gray, cube-like office. The security demons had never seen a soul simply skip the queue and walk straight through the door. Assuming the boss had okayed it, they allowed her to pass. Brian turned to shut the door and then stopped short when he saw her standing there, lopsided, with only one shoe.

"Oh dear!" Brian stammered. "There's a line. I should have told you. I thought . . . I thought you'd see where it started. This is the help desk." He pointed at a window in the office that faced the lobby. "I lost the demon who worked the window. He said he'd rather do eel control in the Bog of Despair than deal with any more paperwork."

Brian raised a dirty, broken, plastic shade and flipped over an OPEN sign.

The line entirely filled the huge lobby and snaked into the street—there were souls with missing limbs, souls that smelled like poo, souls with snakes or spiders stuck on their fingers, arms or faces. One man had his ears and eyes in the wrong spots. Fine green smoke rose from a weeping woman's hair. There were souls of all colors, some missing limbs, some with torn clothing. A few souls were steaming or had burn holes in their suits. Farther away, a large blue demon and a gray-winged gargoyle were breaking up a ten-soul fight. The gargoyle flapped a few feet off the ground, thrusting a pitchfork between the combatants, while the blue demon simply laid about with his fists.

A few souls shuffled along, trying not to attract attention from either security or their fellow damned. The long line had taken a natural toll on tempers. One man in the back was swinging an ax in a futile attempt to intimidate those in front. A blue demon boxed his ears and relieved him of the weapon.

"Sorry," Brian said. "You were meant to go upstairs. I should have told you." He sighed. "I was in such a hurry. It's been a little crazy since I lost my assistant. Again."

"Oh, Brian." For an instant she felt more pity for him than herself. "How can you handle this line all by yourself? Can't they get you any decent help?"

"Demons stink at paperwork, and we've had a sudden influx of souls. What's going on in the Upper World? Can't you people behave anymore?" He shook his head. "I can't blame the demons. It's too much for them."

"It's too much for anyone," Liz said. She stared at the mayhem, appalled.

"Thank you." Brian's brow furrowed. He peered over his glasses. "I appreciate your understanding."

Perhaps it was a fluke; even Hell had its coincidences. Perhaps no one had ever been single-mindedly anxious enough to bypass the line without realizing it and simultaneously lucky enough to bypass security. Perhaps if Liz had spent any time in that line, she would have been just as angry and exasperated as anyone else. If she *had* been sympathetic to his managerial distress, she certainly wouldn't have had a chance to express it.

She would later find out that for Brian, created to supervise the squalling chaos of Satan's kingdom, it was the first touch of kindness he'd experienced in centuries, the first sympathy for the howling line, the huge stacks of paper spilling over his desk and onto the floor, the cold, barely touched coffee.

The raucous cursing of the demons, echoed by the more pitiable cursing of souls brought Liz back to reality. The man in front of the line was holding his severed head in his hands, his neck spewing a fountain of blood. The head had realized that Liz was causing a delay.

"Throw her out!" the head hissed. Blood leaked from the corners of its lips. "She cut in line! I've been here for a year!"

The sentiment spread quickly. With a unified shriek, souls pushed against glass. Howls of despair and anger rippled through the queue. Brian and Liz stared at each other, both realizing what a grave mistake she'd made. She would have to walk through the lobby to get to the DCB on the top floor. She would surely be torn into a thousand pieces before she could make it.

THREE

The New Job

"I'M SORRY," LIZ MUMBLED, MOVING TOWARDS THE DOOR.

Brian grabbed her arm. "Wait," he whispered. "How would you like a job?" Souls upon souls pressed hard against the window. "According to the rules, souls can't be in any decision-making positions concerning the complaints, housing requests, etc., but you could help by making sure the forms are filled out properly in the first place. This line has been getting longer and longer. Maybe, instead of firing a demon once every two weeks, I could just change the job description." He let go of her arm. "Sorry," he said. He chewed his lip thoughtfully. "I'm racking my brain, but I can't see why it won't work."

Liz nodded eagerly. She would do anything to avoid going back out and crossing the lobby. Her afterlife was in his hands.

He ran his fingers through his hair. "I don't see why not, if you simply help with forms and run errands. You would be assigned to work here. I mean, not that you want to work here, but it might be better than. . ." he jerked his head towards the angry crowd. Some of the souls were pointing at her. The soul of an older woman made a slashing motion across her throat.

Brian nodded decisively. "Are you on board? I'm in charge of assigning souls to punishment or work assignments in Perdition City. Usually not in Admin. I think I can make it work."

"Yes!" Liz said, "of course! I would love to help." An exaggeration. Since the alternative was being torn limb from limb, the job offer had a certain appeal.

Someone flung a shoe at the window. She was pretty sure it was the woman who'd made the slashing motion. Brian ignored it, pulled a form from a cubby behind them, and handed it to Liz.

"This is a medical requisition form. I'm guessing that's what your first customer wants." He pointed at the headless man, who shifted his burden to one arm so he could flip them off with the other hand. Brian ignored this as well. "Here are housing reassignment requests, general complaints, paperwork pull requests, etc.," he said, waving his hand at the wall where stacks of forms resided in cubbies with small, dirty labels on the front.

"Most clients haven't got a clue how to fill out the forms and goodness do they get angry when they have to go back to the end of the line," he leaned over Liz and pointed at the form she currently held. "Make sure all sections are filled out in ink. Make sure they check here, here, and here, and initial here. You stand right over there. If you do that, I can spend my days administrating this place." He pushed Liz towards the window. "I have final authority over the results of the DCB, you know. The test that determines your punishment assignment. You weren't hoping for the Lake of Fire or something?"

"No," Liz whispered, not trusting her voice, "I wasn't hoping for anything in particular."

The decapitated man's head yelled from his arms, "Hey! I'm still waiting."

"She's here to help," Brian told the angry gentleman in his friendly and efficient tone. "And you're in no shape to fill out that form yourself, sir. Unless you would like to risk putting your head down. The last gentleman who tried that found his head quite famously used as the flaming attraction in the Demon's Cup Fire Ball Tournament. Good luck reattaching it at that point. And you *will* go to the back of the line. Of that, I can assure you."

The man saw the sense in this. "Whatever," his head said, frowning. His hand tossed the form onto the counter and then wiped blood from the chin. Liz handed him a Kleenex from the box beside the window, took his form and kicked off the one shoe she had left. She was shaking. Determined to do whatever it took to stay out of reach of the angry mob.

"Most clients will need new forms from the cubbies; they've already screwed up the old ones beyond repair," Brian said. "We'll spend some time after the line closes entering the data. Right now, I have some other work to do. Let me know if you have questions."

So, Liz began her tenure in Hell. She often wondered if she had avoided the punishment she would otherwise have been designated, or simply found the perfect way to torment herself. She'd dealt with the public as a librarian: pulled peanut butter sandwiches out of the book drop; been screamed at because they were out of the book that had been assigned to every tenth grader in the city; several times she'd found some weirdo in spandex pants masturbating at the computer desk in the back close to the children's section. Once, she'd even spent an entire morning chasing a squirrel through the reference books. She tried to remember that she hadn't much cared for her former job either. If she could hang onto that thought and avoid thinking about the fact that the afterlife went on forever, she could get through the day.

As the days went by, Liz discovered that Brian was the top authority in Hell when Satan or the rest of the senior executives weren't there. Hell's C-Suite preferred not to hang out in Hell any more than they had to. Brian had a teleconference with Satan about once a month. He occasionally received orders from Mammon, Beelzebub, Lucifer—whom Liz was surprised to find were different entities than Satan—as well as Magoth, Belphegor, Lilith, and Leviathan. The hierarchy of demons was tumultuous; they fought and scrapped to get to the next level, better pay and benefits—from lowly D-1s all the way up to D-12s. However, none of the demons that Liz ran into, even D-12s, were above Brian in the pecking order. All the demons followed his orders, even if they were somewhat rude about doing so.

Brian used his clout to assign Liz an apartment five blocks from Admin and even managed a small clothing stipend to replace what she'd lost at the station. Liz had a seventh-floor apartment on the back side, above a dirty stone alley. A black stream coated with ash either oozed or roared its way through a ditch depending on weather conditions.

Smoke and ash storms spawned by The Lake of Fire region to the west rolled through her new neighborhood frequently, turning all the buildings on her block the same monotonous gray. Tattered, smoke-ruined curtains fluttered behind windows like trapped bats. The apartments had iron bars and metal screens on windows to prevent small creatures— strange scarlet spiders, blue and green lizards with fangs, black bats, and the like—from simply crawling in and making themselves at home. Her building was on a slight rise, allowing a view of the dank, gray city. The sky draped over the landscape like a thick blanket, sometimes glowing with fire or lightning behind cracks in the dense clouds, but more often somber and leaden.

Liz's building faced a demon dormitory, which had its own bar built into the first floor. Raucous sounds of partying assaulted the neighborhood all night long. At night, demons chased souls into the alley to abuse them. Once, around midnight, two gargoyles got into a drunken scuffle and took the skirmish to the air. Windows were smashed; bricks and concrete dust blocked the front door for several days.

A few other souls were assigned jobs and living quarters in Perdition City on the same day as Liz, two of them assigned to her building. Theo, a master plumber who had owned the biggest plumbing company in Cincinnati while embodied, was pulled from line and assigned maintenance work at the train station. Before Brian even left the station the morning Liz arrived, the Federated Demons Union had lodged a complaint on behalf of Georgie, the demon Brian had asked to check the men's, who felt that plumbing should not be under his purview. Theo was a large, pleasant man with brown hair and brown eyes, whose pants—in true plumber fashion—did not provide adequate coverage of his hindquarters. He reminded Liz of her Uncle Irving.

The other soul was a woman named Ellie, who had been an English adjunct while embodied. Ellie's place was on Liz's floor, a couple doors down. When Liz got off work the first day, she found Ellie struggling to carry several heavy stacks of books up seven floors. A tall woman in her sixties, Ellie had short iron-gray hair, hoop earrings, a black leather jacket, black jeans, and short black boots.

"Can I help you?" Liz pointed tentatively towards a stack of books. The woman pushed up her glasses, stared at Liz, then shrugged.

"I can't turn that down," she said. "It's going to take quite a few loads. I hope you're prepared."

Liz picked up a book and sniffed. "This smells like sulfur and mold."

"Smells like the Devil's ass," Ellie grinned. "Be careful of that stack closest to the staircase. The books on the bottom bite." She held up a bandaged hand.

"I saw them pull you from line. I didn't catch what for. What's your assignment?" Liz asked as they struggled up the stairs with the books.

"Teaching regulations at the Infernal Business Academy," the woman said with a sigh. "Come over for coffee sometime and we can bitch about Hell."

Liz's place came furnished, though that wasn't necessarily a selling point. It featured a hideous orange couch in a scratchy fabric. The couch was splashed with large caustic-yellow, chartreuse, and Pepto-Bismol pink sunflowers and looked like it had been designed by Easter bunnies on acid. A two-foot-tall cat-like demon who walked upright also inhabited the place.

Dennis, as he preferred to be known, was assigned to Liz as something between a pet and a personal tormentor. This was how Brian had convinced Satan that standards were being adhered to even though Dennis and his ilk weren't *professional* tormentors. Regulations required punishment, even for souls with work assignments, so every lost soul in Perdition city lived with some sort of nether creature.

For instance, Ellie had a small, mud-colored dragon named Greg. He spouted more smoke than flame. Ellie could never keep a pair of curtains on the windows, as most available window treatments in Perdition City were cheap and therefore extremely flammable. Theo, the plumber, was plagued by a tiny demon named Alberta, a little orange marmoset with two blue horns instead of tufts of hair. She had three rows of teeth and spent every day eating through furniture legs or any other possessions she found tasty. Theo eventually scavenged a couple metal lawn chairs and a lava table, otherwise he would have been sitting on the floor for eternity.

All three of them settled into eternal punishment in Perdition City with other souls who'd been assigned the same fate. After a few months, Liz caught on that Hell had a routine like the Upper World—a dim daylight period for work or punishment, depending on one's assignment, and a dark, frightening nighttime, which Liz spent locked in her apartment.

Though the scarlet darkness of Hell's night was terrifying, it morphed into a dense gray morning worse than the nightmare preceding it. Lurking horrors hiding in the darkness simply became visible, banal, and commonplace in the flabby daylight of the Underworld. Night brought on a primal fear, a terrified existential awareness; morning bred a suffocating repulsion. More souls flung themselves into the Abyss in this dreary morning unveiling than at any other time.

Liz's favorite evening pastime was overanalyzing every earthly mistake, wondering how she'd ended up damned to an eternity of paperwork while Dennis whined, watched bad TV, and demanded tuna. She worried late into the night, falling asleep just in time to awaken to the howls of Dennis—fifteen minutes before the alarm sounded, no matter what time she set it.

This cacophony was accompanied by hissing and claws slapping Liz's face. "I'm starving! Help!"

After she'd fed him and made herself a bowl of soggy and yet still somehow gritty oatmeal or a piece of limp toast, Liz dressed for work. She'd learned to carefully check her underwear drawer, as Dennis preferred to relieve himself there. Typically, she required a few minutes to clean Dennis's barf off her shoes before setting out for work.

Every day, she trudged downstairs to face another day in Hell. The elevator was always broken; public transport never ran on time. There were rumors that some souls had been trapped on the BlueLine of the under-underground for over a hundred years. She'd noted that on every train schedule or map, sure enough, the BlueLine had been marked through with a sharpie. On her way to the office, five blocks from her apartment, she ducked to avoid vampire bats, sidestepped potholes of bubbling mud, and jumped over demons or souls sleeping off the previous night's revelry in alleys and on sidewalks.

Sometimes she walked a few blocks with Ellie or Theo, although Ellie's job was in a different part of the city and Theo's often required him to get up extremely early or stay late at night. More often, Liz ended up walking to work with Hagatha, an extremely large she-devil who lived in the demon dormitory across the street. Hagatha was head of security for Admin. Liz's opinionated demon co-worker made her nervous, but Hagatha's presence kept her safer than she would otherwise be.

Liz resigned herself to her new, barely-there existence, except for one thing: she couldn't stop wondering why she'd been sent to Hell in the first place. She thought about it all night; it buzzed around the back of her brain all day. At least her mind was occupied while attending to the souls. Being spit on, cursed, and otherwise abused took her mind off things.

The reality of corporate life in Hell didn't keep them from trying to make things more efficient. Brian once attempted to requisition iPads so the information souls provided would be automatically entered into the system. The request was denied. Liz could understand why—the demons would have made short work of them, and the souls couldn't be depended on to be responsible for their own limbs, much less something as fragile as a tablet. They couldn't even take care of the cheap ballpoint pens; those were stolen, broken, eaten by demons, sometimes consumed by souls. Every two months there was a new database, each worse than the last. Hell's corporate system was designed more for affliction than efficiency.

Still, the lack of growth depressed Brian. He tried to implement policy without complaining. Sometimes, though, against his better judgment—he ended up confiding in her.

"No one ever consults me," he sighed one day as they closed the blinds and had a fifteen-minute lunch at his desk. "Or you, for that matter. We could make this place so efficient if they'd just listen."

"Maybe you could talk directly to him?" Liz suggested. "During the teleconference. Maybe get something on the agenda?"

"He's Satan," Brian rolled his eyes. "I mean, you don't know him the way I do."

Liz was busy flicking a fly off what she dearly hoped was an egg sandwich. She pulled her chair closer to his desk and banged her knee. Stifling a yowl of pain, she continued, "What were you saying about Satan?"

"It's not his fault. He just can't help making things worse all the time. I mean, in theory he wants this place to work, to give people the punishment they need. Great Lucifer's tail, it's in the mission statement! Between you and me, we simply don't have the funding." Brian shook his head. "Satan gets distracted. He and Mammon and the rest of them have been spending a lot of time in Vegas. I don't even know if they *look* at my numbers. Half of next year's budget is probably tucked in some stripper's thong by now. I hear it used to be different before he made me the manager. I feel like. . ." he took off his glasses and rubbed his eyes. "You know. Like I'm failing."

Liz patted his sleeve. "Not to be blasphemous, but he should thank God he's got you."

"I can always do better, I guess. That's what it says in the handbook. However well you think you're doing, you can always do better. Unless you're Satan. The handbook says he's perfect."

"Who wrote the handbook?"

"Guess." Brian sighed and took a bite of his sandwich.

"It occurs to me that I haven't seen Satan since I've been here," Liz said. "I always thought that if you ended up in Hell, you'd see Satan every day. Poking and prodding you with a pitchfork. Turning you on a skewer over a nice, toasty fire." She wrapped the sweater she'd pulled from Lost and Found more closely around herself. She sometimes quietly envied the people assigned to the Lake of Fire. Admin was always cold and clammy, smelling vaguely of mildew.

"You want to be poked and prodded? Have you tried the new database?" Brian asked, then gestured at the computer. "I've been trying to enter death dates all morning. For some reason the system won't recognize this century. Dammit. This wasn't happening yesterday."

"No, no prodding for me, thank you." She smiled. "I'm glad I've never seen him."

"He *has* been spending more and more time in the Upper World. The last time he visited was before you were disembodied," Brian shrugged. "As I noted, he likes to party. If you had a choice, where would you party? Here or back on earth?"

"You have a point," Liz said. "Still, it seems like he'd have to come occasionally to see how things were going. It's his job, right?"

"Well, be careful what you wish for," Brian leaned back in his chair, which groaned and squeaked under him. "When he shows up, it's usually to do surprise inspections and yell about how everything is going downhill. He demands absurd changes. Impossible stuff really. Then he asks me to cash a check, so he can go back to Vegas and pick up strippers and showgirls."

He jerked his hand towards a skull-shaped red phone perched on a shelf above his desk. "When the hotline rings, you're in for a hard time. We get some sort of crisis that sends him over the edge at least a couple times a century."

"Sounds like we're just as well off without him then," Liz said.

"Not exactly. There are things we need him for. He set this place up a long, long time ago. Made some deals, found the funding. He makes the lease payments. I don't have any idea where any of it comes from mind you, or what kind of budget to expect from quarter to quarter. Much as that information might help us. Nevertheless, I much prefer him up mucking about among the living. Trust me." He cleared his throat. "Anyway, I don't want you to worry about it. That's my job."

"Of course."

He gave her a half-smile, a rare and awkward expression for him, like a hippo trying a tentative dance step. Ludicrous. And at the same time, ever so slightly endearing. "Pull up the blind. I guess we'd better get back to work."

She re-opened the window, taking a charred and still-smoking form from the fingers of a sad little man, who trailed ashes over the counter.

More than once, Liz asked Brian how people ended up in Hell, especially people like her: the anxious, the obsessive, the rules oriented. It couldn't be merely a lack of religion. Hell hosted plenty of religious people of all sorts from all over the world. In fact, they were one of the most prevalent groups in the Help Line. Liz didn't know whether there were more of them, or if they simply complained more than atheists.

A few weeks after their conversation about Satan, Liz asked again about why she'd ended up in Hell.

"Honestly," Brian said, frowning, "all I see is the flame stamp on the paperwork. I've never seen a mistake one time. At least as far as I know. I mean, no one ever gets reassigned upwards."

He leaned back in his chair and shook his head. "No mistakes in Hell, that's our goal." A sad, little laugh escaped his lips. "Only satisfied customers. The best service."

Liz forced a smile as she wiped down the counter. "It would just be so much easier if I knew. I spend all night worrying about it. I kinda can't let it go."

"For what it's worth," Brian blushed, "if it were up to me—well, you're a nice person, Liz." He swung his chair around and started typing on his computer. Liz felt a sudden tiny flicker of gratitude. The good feeling was immediately squelched when she asked the next soul how she could help, and cockroaches ran out of its mouth and ears instead of speech.

During another lunch break the same week, when she couldn't help asking the same question again, Brian gave her the same answer.

"Still no idea," he said. "Sorry."

"No, of course," Liz said. "I don't know why I keep asking."

He chewed a mouthful of his lunch for a minute. "This soup is so thick, I'm not sure it still qualifies as liquid." He scooted a stack of paperwork aside and set the plastic container full of beige sludge down on the edge of his desk. After a forlorn moment, he relented and started shoveling it around with his spoon.

Liz stirred hers with some effort. "The delivery demon *said* it was soup. At least it's not moving like the noodles yesterday."

After a minute of silence, Brian muttered, "I can tell you one thing. Recently, we started getting a lot more souls all at once, and honestly some of them seem . . . nicer. Less rowdy. No one's explained it. It's played havoc with the budget; I can tell you that much."

"So, it was different in the beginning?" Liz asked.

"I wasn't here—not until later. I don't know exactly how they operated in the beginning." He licked his lips, poking the soup more vigorously. "We're really not supposed to talk about that."

Liz had long registered that Brian always glanced up at the hotline phone whenever she stumbled onto a forbidden topic. The base of the phone was a red skull, while the faceplate of numbers formed a permanently surprised mouth. The headset was shaped to resemble a bone. She'd never seen the phone ring as long as she'd been there. He stared at the phone, drew in a deep breath, let it out sharply.

She felt guilty when she brought up topics that made her boss uncomfortable, although it hadn't stopped her from asking questions. However, one topic had seemed taboo right from the start—The Abyss. Just thinking about the idea gave her cold chills.

"We need to get back to work," Brian turned away from the hotline phone, finished his lunch and tossed the container into the trash. "Remind me to reconsider next time I tell you I'm in the mood for soup."

FOUR

A Ticket Out?

LIZ WAS SINKING SLOWLY, SADLY INTO HER NEW ROUTINE: work and worry, worry and work. She occasionally managed to have coffee with her neighbor, Ellie, who was getting used to her new job as well. Normally, they shared coffee at Ellie's apartment—the dreadful instant coffee Ellie stole from the teacher's lounge at the School of Infernal Business. Ellie, an English adjunct while embodied, had been pulled out of line to teach a regulations class for demons because Satan had decided that the Operational Regulations courses 101 through 400—required of all demons majoring in Administration—were poorly taught.

Brian explained that his was all because Satan had been served a Coke instead of a Diet Coke on his most recent visit to Hell. During the quarterly board meeting, Satan seemed in an equable mood as Brian served drinks. But when Brian came back in with the sandwich platter, a cut crystal glass whizzed past his ear. The flying goblet nicked his earlobe slightly, continued its flight across the conference room, then shattered on the brand-new projector screen, leaving a pool of brown liquid and ice. Brian wasn't taken aback by the tantrum, per se; it was the fact that typically tantrums came after Satan took a few bites of his food rather than a sip of his drink. Mammon crossed her slim legs and lit a cigarette. Beelzebub tapped his pen nervously on the table, and Lucifer excused himself to use the restroom. None of them wanted to take on Satan in this state.

"I'm sorry, sir, is something wrong?" Brian asked.

"This. Is. Not. *Diet*!" Satan screamed, red-faced. He pointed at Brian. "Who is responsible for this . . . this travesty?" He turned sideways, pulled off the jacket of his designer suit, and pointed at his stomach.

"Look at this waistline. Look at it, Brian. Do you have any idea how hard it is to retain a waistline this perfect?" Satan's tone had dropped into a silky purr, much more dangerous than yelling. Tall and slender, thick wavy blond hair—of which he was inordinately proud—appearance meant a great deal to him. He wasn't quite so handsome now, though. His cheeks were the color of beets, and his eyes bugged out. His horns, normally smoothly hidden, were beginning to show through his magnificent hair.

"No, sir," Brian said. "I'm sorry, sir."

"What in Hell are they teaching in Operations and Regs these days?" Satan shouted. "Someone must pay for this, Brian, my boy. And you'd better figure out whom."

Brian had tried to point out that the serving demon was new, that the soda fountain's diet had been mistakenly switched with regular and that Operational Regulations didn't cover whether Satan should be served a calorie-free drink; and that the servers in the building were not technically part of Admin and were not required to take Operational Regulations. His pleading was to no avail. Satan decreed that he should find some way to revamp the entire series of Infernal Operational Regulations classes. When Satan decided who was at fault, even if he was wildly wrong, there was no changing his mind.

Brian made a special trip across Perdition City to speak with Dr. Archana Batsen, dean of The School of Infernal Business; she blamed Dr. Vanth Lempo, Dean of Infernal Regulations, who in turn blamed several of the professors in the department. They, of course, blamed an adjunct; a young aca-daemon just out of grad school, who was sent to the Western Wilds to do menial labor post haste.

Satan was mollified, barely. Most of the faculty disdained teaching and instead spent their time writing papers to curry favor with Satan—titles like, *Financing Infernal Punishment*, *Souls, Capital*, and *The Importance of Materialism*, etc. Brian had had to think outside the box to fill the vacancy.

When Ellie's former job appeared in the database, she'd been pulled out of the DCB line and given orders to pore over a huge stack of textbooks to break them down for demon students who couldn't be bothered to read for themselves, and who, in fact, often used textbooks to start fires or as snacks. She was told to add the importance of serving Diet Coke to Satan as the first item on the syllabus.

"Never Pepsi, diet or no. A server would be halfway to the Abyss with a Fendi shoe print on the butt mere seconds from that mistake," Brian told her.

As for Ellie, she took the assignment in stride. "Oh well," she rolled her eyes. "The pay's probably not any worse than my earth job." She was given a huge stack of heavy books to carry back to her apartment where she subsequently befriended Liz.

As time wore on, Ellie discovered that the School of Infernal Business (SIB) was more remunerative than her earthly job if you took into consideration that housing was technically free. However, SIB pupils were slightly less disciplined than typical college freshman, and even a little rowdier than the high school juniors to whom she'd taught American Literature for a few years. Still, her expectations were low. She'd often joked while embodied that someday she would write a memoir/self-help book with the title "Lowered Expectations: the Key to Happiness."

Ellie wasn't terribly surprised she'd ended up in Hell. She cursed. She drank. She'd slept with whomever she pleased after leaving her abusive husband in her early forties, though she occasionally toasted him when she was out with friends. The divorce settlement had provided her with half of his money, from the furniture store his parents had left him, which allowed her to survive as an adjunct. It wasn't a great deal of money, but it had worked out pretty well until she was sixty-two, when skimping on medical insurance finally did her in. She'd died of cancer after her lousy insurance company refused to pay for a CAT scan.

Sometimes Ellie invited both Liz and Theo over for coffee. The three of them bonded that first day. Ellie had the only warm coffee in the building, owing to the fact that her demon companion, Greg, was a small dragon, about the size of a largish bulldog. When he wasn't belching smoke or setting her curtains on fire, he spent a good deal of time sleeping soundly enough that she could set the coffee pot on his back; it fit nicely between two rows of upright scales that ran down his body from his ears to the tip of his tail. Greg did a far better job of keeping the coffee warm than the temperamental hot plates that came standard with every apartment.

One evening, around six months after they'd all settled in, the three of them were gathered at Ellie's for coffee. As always, she poured the molten fluid into makeshift cups she'd found. Liz's was a small mug, made for an imp; it needed constant refilling. Theo had a soup bowl with a chip out of one side that required him to tip it awkwardly until he'd drunk a few sips. Ellie's cup was missing a handle and said *KEEP CALM AND GO TO HELL* on the side. One of her demon students had given it to her. Or rather, had thrown it at her head, but Ellie never liked to look a gift horse in the mouth or any other orifice.

"Piping hot! If only it tasted less like liquid asphalt," Ellie said. She warmed her feet against Greg's sides.

The little mud-colored dragon snorted and twitched his sharp brown ears, and Ellie put out a foot to balance the coffee pot. Liz was jealous of the seeming ease with which Ellie had made herself at home.

Even in the afterlife, other people got the hang of things more easily than she did.

"So, what do you guys think about this place?" Ellie asked. Liz was settled in an ugly yellow and green plaid chair; Ellie and Theo sat on a square couch that either had an interesting abstract pattern in rust, brown, and gold, or was stained so terribly no pattern was visible. "Not my living room—I mean Hell. I personally expected it to be more horrible. And if I'm being honest, more exciting. You know," Ellie waved a hand, "demons inventing new and more exquisite tortures every day, needles under the fingernails, the smell of skin slowly roasted to a crisp over a million fires, organs being torn out only to regrow so that they could be ripped out again, screams of the damned barely audible above my own, yadda yadda."

"I, for one, am not disappointed," Theo said. "It's plenty awful for me. This is the first evening I'm off before ten in two weeks, and I'm pretty sure that's only because Nergal ate the work orders. Nobody put him on the schedule for a lunch break."

"Oh, I'm not complaining." Ellie set her cup on a stack of beat up black and red textbooks she used as a side table. "Just puzzled."

"Me too," said Liz. "This place feels less like the Hell I learned about in church and more like some sort of weird limbo. For the record, I hate it."

"Yeah, it's total crap. I mean, of course," Ellie said. "It's not like I thought it wouldn't be. At the very least, I thought we'd get a tinge of revenge. Meeting famous people in the worst of circumstances. Experiencing the peculiar delights of seeing the truly wicked punished as they deserve. But this is kind of . . . half-hearted, don't you think?"

"Pretty tepid for an inferno," Theo said. "Not that I want it to change. It would surely be for the worse. God knows, a bureaucracy like this never changes for the better."

"Yeah," Ellie said. "But think! Even the worst punishments here are pathetic. We've all seen a demon tear someone's arm off or whatever. It's painful, but limbs reattach or eventually they grow new ones. I mean, medical attention can help a little, you can keep the original limb or whatever, but still. That doesn't seem like how Hell is supposed to work from what I remember of Dante."

"It's like Prometheus' liver," said Liz. "Eternal torture requires eternal regeneration." Dennis had chewed off the end of her pinky finger when she forgot to bring home rancid fish one day, and it had finally grown back. With no fingerprint, but still.

"Yeah. That's exactly it. The pain is perfunctory. Unenthusiastic," Ellie frowned. "The first week, a student in the front row of Intro to Retributive Administration put a pencil through my eye. It hurt. And then it healed. I gave them two days off. A kind of vacation. And I can't see out of it *quite* as well. That's eternal punishment?"

It was the same throughout Hell. Souls crawled in and out of the lake of fire, never fully consumed. The prideful, assigned to forever gaze at themselves in the burnished, mirrored ice of Arctic glaciers, froze off tips of noses and fingers, then glued them back on or waited for them to regrow.

"This place is as ridiculous as it is awful," Ellie continued. "I was at the pharmacy on Friday, and I saw one of those ludicrous skeletons fall off a ladder. Took two of its chums to fit the femur back in its hip. It was like *I Love Lucy* with skeletons."

First aid and repairs, often carried out with duct tape and weak hydrogen peroxide, were the purview of the woefully understocked Dr. Bones—a pharmacy chain run by goofy skeletons. "I was in Dr. Bones yesterday, and I saw a skeleton clerk lose a hand in the cash register. You should have seen the line by the time it managed to get its fingers back on." Theo snorted. "No offense to you and your boss, Liz. This city is pretty poorly run."

"Brian's doing the best he can," Liz said, a little defensively. "He doesn't have the budget."

"Oh, I daresay," Ellie patted Liz's arm. "My job is vile but I wouldn't want yours, even for an earthly cup of coffee."

"I'd trade with her," Theo said. "Doing plumbing and maintenance around this place is no joke."

"I'll bet. Still, that line. Poor Brian. I guess he's just the big guy's scapegoat, huh?" Ellie asked.

Greg awoke, stuck his butt in the air, and let out a weak, smoky flame. Ellie managed to grab the coffee pot before it toppled. She set it on a side table and stamped out a spark on the dingy rug.

"Yeah." Liz felt oddly protective of Brian. "We get tons of people with bad injuries in line. After they get the proper forms, it takes longer to get seen in an emergency medical center than it did to stand in the Help Line, especially here in Perdition City. No wonder souls come up and spit bile on my counter. We don't make the rules. We just try to follow them."

Theo grunted and stuck out his coffee cup, which Ellie refilled.

"Even aside from the weird medical stuff, I don't get this place," Ellie said. "I mean, I understand now that the idiots in the Upper World who think they know everything about the afterlife have been bluffing. Turns out they don't know shit. Look at all the religious people here, right? I completely fail to see the point of this place."

"The fundie Christian ones are the worst," Theo said. "A whole lotta white evangelicals complaining about everything. I haven't met any of the few nice religious people I knew. Some of them gotta be dead." He sipped his coffee. "Guess they could be anywhere though. Too many people in this damn place. I wouldn't know where to begin. Come to think of it, only guy I've seen here is my pal Carlos from high school. Saw him outside the restrooms. He wasn't particularly nice or religious."

Ellie sighed. "Yeah. There are way too many people down here. And there's something else. The ticket counter. Why is there a ticket counter if you can't leave? What's the point?" She leaned forward conspiratorially. "The other day at school, I overheard something Dean Lempo said, something odd. He's a doddering jackass, grayish, wrinkled skin, missing about half his teeth, tail limp as a dishrag. I've heard rumors that he's been around longer than some of the other demons."

Theo set down his soup bowl with a thud and coffee sloshed out the side. "That doesn't make any sense," he said. "This is eternity. How can one of the demons be older than the others?"

Ellie shrugged and threw Theo an old tea towel to mop up the spill. "Don't know. It's just what I've heard and observed. Anyway, I was sitting close to his table in the lunchroom, and he said something about "back when the train ran both ways." And the other demons shushed him. Of course, I pretended not to hear. I don't want to end up in the Western Wilds anytime soon. Know nothing. Say nothing. That's my policy. What does it mean?"

Theo shrugged. "I sure as hell don't understand it. Of course, no one pays me to think about anything."

"Maybe it's to torment us," Liz said. "You know, like, there's a ticket counter and we can never buy a ticket."

Ellie nodded. "Yeah, that's what I thought too. After all, a lot of the environment down here mirrors what we had on earth, only in such a way as to make us feel trapped and hopeless. What if the train used to run both ways?"

"Don't know how it helps us if it did," Theo said. "It sure as Satan doesn't run both ways now."

"And it hasn't for as long as anyone here can remember," Liz said. "Brian never said anything about trains running *out* of Hell."

Ellie shrugged. "It's an interesting possibility, though. Made me wonder. What if souls used to be able to get out of this place?"

FIVE

An Outing with Hagatha

IT DIDN'T TAKE BRIAN LONG TO ASSIGN LIZ DUTIES THAT took her out of the office, a huge relief for the busy manager. He sent her to the station to refill the map racks or to the Housing Council, run by a pack of wizened, leather-skinned imps who liked to scream out their reasons for denying housing requisitions.

"This form requires triplicate copies—you only provided double! Denied!" the imps would scream as they raised their arms and with unnecessary force rubber-stamped the paperwork with a "D" surrounded in flames.

"The answer for question number 368 is blank! *Denied!*" they would holler and stamp with obvious glee.

One morning, Brian sent Liz to the Perdition City Station to replace the poster sized maps, which were continually being torn down, and to refill racks with brochures. Hagatha, a D-9 with the highest security rank in Admin, was sent along to keep Liz safe. Hagatha, towering over Liz and several inches taller than Brian, had deep scarlet skin, almost purple, and a shock of raven hair that stuck up from the top of her head between her pointy ears like a Mohawk. She loped along, goat hooves clicking on pavement, as they made their way to the train station; Hagatha occasionally slowed to grab something from one of the confused new souls heading into town. She made Liz nervous, though not as nervous as she would have been without her.

The blue demons and the ghoul conductors understood Liz's role at the office, which admittedly didn't guarantee good behavior since they loved to tease. However, they would only push their luck so far. On the other hand, the souls at the station could be dangerous upon arrival. They were confused, stressed, and understandably erratic.

"How did you become disembodied?" Hagatha asked Liz on the way to the station.

"I stepped in front of a bus."

"Why the fuck did you do that?" Hagatha asked, puzzled. "That was stupid."

"True, but I didn't mean to," Liz said. "I had a fight with my boyfriend the night before; I was on my way to a meeting at work; I was stressed. Wasn't watching where I was going."

"How'd the fight go?" Hagatha pressed. "Did you kick his ass?" She made a kicking motion in the air, nearly making contact with a skull-headed monkey, who made a fist and chattered angrily at them.

"We just yelled at each other," Liz said. "Nothing physical. I was upset because he got drunk at a party the night before, and he was flirting with some other girl. Or at least I thought he was."

"Who gives a shit?" Hagatha said. "So what?" She grabbed a piece of half-eaten fruit from a soul passing by. She flung it down her throat and spat out a pit.

"I thought he was special." Liz barely missed stepping on a large, not yet dead rat.

"No one is special," Hagatha answered, scooping up the rat and swallowing it whole. "First rule of Hell. Also, second and third rule of Hell. The only reason anyone in Hell gives a crap about anyone else is if that person can do something for them. Like Brian, for instance: the only reason he gives a rat's ass about you is because you do all that work for him."

"Of course."

"That's how things *should* be," Hagatha went on, with a decisive nod. "I take care of you because he wants you to do a bunch of crap for him and he's the one who gives me my Hell Coin on payday, so . . . " She shrugged. "It's all about the kickbacks."

"Sounds reasonable." Liz preferred to agree with Hagatha.

The demon playfully punched her companion's shoulder, knocking her into a wall.

"Ha! You'd make a good demon. Humans are usually pretty damn irrational and whiny. There's no such thing as a friend in Hell. Remember that."

"I always though you and Gadreel were kinda friendly," Liz said, thinking of the large blue demon who worked with Hagatha on crowd control in the lobby.

"What?" Hagatha snorted as smoke billowed from her nose. "C'mon. I like Gadreel okay; he has my back. I have his. That's all. Like, if he tried to take something from me, I would beat the uholy Lucifer out of him, you know?"

"I see." She shrugged. "I guess I haven't quite let go of some of the ideas I picked up from the Upper World."

Hagatha shrugged. "It happens. You have to acclimatize."

"I guess so," Liz said.

Hagatha slapped her on the back. "You're in the right place. No doubt about it."

As they approached the station, the she-devil took a long deep sniff.

"Ah! I smell it!"

"What's that?"

"Fear, confusion, dread and despair." Hagatha licked her lips. "Delicious!"

They pushed their way through the crowds of wailing souls, some tightly gripping their luggage. Nergal, who liked to tease Liz, pointed at her, and raised his eyebrows.

"You're a tasty morsel," he grinned, rubbing his stomach.

"Hey, asshole!" Hagatha said. "Want me to come rip your fucking arm off?"

He shrugged. The she-devils were a good foot taller than the blue, Baalzephon demons, and built like Valkyries. Liz had seen Hagatha toss bigger demons than Nergal into the street for annoying her.

Liz went about her business quickly, re-pasting posters of the map on station walls over old torn ones, placing brochures in small wire racks scattered around the platform. Two of the dozen racks were twisted beyond usefulness; she made a note to request some more. Theo was removing the rotting benches on the platform. He noticed her and gave her a little wave.

The thing Liz hated most about the train station was the newly damned, pressing against her, begging for help or information. It re-awoke her own terror at finding herself in Hell. Some were angry and lashed out. Hagatha quickly sent them on their way, shoving maps at them, kicking them, slapping them, telling them to go to the Admin Building and get in line.

One soul managed to evade Hagatha long enough to tug at Liz's sleeve; a small, disheveled man in a suit that was too big, holding a hat in his hand.

"Is this the afterlife?" He stared at her with big, brown, liquid eyes. "I thought I would just quit existing." He started to cry. Childlike, he wrapped his fingers around the end of Liz's sweater sleeve.

"Please, ma'am?" His lip trembled. "Can I just quit existing? I'm tired. I'm so tired."

Hagatha was there in a flash. She shook the poor little man off and thrust a map into his hand. She pointed at the center with a bony claw.

"Right there, buddy," she tapped the map. "Take off and jump in. That'll be the end of you." She kicked at him, and he shuffled off, clinging tightly to his map. Liz watched him shamble away. She felt a pang of pity, a fact she did her best to disguise.

On the way back to the office, Liz asked, "Have you ever wondered why more of us don't just jump in the pit? I mean, why we bother existing? The lost souls, I mean."

"You tell me," Hagatha said.

"I don't know," Liz said. "I want to be here, to be me, even if there's nothing to look forward to except this for the rest of my afterlife," she waved her hand around the smelly crowded street filled with demons.

Hagatha slowed down to keep pace with Liz for a second. "Why bother worrying? You and I have sweet jobs, and all the pay we can drink. Souls always wanna overthink things." The she-devil shook her head and lowered her voice. "Besides, no demon in my memory has ever gone into the Abyss. Know why? Becoming nothing is terribly painful, and it doesn't totally work every time. A demon I know named Jeremias talked to some of the soul fragments close to the Abyss. He says he made out some of the stuff they were saying, even though I've only heard them talk gibberish. No one's even sure how many souls just get fragmented instead of becoming nothing. Or even if any manage to *totally* become nothing."

"Why?" Liz asked. "Why not tell souls that?"

"Don't know. It's policy," said Hagatha. "Don't care. What difference does it make to me?"

She eyed Liz suspiciously. "Why do you care? You're not going to throw yourself down the pit, are you? Brian would be pissed. The line's half as long as it was before."

"No," Liz shivered. "Not at all."

"Any other stupid questions?" Hagatha asked.

Deciding to push her luck a little, Liz nodded. "Actually, there is something I've been wondering about. Why is there a ticket counter at Perdition City Station? It seems weird since we're all stuck here for eternity. If you can't buy a ticket, why bother with a ticket counter?"

Hagatha shrugged. "Don't know. It's been sitting there, boarded up since I can remember. And for the record, that remark about stupid questions was meant to make you feel stupid. It's what we call sarcasm around here."

"It doesn't matter anyway. I guess we're not going anywhere."

"There you go!" the she-devil said. "That's the spirit. Get everything you can out of everyone you meet and don't question stuff all the time! You're waking up to reality, baby."

She leaned towards Liz. "Don't tell anyone I told you any of that, especially that shit about Jeremias. Or else." She opened her mouth and hissed through two possum-like rows of teeth.

"Of course not," Liz said. "I'm not sure I believe you, anyway."

Hagatha barked out a laugh. "Now you're catching on."

SIX

The Foundations of Hell

WHEN THEY RETURNED, BRIAN WAS WORKING THE WINDOW. Hagatha walked Liz into the office. "She has all her limbs and she's back to do your bidding. Can I go home now?"

"What?" Brian blinked. "You mean for the day? Of course not. Gadreel and Jezreel would tear me limb from limb if I let you go early."

"Just thought I'd ask." Hagatha slammed the door behind her.

Brian gazed at Liz. For a moment, a smile flickered on his lips. "Glad you're back. We're getting behind. Hey, before you get back up here, can you open that package? It's a bunch of new brochures. Satan sent them from Up Top. He's rolling out another new promotion. Hope it's better than their last 'upgrade.' The new software is the worst yet."

"New flyers?" Liz asked, opening the box. A glossy corner of thick paper peeped through foam peanuts. "Wow. We usually just photocopy old ones. You must be a magician with the budget."

"I didn't do it," Brian said. "Satan must have paid for them. If I did find extra money in the budget, I certainly wouldn't waste it so frivolously. I have no idea why he thinks we need new ones."

Liz pulled a slick trifold brochure from the box. On the front was a picture taken at an odd angle from one side of the Abyss. The mouth of the great chasm was hidden from view. She saw a cloudburst of glowing haze where the River Nepenthe spilled into it. The colors were soft, soothing, and obviously photoshopped. The tagline was: *Tired of the rat race? Fed up with Existence? Ever thought about . . . Nothing?*

Inside were photographs, one a beatific soul flinging itself into the Abyss, Lava Falls in the background, the lava a glorious apricot. Against the drab lights of Hell, it was almost enticing. As Liz unfolded the brochure, photos of unhappy souls emerged: waiting in line, missing limbs, stealing food from trash cans. There was a picture of a soul being thrown to a bog eel, and that same soul, half-digested, crawling back up to shore. In each case, the brochure suggested, without saying so directly, that unhappy souls might find the answer to their problems in the Abyss.

"These are—something," Liz told Brian as she took his place at the window. "I've never seen anything like them. The weirdest thing of all is the quality. It's surprisingly good."

"You're right." He gave a whistle. "And they seem to encourage jumpers. They might not meet regulations. Put them aside for now. We still have some we can use."

Brian seemed frazzled by the end of the day, so when Liz closed her window and pulled down the shade, she suggested they grab a cup of coffee somewhere. "We could go to the Wake-Up Witch or the Caffeinated Goblin. Neither one is that much better than the coffee here," she conceded. "The great thing is . . . it's not *here*."

Brian stared at her—obviously confused by the thought of leaving before midnight.

"I suppose anything would be better if it wasn't here. Maybe sometime. Not tonight." He waved his hand helplessly over a stack of papers on his desk. As Liz closed the office door, she noticed him staring at her. When she caught his eye, he blushed and turned back to his work.

She pulled on her sweater with a sigh and walked through the lobby. The night shift had just clocked in; Gadreel dropped the soul he was shaking and walked out with her. He lived in the same demon dormitory as Hagatha, the one across from Liz's own building. They passed the long line snaking down the sidewalk. As always when the souls saw Liz, there was a round of sighing and cursing. It meant the line was closed and they wouldn't get any further that evening.

The young man who'd thought he was on a bad mushroom trip the day Liz arrived was within sight of Admin now. He was camped on the corner of Main and Phlegethon, a block from where she'd seen him the day before.

"Hey, dudes!" he said. "Be seeing you in a day or two." He grinned and gave them the thumbs up.

Gadreel rolled his eyes. He walked with her another block and then stopped in front of a raucous demon bar called The Blazing Desolation. The music and demonic laughter pumping out was so loud that Liz had to read Gadreel's lips when he turned to her and said "Time to party!"

They nodded at each other and parted ways. Liz wasn't in any hurry to get home to Dennis. Perdition City nightlife was heating up and she didn't like to be on the streets alone, so she picked up her pace.

As she walked into the lobby of her building, she met Ellie, whose arms were so full of large black spiral-bound notebooks and manila folders that they came up to her nose.

"Hey! Can I help you?" Liz rushed over when she noticed the stack wobbling and caught several books as they toppled. She took half the load and they started for the stairs. "Do any of these bite?"

"Not these," Ellie grunted from under the weight of her stack. "Nor do they have legs. Small mercies. Should be perfectly safe."

"Wow, these are heavy," Liz said. "How do you manage?"

"Not well. My arms are cramping," Ellie said. "I'll explain when we get upstairs. How about some coffee? Or beer if you'd prefer. It's not cold, and I'm sure it's lousy. Hey, it's alcohol. Anything to take the edge off."

"Sure. Let me help you with these, then I'll run home and feed Dennis, so he won't poop in my underwear drawer."

When Liz returned, Ellie was in the kitchen pouring them both a tepid beer.

"Guess what you carried up for me? Actually, don't guess. Read," Ellie commanded from the kitchen.

Liz picked up a large spiral-bound notebook from the coffee table. The metal rings strained to hold all the printed material. The peeling red-lettered label on the front said *Contractual Records and Agreements: Regulations, Provisos, Amendments, and Exceptions. Underworld Plots 666-713, and Adjacent Unclaimed Territories.*

"Some sort of real estate records?" Liz suggested.

"Yep." Ellie handed her a beer and sunk into the couch. "Remember how I told you that a couple days ago the dean and the school president had a tiff? You know, the old demon who was talking about the trains running both ways?"

"I remember." Liz put her feet as close to Greg as she dared. The warmth emanating from his body was delicious.

"He got demoted and sent to teach Swamp Regs at the satellite school in the Bogs of Despair. The worst possible job in the system for a tenured professor, much less a dean."

"Was it because of what he said?" Liz asked. "About the trains?"

"Nah," Ellie said. "It was because he told the head of the Geology department that Dr. Batsen, the school president, was a suck-up and a hack. Word got back to Dr. Batsen, and she and old Dean Lempo had a fist fight. Now there's something that would have made teaching worth my time when I was embodied. She spat poison right into his eye." Her tone was dreamy. "It was kind of amazing."

"Wow," Liz grinned. "The demons in Admin usually only fight with the souls. Probably because they're afraid of Hagatha."

Ellie shrugged. "At least it's entertaining. Anyhoo, I managed to get into Old Lempo's office after he got himself fired. I had a bit of a sniff around and found these," she waved at the ledger books and folders, "in a file cabinet under his desk. It had a key, and it was always locked. So, I figured whatever was in there had to be interesting."

"Unholy Hell, Ellie!" Liz put her beer down. "What made you decide to steal them? And how did you snag them if the drawer was locked?"

Ellie laughed. "I wandered back in after the janitor cleaned out the office. He must have opened the drawer to throw things away. He's such a lazy fuck; he went on lunch half-way through. You know how demons are about taking every available break. I snuck in and when I saw some stuff about Hell Corporation, founding grants, and real estate deals, I took them. Nobody seemed to notice or care, which I figured would be the case." She took another swig of beer. "The Dean's specialty was Netherworld real estate and the regulations pertaining thereto. All property in the infernal realm comes with mountains of policy attachments. You can't buy real estate here. It's leased in perpetuity."

"Okay, two questions. One, aren't you afraid you'll get in trouble? And two . . . leased for eternity? From whom?"

"First, what are they going to do?" Ellie said, lifting one eyebrow. "Kill me? Anyway, I'm curious about this place. That ticket counter got me thinking. This looks like the same crapola I always carry home. Besides, I bet that janitor could have cared less what was in those drawers. He's a real lunkhead. He looks like a chubby, upright lizard with one squirrelly eye and duck feet. He leaves trash spilling out of the cans in the hallways until people start tripping over it."

"And?" Liz said. "What about the grant and the lease?"

"That," Ellie said, "is what I aim to find out. Who knows? Maybe we find out why Hell was created in the first place or how we got chosen to be eternal residents thereof. It'll probably take me forever to get through it all, but it's something to do and technically, I do have forever." She shrugged. "What have I got to lose? Theoretically they can't throw me in the Abyss. Anyway, would it be so bad?" She took off her shoes and put her feet on Greg's back.

Liz laughed. "Well, I won't tell anyone. Please, you have to promise to let me know if you find out anything interesting. And I have something to tell you about the Abyss." She told Ellie about the new brochures.

"You keep me updated on the new policy to get rid of us all," Ellie said, "and I'll tell you if I find anything that seems pertinent to the trains. Deal?"

"Deal."

SEVEN

Rock Bottom?

LIZ WENT TO BED THAT NIGHT WITH DENNIS SLAPPING her nose at random times or suddenly running to the end of the bed and biting her feet. It wasn't until Dennis curled unconscious, butt in her face, producing a whiffling, piggish snore, that she began her nightly ruminations. Normally, she combed memories of embodied life, trying to untangle the reasons for her afterlife assignment. That night, she shifted her anxious thoughts to Ellie's discovery. What did it mean?

What about the brochures? Admin wasn't allowed to order or even strongly encourage souls to jump, but those brochures were practically a celebration of nonexistence. What about the fact that not long before she arrived, many more souls had been assigned to Hell—different in temperament from the souls before them? What about Dean Lempo, the one who said the trains used to run both ways?

She moved each fact around in her mind, trying to piece the puzzle together. She finally fell into a fitful sleep. Around three a.m., she found herself waking up to the stench of Dennis's foul breath.

Standing on her chest, wet nose pressed against hers, he complained, "I'm hungry."

Liz stumbled to the kitchen, scooped out some rancid tuna, and watched as he ate it in one gulp. When he was satisfied, they returned to bed. She had a hard time falling back asleep. The whimpering cries of a soul being tormented drifted through the window; she propped herself up against the pillows, pulling the damp, stained quilt around herself, awash in self-pity and anxiety. Three a.m. was exactly the same, life or death, she thought miserably. The witching hour. It suddenly occurred to her that there while she might be able to solve the mystery of why she was here, in the end, it didn't matter. Nothing did. Nothing they did or learned would ever make a difference. She wondered if flinging herself into the Abyss *was* a viable option.

She'd spent an entire lifetime as a perfectionist, always trying to measure up. She'd studied hard, made straight A's, staying up until the wee hours writing papers, preparing for exams. In high school, she'd often given half her meal to that girl whose mom wouldn't sign her up for free lunch. In college, she drank sparingly, never to excess, frequently reminding herself she was there to study, not to party. When she'd started at the library, she came in early, worked off the clock. Her father, a doctor, had drilled a puritan work ethic deep into her soul. She brought extra yogurt and stocked the fridge in the break room in an attempt to get along with all her coworkers, even Stinky Jim, who didn't bathe nearly as often as he could have. She'd put up with all the dreadful sticky-fingered children on Story Mornings with a smile. She'd dutifully gone to her aunt's house once a month for dinner and pretended to like her bland chicken casserole with the crushed cracker topping—even Hell's food hadn't made her nostalgic for her aunt's culinary disappointments.

Perdition City was more of the same, a horrible extension of her life on earth, worse because she now knew it would last forever. While embodied, the pointlessness of existence had been swallowed up by dreams of the future: marriage, kids, promotions, that book she was going to write. They'd somehow drowned out the creeping nihilism of a tedious job, loneliness, stress, and fights with Rob. The afterlife had ripped the blindfold off. There'd never been any purpose. Even if Ellie discovered why they were there, none of it would make a difference. This was it. Forever. She found herself sniffling into the faded gray bed sheets, until Dennis bit her big toe.

"For Satan's sake," he whined. "Shut the fuck up."

Liz kicked at him. He immediately began snoring like a chainsaw again. A wave of self-pity swept over her. The wave crashed on the shore of her consciousness and left something in its wake—relief. This was Hell, rock bottom. She'd circled the drain, been flushed. She felt almost . . . cheerful. It was finished. The stress and scheming—her attempts to be the perfect student, the best employee, the best friend, the best girlfriend—were useless now. She understood why Ellie had taken the books without giving a damn whether she'd get caught. Liz had failed as far as she could fail, as far as it was possible to fail; an odd, wobbly composure took up residence in her heart. The worst that could happen to her was the Abyss. Maybe, just maybe, she would choose that ending for herself at some point. Until then, she was free. Her existence depended on nothing, was going nowhere.

From her bed, she investigated the alley. A soul was drunkenly trying to fend off an amorphous gray demon, which shapeshifted, turning itself into an oily serpent, while the soul attempted to hit it in the face with a broken stiletto heel. Sticky red steam rose from the grates. Wailing and harsh laughter drifted upwards. Liz closed the crooked blinds, wrapped herself in the mustard-yellow quilt and slept soundly until seven a.m.. She even managed to remain unconscious through what Dennis later described as an enthusiastic nose flogging.

"I wanted breakfast!" he groused after she got up.

She hummed a little tune as she unwrapped a particularly smelly fish head for Dennis and chucked him on the chin with her thumb.

"Bye love," she said. "I'll see you this evening."

He hissed.

She noticed that he forgot to barf on her shoe—a small favor. More than she'd hoped for. Warmth spread through her body, but she checked herself. This was the bad place. The worst place. It would not—could not—disappoint if one remembered that. Still, the tiny wavering sense of relief held on in some corner of her soul. She existed in the most miniscule, least meaningful way possible. Maybe that was enough.

EIGHT

Existence is Enough

WHEN LIZ ARRIVED THAT MORNING, BRIAN SAID, "WELL, you look rested."

He stumbled as he rose from his too-short office chair and handed her a printout. The lever that allowed the height of the chair to be adjusted had given out about fifty years before, according to his estimate. "Almost lively."

"I slept better than usual," she answered, reaching for a fresh box of Kleenex to set on the counter. Pulling the string on the dusty old blinds, she opened the window to a sea of lost souls, undulating against the dim light leaking through the dirty two-story lobby windows.

"Is Dennis okay?" Brian pulled down his glasses and stared at Liz. She was uncomfortable because she knew there was something fresh and different about her. She wasn't sure if it was wise to let anyone see.

"He's in fine form, believe me. He snored so loud; I dreamt I was driving construction equipment all night."

"Good old Dennis. You'll dream about drowning in paperwork tonight. Remember the new system we got in last week? We lost about fifty years' worth of data, so I guess I'll be working late."

"I'm sorry," Liz said. "Want me to stay?"

"Nah. You've got your day cut out for you already."

Brian pointed at the complaint window, which was not yet open. A woman was standing outside, frantically banging a hand against it. A very large hand, attached to an arm wearing a man's watch. The arm was covered in hair. It did not belong to her.

"Open up, goddammit!" the woman screamed.

Liz flipped the sign to *open* and pulled up the window shade.

"You're really learning not to let them get to you," Brian said, walking up behind Liz at the window later that day. "You seemed remarkably unfazed by the guy who vomited steaming bile and tried to crawl into the window to make changes to his form."

"This is Hell. I've lowered my expectations," Liz smiled.

"They can never be low enough." He frowned a little and shook his head as Liz handed him a stack of forms. "Keep that in mind."

"By the way," Liz said. "Thanks for helping me push him back until Hagatha got here."

He shrugged. A furtive half smile played around his mouth. "Satan knows I can't lose my only help."

That day, there was very little the souls could do to rattle Liz. She felt Brian's eyes on her as she worked with souls, handed out forms and Kleenex, or wiped down the counter after someone spewed blood or spat on it. All that week, Liz slept through the wee hours. She'd spent a lifetime worrying and just couldn't manage it anymore. On Friday, Brian walked up at four fifty-eight p.m. and flipped the sign over to *closed*.

"Let's go to the café and grab some dinner," he suggested. "They've been waiting so long that one more weekend won't hurt them. Besides, I'd like to get there before there's a crowd."

Liz was intrigued. She'd never seen Brian leave the office, other than a quick trip to the Housing Council or another office, and those tasks were usually left to her now. They walked past the line. A few souls began to howl with indignation. Someone threw a dismembered foot at them. Someone else belched out a cloud of foul-smelling smoke.

A nervous-looking soul addressed the crowd. "Please. Can we all calm down? Please?"

"You've got two minutes left!!" shrieked a nicely dressed, middle-aged female soul. She stabbed the nervous-looking soul in the eye with a ballpoint pen in frustration. "I've been here two fucking years!"

"Hey! Ow!" the nervous soul yelled, "this is exactly what I'm talking about!"

"You left the line six times," a large male soul pointed out. He pushed the middle-aged soul, and they began to wrestle.

A soul dressed in a teal green velour tracksuit turned to the soul behind him, grabbed it by the ears and began to twist in an effort to remove the head, probably to throw it at Brian and Liz as they passed. The soul whose head was being twisted gut punched his attacker, who fell backwards and took out five or six others like bowling pins. One soul turned beet red; smoke began to pour out of his ears and nose. As he waved his fist at Brian, flames burst out from his collar, singeing the material. A gargoyle flew over with a fire extinguisher spraying everyone in line with foam.

Gadreel used his walkie talkie to call in more demons, foreseeing the inevitable crowd control problems; in the meantime, security began to push the mob back. Jezreel simply walked down the line, randomly hitting souls with his club. Security gargoyles picked up souls, lifting them in the air, throwing them back into the crowd.

"Well, at least the line will be a little shorter when we get back on Monday," Brian said with a wry smile, as Hagatha launched a screaming female soul through the revolving doors. They stood back for a moment as the soul spun like a load of laundry in the spin cycle until she was deposited in a heap on the sidewalk.

"I don't know how you've done this century after century." Liz leapt over a potted plant that came skidding across the foyer as they reached the door.

Brian shrugged. "Actually, this part of it has gotten better since we started getting in more souls. More souls equal fewer fights." He shook his head. "I wish I understood why. A hundred years ago, there were fewer souls and more fights and violence. Who can say?"

At Dante's Café—a squat, dirty diner that sat on a pier where the Sea of Dread washed up in moaning waves—the server showed them to a corner table. Small islands of trash floated on the brackish water outside, while the smell of dead fish skulked in through grimy windows. Dante's was one of the better restaurants on the pier. Brian and Liz both ordered omelets and fries; the eggs were dry, rubbery, and burnt. And the fries were cold and clammy, but they were typically the least noxious items on the menu.

"Hold the ants this time," Brian joked to the server, a mirthless gray fellow with a long face and a missing right thumb. He meant to be funny. But there were, occasionally, insects in the food.

"I'll do what I can, sir," the server sniffed. He removed himself with a long, drawn-out sigh and drifted into the kitchen at the back of the diner.

As the kitchen door swung shut behind him, they heard their server say something. The demon chef bellowed in response. "By Great Lucifer's tail!" the demon chef yelled. "Are you accusing me of putting ants in the food? As if I would waste gourmet pepper ants on the underbred assholes who eat in this place!"

"There's definitely going to be ants in the food, isn't there?" Liz sighed. "By the way, is the server a lost soul? Sometimes, if they've been here long enough, I can't tell them from the demons."

"Yeah. He's been here almost as long as I have—worked at a medieval inn in England if I'm remembering correctly. Demons make terrible servers, you know. They make terrible chefs too, but the Demon's Local forces us to reserve head chef jobs for them. I'm always getting requests to pull souls out of line for service jobs. There's certainly no question that he's being punished properly." Brian smiled. "Sometimes a job that's more of the same is one of the worst punishments you can get in Hell," he said. "No offense to you."

"None taken," Liz said. "I concur. You're a pretty good boss. All in all, things could be worse."

"Thanks, I guess. I'm not sure Satan would agree. He says I'm not hard enough on the employees. And I'm always behind."

"You do exceptionally well for the circumstances you're in," Liz said, leaning forward. "C'mon! Take it easy on yourself."

He blushed a little and turned away. They sat in silence for a moment, the cracked vinyl of the booth squeaking and crackling under them. Brian stared down and picked at food that had been stuck on the table since time immemorial. Liz found her skirt stuck to a poorly applied strip of duct tape and had to scoot sideways a few inches. She wasn't sure why they were there, and she was starting to get a little nervous.

Finally, Brian reached across the table and touched Liz's hand—for just a second. The Sea of Dread was working itself up into a frenzy; the moaning morphed into wailing and the wind whipped some garbage and flung it against the windows. Brian struggled with his next words as he watched the sea rise.

"Liz, I didn't come here to talk about me. It's you I'm worried about," he said, his voice low. "What's going on? You seem . . . well, not happy, exactly. Not stressed or freaked out. And you're getting even more work done than normal. What gives?"

"I just realized where I am," Liz answered. "And somehow it makes things okay."

"What in Unholy Hell are you talking about?" Brian jerked forward, and spilled his sluggish, opaque water on the table. He glanced around the café and seemed relieved that they were alone. He pushed his glasses up on his nose and leaned over the table, then backed up and wiped crumbs from the front of his sweater.

"This is . . . you know, the bad place. The worst place," Liz said. "It can't get more horrible than this, so what's the point in stressing?" She shrugged. "Other than the Abyss, of course."

Brian held up his hand to shush her. The server put down the bread plate and waved his hand over it with an elegant gesture. Brian inspected the bread, shooed off a fly from one dinner roll, and shook a slug from another, taking the one with the recently removed slug for himself.

"It's fine," he sighed.

"Very good sir," said the server, shuffling back to the kitchen. As soon as he swung through the door, the mutual cursing began again between server and chef.

"You're not going to jump into the Abyss, are you?" Brian asked. "Because I was just thinking the other day that I don't know if I can get by without you. Sometimes souls experience moments of clarity before they jump, or so the demons who work the Abyss tell me."

"No, of course not," Liz sawed into her roll. "I just hit bottom. The bottom of everything. Things aren't going to get better. I know that now. For the first time in my existence, I don't think they're going to get worse. And if they do, for once, I know exactly how that will look. Thing is, that makes me feel better about—I don't know—everything."

"Don't take this the wrong way, but I don't want you to be happy," Brian said. "That's just a set-up for disappointment later. Torturous disappointment. It's just—not done here. The happier you are now, the unhappier you'll be later. Trust me. I was almost happy once. It didn't work out."

"Oh, Brian," Liz leaned forward, touching his hand. His skin felt surprisingly warm, and she let her hand linger. He drew in his breath. He didn't move his hand from under hers. Was something happening between them? "I'm not happy. I promise. I just don't have the energy to be worried about things anymore. I'm settling in." She left her hand on his; he didn't pull away.

Outside the window, scraps of paper drifted on the ashy wind and fluttered off the pier into the water. The space under an overflowing trash can teemed with footlong black and green dung beetles. A large flying rat fought one of the beetles for an enormous rolled-up ball of excrement. A tall ochre demon with a wicked, spiked tail kicked at both and they tumbled off the edge, the rat flapping and screeching skyward, dung beetle disappearing into the water. The demon tossed the ball of crap down his throat and promptly barfed it back into the trash can. This was perhaps not the best scene for a serious discussion—much less a bit of romance.

Brian looked down at her hand. He reached out with his other hand and ran his fingers along a scratch near Liz's knuckles, created by Dennis the previous morning. "I like you, Liz," he said. "And that scares me. I don't like anyone. I'm not *supposed* to like anyone."

"It's okay to be scared, Brian," she smiled. "I promise I'm not trying to tempt you to some state of blissful awareness or any of that stuff. All my human life, I spent worrying about doing the wrong thing, saying the wrong thing, making the wrong decisions. Now I don't have to worry anymore. I've already done all the damage that can be done. Now I can just be. Just endure." She drew back her hands, took a large bite of her roll and then realized something was missing. "Can you pass the butter?"

"I get what you're saying. You just have to be . . . careful." He handed her a squashed-up foil package containing the "butter," an oily yellow substance that tasted almost exactly not like butter. "Hell has an equilibrium. Satan doesn't like it disturbed unless he's the one screwing it up. The last few years, things have been different, and I can't put my finger on why. So many souls, the budget tighter than ever. It worries me. And then those brochures. They aren't forcing anyone to jump in the Abyss, but they surely come close to breaking the only rule Hell ever enforces. This is no time to relax."

"Surely relaxing a little and not stressing every damn minute won't break up the balance of Hell," Liz said, "or make us want to become nothing. I mean, I think it would make us less likely to jump."

"I'm just saying that even if you do feel some strange form of contentment . . ."

"I don't," she interrupted him. "That's the thing. It's the opposite of contentment. There is no *content*."

"Even if you do," Brian continued, "might be best to hide it. Okay?"

"Fine," she said. "I will do my level best to appear unhappy, if that makes you happy." She rolled her eyes and smiled. Clearly, Brian couldn't figure out exactly what to do with that, but he smiled back anyway.

The waiter returned and re-filled their glasses. Liz swished hers.

"No bugs," she was poking Brian a little. "Little favors, huh?"

"Don't," Brian said. And then burst out, "Is that all? Everything is okay because you realized you're in Hell?"

"Yeah. I think that's it." They ate in silence for a few minutes before Liz decided to take a risk. "Brian, do you know if the trains used to run both ways? And why there's a ticket counter at the station?"

He stopped mid-bite, stared at her again, then pushed the eggs around on his plate until Liz was concerned she'd broken him.

"I'm sorry," she apologized. "I shouldn't have asked that."

Brian let out a deep sigh. "Listen, we need to talk. It can't be here or now."

NINE

Brian Knows Something

MONDAY, AFTER SHE FINISHED CLEANING UP THE COUNT-
er, Liz stopped behind Brian's desk. He was hunched over, the weak
reddish light from the desk lamp and the glow of his ancient computer
wobbling over his chin, washing out his face in an eerie green and amber
glow. His dishwater blond hair had a few gray streaks. He looked so sad
and troubled that, without thinking, she touched his left shoulder and
leaned against him, just for a second.

"Don't work too hard."

He closed his eyes, brought up his right hand, brushed hers, then
gently removed her hand from his shoulder.

"You should go now," he said. "I'll be working late. You go on
home tonight. Seriously." His voice cracked a little. He scooted his chair
away and picked up a stack of papers from the other end of his desk.

"Sorry." Liz wanted so much to ease his burden and help him feel
better. Now she was worried she'd offended him instead. He hadn't been
as talkative since their conversation at Dante's. She put on her sweater
and walked out into the muddy gray twilight, head down, past the
infernal lamentation of the line and the baying demons trying to control
the crowd.

Later on that evening, Dennis was watching reruns of "The
"The Apprentice". Bad TV was one of the more effective punishments
of Hell, and Dennis enjoyed it more than any of the other personal
tormentors in their building. He always kept the remote in his claws
and liked to blast his favorites at top volume. He'd barfed up all his

dinner and was angrily demanding more, yelling over the noise of the television, when Liz heard a knock at the door. This time of night, most of the souls in the building were long since locked behind their heavy apartment doors. Was it a wandering salesman trying to sell hot lava brew makers? Or a demon, drunk or high, who'd forgotten that she worked with Brian? Worse yet, could it be a soul from the Help Line? She'd been followed home before. She stood quietly in the corner, waiting, hoping that whoever it was would go away. The knocking continued and grew more urgent. She grabbed Dennis, prepared to throw him at the intruder.

"Hey! Ow!" Dennis yowled. "I'm watching TV! Help! You're fired!"

A few seconds more and he would have had her hand off—but then she heard a familiar voice outside the door.

"Open up. It's Brian."

She put down the demon cat with only minor damage taken to her arms and legs and opened the door. Dennis stalked away, green tail bristling to its arrow tip, and retreated into the bedroom where Liz was certain he would barf on her bed. Brian pushed past her into the apartment. He turned, locking the door behind him.

"If anyone asks, this was a work meeting."

"Okay," Liz said. "*Is* it a work meeting?"

Brian walked over and with a trembling hand closed the bedroom door on Dennis, who was working himself up to a good retching. Her boss sat on the horrible couch, grimacing.

"Do you want a lukewarm beer?" Liz asked as cheerfully as possible. He shook his head and sat there for a minute more, saying nothing. She *had* offended him. She just knew it. Just when she thought nothing could bother her, she was going to get fired. She'd be sent to the Bogs of Despair, or she'd be sent to the Ghastly Geysers to clean out the farting pools that bubbled with sulfur and methane . . . or . . .

"You know what? Yes. I'd love a beer." Brian said. "Thank you for the offer."

Liz brought the beer and sat in the ancient, broken armchair, across the scratched parquet coffee table. She popped open the beer and scooted it towards him. He definitely had *something* on his mind.

"Sorry, it's Bud Light," she said. "We are in Hell, after all."

Brian gave her a weak smile and sipped his beer. He picked up the remote, stared at it as though he couldn't figure out what it was, then put it back down.

"Okay," Liz said. "What gives? You look like death."

He twisted the can in his hand still saying nothing.

"Sorry. Bad afterlife joke. I feel like I'm the only one talking here," Liz paused. "I assume you came here to say something." She was too nervous to wait much longer. She popped open her own can of beer and spilled a little on her blouse. Things were getting more awkward by the minute.

"I do have something I need to say. It's hard—I don't know how to start. It's that stuff we were talking about the other day at lunch."

He swallowed hard. "Yes. The trains used to work both ways. I'm pretty sure, anyway."

Liz let out a sigh of relief. Maybe she wasn't going to get fired. And then she caught what he had just said. Her mouth dropped open.

"Are you kidding me? They did? Why don't they now?" She pulled her chair closer to the table. "Brian, what the Hell? What happened to the trains? Where did the trains go when they left the station?"

"I don't know a lot," he said holding up his hands to stem the barrage of questions. "I wasn't always—here. The rumor is that trains used to leave with passengers, souls assigned to damnation but later released. I've heard enough idle gossip to believe that before my time, souls could somehow leave this place."

"Where did they go?" Liz leaned forward, reaching for Brian's hand. "Surely, they couldn't go back to earth? To Heaven? Where?"

"I don't know," he said. "Honestly, I don't. That's all I can tell you. I heard Satan and Mammon discussing it one day as I was coming into the conference room. I stopped outside the door because I was worried it was something I wasn't *supposed* to hear. They slip up sometimes when they think no one is listening."

"Holy Beelzebub," Liz flopped back in her seat, and felt the end of a broken spring punch her in her back with equal force. "Ouch." She sat up, rubbing her sacrum.

"You have to understand, I'm not supposed to know any of this stuff, much less talk about it. I don't really *know* anything. If you discuss it with anyone, please leave my name out of it. You didn't hear it from me. Promise?"

Liz thought for a moment. The sound of retching, followed by wet thuds, came from the bedroom. Ash pinged on the metal grates outside the window. A storm was coming. She shivered. "Yes, I promise."

"I'm sorry. That's all I know. If I could tell you more I would." He slumped over and sighed, his head in his hands.

"I believe you," Liz said. "It's okay. Don't feel bad."

Eventually, speaking to his shoes, he mumbled, "There's something else you should know, Liz. It's hard for me to say. It may be more dangerous than the train stuff."

He rose from the couch and paced to the window, where the dark night of Hell was well underway. A scream pierced the night; raucous laughter bubbled up from the street below.

"What is it?" Maybe she *was* being fired. If she was, she wished he'd get it over and done with.

"It's so hard for me to say. I wasn't created to like someone or . . ." he trailed off, muttering so quietly that Liz couldn't hear what he said.

"You're talking into the curtains. What did you say?"

"Or to have feelings for someone. That's what I said," he turned and stammered out. "I have these weird *feelings* when you're around. I don't think I'm supposed to."

She sat very still. Dennis was digging through the underwear drawer in her bedroom, the scraping of his claws against wood punctuated by angry mewls. Then they both heard it, a low rumble of thunder in the background.

"I need to get the duct tape and a piece of plastic," Liz said, absently. "Sounds like a smoke storm is coming. It'll rain ash right in that broken window."

"It's an omen," Brian said morosely.

"Oh, c'mon. It's just a storm." She crossed the room and stood behind him. Then, gathering courage, she placed a hand on his back.

They stared together at the thick column of ashes gathering and swirling in front of the distant plume of red light rising eternally in the west. Brian seemed mesmerized. He took her hand and led her back to the couch. He sat in front of her. This time he looked directly into her eyes. She felt his hand tremble.

"I like you a lot, Liz," he said. "I've never felt like this. I get butterflies in my stomach when I see you wearing that skirt with the flowers. And I feel warm when you sit next to me at lunch time—even though it's not warm. The fact is—I worry about you when we're not together. I'm sorry. I'm sure that's probably not how you feel about me. And I shouldn't feel that way about you. It's not okay. Satan won't like it." He took a deep breath. "*You* probably don't like it. It upsets my stomach. I can't seem to stop. It feels good in some weird way, and I don't want to stop. I'll try though. If it makes you uncomfortable."

Liz quit breathing for a moment. She was stunned because it suddenly occurred to her that the deep affection she felt for Brian might be more than friendship. The man who bandaged her paper cuts. The man who had once slammed down the window on the arm of a soul who'd reached through to pull her hair. This tall skinny man with his tortoiseshell glasses and wide friendly face. She thought of all the times he'd ordered out and given her the best sandwich. The small space heater powered by tiny dragons he'd brought in to warm the air under the complaint counter to keep her warm. She realized how familiar she was with his masculine, smoky smell. His graying hair. What she felt for Brian might go beyond a professional relationship. Even well past friendship.

"It's okay. I . . . I like you too," she whispered. "A lot."

The moment was interrupted by Dennis banging at the door. "Who locked me in here? What's going on? Why can't I hear the television?"

Brian flinched, dropping her hand. "Please don't say anything. For Hell's sake, don't let anyone see that we care about each other. I need to think about this. Please. I shouldn't have told you."

He stood up. "And that's why the forms now have to include three hundred more categories of disembodiment. Whole new ways to die in the Upper World, Liz. I'll need to see you early in the morning. Lots of work to do."

He walked over and opened the bedroom door. Dennis appeared in the crack, narrowed his eyes, and glared suspiciously from Liz to Brian.

"Okay," she said. "I'll be there early. I'll be tired, though. Dennis here will get me up three or four times tonight." She tried to look dejected.

"Well, he's doing his job then," Brian said with a tight smile.

Dennis flipped his tail up over his back and walked proudly to his chair, snagging the remote with his claws on the way. "Absolutely," he purred. "I know how to do *my* job. Unlike some people whose bosses have to make a special trip to tell them things they should have learned at the office." He flipped the television back on full blast, found an episode of Full House, and started howling with laughter. As the door shut behind Brian, Liz stood frozen until Dennis screeched, "Get out of the way of the TV before I scratch your eyes out!" She wandered absently into the kitchen and stared out at the crimson streaks of falling sparks against the dark sky.

So, Liz thought, *I've gone to Hell and I'm in the least dysfunctional relationship of my existence.*

Circumstances were not the best. No doubt about that. Brian was worried, and truth be told, so was Liz. What if someone found out and she was forced to switch jobs? There was a demon library in Perdition City. It did not have the best reputation as a professional or pleasant organization to work for. Would she be sent there? Or the Plains of Eternal Boredom? The Western Wilds? Her breath caught in her throat at the thought of not working with Brian every day. She'd just come to terms with Hell and now she had something to lose again. The realization stung.

Still, despite the fear, a feeling bloomed quick and hot in her heart; a certain "joie de après vivre" that would not be suppressed. It was imperative Dennis didn't find out. She stood by the refrigerator, taking deep breaths, allowing her apprehension and some tiny flowering of love and happiness to fight it out in her heart. *I'm in Hell; I think I have a boyfriend; I'm in Hell; I think I have a boyfriend.* The mantra beat its way through her heart leaving her unsteady on her feet. It occurred to her that both things were true and yesterday she'd only been in Hell. Romance won, for a moment.

Dennis came into the kitchen to beg for fish heads to eat in front of the TV and caught her humming.

"Why are you happy when your boss had to make a special trip to talk to you about work?" he asked, rubbing his snotty nose on her bare leg. "Shouldn't you feel bad for being stupid instead?"

Liz shrugged. "I'm just happy he's gone," she said. "Relief, you know."

"Like how I feel every morning when you leave?"

"Yes. Exactly like that," she repressed a smile. "Do you hum a tune after the door shuts behind me?"

"I certainly do," he meowed. "And I dance a little jig. By the way, I pooped in your underwear drawer. Those fish heads you brought me weren't properly rancid. Try harder tomorrow." He sat on the table, spread open his legs, and licked himself slowly, slurping.

"Okay," she said. "Can we go to bed now?"

"Full House marathon," he said. "It's not over until two o'clock."

TEN

Liz Falls Deeper

LIZ WAS EXHAUSTED WHEN SHE GOT UP FOR WORK THE next day. Dennis had been praised for doing a good job tormenting her and the positive reinforcement had gone to his head.

"Here you go, you little asshole." She spooned some greenish-looking tuna from a can into his bowl. He purred noisily and scarfed the tuna. Liz rushed to get her shoes on, so she could get out the door before he threw up on them.

Dennis just missed her shoe; she could hear him retching right inside the door. She made a mental note not to step in it on the way in.

"Ha!" she whispered through the door. "Wore yourself out didn't you, you little jerk? You're slow this morning."

"Don't worry! I'll be pooping all day."

Liz hurried out into the gray light of the morning. Last night's ash storm had covered everything with a fine soot, including a few demons who'd spent the night on the street. The showers had subsided into an unenthusiastic gra y drizzle spattering the city. She nearly tripped over a dusty demon who flashed spots of bright fire-engine-red under the soot covering his back—on leave in Perdition City from the Lake of Fire no doubt—his lower body stuffed beneath the remains of a park bench, which had been burned and gnawed clean through. He woke as she passed and jumped up, a shower of ashes sluicing from his befuddled face. He reached for her, hooking a claw through her sweater, and yelled, "Back in the lake! You're not properly cooked!" Fortunately, Hagatha was coming out of the dormitory across the street.

"Whoa there, buddy," Hagatha said, grabbing his arm. "This isn't your district."

She gave the red demon a good hard clap on the back and sent his eyes rattling around in his head.

"Sorry," he muttered, shaking himself awake, and loped off in the direction of the bus station.

"Bet he's late. Probably only had leave for the day and got tanked up last night," Hagatha said. "Hope he gets a good beating when he gets back. That'll give me something to think about today." She switched her tail with pleasure. "Aren't you going to thank me?"

"Wait," Liz said. "You only give a crap about me because I work for Brian who pays you your drinking money, and he only gives a crap about me because I work for him. So, you were just protecting your own interests, right?"

Hagatha raised her long possum-like nose and howled with laughter. She slapped Liz on the back so hard she nearly fell into the dead black arms of the thorn bush growing behind the fence.

"Sometimes I think you're not quite as stupid as the other lost souls," Hagatha said. "It's a pretty low bar though. Don't get excited."

Liz was nervous about seeing Brian again. She supposed the best bet at the office was pretending their conversation had never taken place. When Hagatha followed her into the office, she nearly had a panic attack. However, the she-devil merely wanted to request a new pitchfork because she'd broken a prong on hers in the battle with the complaint line on Friday.

Hagatha shoved the broken pitchfork under Brian's nose. "Again! This equipment is rubbish."

"Use your club today. Take the pitchfork downstairs to the metal shop; they can fix it."

"This is the third time I've broken it," Hagatha said, waggling her long sharp claw finger in his face. "It's a lousy weapon."

Brian sighed. "Get it fixed for now and I'll review the budget. I'll see what I can do. I usually don't order new security equipment until the end of the quarter." Hagatha stood glowering in the door. "C'mon," Brian said. "I'll try. Right now, there are souls to torment."

"True." Hagatha pursed her lips. "You're lucky I like my job." She swung through the door and let it slam behind her.

Liz thought she detected a slight smile when Brian turned to look at her. He squelched it. "Get the blinds open, Liz. Let's get started."

They swung back into the usual routine without openly acknowledging anything was different. Still, throughout the day, and over the next couple of weeks, there was something in the way their fingers touched when they exchanged forms. Sometimes, Liz caught the twitch of a smile. The tiny crack opening in the dismal walls of despair stayed open. There was a voice in the back of her head telling her to take care, to remember no one in Hell was meant to be happy, that some equilibrium was being disturbed. She squashed the thought as easily as she squashed the hideous green jujubugs that crawled in her window to spit green slime at her.

In fact, the aftermath of their tryst was amazingly quiet. Liz and Brian did their best not to let on that there was anything between them. The mood lightened just a hair throughout the entire Admin Building, the tiny spark of contentment not exactly catching fire, not exactly sputtering out. Brian gave Gadreel a longer lunch than usual, and he returned with extra sulfur and ghost pepper meatballs which he shared with Hagatha and Sheena, the curvaceous imp who ran reception. When Jezreel's pitchfork slid across the lobby after a brief skirmish with the line of souls, Sheena walked out from behind her desk, picked it up, and handed it to him personally, something Liz had never seen her do before.

Jezreel looked slightly confused and separated a couple of truculent souls without kicking anyone out of line. There certainly wasn't enough goodwill or bonhomie that Hell couldn't swallow it. At the same time a tiny, tiny breath of relief—almost imperceptible—was released into the atmosphere.

One Thursday about six weeks after Brian had come to her apartment the first time, Liz came in to work early and quietly slid a bag of ghost-powdered donut holes onto Brian's desk. After he'd made certain all the blinds were still down, he muttered a quiet thanks.

"Time to get started," Liz announced. She opened a new box of ballpoints. "Oh, bat poop. These are green. The forms have to be filled out in blue or black."

Brian rolled his eyes. "One of Mammon's accountants probably saw a deal, started salivating, and didn't even consider the color of the ink. Check in the storage closet; I think there's another box."

She did as he suggested, tugging at a large box, perched on top of the box marked "pens"; it tipped, spewing a treasure trove of paper clips across the office floor. "Hell's bells! Now where's the broom?" She rummaged for a few minutes without success.

As she fished around in the dark broom closet, she felt Brian behind her. He brushed against her, and suddenly both arms were around her waist. He reached around, placing the broom in her small hand with his large one.

"Here it is," she heard him say gruffly. She took the broom and felt his arms start to pull away—and then they closed around her, tightly. The broom fell to the floor and Liz closed her eyes. A tingling spread from his arms right through her middle. Tender warmth licked like electricity through her entire existence, past, present, and future—an eternity of passion in a split second. Brian's breath brushed her neck. He moaned, a soft animal sound in her ear, and she quivered all over as she felt his lips against the delicate skin under her ponytail.

Liz turned, moving straight into the circle of his arms, her head on his chest, lost in the thumping of his heart. For the only moment in her entire existence—living or dead—she felt pure happiness.

"I like you, Liz," he was murmuring, nuzzling her hair. "I like you a lot."

"I like you, too," she said into his sweater, her words muffled.

"We have to get to work," he said. He didn't move.

"I know," Liz said, not moving either. She felt wrapped up, safe, warm. He leaned over and their lips touched.

At the clatter of cloven hooves outside the door, they broke apart, hearts pounding.

"Get those blinds up!" Brian exclaimed, walking over to open the door. Liz was already at the window by the time Hagatha came in to check on the delivery of her new pitchfork. She hoped no one could see the pink flush radiating all the way down her neck.

ELEVEN

The Smoking Gun

THAT EVENING, LIZ WAS IN THE LOBBY OF HER APART-
ment building checking her mail, still tingling with something that felt all too much like happiness. She had pulled on a leather glove to fish carefully in her mailbox—she'd learned the hard way that the Infernal Post sometimes delivered more than she bargained for—when she felt someone tap her on the arm. She jumped several inches. She turned, purse in hand, ready to thrash her stalker and only relaxed when she saw Ellie.

"Whoa, settle down." Ellie checked the dingy lobby to make sure no one else was there, even leaning down to glance under the perpetually crooked plastic chairs that sat inhospitably on a corner of the dirty linoleum tile. "Come straight up to my apartment. Do not ask questions. Just get your ass upstairs."

She turned and dashed back up the stairs, wearing pajama pants rather than her regular day clothes. Baffled, Liz stood for a moment, clutching her mail. Ellie didn't usually get home before she did. She jammed the discount flyers from the Anubis Mall and a delivery menu from the Roast Beast Bistro into her purse and headed upstairs.

When Ellie opened the door to her apartment, Liz asked, "What's up? Why are you in your pajamas? Didn't you go to work?"

Ellie grabbed her and pulled her in. "Hush, don't wake him." Greg was asleep again, small snorts of smoke rhythmically spurting from his nose. As always, Liz thought of Dennis and felt a small pang of jealousy. "Come into the kitchen, I'll explain."

Liz plopped onto a rickety chair and Ellie pushed a cup of tea into her hands. "First of all, yes, I took a few days off work."

"How in Great Beelzebub's name did you manage that?"

Ellie calmly picked some mealybugs out of the sugar bowl and slid it across the table.

"I gave the students a field work assignment and a long weekend," Ellie shrugged. "The administration—they're a bunch of bastards who would walk five hundred miles through hot lava just to kick your shin. On the other hand, they don't really give a crap about the students or learning in general. So, I can get away with quite a bit if I don't bother them. Honestly, the fewer students there are, the less miserable the staff and faculty are. Schools are so much better without students. I always thought so. Even up top."

"I assume you took time off because you wanted to go through all that stuff you brought home?"

"Yep," Ellie nodded. "Tuesday night, I found the pertinent documents. Wednesday, I gave my dear pupils their 'field assignment.' I got up bright and early this morning and I've been going through stuff ever since. In a word, it is extremely *interesting*." She got up and opened her kitchen door a crack to check on Greg. "He is the laziest little demon I've ever seen. Bless him. I'll take a couple of fires a week in exchange for twenty hours a day of unconsciousness. Also, he can't read. If I can keep this stuff out of his reach, we should be good. He's more likely to burn it than to give a fig about it. Better safe than sorry though."

"So, what did you find," Liz asked. "What does it mean?"

"Okay," Ellie took a deep breath. "I found two things of interest. You said you heard rumors from somebody in Admin, who shall not be named, that the hearsay about the trains is true." She pulled out a folder and passed it over. "Read this first."

Liz read a few lines. "A grant allowance for Hell?" She ran her finger down the page. "They're receiving money from an enterprise called The Mountain Group for . . . rehab?"

"Exactly. Now, what about this section?" Ellie leaned over, pointed to a spot she'd highlighted with a sticky note.

Liz read aloud: "Hell Incorporated agrees to bear responsibility for all real estate purchases or rentals, facilities, etc." She scanned lines. "There are provisions for staff salaries, allowable expenses. Typical restrictions that come with grant money. 'Hell Corporation agrees souls will be prescribed individualized treatment plans . . . rehabilitation goals . . . given tickets . . .'" She read faster. "Sweet Lucifer! Tickets across the chasm to Valley Station. 'Hell Corp agrees that the upkeep of the train system is their responsibility'. . . hang on. 'System failures lasting more than five millennia will result in cessation of funding and require repayment of all monies distributed by the grantor to the grantee throughout the entire span of the contract . . . Grantee agrees to all repayment and resolution of contractual issues as outlined above.'" Liz stopped, mouth open, processing this new information. "It's true. The trains are supposed to be running out as well as in."

"Yeah," Ellie said. "If there's no contract that superseded this one. Best I can understand, this place wasn't set up to punish souls forever. H Corp was initially given the charter of rehabilitating souls—whatever that means—to send them on to another station. I don't know what constitutes rehabilitation or where the other station is located, which is why we're going to spend the evening reading through this junk. The upshot is that this was always supposed to be more like what we would consider Purgatory than Hell. Wait, there's more. Just a second." She listened carefully to make sure that Greg was still snoring in the next room.

"Okay," Ellie said. She pulled out another folder. "Now look at this one."

Liz's heart was beating out of her chest. "It's a lease for the parcel upon which Hell is located. Wait, the rent is satisfied by . . . oh for Satan's sake . . . by the souls who fling themselves into the Abyss? What? Why?"

"I don't know. I haven't had a chance to read all the way through either of these documents yet. We'll spend some time going through them in detail. Then we do it again tomorrow. At least it's a Saturday. I told Theo to have a sniff around the ticket office—just in case there's anything about the trains. I think he's taking tomorrow off to go to the mall for a belt, so we might have to wait until next week to see if he digs up any clues at the station. If you're off in the morning . . . "

"I'm helping Brian catch up on some paperwork in the morning, then we're having lunch." She blushed.

"I'm sure that's work-based."

"Of course."

"I see," Ellie sighed. "Listen, I'm not going to tell anyone. Besides that, you might get the scoop. Worm some gossip out of the man. You'll be with him half the day. This mystery has given me a reason to carry on with this sham of an afterlife."

Liz sighed. "The rumor around Admin is simply that the trains used to run both ways. He doesn't know anything more than that."

"Brian might not know what he knows," Ellie said. "Understand? He may know things that don't seem pertinent because we haven't put everything together yet. So, keep your ears open. Listen. Keep asking questions. Some tiny scrap of information might be the key to the whole thing."

"Before we go on, tell me honestly, do you think this will do us any good?"

Ellie shrugged. "That's what we're trying to find out." She poured more tea.

"One more thing worries me. Why do you think this stuff was left where you could find it? Doesn't it make you a little nervous? Why weren't all these documents locked up in the office or something if this is such a big secret? Were they left there on purpose to confuse us or make us think we'd found something when we haven't? So we'd get our hopes up and feel even worse afterwards?"

"I already thought of that. First, if I can have the slightest bit of hope for even a nanosecond, I'll take it."

Ellie took a sip of her tea and leaned over the table, dropping her voice even lower. "Besides, I work there every day. I haven't seen one instance of any process that rises to even the most basic level of organization, much less cunning. Professor Slipskin, Dean Lempo, and Dr. Batsen all got their positions by shamelessly flattering Satan and throwing other demons under the bus. That's the extent of any strategy I've seen. None of them are particularly knowledgeable about their topics or anything else. They theoretically "teach" real estate regulations or finance or whatever, which mostly means letting adjuncts handle things while they keep their noses crammed up Satan's butt. That drawer of folders hadn't been disturbed for a very long time when I found this stuff."

"So, you don't think they would do this just to make trouble for you or get our hopes up to dash them?" Liz asked.

"They may be a pack of pricks, but they amaze and astound me with their incompetence every damn day. I know it seems unbelievable. I think someone just forgot that this stuff was there. In fact, if anyone asks the janitor, he'd say he'd never seen it to save his own skin. I'll stand by the assumption that it got left in that drawer for no other reason than because they're morons. Occam's razor and all that." Ellie went to the cabinet and took out a black cardboard container covered with shrieking cartoon specters. These were Ghoulios—hard dry cookies with two burnt-looking circles encasing a thin oozy frosting between them. Liz took one and dipped it in her tea where it promptly crumbled into gluey bits that swam to the edge of the cup and crawled out. Liz ran her forefinger around the edge of the cup, catching the tiny moving frosting blobs, and then licking them before they could escape. Ghoulios were conceptually disgusting, but one of the few decent-tasting items in Hell once you got used to them.

After she'd captured the last of the fugitive cookie bits, she said, "Okay. I just don't want to be the first soul to get tossed into the Abyss against my will."

"Liz," Ellie said, "If there's even a smidgen of a speck of a nanoparticle of a chance we get out of this cesspool . . . let's risk it. Who knows? Maybe you'll end up somewhere you can actually let people know who you're dating."

The dingy clock on Ellie's gray wall ticked away eternity in the silence. In the distance, a low rumble heralded another ash storm.

"Let's do it," Liz rubbed her eyes. "What have we got to lose?"

"Exactly," Ellie looked at Liz over her glasses. "One more thing. I hate to say this about Brian, but you might want to use some caution in telling him things. I'm not saying do or don't tell him. I'm saying that just because you're dating someone doesn't mean you can trust them. In fact, in my experience, it exponentially lowers the odds that you can. He might not even *want* to know. Who knows what Satan could worm out of him under duress? Understand what I'm saying?"

Liz nodded. "Yes. I'll be careful."

"Okay," Ellie said, thrusting a folder at Liz. "Start reading. And after you get done with all your 'work,' get your butt back over here as soon as you can, got it?"

TWELVE

There's a Problem with Nothing

IT WAS LIZ'S FIRST TIME WORKING SATURDAY. SHE WAS excited and nervous after the previous night; it certainly seemed that Satan was playing fast and loose with the contract he'd signed. She hardly dared hope she could ever leave this place. If she did, what would that mean for her and Brian? Brian *had* to be brought into the loop. She had no idea how or when.

On weekends, the line camped in place. Souls stretched from the street into the lobby to maintain their place. The window was closed, so that Brian could wrestle the mountains of data into submission. Liz had convinced him that today he could take an hour for lunch, since she'd be helping. One of the weekend security demons met her at a prearranged spot several blocks away and walked her to Admin. As Liz got closer to the building, she saw why Brian had been adamant about security. The complaint line took on a whole new personality when it was parked on weekends.

As she approached the door of the Admin Building, a tall young man in a polo shirt leaned out of line towards them. "Get in there and open the window," he yelled at Liz. "Bitch!"

Nimue, the security succubus who'd been sent to walk with Liz, casually stretched two of her fingers out and jabbed him in the throat with beautifully polished, deep purple nails. He fell to the ground, gasping for air. The succubae had the appearance of beautiful, scantily clad women with long, shining manes of hair, as if they were supermodels who happened to have batwings and live in Hell. As such, souls often underestimated the danger of harassing them. Unfortunately for those who tested them, the succubae had many abilities that weren't immediately apparent. For instance, they had incredibly long, chameleon-like tongues.

Hardly two seconds had passed when another soul tossed a shoe at them. Nimue caught it neatly, snapped out her long sticky tongue, and popped the soul's eye out. She put the eye in the shoe, handing it back to the wailing soul with a pert smile and a wink.

"Now you can add a medical req to your list of forms when you finally get inside on Monday. Get some pain meds for regrowing that eye." She flipped her thick, black curls over her shoulders and giggled like a schoolgirl.

When Liz made it into the lobby, she found she didn't need Nimue's services anymore. Unlike the souls outside, souls in the lobby were remarkably tranquil, sitting down, dozing, staring into space, or sleeping against each other.

"What's up with the lobby? I've never seen it this quiet," she commented as she walked into the office and put down her purse.

"The line is always rough on the weekend. Grigor sprayed the lobby with sleeping gas a few minutes ago," Brian said.

Liz lifted the blind and peered out. Grigor, head of weekend security—a short, stocky, fur-covered demon with two sets of ivory goat horns—was leaning against the wall calmly reading the *Perdition City Blasphemer.*

"Makes things easier, I guess."

Brian walked over to the door and locked it. "It doesn't affect the demons as much, but it settles them down a little, too. We shouldn't have to worry about them bothering us today. Guess we should get to work, huh?"

"We've got a lot to do, but there are two of us." Liz walked over to the closed window and picked up a stack of forms that needed to be entered into the database, flipped through them, and paper-clipped the oldest ones. "We should start with these."

"Yeah," He pulled the extra office chair up to his desk and stood up to let her scoot past him with her stack of forms. "Let's get going. Later we can take a nice long coffee break. Around ten-ish?"

"Sure," Liz said. She brushed past him and set the papers on the desk. She didn't sit down. Instead, she gave Brian a little hug. He put his arms lightly around her shoulders and looked into her eyes.

"I refilled the coffee cannister. All I could find was Moloch's extra bold. We should cut it with Mud Canyon decaf, or you'll be up all week. I guess we really should get to work now." He didn't move his arms. Instead, he pulled her into a tighter embrace.

"Mmmm . . . good plan. We should get started," she said as she felt his hand slide under her sweater, his lips dropping kisses into her hair. She pressed her face against the wool and wrapped her arms around his waist, holding him as tightly as she could. "Oh, Brian. I've wanted to be alone with you for so long."

He lifted her so he could kiss her properly, and she wrapped her legs around his waist.

"Liz," he whispered in her ear. "You have no idea how much I've wanted to kiss you."

Her only response was a kiss. The two of them slid to the floor.

Half an hour later, Liz was rebuttoning her blouse and pulling her tights back on. Brian was running his hands through his hair and looking for his glasses.

"Hard to find your glasses without your glasses," he mumbled, blushing. He dug through stacks of forms.

"Here," Liz plucked them from under the desk. He bent down, and she slid the glasses onto his face.

He picked her up and hugged her again. "I like you so much, Liz. It can't be right. It makes me so nervous, but I do."

"Don't be nervous. I like you too. Obviously," She kissed him and straightened his glasses. "Now I guess we'd better get to work. For real. Guess we can skip that coffee break."

Reluctantly, he put her down. For the first time since she'd met him, Brian broke into a huge, spontaneous smile. "I guess so. I just feel like I'm . . . I don't know . . . something I've never felt before."

"Happy?" Liz asked.

"Yeah," Brian blinked slowly. "Maybe that's it. Maybe I'm happy." He shook his head. "I know better, but now that it's happened, I can't stop myself. Scary, isn't it?"

She smiled at him. "No. It's good. Scoot over and let me help you get some of this work done."

She pulled up a chair close to him and fired up the desktop. "It may be next weekend before this thing comes to life." She banged the monitor. "By the way, I volunteer to work next weekend too."

Brian leaned back in his chair. "Happiness is weird. I don't know that I'm made for happiness."

He reached over and gently pushed a tendril of hair behind her ear.

Liz smiled. "Don't be a worrywart, things will never be too good in this place. Just think about that if you get scared. There will always be enough stress and despair to balance out happiness."

Neither of them said much. Their fingers brushed as they handed forms to each other, and their knees touched occasionally when they moved their chairs. A haze of contentment hovered in the damp, run-down office, and though the conversation about the trains she'd had the night before occasionally floated into her consciousness, Liz let it float away, loath to break the mood.

A few minutes before eleven, Liz was entering housing data and Brian was going over some correspondence from Mammon when the phone on his desk rang.

"Now what?" Brian reached for the phone. "Who's calling on the weekend?"

Liz shrugged and kept entering data. The caller on the other end of the line was talking loudly. So quickly she couldn't make much of anything out.

"What's that?" Brian asked. He listened to a few minutes of one-sided conversation, unable to interject. "Yes . . . I see . . . well . . . what about . . . " he cupped his hand over the receiver. "Hey, can you grab me a notebook and a pen?"

Liz found the memo pad under a pile of paperwork, pushed it towards him, and grabbed a pen from an empty lava smoothie cup where she'd corralled them. Brian's hand rested near the memo pad, waiting to scratch down notes. He wrote down a few words and then stopped, confused.

"If it's nothing, I don't see the problem. Could you send a report?" Brian asked. The other voice rattled off something angrily that ended with the shouted word "nothing".

"Yes, I realize there's no place to put 'nothing' on the report," Brian rolled his eyes. "Put it in the comments section at the bottom. Email me right away."

"What was that about?" Liz asked.

"Not a clue," he sighed. "If I had to guess, I'd say Zenebrius is inebriated again. He's the D-7 in charge of Outpost 989 in the Western Wilds. Probably no big deal, but I wish demons could concentrate on their jobs occasionally."

Since demons—particularly D-7s and below—weren't the most literate of creatures, it took an hour before Brian received the email report from Outpost 989. Option lines and check marks in the incident report were blank. In the comments section at the bottom the demon had typed:

Therz a noTHing hear. 3 of us hav seen. Jozz's been missing. wE think 2 daze. Could be the nothinG.

Brian stared at the email for a few moments. "What in the world? Are they *all* drunk?" He shook his head. "In a nutshell, this is why demons can't work admin."

Liz scooted over and squinted at the email. "Who's Jozz? Is it weird that he's missing?"

"Jozz is a D-4, assigned to the Outpost. Like everyone else out there, he got fired from all his previous jobs, because he was always late, drunk, and making excuses."

"Isn't that typical?" Liz asked.

Brian snorted. "To an extent. Most demons can party hard and still do their jobs. Unlike souls, demons have to ingest an awful lot of alcohol or Nepenthium to be incapacitated. Zenebrius's crew does just that. Fortunately, there's not much for them to screw up out there. Most likely Jozz is stoned, wandering the desert. No one *actually* goes missing in Hell. I mean, you might get lost for a century or two. Only if you don't care about your next drink. Jozz will wander back when he gets thirsty." Brian threw up his hands. "I'm not sure what to do about it without going out there."

Brian continued reading his mail and Liz went back to work. After another ten minutes, she heard him groan.

"Water's down in the Toxahatchee again. River eels are tunneling, and Satan only knows where they'll end up." He ran his fingers through his hair, setting it on end. Then he turned with a sheepish grin. "You did tell me Hell would take the edge off my happiness. I guess you were right."

She scooted over to look at the email with him and patted his leg. "Yep. We don't have to worry about being overcome with happiness around this place."

Still, Liz felt . . . happy. She'd never had a lover before who was also a comrade. Her first boyfriend had been a classic bad boy. They'd had nothing in common. Except her best friend, whom he'd slept with behind her back. Her last boyfriend, Rob, the one she'd argued with before stepping in front of the bus, was so busy with his job as a contract lawyer that they were like ships passing in the night. They barely spoke on weekdays. And Rob wasn't a homebody; he liked hanging out with their friend group or partying on the weekend. With Brian, there was a level of intimacy Liz had never known in the living world. They were together day in and day out, side by side. With Brian by her side, she wondered if there was anything Hell could throw at her that she couldn't deal with.

"Has it happened before?" Liz asked him, returning to the topic at hand. "The eels, I mean?"

"From time to time," he said. "On the day you arrived, a bunch of demons diverted a canal to make a swimming pool. An eel tunneled into the men's room at the station in protest. It's a huge pain in the ass. I'll either have to check it out or send someone in the next few days before the situation gets out of control."

"Sorry," Liz said. "Is it always this bad working on weekends?"

Brian smiled. "I'm not going to complain about working this weekend at all." He blushed and kissed Liz's hand. "Wanna work tomorrow? I mean, I know it's Sunday . . . only if you want to."

"Yes," Liz punctuated her response with a kiss.

THIRTEEN

Who Can You Call?

LIZ WENT STRAIGHT TO ELLIE'S APARTMENT AFTER HER lunch with Brian at Taco Torchiere—a new eatery in the Little Pitchforks district of Perdition City. As her digestive system attempted to process her entrée, two viper tacos with snake tongue relish and a scarlet widow chalupa, all three in chili-red taco shells, Liz decided that Taco Torchiere was less a restaurant and more a marketing tool to help Dr. Bones pharmacies sell Hell Tummies Antacid—even though she'd picked off the garnish of tiny fried spiders. She stopped and bought a large bottle of Hell Tummies, which portrayed a sad-looking male soul with a huge round belly and red face on the label and the tagline "Quell Hell Tummy."

"Took you long enough," Ellie said, when she opened the door for Liz.

"Sorry, we went to the new taco place on 666."

"Geeze, are you insane?" Ellie shook her head. "I heard a yeti demon melted after eating a couple steam tamales. They had to copter him back up north in a bucket."

Greg woke up, snuffled, then rolled onto his back snoring again, his little claws sticking straight up, directly across their path to the kitchen.

"Has he been conscious in the last couple weeks?" Liz asked. "I feel like he's napping every time I've come over."

"He's only awake long enough to eat or move to a different napping spot." Ellie gently lifted the snoozing dragon and moved him carefully to the rug next to the couch. When they reached the kitchen, she continued,

"If we do get out of here, I'm almost going to miss that little doofus. Wonder if I can take him on the train."

Liz stifled a laugh. "I can only imagine taking Dennis on the train. The bitching would be legendary." Dennis had recently taken to sitting next to her on the couch instead of in his chair; he claimed it was warmer, and it allowed him to rub his snotty little nose all over her sweater. She sometimes wondered if he felt some sort of twisted affection for her.

Ellie shrugged. "In a weird way, I think it's better than being alone. I wonder if it's a holdover from the rehab requirements. You know, having a companion could be therapeutic—but like everything else around this place, it just got screwed up."

"Sometimes I think it's better," Liz considered. "Mostly, I think I'd rather be lonely."

Ellie laughed as she pulled a couple of folders with Post-It-note bookmarks from the stack.

"Have a seat. I haven't found anything that would contradict what we learned yesterday. Although, I did learn some details. The grant money is set up to pay per soul—and get this," she opened a folder and pointed at the highlighted text. "His salary increases as the population of Hell goes up." She raised an eyebrow. "Here's the appalling part. I can't find any incentives for people *leaving* Hell. There's an *expectation* that it will happen. Read here and here. There are some vague parameters to identify souls who are ready to receive outbound tickets. But the incentives to move souls out aren't nearly as good as the incentives to bring souls in."

Liz furrowed her brow as she read through the highlighted section. "And I guess that since the leasing company gives kickbacks for souls that jump into the Abyss, it works for him on that end too?"

Ellie nodded. "Think about it. The more souls he crams into this place with no hope of leaving, the more despair the big guy creates, the more souls jump. I think it's just that simple. And cynical."

"What can we do, though?" Liz asked. "I mean, how do we make someone realize he's not fulfilling his contract? How do we sue Hell?"

"That's the question, isn't it?" Ellie slumped forward, chin in hands. "I think we need to contact the group that gave him the grant. Obviously, the real estate company that leased the property won't be much help. And I'm not sure I *want* to deal with entities that just want souls to annihilate themselves. I think what we're trying to find is some way to trigger an investigation or an audit from The Mountain Group."

"So, we keep poring over this stuff, for a name or some sort of contact information?" Liz waved her hand over the stack of folders.

"I haven't seen anything yet. We shall keep trying," Ellie sighed.

"Even if it's not in here, surely there are records somewhere in Perdition City," Liz bit her lip. "Maybe Admin?"

"Hell's bells and bagpipes, I sure hope so," Ellie rubbed her eyes. "In the meantime, we go back through all *this* stuff to see if we can find someone . . . anyone . . . to contact."

She had just handed Liz a black bound folder and a highlighter pen when they heard a pounding at the door.

"Sheesh!" Ellie said. "Is somebody trying to break the damn door?"

She went cautiously to the door and opened it with the chain lock still attached. Liz stood behind her with a heavy book in her hand in case she needed to swat a wandering demon salesman or overexcited soul.

"Theo!" Ellie said after she peered through the crack. "What are you doing here?" She opened the door and Theo pushed in, flushed and excited.

"I found something!" He hitched up his pants.

"Not a belt, clearly." Ellie pointed at his pants, which were still drooping.

"I thought you were going to the mall today," Liz put down the book, relieved that she didn't have to hit anyone.

"Nope," Theo said. "I got into the ticket office this morning. Then I got stuck there. The demons were all gathered around there smoking, so I had to wait. Hey, that part's not important right now. Can we go into the kitchen?" His big voice boomed around the apartment and Greg opened one eye, snuffled, and blew some cinders onto the rug. Then the dragon ambled over to Ellie and breathed weak flames onto the bottom of her jeans. She patted out the flames.

"Hungry," Greg said, in a husky voice that bubbled with smoke. He was a dragon of few words.

"I'm going to get Greg some treats and then we can go into the kitchen." Ellie reached for a large bowl that looked like the top part of a skull and handed Greg a bone. He shuffled back into his corner with the bone, crunched it down, and immediately began to snore.

"What in Hell are you giving him, and can I get some for Alberta?" Theo asked, awe-struck.

Ellie ushered them back into the kitchen. "Tell us what you found first. If it's good, maybe you won't have to worry about Alberta much longer."

"This!" Theo pushed their folders to one side and plopped something small and rectangular on the table. Liz and Ellie both leaned over to look at it and at the same time said, "A business card?"

"Yep," Theo said. "And this." He unfolded another, larger piece of paper from the pocket of his pants and placed it on the table.

"A railway map? Oh wow," Ellie spread out the map, pinning down one corner with a heavy folder and another with the sugar bowl.

Liz pointed at the map. "There's Perdition City Station, and there's the Netherworld Station. And what's this?"

"That?" Theo said, "that's a bridge to somewhere called The Mountain."

The map showed a complete layout of Hell, as well as the internal subway and train lines. Train tracks stretched out from Perdition City Station in two directions. The northern track was labeled Netherworld Station. Liz knew this was the sorting station where souls were sent on to their various destinies after disembodiment, although for most souls—including herself—memories before reaching the Perdition City Station were fuzzy at best. As far as she knew, the Netherworld Station was the only outside contact point with Hell. This map showed another track starting out at the Perdition City Station, going East where it crossed the Sea of Dread on a railway bridge and then traversed a blank spot on the map labeled the Chasm. On the far corner of the map, there was an arrow pointing to the words "The Mountain."

"There was another track," Ellie blew out a long breath. "Or there was supposed to be. *That's* where rehabbed souls were sent."

Liz picked up the business card. "What's this?"

"Read it!" Theo was beaming.

Ellie leaned against Liz and the two women squinted at the card. It was made of thick paper, once white, with gold swoops on all four edges. In the middle a jagged forest-green line outlined a stylized mountain. Superimposed in plain black sans-serif font over the mountain was:

Sam K. Azrael
Auditor/Inspector
Accounting Division
The Mountain Group

Under his name was an email address and a phone number. "Well, I'll be damned," Ellie said.

"You already are," Theo said. "Let's see if we can fix that." He sat down in a kitchen chair and leaned back, stretching triumphantly. His pants celebrated by sliding down his hips.

"I guess this is the guy to call," Liz said. "I almost didn't believe we were going to find anything," her instinct for joy tempered by thoughts of Brian. Whatever Ellie said, she would now have to tell Brian what was going on. If Satan found out what was happening, or The Mountain Group contacted the big guy before Brian? Liz shivered. She didn't want him blindsided by *that* conversation.

"Don't get too excited," Ellie said. "First, we have to see if we *can* contact this guy. Then it's a matter of if he responds. Can we dial out of Hell?"

"I honestly don't know." Liz bit her lip. "Brian dials nine to get a line out of Hell so he can call Satan, Mammon, or Beelzebub. They're in the Upper World. I don't know how to dial out for the Netherworld, or wherever this guy is based. Brian exchanges emails with Satan and the rest of the board too. I don't know if peasants like us can email outside of Hell. I've certainly never done it. Maybe? Maybe someone knows how?"

Theo leaned back against the wall. "We'll soon find out," he said. "I went into the office at the station before I came here and emailed him. Didn't get a failure error, so I think it sent."

FOURTEEN

An Unexpected Meeting

ON HER WAY TO WORK THE NEXT DAY, LIZ THOUGHT about what to tell Brian. Ellie still wasn't in favor of bringing him in on the discovery; her reasoning was that just because Theo had emailed someone from an old business card he'd found, it didn't mean they'd respond. Besides, if Satan got wind of what they were doing, he would surely try to stop them. Brian might feel uncomfortable knowing any of the information and as Satan's underling, he was in a particularly vulnerable position. Liz, on the other hand, argued that she didn't want to spend her afterlife apologizing to Brian. Ellie finally agreed. Liz had only a short time to plan what to say.

She'd just come to terms with eternity; she could hardly convince herself that anything could ever change. For better or worse. Brian had been manager for centuries upon centuries. *He'd* never seen the trains run. The mere existence of Hell's immutable grind, endless routine, oppressive sky, the skin of dust and ash that coated everything—all those things argued against the slimmest possibility of change. Some part of her didn't think there was any point in disrupting the status quo. Part of her almost wished she didn't have to say anything at all, at least until they knew for sure. The possibility was real, and she could only imagine how hurt Brian would be if he found out from someone else.

She felt more and more nervous as she approached work. Nimue escorted her again. Liz hardly noticed the trail of lost eyes and choking souls the succubus left in her wake. Instead, she concentrated on her newborn hope. She pictured herself in a clean, airy apartment, Brian reclining on the sofa reading. Maybe there *was* some other way to spend eternity. What would happen if it didn't work out, if they just made Satan angry? She pictured Satan pushing Brian into the Sea of Dread, where the dire worms would . . .

"Hey!" Nimue broke into her thoughts. "Can you be a little more careful about getting close to the line? I almost broke my nail when I punched that lady." The succubus pushed Liz farther back on the sidewalk. "Pay attention. I just got a manicure for Lucifer's sake!"

"Sorry," Liz mumbled, bringing herself back to reality.

Increasingly hostile butterflies morphed into hornets in her stomach. She hadn't thought of any brilliant way to break the news. Was it best to simply spill her guts as soon as she walked in? Brian would worry, of course. She would reassure him. She wasn't leaving Hell without him, and she wasn't going to let anything happen to him. It was too late for regrets; Theo had already sent the email. The wheels of the plan were in motion. Besides, Ellie was on the case and wasn't going to stop for anything. Liz and Brian would figure out how to handle issues together. Wasn't that part of a solid relationship? It would all be fine.

She walked into the office and dropped her purse in an empty file cabinet drawer. "Brian," she said, "can I talk to you about something? Ellie, Theo, and I found some—"

Brian, who'd been standing by the file cabinet waiting for her, kissed her on top of the head and interrupted. "I'm sorry—I have to go down to the basement with Grigor right now. It's an emergency. All those boxes of brochures from Satan are blocking the weapons room. The demons are making a terrible fuss. Grigor's gonna grab a few extra pitchforks and I'm going to supervise moving the stuff. If I can figure out *where*. I'll be back soon."

He rushed out before she could say anything. Liz busied herself entering data until eleven. Just as she had decided she should send Grigor back down to the basement to see how things were going, Brian returned. He locked the door, walked over, and kissed the back of Liz's neck. One thing led to another and information about the trains, and Theo's email, went right out the window. Sometime later, she found herself searching under the desk for Brian's glasses and her bra. Important items located, she did her best to pull herself together.

"It's lunchtime," Brian said, as he readjusted his glasses and retied his bow tie. "Dante's? Weren't you going to tell me something? I'm sorry. I came back in and saw you sitting there and . . . " His cheeks turned pink.

"Sure, Dante's is great. I can barely feel my tongue after the viper tacos yesterday," Liz said. "We might as well eat at Dante's, where we can't taste anything anyway." She groaned inwardly. It certainly wasn't the best place to have the conversation they needed to have.

Brian gave Liz a bear hug. "For once, I kind of love weekends."

When they arrived at Dante's, Grayface seated them in their usual booth. They were the only ones seated along the wall of windows facing the Sea of Dread. Brian laughed when a demon gull awkwardly flattened itself hard against the glass, beady eyes intent on their bread plate. He caught himself and pressed a fist against his mouth, stifling a chuckle. "Sorry. I shouldn't, you know, shouldn't be having this much fun."

"I don't know why you're apologizing," Liz said. "I like seeing you happy."

He squinted and turned his head for a moment, anxiety dulling his features. "Yeah," he said. "It's strange how good happiness feels. Feels almost worthwhile to tempt fate. It's the craziest thing."

Liz touched his leg under the table with her foot. "I think it's fine if you relax just a little."

"What did you want to talk to me about?" Brian asked. "Sorry I've put you off."

"Listen," she began. She looked around and no one seemed to paying much attention so she plunged on, "You remember when we were talking about the trains before? Ellie found some documents at the School of Infernal Business that might explain things."

"What do you mean?" He was leaning over, reading the menu. He passed it to her since Grayface had only brought them one.

"I mean about why the trains don't run both ways anymore." She took the menu and perused it, then tore the edge of her napkin to wipe a sticky spot. "I've had all the omelets I can eat. I think I'm going to try the beastloaf."

"Brave choice," Brian raised one eyebrow. He set the menu on the edge of the table so Grayface would know they were ready to order. He lowered his voice. "What did you find out? Did the trains really run both ways?"

"Yes." Liz took a deep breath. "They should still be running. This place was set up on a grant. Souls shouldn't be kept here for eternity, according to the contract that Satan signed. It was meant to be rehabilitative. We think there's a possibility that we could contact someone to trigger an investigation or an audit or something. And then maybe . . . "

"The trains would run again," Brian finished for her. He leaned back heavily against the greasy vinyl of the booth. He stared past Liz and into the dirty glass window. "Wow. Maybe we *could* get you out of here. Not that . . . not that I want you to leave. You don't deserve to be here, Liz." He continued to stare out at the Sea of Dread as it moaned and slapped the pier. "There it is. Why I'm afraid of happiness. It can be so easily taken away. The thought of you leaving . . . " He trailed off. "Hell wouldn't be the same without you."

Liz thought she saw tears behind his glasses. "I wouldn't be leaving without *you*, silly," she said. She reached forward and grabbed his hand, not caring if anyone saw her. "I mean, you could quit your job, right?

Besides, if the trains went *both* ways, Hell might be better. With fewer souls to take care of, the budget might work. I would be totally content here if I knew I could leave and visit Ellie and Theo. Anyway, I'm trying not to get my hopes up. We don't know what's going to happen."

"I hope it works out," he blinked, patting her hand. "You deserve the best. We *will* make it happen." Brian sat ruminating, and Liz didn't know what to say next. "Let's go back by way of the boardwalk. We can talk details, take the slow route back to the office. Weather is okay." The sullen clouds were steel gray, the breeze sluggish, and nothing was falling from the sky for once—altogether a rather decent day.

"Okay," Liz said. Brian sat blinking, staring past her. "I think when you know everything, maybe it won't be as worrisome." She thought about the new brochures, the contract with the strange entities who wanted souls to fling themselves into the Abyss, and wished she felt as confident as she sounded.

Brian continued staring at the water. "It's a lot to take in." His voice wobbled. "I do want things to be better for you."

"For both of us," She squeezed his hand. He didn't squeeze back. "For both of us." She paused. "There's always the horrible possibility that this might not be true. I asked Ellie if she thought the stuff was left there to get our hopes up. She thinks that's beyond the level of competence anyone can expect from Hell."

"She's right there," Brian traced the stains on the table with his thumb. "You know what? I'm hungry after moving all those boxes. And everything else that happened this morning." He gripped her hand and met her gaze. "It's just shocking. I need time to process. I'll be okay. Let's just eat." He gave her a weak smile. "If we can get Grayface over here to finally wait on us."

"Excuse me!" he called out, "Do you mind if we order?" He waved his hand at the server, who was slamming through the kitchen door and into the dining area.

"Be right there, sir," Grayface sniffed. He stopped at the kitchen door to yell at the demon chef. "Table three feels that the ghoulash has not been properly seasoned. Not enough ghost pepper." There was a roar from the kitchen. A rolling pin narrowly missed Gayface's head as he casually ducked and smirked, pleased by the chef's outburst.

"May I take your order sir—and madam?" he asked as he reached Liz and Brian's table. "The ghoulash is off today, by the way."

"Is it ever *on*?" Brian asked.

They ordered and ate in near silence; Liz quickly regretted the beastloaf, which hit her anxious stomach like an anvil. She'd just dumped an awful lot on her boss/boyfriend. He'd be the one to bear the brunt of Satan's anger if Hell was audited. Not that anything would be Brian's fault. Brian's job was to be Satan's fall guy—to figure out how to clean up the messes that Satan didn't care enough to fix.

Just as Brian was finishing his soggy murk-fish, and Liz had finally quit trying to saw off any more beastloaf from the immovable charcoal-colored square in the middle of her plate, the door of the restaurant banged open. A short man entered; clothed in a trench coat, a black fedora, and thick, square, black glasses. Underneath his coat, he wore a suit and tie. He was remarkably clean and yet rumpled—as if he'd just arrived in Perdition City from the Upper World in a suit that he'd borrowed from someone two sizes bigger than himself. He was pulling a plain black suitcase on wheels behind him.

Grayface shuffled towards the door. "Would you prefer a table or a booth, sir?" Not that it mattered. The server sat customers wherever he pleased, usually the opposite of their requests.

"Neither," the little man said. "Thank you. I'm looking for someone," he licked his lips, scanning the room table by table until he landed on the booth where Liz and Brian were seated. He opened his coat, took out a notebook, and flipped through the pages. He stopped on a page, read it, looked at Brian, reread his notes, and then hurried over to their table.

"Brian?" the little man asked.

"Yes?"

"Manager of Hell?"

"Yes?" Brian said uncertainly. "Can this wait until Monday? If you have a complaint or something there's a line in the Admin Building you can join."

The little man plopped into the bench seat next to Liz, who scooted over to make room for the interloper.

"I don't think this can wait," the little man took off his fedora and set it on the table. "There's been a bit of a misunderstanding. I know I should have come earlier, but my goodness. Such a caseload. You know how *that* is. I got an email from a gentleman named Theo from the . . ." he glanced at his notebook " . . . Perdition City Station. He found my card at the ticket counter and emailed me yesterday afternoon. I came straightaway when I realized what was happening. Trains not running and all that."

The little man looked across the dingy restaurant at a table of pale, sad souls sipping brackish water. His eyes rested on a blue Baalzephon demon slumped in another booth, head on table, long tail curving out onto the dirty black and white tiled floor. Liz saw him shiver when he caught sight of a largish cockroach carefully pushing a breadcrumb across the floor. The man put her in mind of a bug-eyed little goldfish that had just been plopped into a tank full of piranhas.

"Interesting place," his eyes darted about, searching for something reassuring and coming up empty. He gave them a weak smile.

Brian lowered his voice to address Liz. "Those details we were going to discuss—is this one of them?"

"Probably?" Liz admitted. Why hadn't she just told Brian straight away when Ellie had first found the documents? "I didn't know until yesterday afternoon that Theo had found a business card and sent an email. That's one of the things I wanted to tell you."

"Theo, yes," the little man said, happy to grasp some common ground in the conversation. "The gentleman who contacted me, as I said. I'm Sam Azrael. I'd like to apologize. You see, until I received the email . . . to be honest . . . " Sam scrunched his shoulders. "I had simply let this case slip through the cracks. I'm very sorry. I'm hoping we can straighten things out without too much trouble. I haven't even told my boss exactly why I'm here yet. I thought we could discuss the issues and see where we're at."

"Did you reply to Theo's email?" Liz asked. She might have to beat Theo's ass if he'd known about this and hadn't warned her.

"No. Apologies to Mr. Theo. We have very specific rules about whom we can work with on an audit. I had to go back through my data to ascertain the current administration structure. Of course, I'm sure we can come to some agreement about what we will and won't report in reference to our respective job duties."

Brian took his glasses off, rubbed his eyes and sighed deeply. "I can't believe this," he said. "I thought this weekend was going so well."

"I apologize for ruining your weekend," the little man said, "but I think . . . "

Brian held up a hand. He glanced sidelong at the little man. "This may not be the best place for this discussion."

"Can we talk after lunch? I'm starving. Meantime, here's my card." The man took a card out of his pocket and slid it across the table. On the front was the stylized logo of a mountain in green ink: 'The Mountain Group' with his contact information superimposed on top.

"You can call me Sam. Think of me as an auditor, an inspector, and a case worker all wrapped up in one." He smiled weakly. "I do apologize. I should have been here centuries ago. You're not my only nonprofit and cases have been stacking up like you wouldn't believe. The after-verse is a wide and varied place. You know how it is," Sam waved his hand in the air. "So many emergencies. Somehow your case dropped to the bottom of the stack. Anyway, here I am. I'm sure we can fix it now." He turned away and Liz heard him mumble, "I hope."

Sam waved his hand at Grayface for a menu. "I'm awfully hungry, if you don't mind."

There was an awkward silence, then Grayface skulked over with a menu.

"What can you recommend today?" Sam asked Grayface, as he perused the ancient, greasy, laminated list of inscrutable pictures.

"I never like to speculate about the tastes of my customers," Grayface said. "However, the ghoulash is off today."

"In what way?" Sam asked, running his finger down the menu to find a picture of the offending dish.

"Not spicy enough," Grayface said, yanking the menu away from Sam. He turned it over and pointed at a blurry-looking red and black mess.

"That's what I'll have," Sam said. "I'm not fond of spicy foods."

Liz opened her mouth to speak, but then stopped. Sam K. Azrael could discover the delights and disgusts of Dante's menu fot himself.

"Would you care for the blood orange juice to go with it? Chef squeezes it himself," said Grayface with a smirk.

"I suppose that might be . . . " the man started. Brian shook his head from across the table.

"How about a coffee?" the small man asked.

"Fine, sir. I will have to *make* coffee, so it may be some time." Grayface snatched the menu back, frowning. He walked off towards the kitchen with his nose out of joint. "Number three, complimentary blood orange!"

Sam laughed nervously.

"Weather is a bit dicey in this place, isn't it?" He glanced out at the gray day and the sullen sea.

"It's not too bad today," Liz said.

"Pretty decent, actually," Brian agreed.

Grayface interrupted this pleasant small talk by plopping Sam's ghoulash, coffee, and complimentary blood orange juice on the table with a flourish and a smirk. "We happened to have a bit of coffee left at the very bottom of the pot, as it turns out."

Sam poked the strange-looking mass in front of him. "Did it just move?" he asked.

When no one answered, he picked around his dish with a fork for a moment, then tentatively lifted a forkful to his mouth.

After a few slow chews, his face turned purple. Smoke escaped his nose, and his eyes began watering so hard he had to use his napkin until it was soaked. Unable to stop the flow of tears, he started drying his face with Liz's napkin. He took a sip of the complimentary blood orange juice and then promptly spat it back into the cup. "What in the name of all that's holy?" he choked.

He picked up his cup of coffee, which for once was boiling hot, and drained it. "Yipes! For heaven's sake!" He snatched Liz's half-full water cup and drank that too. He reached for a single roll of bread that was left sitting in the breadbasket and ate it quickly, perhaps hoping it would quell the sensory blast of the ghoulash. He coughed and choked for a few moments. Liz patted him on the back until he regained his composure.

"The ghoulash is not spicy enough? For whom? A fire salamander?" Sam managed to croak out.

Grayface appeared instantly, smirking. "Are you done sir? Would you care for some dessert? We have devil's food cake, lava cream pie? Chocolate ant flambe?"

"Thank you, but no way." Sam coughed a little more into a Kleenex Liz had dug out of her purse and mopped his face again.

"Shall I give your compliments to the Chef?" Grayface asked.

"Heavens no," Sam said, still watering at the eyes. "It was, in a word, dreadful. Far too spicy."

Grayface grinned. "I will let him know, sir."

Brian pulled out his wallet. "In that case, we'd better be going before Chef gets the feedback." He threw down a bill. "Keep the change."

Grayface tucked the bill into his apron. "Thank you, good sir. You're quite generous." He waited a beat. "Customer says the ghoulash is too spicy!" Grayface yelled, on his way back to the kitchen.

Brian, Liz, and Sam filed out under the overcast sky.

"Dreadful place," Sam said. Through the window, they saw a heavy pan come flying out of the kitchen and land in the dining area. Grayface jumped over it. "Listen," Sam continued. "I need to drop my suitcase at the Brimstone Inn and let them know I've arrived. I've managed to reserve a room. If you two wouldn't mind accompanying me, we can talk on the way. Plan our next steps."

FIFTEEN

What Happens to Hell?

BRIAN AND LIZ DECIDED TO TAKE THE SAME ROUTE along the pier they'd planned before Sam's arrival: a slightly longer distance to the Inn, and one with very little foot traffic. The Sea of Dread was perpetually moody and many of Hell's inhabitants preferred not to risk its ever-changing temperament. Fortunately, it seemed to have settled into a steady state of somber depression for the moment, and, like the leaden sky, was behaving remarkably well with only an occasional moan and slap of water washing up on the wooden decking.

"Alright, I would very much like someone to explain this all to me. Maybe start at the beginning." Brian stepped between Sam and Liz. "Pretend I don't have any idea what's going on."

"It's simple. The trains should be running," Sam admitted. "And if they don't start running again soon, I'm afraid The Mountain Group is going have to ask for the repayment of centuries' and centuries' and centuries' worth of funding."

Brian stomped along for a few moments. "Well, fuck," he said.

"Unfortunately, I think we *will* have to meet with your boss. At some point," Sam said. "I hear he's a bit difficult?" Sam's voice lifted at the end, perhaps in hopes that someone would contradict this fact.

"Depends on how much you like having things flung at your head. Or how good your reflexes are," Brian said. "And yes, we'll have to involve him. I certainly have no way of repaying the grant."

Sam cocked his head. "Maybe that won't be necessary. Since I'm not *quite* up to date with this case, what do you say we take a few days and get all our little ducks in a row before we involve *anyone's* boss? Knowing where we stand before we bring in the big guns might be the best strategy." He cleared his throat.

Brian shrugged. "I'm certainly in no mood to call Satan right this minute. I sense we're only putting off inevitable doom. So, since I don't know anything about this, I'll need facts before Satan interrogates us. And believe me, he'll have questions about everything. It will be like he never signed the contract."

"Oh dear," Sam said. "That sounds . . . unpleasant."

Brian was walking so quickly that Sam and Liz were practically jogging to keep up with him. "*Exactly* how long has it been since you've inspected Hell? I've been here for centuries, and no one has ever inspected anything, as far as I know. Except Satan. And he's usually just investigating whether his towels are soft enough and there's a steady supply of Diet Coke."

Sam sighed. "We're supposed to audit our grantees every two centuries or so. It varies by contract. I'll admit to being behind. I can't tell you how thin we've been spread. The Netherworld Office alone needs to hire at least fifty more auditors. In fact, I *should* have brought a team here, but things are crazy right now and I thought I'd check things out and talk to you before I call in the troops, so to speak."

"And *you* don't want to get in trouble, right?" Liz asked. "I get the feeling no one at The Mountain Group is aware you've overlooked us for this long."

"Partly. I'm already on probation. I'm not a multi-tasker and you have no idea how hard my job is. Imagine auditing Valhalla, for example. Yes, it's small. The contract is tremendously complicated. The mead requirements alone are insane! Souls get injured in the battles and trust me, despite the promises, they aren't always one hundred percent by the next day. You don't have any idea how often we've had to quibble with

Odin about how he's using the grant money. And Loki is his lawyer, for infinity's sake! Imagine that! Eternity doesn't stretch out sideways until you get more than halfway up the mountain. One day follows another on most of my cases, just like it does here in Hell. I do hate a linear timeline. So much opportunity to get behind. The case workers in true eternity, up in the mountain towns, don't have this problem. It's not linear, you see."

"What is all this talk about the mountain and timelines?" Liz leaned around Brian to quiz Sam. "Is the mountain like heaven?"

"The mountain is where we're all meant to go," Sam said, "you know, eventually. When we can. When we're strong enough. In the case of entities like myself, when we get a promotion. It turns out that souls weren't quite strong enough to go straight to the top as soon as they passed from the material world. If I'm being honest, the concept of Heaven in the Upper World is far more absurd than the concept of Hell. Much farther off. You see—"

Brian leaned down. "For just this second, can we get back to Hell's problem? Sorry, Liz."

"It's okay," Liz said. "You're right."

Brian went on, "If we can get the trains running again, could we avoid repayment of funds? I mean, look around, it's not like we have a sky-high budget here." He waved his hand around the dingy boardwalk with rotting planks, the bent and overflowing trash cans, the gray city brooding on their left.

"Maybe. Hell *will* lose its funding if the trains *don't* run, and in fact, The Mountain Group will have to be repaid. That was part of the agreement," Sam pulled his overcoat tightly against the damp. "There are other parameters that need to be met as well. Hell was meant to be rehabilitative. If we at least get trains running, send a few souls across the chasm, I think I can get my people to stop the clock."

Brian buttoned his coat. The wind was picking up. "How did we get this far off track?"

"I don't know," Sam said, wrapping his scarf more tightly around his neck. "Satan seemingly understood the purpose of this place. He was initially part of The Mountain Group—on the board! He objected to the whole "soul essence" experiment. Felt it was more effort, more cost than it was worth."

"What *is* it worth?" Liz asked. "What's soul essence for a start?

"Well . . . errr . . . " Sam cleared his throat.

"You don't know?" Liz narrowed her eyes at him.

The wind started moaning and no one spoke for a moment. The clouds were beginning to grow darker.

Sam acknowledged. "The ingredients are a corporate secret. And it's trademarked. They don't tell us *everything*. Just that souls were created to go up the mountain. Satan, however, knew all details. For reasons known only to himself, he was furious at the experiment, stormed off— went rogue for a while. Then he came back, said he'd seen the light. He wanted to help. Satan and Mammon came up with the rehab idea. The grant was written. Hell was established."

Sam shivered and rubbed his gloved hands together. "It honestly seemed like a better idea than Valhalla for instance. Souls lingered there, never wanted to start up the mountain. Souls from the Upper World who started climbing immediately upon disembodiment soon puttered out. A place with spas, and gyms, and meditation, etc. seemed like the perfect answer. When souls were healthy enough for the trip, Satan was to send them up the mountain. The Netherworld track was completed on the day of the ribbon cutting ceremony. Satan's construction crews had already started building the tracks to the mountain over the chasm." He stopped. "There were so many other cases, and we switched databases. My scheduled audits were a mess."

"We get it. It's not your fault." Liz rolled her eyes.

Brian rubbed his temples as they walked along the pier. "Never mind all that. What's our time frame?"

"That's the tricky bit," Sam said, "Due to the unfortunate circumstances we find ourselves in, we have exactly six months."

"Six months!" Brian said. "Six months is the blink of an eye in Hell! Satan sometimes doesn't visit for decades at a time. And if you take away funding *before* we get the trains running, I don't see how we can make the trains run. It's a catch-22."

"Also, the fact that we haven't been audited is your fault, isn't it?" Liz blurted out. "Isn't there a clause that adds time to if The Mountain Group doesn't meet obligations?"

"There's a clause," Sam admitted. "But it reads—paraphrasing until I get to my notes—the grantor reserves the right to conduct an audit of the grantee's outcomes per the contract every other century. The grantee agrees to perform internal audits once per century and to share all audits with the grantor. If the grantee fails to properly perform obligations under the grant contract or violates any terms therein, the grantor retains the right of termination. In other words, we *can* audit you if we choose, but you're *obligated* to hire an auditor regardless. If it comes down to the wire and conditions are not met, we sell off whatever assets you have left and settle the debt."

"What will happen to the souls?" Brian asked. "And the demons?"

"There may be some recourse for the citizens of Hell if the grant is rescinded. If your organization is shut down, or you go into bankruptcy, we may be able to apply for the inhabitants to have special refugee status," Sam said. He pulled his collar up against the wind.

As if picking up on the angst in the air, the sea breeze grew suddenly sharp and kicked spray across the boardwalk.

"How would that work?" Brian gasped. "Refugee status where?"

"Likely somewhere in the Netherworld. It's doable, and it is dreadfully complicated. Trains run *out* of the Netherworld station to various destinations. You must get a special dispensation to run them *into* the Netherworld. It can take time," Sam said. He stepped delicately over a dung beetle rolling its treasured sphere and wrinkled his nose at the smell. "Never fear, I imagine my bosses would prefer that Hell stays open. But only in the capacity in which it was intended. You've never seen the contract or any of the addendums?"

"No." Brian huddled into his trench coat, morose.

Liz slid her arm through Brian's. "And if we don't get refugee status?"

"Errr . . . I think that we should just assume we can get it worked out." Sam pulled his hat down over his face.

Brian stopped suddenly. "If we don't?"

Sam shuffled to a halt, shrinking into his coat. "If Hell is rendered nonexistent, then of course the inhabitants would be . . . " he mumbled something incoherent.

"Nothing?" Liz offered.

"Yes," Sam acknowledged. "It simply won't come to that. Let's assume we solve the problem."

"For Hell's sake," Brian mumbled. "Fuck."

"You know what?" Liz blurted out. "Ellie has read through all the contracts." She tugged Brian's sleeve. "We should call her. I think she might have as good a handle on things as our auditor here." She glared at Sam.

"Yes," Brian said. "We need all the help we can get."

Sam kept his head down. A wave splashed over the boardwalk; the Sea of Dread was done being merely sullen—it began to wail and moan in earnest. A black, bug-eyed fish shot onto the decking. The creature flapped against Sam's shoe. He shrieked and kicked at it, until it stuck out its tongue and flopped back into the water. It wasn't until they turned onto Gehenna Street, where the Brimstone Inn was located, that they could hear each other speak again.

The Brimstone Inn, the oldest and most imposing hotel in Perdition City, stood on the corner of Broad and Gehenna. The hulking structure encompassed many city blocks. It was meant to be a tridecagon, but as demon builders cut corners, building plans took some odd turns, and resulted in something that *was* impressive—in the utter lack of aesthetic pleasure it produced in the viewer. The top of the building had an elaborate sawtooth pattern running all the way around the perimeter, with occasional sharp turrets, randomly placed.

"I'll call Ellie," Liz said as they crossed the lobby. "I'll see if Gla'ap will let me use the phone at the desk."

The interior contained thousands of rooms; each had an arched window of rippled scarlet glass, leaving those inside bathed in distasteful, blood-colored light. The enormous arched portico was painted scarlet and had a carpet of the same color running through it all the way from the lobby and down the broad staircase to the street, giving the impression of a great mouth with a tongue lolling out, waiting to swallow passersby. It was impossible to tell the original color of the brick exterior as it had turned black centuries ago from the smoky air.

Liz occasionally worked with Brimstone staff, as there were a few souls with permanent residential or employment assignments there. A clumsy gargoyle with huge batwings named Gla'ap managed the place. She was one of the only citizens in Hell who truly wanted to be helpful—as far as Liz could tell—but spent most of her time accidentally knocking things over or scattering paperwork with her wings. The motley assortment of skeletons, monkey demons, ghouls, and bitter souls who worked as employees did nothing to improve the hotel's dreadful service.

"I'll pop in and check my bag while you call your friend," said Sam. "The sooner we figure this out the better."

"Carry the bag to the room yourself," Liz said. "Whatever you do, don't give it to one of the monkeys. You'll have to tip them your right arm to get it back. Possibly literally."

Sam checked in and started lugging his bag up the grand staircase with a monkey tugging at it until Brian walked over and tipped the tiny bellhop some Hell Coin to go away.

Gla'ap handed Liz the phone from behind the ornate black desk, accidentally catching Liz's sweater with her claw, and unraveling the end of the sleeve before disentangling herself. Liz dialed Ellie, who answered quickly.

"What's up? You coming over?"

"Yes," Liz glanced at Brian. "And I won't be alone."

"I'm in my PJs, drinking beer," Ellie said. "Should I hunt for real clothes?"

"We met a Mr. Sam Azrael today," Liz said. "He got the email and decided to contact Brian."

"Sweet Lucifer's fiery balls!" Ellie gasped. "Get your asses over here. I'll put on pants."

SIXTEEN

What's the Plan?

"HEY GUYS," ELLIE SAID AS SHE OPENED THE DOOR. "TRY not to wake up the little fire ball if you don't mind." She nodded at Greg, who was snoring away next to the couch as usual.

"What would that take? Dynamite?" Liz handed Ellie her coat.

"You have a point. Theo had to work today. He's coming over as soon as he gets off," Ellie said. She took in Sam's rumpled suit, cheap shoes, and air of general deflation. "The Mountain Group guy, huh? Let me guess—you're not the CEO." Liz could sense Ellie's disappointment. Sam Azrael, Auditor, did not inspire confidence in his executive prowess.

"I was hoping we could get to work and figure out what's going on before we get the CEOs involved. Mine or yours," Sam said.

Ellie swung open the kitchen door and pointed everyone towards the table. "I'll take what I can get. Let's do this thing."

The documents were stacked on the table. There was also a box of Ghoulios, some ghost powder donuts, a coffee pot and Ellie's mismatched mugs. Sam sat down and took a coffee.

"I think you'll find that Satan is double-dipping," Ellie said, she gave him a binder with the familiar Mountain Group logo on it—the grant contract, then handed Sam a black binder rimmed with red from the top of the stack. She flipped through the first couple of pages of the black binder, and tapped her finger on a line of text. "It's my understanding that he's taking money from The Mountain Group to rehabilitate souls, part of which can be used to lease property; so far so good." She tapped the page again. " This contract covers how he leased the property. Satan isn't paying this group. Not in Hell Coin anyway. He's paying them in . . . well . . . just read it."

Sam skimmed both contracts side-by-side, the real estate contract for the property surrounding the Abyss, and the grant from The Mountain Group. He put down the grant documents and silently read through the real estate contract twice.

"Odd," Sam said, as he began to read. "Our records indicate he leased the property from Nether Properties, as he was authorized to do I've never even heard of this group." He leaned over the contract. "Nulentian Realty, Inc.? Brian? Do you have a clue who these people are?"

"Never heard of them," Brian said. "I don't have anything to do with the lease payments. I honestly don't know anything about how Hell was founded, nothing more than what I've learned from Liz. I get a budget to administrate day-to-day afterlife and that's the end of it."

Everyone drank coffee in silence for a moment while Sam pushed up his glasses and ran his finger down the document. Ellie handed him a red pen. He underlined furiously, then flipped forward rapidly. He stopped, finger resting in the middle of one page. He shook his head, started at the top of the page, skimmed down, and stopped again.

"Wow." He reread the page again. The pen fell out of his fingers and dropped to the table. "Does this really say what I think it says?"

"Yep," Ellie said. "It appears that the real estate upon which our lovely homes are located is free as long as a certain number of souls destroy themselves—jump into the Abyss," Ellie clarified. "Why? It's not clear in the contract. Obviously, on his end, the fewer souls there are to house and torment, the less money it costs him.

Sam stared at the documents. "I hardly know what to say. I need to look all this stuff over in more detail. Can we take it to the office?" He bit his lip. "Actually, it's better if I stay here. No need to start tongues wagging. I'll need to talk to management before I decide how we're going to proceed. I don't know what to tell them at this point."

"Here's something else to consider. Has anyone asked themselves what Satan is going to do when he's confronted with this?" Brian asked.

"I expect he's going to set up the rehab centers he promised, and start putting souls on the train to the mountain when they've gained strength. And cough up the money to do it," Sam said firmly. "I know that he terrorizes the help around here, but The Mountain Group pays him. He seems motivated by finances—and besides, I've never seen The Mountain Group lose a case."

"Have you met him?" Brian reached across Liz for a ghost powder donut and dunked it into his coffee while he waited for an answer. The donut burped up a tiny "boo" when dunked, and a dusty coating of ghost sugar hovered above the cup.

"Not exactly," Sam admitted. "I mean, I met him the one time I was here. He seemed . . . reasonable."

"Well, he's not," Brian assured him. "I suggest that once you figure this out, you go up the food chain as far as possible as soon as possible and get some of your higher-ups down here to work with him, threaten him, bribe him, whatever. He only responds to people who have the same kind of power he does. The only time I've seen him lose an argument was when he got into it with some character named Zeus—something about stealing a lightning bolt. That guy had some stellar lawyers and Satan had to cough up the stolen bolts and write an apology letter. If you don't have that kind of power, things are not going to go well."

Sam studied Brian over his glasses. "I may not be powerful, but The Mountain Group is. Once you can get the legal team to pay attention, they dig in. These violations are flagrant and unfortunately for my career, I'm afraid management is going to be *very* interested." He put his chin in his hand for a moment, downcast.

"I think we have bigger problems than your career trajectory right now," Liz asserted, concerned that he wasn't taking the threat seriously enough. "Besides, some of the stories Brian has told me suggest that Satan might be more dangerous than you think."

"If we can't get the trains running, we close Hell down. Surely, even Satan understands that. The Mountain Group always wins. There's just no contest—they've never lost a case."

"Think of it this way," Ellie rolled her eyes. "They didn't have *you* helping them in court." She'd been standing by the counter. She plopped into a chair next to Sam. "I want out of here. That's the long and short of it. If Satan is going to make things difficult, and we need the whole C-suite of The Mountain Group and their lawyers to show up, let's make that happen. We need a plan. We can't wait too long to figure this thing out, okay? No one here gives a damn about your job. Just to be clear."

"Just give me a few days to put together a report. My boss will talk to her boss. I'm certain they'll send someone from legal, someone from accounting, and no doubt someone from operations. Even some of our logistics people to help get the trains running again," Sam said. "Once Satan sees the evidence piling up, even he will realize what he's up against and we'll get this taken care of posthaste."

Brian shrugged. "Don't set your heart on it. And I'm not worried about you guys winning. I'm worried about all the souls, demons and nether creatures who live here if Hell closes. Will we *all* get refugee status? Can we get everyone out of here in time? What happens to my employees? You understand that many of the demons were created to work here, correct? They don't have soul essence or whatever your trademarked product is."

"These are all the things I need to consider before I talk to my boss," Sam pursed his lips. "I suggest we get started."

Liz opened the box of Ghoulios and handed them round.

Sam took a cookie and stared at it as though it might bite. He dipped the cookie in his coffee and jumped as the crumbs dashed down the sides of his mug.

"Grab 'em before they get away." Ellie pointed at the crumbs. "Are you talking about Heaven? For refugee status or whatever?"

"All entities are created to go up the mountain eventually. Souls go after disembodiment. That's the rule." Sam's fear turned to pleasure as he licked the Ghoulio crumbs from his fingers. "Likely, souls have been weakened, not strengthened by living in this place."

"Do you live on the mountain?" Liz asked. "What's it like?"

"My office is in the Netherworld," Sam said, "Eventually I expect to be promoted and I'll move up the mountain like everyone else. It will be another couple eons after they see the mess I've made of this case." He wrinkled up his nose.

"So, you don't know anything about it," Liz sighed.

"I know that every occupant of every place that's ever closed—from Olympus to that place with the talking animals, you know the one with the wardrobe as a portal—has been sent farther up the mountain. The Olympians' new village is high enough up the mountain that I don't have contact with them anymore." Sam spread out his hands.

"How did *you* get *here*? Today I mean," Ellie asked him.

"I caught the train to Hell at the Netherworld Station."

"How are you going to get back out?" Ellie asked. "Have you thought about that? Since the train doesn't run back to the Netherworld?"

Sam blinked several times. "I assumed that my status as someone with The Mountain Group would allow me to take the train across the chasm. I can't go up the mountain, but I could catch a train back to the office in the Netherworld from there."

"There is no track across the chasm," Brian said. "I'll take you to the station later if you like. I can assure you, there's no track."

"There were miles of it when I attended the ribbon cutting," Sam said. "Some of the VPs and I borrowed the Flying Dutchman to get here. My word, I was airsick by the time we got back. We flew out over the track and inspected it. It was halfway done."

"Well, there's no trace of it now," Brian said. "None at all."

"Except for on this map." Ellie pulled out the paper that Theo had found at the station.

"That does complicate things," Sam was pale.

"Guess you do need to get those trains running then." Ellie rose to place her cup in the sink, then left them in the kitchen to answer the door. She returned with Theo, whose pants were held up with a bright yellow vinyl belt.

"This stupid belt was all they had at the mall," he grumbled as he came into the kitchen. "Did you save some ghost powder donuts for me?"

"Yep," Ellie said. "But before we get to the donuts, I'd like you to meet Mr. Sam K. Azrael."

Theo beamed and nearly shook Sam's arm off, by way of greeting. "I told you I didn't get an error message. It worked!" He filled up a plate with donuts and cookies. He looked around the kitchen from Brian, slumped back in a chair; to Liz, who was pulling at the raveling edge of her sweater; to Sam and Ellie. "This is going to take more than a couple days, isn't it?"

Ellie nodded.

"In that case, I'll have a couple beers with my donuts."

SEVENTEEN

Out Into Hell

LATER THAT EVENING, ELLIE SENT BRIAN AND LIZ ON A mission to pick up more coffee and snacks. They strolled back slowly, from Ghastly's Groceries as twilight came on, red and gray, as damp, moaning winds from the Sea of Dread skittered into the city. The angry crimson glow of an ash storm brewed in the west, out over the Lake of Fire and Lava Falls. Liz hated when the weather patterns clashed over Perdition City; the resulting winds alternated fire and sea scum as they tumbled around the city, scattering trash and cinders and playing havoc with her hair.

"Weather looks awful," she said. "It's going to be a rough week."

"Yeah." Brian kicked at a pile of dead leaves glumly.

They walked several more blocks without talking. Finally, Brian stopped by the cracked glass front of the Perdition City Gift Store. The windows were full of cheap key chains; tacky chartreuse, drab brown, or salmon color t-shirts covered in poorly drawn demons; and coffee cups bearing slogans like "Lava Hottie" or "I Went to Hell and Couldn't Even Afford a Lousy T-shirt."

Liz put her hand on his arm. "Penny for your thoughts? I'm sorry we sprung all of this on you. It wasn't fair. I should have told you earlier."

"I *am* having a hard time taking all this in, Liz." He quickly added, "It's not your fault. I just can't wrap my head around it. Hell shutting down? What would I do?"

"You'd come with me . . . with us," Liz said. "We'd figure it out. Wouldn't you like to be free of this place?"

"I don't know if I can do that," he murmured. "You have to understand, I was made for Hell. I know Sam said all the inhabitants would qualify for refugee status, but I'm not sure he's talking about *us*. You know, me, the demons, Dennis. I don't even know if I *have* a soul."

"What are you talking about?" Liz put her arm through his and pulled him toward a dark alcove where a rusty black bench was half hidden under a thorny tree. "Of course you have a soul! You have one of the best souls I've ever encountered."

They sat. Brian stared up at the black and scarlet clouds chasing each other through the evening sky.

"Liz, I have to tell you something. I'm not sure about all the demons or other creatures who work and live here, but as Hell became more crowded and Satan needed more help, the rumor is that he and Mammon snuck back over to the mountain and stole some byproducts of soul essence and other components from a warehouse. Took any personality traits they thought were pertinent—whatever they could find. The last round of demons and myself were thrown together out of junk and spare parts. *I* was created specifically to run Hell. *I* exist only for that purpose, even more so than the rest of them. I'm not trying to say I'm special. Satan made me to *not* be special. Particularly . . . "

"That's ridiculous," Liz placed her head on his shoulder and her finger on his lips. "There's more to you than spare parts. You told me you weren't meant to like someone. Then again, you do like me . . . right?"

"Of course," he said, shifting his weight. "Although, what if affection is a weakness that Satan gave me, so I'd care about doing my job? What if it's not good enough for a real soul like you? What if you could do better when you get to the other side?"

Liz reached up and touched his cheek. "Brian, the only person who can decide what's best for me is me. I don't care what Satan *thinks* he made you for. We need to keep exploring what we have. Can't you see?

We can figure it out if we stick together." She pressed against him until he relented and put his arm around her.

After Brian made sure no one could see them, he leaned down and quickly kissed the top of her head. "I'll try. I wasn't exactly made with an extra helping of self-esteem."

She laughed, relief flooding her chest. "That's okay. However you were made, it suits me. Besides, if this place can be rehabilitated, who's to say I can't stay here? I mean, if the trains are running again, and there are farms, gymnasiums, and parks, I could be happy *here*. I could take a train and visit Ellie if need be. If you don't leave Hell, maybe I won't either."

They sat pressed against each other until the rotating clouds began to form an unstable cone.

"Looks like an ash devil," Liz sighed.

"Yep. C'mon. Let's get you home. We need to be at work early tomorrow. This is going to be the craziest week Hell has ever seen."

Since Brian had convinced Sam that a long line of howling souls filling out complaint forms while spontaneously combusting or holding bleeding appendages wasn't conducive to serious mental work, the auditor agreed the main thrust of his efforts should be conducted in his room at the Brimstone Hotel. Besides, Liz assured Sam that the Brimstone staff were famous for ignoring guests. The employees erred on the side of laziness over malevolence, as the latter required a great deal more active work. They decided to meet the next day around dinnertime at Ellie's place.

Liz and Brian returned to work Monday morning and attempted to act as though nothing had happened over the weekend. Liz was so giddy and anxious by turns that she took a handful of Hell Tummies. Brian remained firmly on the anxious side of the equation, ruffling his own hair, and pushing his glasses up and down continuously.

They still had half an hour before it was time to open the blinds. Brian peeked out to survey the line snaking out through the lobby and into the street. "Imagine the logistics of getting all these souls out of here." He chewed his bottom lip.

"Hell will stay open, and the trains will start running," Liz argued. "I don't think The Mountain Group will be eager to shut this place down. We'll be able to accomplish things in stages even if worse comes to worse. We'll have help."

Brian returned to his desk without responding and slumped into the chair.

"I'll make some copies of these forms while you check emails," Liz said. "Let's just try to get back in the swing of things today. We're going to meet Sam tonight, right? We just have to pretend that everything is normal today."

"Okay," he said, "it's a deal. No point in borrowing trouble."

Liz filled the printer tray, pressed the button, and stood back to see what would happen. As usual, the tired old machine printed three forms, jammed up, then belched sad wisps of smoke. She was wrestling with the paper drawer when Brian groaned. "What's up?"

"Two more demons disappeared from the Outpost. Gargdorf, a D-4, and Aphonia, a D-3. And Jozz still isn't back. And more nonsense about *nothing*," Brian took a deep breath and then blew it out. "Just what I need this week. I may have to send someone out to try and make horns or tails of the thing."

Liz was trying to think of something comforting to say when a sudden noise drove all rational thought from her mind. It sounded like a chainsaw cutting through a handbell choir, jangling, and buzzing. She clapped her hands over her ears. The shattering sound continued.

The red skull phone perched over Brian's desk was ringing so hard it was bouncing in place. The faceplate of numbers, the permanently surprised mouth, gave the appearance that the phone was howling. The bone headset rattled, shaking dust everywhere.

"Is that Satan?" she yelled.

Brian's lips moved. She couldn't hear him. She didn't need to. His expression told her everything.

The grinning skull kept up its macabre song and dance routine, becoming louder and louder. Brian reached for the headset. The sudden cessation of the noise was a welcome relief.

"Hell, Main Administration, Perdition City, Brian speaking." His voice sounded weak, but steady.

"Oh, fine," he was responding. "Very well, actually."

The voice on the other end of the line was quite loud, Brian had to hold the headset out from his ear a few inches. The connection wasn't terribly good, so Liz heard, through a series of buzzings and hissings, the words *hotel suite, conference rooms, the boys and Em,* and *next week.*

"Yes," Brian said. "Of course. For how long?"

"We know . . . those asshats . . . can't say . . . no access," Liz heard the voice on the other end say. *"Penthouse . . . Diet Cokes."*

The voice went on and Brian replied, "Yes, sir. Immediately."

As muddled as the voice sounded, the fact that Satan was on the other end of the line unsettled Liz, deflating her newfound hopefulness like a pin in a balloon. The line outside the window was becoming rowdier; Liz could hear Hagatha howling at them to settle down. She checked her watch. Nearly time to start.

Brian replaced the red bone in its place on the base of the skull phone, whose green glass eyes now seemed to glitter with satisfaction.

His throat bobbed. "Satan is coming for a visit. Somehow, some way, he knows we're being inspected. Wants the conference room set up. He's bringing Mammon and Beelzebub with him, probably some of the other board members. I've got to get the penthouse suite set up in the

Brimstone Hotel for him and find suites for everyone else too. I hope Sam is as ready for this as he thinks he is." He lowered his voice. "He now has five days to get his ducks in a row.

Hard deadline."

"Let's remain calm," Liz said, "It's early, but Sam has all the evidence he needs. Everything is going to be okay."

"Yeah. I mean, it's not like Satan was going to be any happier two weeks from now if The Mountain Group called him onto the carpet. Or two months, or two years," Brian said. "Satan says not to let anyone look at any of the documents. Too late for that, I guess."

"Well, technically you didn't show anyone anything. Ellie didn't get the documents from you," Liz said. "I don't think you should worry too much. He needs the money, and he needs Hell to stay open. Surely, he'll behave himself."

Liz couldn't quite convince herself of that, having heard the nasty voice on the other line. She thought it might be best if Brian believed it.

"I hope that's true," he said. "We'll see. But I have another concern right now. That's you."

Her heart dropped.

"The last thing I want to do is make things worse for you," she said, forcing a smile. All Brian's warnings about being happy came rushing back to her.

"I'm sorry."

"I'm not sorry. Not at all," he said. "Maybe I should be. I should never have put you in this position. Now that I think of him coming here . . . seeing us together . . . if he knows how we feel about each other, I'm afraid he'd react terribly. I'm used to getting Diet Cokes thrown at my head. I couldn't take it if he did that to you. Or if he did something, you know, worse. Which. I mean. He could."

"Listen," Liz shrugged. "I don't care. I mean, what's he going to do? Throw me in the Abyss? That sort of thing would surely derail the money train. Besides, he can throw a fit all he wants; I firmly believe things are going to get better now that we know the truth, even if they get worse for a little while."

"I couldn't bear him tossing you to the bog eels, Liz," Brian whispered. "I really couldn't. Short of throwing you in the Abyss there are a lot of terrible things he could do. Terrible places he could send you. What if he sends you to the dust mines? Or to herd fire lizards on Krakatoa Mountain?"

They were interrupted by the door banging open.

"What in the warty bottom of Beelzebub's hairy toes is going on in here?" Hagatha glared at them. She pounded her pitchfork on the floor. "Can you open the fucking blinds? I have enough trouble keeping those asshats in line without you guys opening late."

Brian nodded at Liz, and she pulled up the blind and took the first form. Hagatha stomped back out to the lobby, tail twitching.

"Please sign here and here, and initial here," Liz said to the first soul in line—a sad-looking woman covered with muck and algae. A green beetle fell from the soul's ear, which Liz expertly flicked right out the window and back into the lobby. Brian stood by his computer chewing on the end of his pencil, deep in thought. By the time the fifth soul reached the counter, Brian touched Liz's elbow. "I have an idea. And it kills two bats with one lava rock."

"I'm listening," Liz leaned forward and took the form from the soul, retrieving the ballpoint pen just as the mucky female soul attempted to swallow it.

"You're going out to see what's going on at the Outpost and at the Toxahatchee," Brian said, "The big guy is bound to be on the warpath about anything going wrong during the audit, and if I've sent someone out to check, at least he knows I'm on it. Also, it means you won't be here when he is. I would feel a lot better—"

Liz started to protest. He waved her away from the window and took a form from the next soul.

"I'm going to take over the line," he said. "Go get Hagatha. Tell her to come in here *right now*. You'll have to be firm. I'll call in a temp after lunch."

"Get Hagatha?" Liz was rooted in place for a moment, contemplating a trip into the outer reaches of Hell. She'd never gone any farther than the center of Perdition City.

"Yes," Brian said. "Just drag her in here. Please? Also, don't say anything about the inspection or The Mountain Group to her. I think we need to see where this is going before all of Hell finds out. As far as she knows, you guys just need to fill out some on-site incident reports."

"This situation is getting mighty complicated," Liz said with a sigh.

She walked into the lobby, where Hagatha was lifting a bellowing, red-faced man, his collar caught on the tip of her pitchfork. He flailed against the grimy window, feet dangling over a dusty, fake potted palm.

"Did you just say something about my ass, dude?" Hagatha was saying. "Seriously?"

The red-faced man tried to choke out an answer. He could only manage a helpless gurgle.

Gadreel stood nearby watching in amusement, occasionally half-heartedly poking souls who wiggled out of line with his sharp, red-tipped spear. Liz tapped him on the arm.

As he turned to face Liz, Gadreel raked down the line with the back end of his spear, toppling about six souls.

"C'mon guys," he said, when they began to wail. "Settle down." He turned to Liz. "Not enough coffee in the afterlife for this job. What do you need?"

"Gadreel!" Liz yelled over the rising din of low-level squabbles, "Brian wants Hagatha in the office!"

"Why are you asking me?"

Liz pointed at Hagatha, who was now lifting the poor man even higher, dangling him in air like a fish she was contemplating throwing back. "I don't think she can hear me."

Gadreel shrugged his massive, muscular blue shoulders and scratched his chin with his free hand. "She's busy. You want me to interrupt that?"

Hagatha was now shaking the soul to and fro, as pleased as a child with a rag doll, watching his flailing limbs. Ashes and dust rained from the poor soul's clothing.

"You oughta *thank* me! I just cleaned your suit!" Hagatha screamed.

"Brian said now," Liz repeated.

Gadreel raised an eyebrow. "Fine. Hope he's going to help me pull my horns out of my ass when she turns me into a pretzel."

He let his spear fly, and it landed in the potted palm, shaft ploinking into an upright position just between the flailing soul's legs.

Gadreel grinned. "Did you see that? Pinpoint accuracy."

Hagatha turned and hissed at them.

Gadreel lifted his hands in a gesture of surrender. "Boss wants to see you in the office," he bellowed. "*Now!* Says this one, anyway." He pointed at Liz, who tried to make herself appear small and submissive.

Hagatha threw the soul with a twist of her wrist. He sailed through the air and smacked into the wall.

"Great Satan's balls!" she said, banging her pitchfork on the floor. "I'm busy. What's this about?"

"Don't shoot the messenger," Liz squeaked.

"Don't look at me," Gadreel said. "I know nothing."

"Just trying to do my fucking job here. As if anyone cares," Hagatha snarled, stomping across the lobby to the office.

When Hagatha banged through the door, Brian was mid-conversation with a soul.

"One second, sir. I'll be right back." He slammed the window shut and turned to address Liz and Hagatha. "You two are going on a business trip."

"Is traveling in my job description?" Hagatha sat on his desk, leaning forward, nose poking through the tines of her pitchfork. She raised one eyebrow. "Well?"

"Security detail is," he said. "I've had a couple of weird reports I've been meaning to get to. Now I can't. Big Boss is coming. I can't leave so I'm sending Liz. The first situation is down at the Toxahatchee. Water is low under the Lucretia bridge and the eels are starting to tunnel. After that, I need you two to check out a report from the Last Outpost."

"Out there? Traveling is a tough assignment," Hagatha said. "Might be above my pay grade. You know what it's like outside the city. Not exactly a picnic in the wastelands."

"I could send Gadreel or Jezreel," Brian said casually. "I just thought you were the best."

Hagatha's eyes narrowed. "I didn't say I wasn't the best; I said I don't *want* to. Of course, I'm sure she'd be toast if you sent either one of those lame-ass fuckers."

"That's why I'm asking you. Or rather, assigning you to the detail."

Two souls were pressed up to the window, battling for a place in line and pounding the glass. Hagatha strode over, opened the window, and stuck her long face through. "Shut the fuck up!" she shrieked and slammed the window shut again.

"You're going," Brian said as the line settled into a moment of quiet. He handed Liz a manila folder. "Here are the reports. We've already been over most of the stuff. And before you ask," he pulled down his glasses and peered at Hagatha. "This is all we know. That's why you're going—to figure out what's happening."

"Why now?" she whined. "Can't it wait?"

"I already told you. Satan's coming," Brian repeated. "I need to be here to greet him."

"Isn't he gonna be pissed when he sees the line is super long?" Hagatha asked. "Didn't you say all the demons you tried out on paperwork made things worse instead of better? Maybe you should keep Liz here."

"Satan doesn't give a crap about inconveniencing souls," he argued. "I will say that if a river eel shows up in his toilet, he's going to be pissed."

"Oh, alright." Hagatha jerked her head dismissively towards Liz. "Two questions remain. First, why her? Why not a demon?"

"Last time I sent a demon to fill out an incident report, it took six and a half weeks to get a report back. When I did get it, it was covered in peanut butter and jelly and smelled like gin and vomit. Bear in mind that the incident occurred on the far side of Perdition City, not on the far side of Hell. Not to mention the fact that once I wiped off the jam and interpreted the misspellings and grammar errors, it was pure nonsense. I had to make the trip myself anyway. There's going to be a boatload of paperwork involved, no doubt, and Liz can do that better than anybody I know. Not only are you the best security for the mission, you're D9. You have the authority to start a work detail if need be."

Hagatha scowled. "Fine. I get it. Second thing: why do we give a bat's ass what happens in the Craggy Mountains? I get the river eels. We don't need a river eel swimming up the boss's ass from his hotel room toilet. So what's out in the desert? A couple of skull-head lizards and three dried-up souls? What are we looking for there?"

Brian cleared his throat. "Um. Nothing." He gazed at the ceiling and waited for the response.

"We're driving across Hell for *nothing?*" Hagatha asked. "Sweet Lucifer's Tail! What are you talking about? *Nothing?* Seriously?"

"They're missing personnel," Brian said. "Zenebrius says that they saw a *nothing*, whatever that means, and then Jozz disappeared. He just emailed us again last night and he's starting to sound frantic. He lost another couple demons. Just head out there. Maybe his nothing is really nothing. Maybe the missing demons will be back before you even get that far. If that's the case, I'll call you guys back. Otherwise, I'd really like you to keep the whole thing quiet and see what's going on. You know how things get in Hell when there's a panic."

"Yeah, I know," Hagatha said. "Although—that's not really my problem."

"It's my problem," he retorted. "And I'm your boss. Which makes it your problem."

Hagatha contemplated her position for a moment, frowning down her nose at Brian. "Satan's balls on toast," she spat, "that's a long fucking trip! I struggled to get this job. It's not easy to get D-Class 9. This job pays well and it's a piece of cake. Besides, my favorite bar is here in Perdition City. How long are we gonna be gone?" She slammed the handle of her pitchfork against the floor, making a dent in the black and white linoleum. "What if I say I won't go? What then?"

Hagatha bent down until she and Brian were nose to nose. He didn't relent. "I have no problem reducing your pay to nothing and demoting you to all the way back down to service level D-3. You can stay here in the city and get a job over at the mall. You can make Lava Smoothies."

Hagatha ran her tongue along her teeth. "This trip might be expensive. And who knows what kinda stuff we'll need on the way. Food, lodging, emergency rations. We might break down and need a new tire or something. I hope you don't expect me to pay for anything."

The standoff continued for a long moment. Brian nodded and strolled into the back office where the safe was located, shutting the door behind him. Hagatha thrust the pitchfork at Liz. "Hold this."

She perched on Brian's desk, arms crossed over her chest, long hairless tail twitching.

Brian returned, and with an expression of great misgiving, he held out a small black credit card. A holographic flame flickered on its matte surface.

Hagatha reverently took the card. "The Black Hole Card? By the hairs on His fiery testicles, I never thought I'd see one of these." She let out a long, low whistle.

"There's a little cantina close to the Outpost. I hear the liquor flows like lava over there. It's cheap. Drink what you want when you get there, expense it. I'll give you a bonus if you get Liz there and back safely. The line *will* be hellacious by the time she gets back, and I'll need her in one piece," he said. "I don't have time to train another soul." He caught Liz's eye and she realized for the first time how worried he was about his plan. The realization was not comforting. "Your first stop is a motel close to the lava beaches called Smokin' Joe's. Joe keeps his eye on everything, and demons talk to him. He doesn't get a lot of business anymore, but he has some contacts. He's only a few miles from the Toxahatchee. Maybe he knows something, maybe he doesn't. Just don't mention it to the big boss if he's still here when you get back. Satan doesn't like him for some reason."

"Because ol' Joe knows some shit, like how to do his own job," Hagatha shrugged. "Just guessing."

Brian threw up his hands. "I'm certainly not getting into that. Also, since Dennis has been assigned to you, Liz, regulations say you have to take him when you travel."

Liz groaned. The possibility of being without Dennis had not occurred to her. In the same instant the sweet relief of leaving him behind dangled before her, it was taken away.

As they turned to leave the office, Brian called out, "Don't go *totally* nuts with the card. Please! Drink, stay at nice hotels, whatever. Don't bankrupt Hell, would you?"

"Don't you trust me?" Hagatha bared her sharp rows of teeth in what she possibly thought was a charming smile.

"Not as far as I can throw you," he said to the enormous demoness. "Now please focus. You guys need to set off as soon as possible."

Hagatha gave Liz a curt nod. "Let's go, kiddo." To Brian she added, "I was having a perfectly good morning shaking up souls. Plus, I planned to go out with some guys later and get wasted. Just so you know, you're ruining my day. And probably the next couple weeks of my life."

"Hit someone on the way out," Brian said. "Get as wasted as you want when you stop at Smokin' Joe's. Try not to crash the over-priced car I'm sure you'll rent."

"You know that if I'm going to get this job done in a reasonable amount of time, I'll need to rent a car with a Frenzy Drive. No other way to cover those distances without sucking up an awful lot of eternity."

Brian rubbed his temples. "A Frenzy Drive? You know what that costs?"

She shrugged. "Want to see us before the year is up? Then I'm getting a Frenzy Drive."

"Just don't go overboard."

Hagatha slipped the card into her lanyard. "Yeah. Of course not."

"Actually, can you wait in the lobby for a minute? I want to give Liz a few pointers about the reports."

"Yeah, fine," Hagatha sauntered away, calling, "I'm not exactly in a hurry to start on this sucky quest anyway."

Brian locked the door behind her, walked over to the window, pulled down the shade and drew Liz into his arms. He pressed his lips to her forehead and kissed her. "Please be careful. I'm going to miss you, Liz."

"I'm going to miss you too," she whispered.

"You'd better get going," he said. Something heavy banged against the window. Liz reluctantly left him and made her way into the lobby.

Hagatha was behind the front desk, already on the phone to the rental car company. Sheena sat flipping through an *AfterGlam* magazine as souls wandered up and asked directions to Housing or the Department of Infernal affairs. She occasionally blew a bubble of tar gum and pointed at a directory behind the desk without glancing up from her magazine. Hagatha pulled Liz behind the desk for safekeeping while she ordered a car to her exacting specifications.

The lobby buzzed with querulous souls, squabbles occasionally punctuated by screams or curses, forcing security to get involved. While Hagatha haggled over the price of the car and added all the extras she could think of, Liz blinked back tears. At the thought of heading into the unknown, she felt a sudden affection for the dirty and disheveled Admin Building—a mere thimbleful of warmth, but it was there. Bilious light leaked through dirty windows and onto sad rubbery plants. Brian was in the office, as was her office sweater, her potted fireberry plant with its purple thorns and vermilion berries, the small photo of Dennis he'd insisted she place on her desk. She ruminated, morose, until Hagatha's claw descended on her shoulder.

"They'll drive the car out to your place and meet us in two hours," Hagatha said. "Wait until you see it." She rubbed her hands together and let out a wolf whistle. "Frenzy Drive, takes premium lava, matte black that soaks up the light. Unholy frickin bat guano! I gotta get some pictures of me behind the wheel. I'm literally gonna turn some guys green with jealousy!"

"Hey, doesn't she work here?" a tall soul inquired, pointing at Liz as they walked through the lobby to the door. The soul was obviously from the prideful north, judging by the ice in her hair. The continuously melting ice dripped on a small soul whose clothes were gently aflame. The elements meeting caused steam to rise from the smaller soul's jacket. The smell of someone who'd obviously been through the digestive system of a bog eel wafted towards them as more souls pushed into the lobby. A cloud of dust kicked up as a soul from the western wilds spun through the revolving doors.

"Who's running the line?" a soul yelled.

A quiver of worry ran up and down the line. Souls pushed each other. The line widened and thrust forward. A gargoyle spat fire at the crowd, "Back up, folks! Don't push!"

Anxiety rippled around the room, even though a few people at the front of the line tried make it clear that the window was indeed open. A scuffle broke out by the potted plants. The people just outside the doors had apparently decided that the line was indeed closing, and they surged forward in panic.

Jezreel stood by the lobby doors. Anyone who pressed too hard went skidding through the exit. The line closed in; souls howled and fussed. Scrums formed in the middle of the large foyer. Gadreel, who didn't like to be bothered, had finally been irritated into action, flinging souls left and right.

Hagatha looked on in admiration. "You know, he's pretty impressive when you get him riled up." She grabbed Liz by the arm and pulled her through the exit doors. "C'mon. We got stuff to do.

EIGHTEEN

Liz and Hagatha Go Shopping

HAGATHA BARRELED DOWN THE CROWDED SIDEWALK, occasionally tossing aside souls and demons so Liz's path was clear. When one brutish soul thrust an arm in front of Liz, Hagatha neatly twisted it backwards. "No touching," she said. "Kindly fuck out of the way."

"My apartment is back that way," Liz wheezed.

"I know that, Captain Obvious." Hagatha picked up an incubus meandering in front of her and adroitly deposited it in a trash can. "I meet you there most mornings on the way to work. I live across the street, remember? We're not going there just yet. We're going over to the Anubis Mall—Nether Leather to be exact."

"I see," Liz panted, running almost flat-out.

Hagatha patted the lanyard holding the black credit card. "I have never had this baby in my claws before and I am entirely unlikely to ever have it again, especially when Brian gets the bill for *this* trip. With Satan coming, he's gonna be distracted. There's a scarlet leather jacket in the window of Nether Leather that doesn't have my name on it. It will soon." She swept her tail around to clear the sidewalks. A tall, slender lizard-creature trailing sticky green vines kicked at them as they passed, annoyed by Hagatha's swagger. Hagatha kept walking as though she didn't notice. As they passed, her long possum tail reached backwards and coiled around one of the creature's ankles just above its webbed foot. It lost balance and rolled into the street hissing.

"Bitchesssss . . . " it yelled after them.

"Get out of my way next time, you smelly freak," Hagatha said dismissively. "I wish these assholes would stay in the swamps. They should know to get out of the way for she-devils. Don't know one that's less than D-7. Class warfare is alive and kicking."

"I got trapped in the mall for the whole weekend when I tried to pick up a shower curtain once. Dennis almost destroyed the place before I got home," Liz panted, struggling to keep pace. "Even getting to the mall isn't easy. Aren't we supposed to leave today?"

"Gotcha covered," Hagatha said. "We're heading to the taxi stand."

Notched into the square gray courtyard of a dingy brick building was a line of large wrought iron cages with doors in front—bird cages big enough to accommodate groups of people and even larger demons. Behind each cage was a tall perch with an enormous bird, many sleeping, heads tucked under one wing. The flying taxis.

"Oh no!" Liz backed away. "I made a vow. No flying taxis. You should see the kind of stuff I deal with in the complaint lines."

Hagatha laughed. "Don't be a baby." She patted her lanyard again. "No chance I don't take advantage of this. You're getting in and you're not making a fuss."

A giant, scruffy raven blinked itself awake, squawked, and settled down on top of the wrought iron cage in front of its perch, gripping the handle with its talons. The door opened. With a heartfelt sigh, it croaked out, "Where to?"

The bird had dull, black feathers that faded to rust at the tips with a stray, gray feather or two sticking up from its head, giving it the appearance of a crazy old man. It was taller than Liz and smelled strongly of cigarettes and chicken poop. None of these facts eased Liz's anxiety.

"Mall," said Hagatha, "which floor is the leather store? Also, is the new liquor store open?"

"Apparel on twentieth," said the raven. "Witches Brew Liquors on the fiftieth, top floor, right outside the Vortex Elevator. Just opened two weeks ago."

"Can you drop us on the twentieth and then meet us roof-side?"

"Probably. There's usually an open window on the east side."

"Cool," Hagatha smiled. "That oughta save some time." She shoved Liz into the cage and followed, slamming and locking the door. The cage had metal seats around the edge and a swinging perch suspended from the center. Liz and Hagatha took seats on opposite sides of the cage.

"Cushion?" Hagatha handed Liz a dirty, round pillow of worn red velvet with a button hanging off the center and located one for herself—a burnt orange square pillow with one lonely tassel barely clinging to the corner.

Though the cage was large, Hagatha took up a solid one half of the space. Liz wasn't sure if the raven would even be able to lift them.

"Name's Edgar. I do my best for my customers' comfort," the raven cawed. "I search through the trash every week for cushions because I have to replace them frequently. Please do your best to vomit outside the cage, as garbage day near my nest is not until Thursday."

"Whatever," Hagatha reclined, perfectly at ease. "Let's head."

Much to Liz's disappointment, the cage lurched off the ground; she found herself gripping bars, trying desperately to wrap her legs under the seat for stability. The swinging perch flew back and forth, just missing her face.

"Grab the bar in the middle if you get thrown from your seat mid-flight," the bird said. "No big deal. Happens all the time."

"Comforting," Liz muttered, as Hagatha laughed.

The cage wobbled into the head of a passing demon with a long giraffe-like neck who swore at them. "Watch where you're going, you great fucking twats!"

Hagatha flipped him off, and the cage creaked upwards. As they lurched skyward, Liz was immediately flung from position. She grabbed the perch, which pitched her back into her seat momentarily. The disadvantage of the cage was its openness. Liz could see the ground getting farther and farther away, all the while hearing Edgar groaning and grumbling about his muscles.

"Not as young as I used to be," Edgar said as they came level with the tallest tree on the block.

"Goodness, I suppose I should work out more. I think I just felt a tear in my pectoralis major," he murmured as they rose to the tops of some of the smaller buildings.

If Liz looked down now, the souls and demons on the street were the size of beetles. She shut her eyes as Edgar flapped still higher.

"Leaping Leviathan, maybe I should have retired last year like the wife suggested," the raven said.

Liz closed her eyes. The cage had steadied but still swayed with every flap of the bird's wings. She peeked out of the side of the cage towards the street, where the crows below appeared as small as ants now, and immediately shut her eyes again.

"What are you worried about?" Hagatha chuckled. "Dying? Too late for that! You're missing the wonderful view."

The flapping and grumbling seemed interminable. Finally Liz heard Edgar grunt, "Mall to starboard."

"Can you get us level with the twentieth?" Hagatha asked.

Liz opened her eyes. Edgar was losing altitude and wobbling towards the Anubis Mall; a monstrously tall, rusted metal building. The top floors had obviously been built on piecemeal, out of entirely different metals. There was a flat roof with a smoothie stand, but the entire building leaned slightly to one side.

"So, you say there's an open window?" Hagatha shouted.

"Yep. There's a window over at Clauneck's Department store that's been broken for the last ten, twenty years. Can't see them fixing it anytime soon." He coughed for a few moments, losing a little height, slowly wheezed his way back towards the building.

"Are you kidding? We're going in through a broken window?" Liz asked.

"It'll be quicker," Hagatha gestured expansively. "Time is of the essence. Weren't you the one who wanted to leave today?"

Edgar reached the building and hovered outside the window, flapping to stay in place.

"This is as close as I get without slamming the cage into the wall," Edgar said. "You'll have to swing 'er in."

"Me?" Liz clutched the side of the cage, determined not to let go.

"He means the cage, doofus," Hagatha said. "Swing the cage in. Yeah, you too in a minute. Okay Edgar, I'll swing the cage until I can grab the window with my tail."

The cage of the taxi was already uncomfortably close to the wall when Hagatha began swinging it. Liz realized that two options for a very long nether body regeneration lay before her—bashing into the wall or falling twenty stories. She strongly suspected both might happen.

"Hold on," Hagatha said, concentrating. "Like, really tight."

The demoness' arms stretched across the cage as she swayed her powerful body back and forth until the metal box swung nearly horizontal. Liz could see the sky, then the bustling street below. She closed her eyes, clinging desperately to the metal bars. *This trip is going to be over before it starts,* she thought, fighting the urge to vomit.

Edgar continued flapping. He was starting to wheeze. "Okay ladies. I'm decrepit. Don't know how much longer I can hold out. Can we hurry this up?"

With every breath, Liz waited to crash. Hagatha just swung the cage harder.

"Keep your drawers on," she shouted. "Almost there."

The morbid curiosity was too much. Liz opened her eyes. The sky, the swarming street below, the wall of the mall through fine mesh at the bottom of the cage. Sky, street, wall. A sickening rhythm that matched Edgar's rasping breaths and Hagatha's grunting. The cage stopped abruptly, angled on its side, door open. Hagatha was holding the cage close to the window ledge with her tail while Edgar continued flapping.

"Hurry out," croaked the raven, flapping against the weight of the cage. "I'll be at the top of the building. Give me a whistle. You paying me to wait?"

"Sure. Why not? You take cards?"

"Who doesn't?" Edgar said. Hagatha pulled the cage closer to the window, tipping it even more on its side. Then she grabbed the ledge with her hand as well as her tail. She swung one leg over the windowsill. Her mighty tail flipped back and circled around Liz, who wrapped her arms around the long possum tail, every flap of the bird's wings making her heart flutter. The cage fell away, and Liz was briefly suspended twenty stories from the ground, held only by Hagatha's tail.

Hagatha slid through the window, and pulled Liz through the opening after her, managing to bang her against the frame with only moderate force. Liz touched the slight bump on her forehead, grateful her skull was still in one piece. She lay in a pile of poorly stuffed pillows and ugly brown blankets. They had fallen through the window into the linen department of Clauneck's Department Store.

"The only reason you have a knot on your head is because you didn't duck when I told you to," Hagatha sniffed. "You should really pay attention to what I'm telling you when you're twenty stories up. I mean, you should always do what I tell you to, but like, more so when you're hanging off a building."

Liz wanted to argue. Relief overcame her ability to speak.

"See," Hagatha bragged, "I probably saved us at *least* two hours. The sidewalk is packed today. There's a line around the block. Even with me tossing souls left and right, it would have taken us an hour or more to get in. The only other line we have to wait in is the one for the elevator. I think I can push some people out of the way. We're in great shape time-wise."

"You mean the Vortex Elevator?" Liz asked. After reading the warning signs, she'd never had the guts to ride it. On the rare occasions she'd gone to the mall, she'd put on her walking shoes and taken the stairs. The creeping escalators had a habit of either being broken altogether or suddenly changing direction.

"Yep," Hagatha went on. "On the plus side, once you ride it, you'll look more fondly on the flying taxi. Of course, getting dropped on the twentieth cut off some of the floors we'll have to ride to the top, so it shouldn't be so bad. Your brain will probably still be in its braincase." She gave Liz a toothy grin. Even thinking about it brought back Liz's nausea, but Hagatha was in no mood to argue. After they exited Clauneck's, they headed for Nether Leather, a boutique on the opposite side of the twentieth floor. The walls were covered with black leather while red velvet chairs were tastefully—for Hell—placed here and there.

"This is not bad. I didn't know there were stores this nice in Hell." Liz gazed around.

"Souls and even most demons don't make the kind of money it takes to shop here," Hagatha said. "Neither do I. Yet. You never know, once you start dressing like those guys, catch their attention, start getting invited to their parties . . . anything's possible."

She grabbed the first sales-demon to pass by, stuck the flat black credit card in her face and pointed. "Bring me the red leather jacket from the window display. And be quick about it. You have a suitcase for the trip?" Hagatha asked Liz. "Souls like to take a bunch of shit with them, I guess. Clothes and stuff?"

"No," Liz said. "As a matter of fact, I do not have a suitcase." She'd had to replace all her clothes after the luggage incident at the station. She'd certainly never imagined traveling and saw no need to replace her bag.

"A suitcase for my pal, too," Hagatha instructed the clerk. "Oh, and throw in a pair of those sunglasses." Hagatha pointed to a rack of expensive sunglasses on display at the counter.

The well-endowed demoness looked down her nose at the card. "What makes you think I have your size?" she asked. "Besides that, where did *you* get a Black Hole card?" She slipped the strap of a red sundress back in place. The dress was insubstantial, clingy, and nearly the same color as her skin, making her appear naked for a moment. She pursed her stained black lips and glared.

"Admin, baby," Hagatha pointed to the ID on her lanyard. The demoness studied the two of them. Then she held out the card and turned it over.

"Still," the sales demoness bit her lip. "Perhaps I should call someone to verify that you're authorized to use this card." She raised one eyebrow.

"We're in a bit of a jam for time, babe. And I thought you might want to add a little something for yourself," Hagatha purred. "But if we have to wait for authorization, then—"

"I see, madam," the salesclerk smiled. "I'll have it wrapped up in a jiffy." When she returned, she held a gold-plated lipstick, some very expensive, studded black leather pants and a pair of spiky red patent high heels that she put aside for herself. She then retrieved the leather jacket and sunglasses that Hagatha had requested along with a red leather suitcase with black trim, interwoven with tiny glittering skulls.

Hagatha nodded. "You have good taste. Enjoy." The cashier turned and swiped on the lipstick, a fiery orange, and licked her lips.

"Wow," Hagatha said, "nice. It suits you, babe."

The sales demoness smiled. "I know."

She swiped the card, then delicately folded the merchandise she'd chosen for herself in black tissue, affixed a scarlet ribbon on the bag, and placed it under the register. Only then did she wrap Hagatha's jacket and sunglasses. She removed the tags from the suitcase and handed it to Liz.

"Do you even need the bag?" Liz asked Hagatha as she slid the jacket out of the bag with the Nether Leather logo and put it on.

"Of course," Hagatha responded indignantly. "There's no use shopping at Nether Leather if you can't make people jealous. I'm sure I can think of some crap to casually carry around in this sack. Now, let's hit the liquor store on the way out. I want to get some Old Nick Whiskey. Something else I've never had before."

The demoness flashed her lanyard again at the Vortex Elevator, for which there was a substantial line. One or two souls tried to prevent her from cutting, but they ended up sliding down the hallway on their asses. Hagatha was pleased to find that every other demon waiting was below D-9 and therefore inferior to herself and, of course, she had no respect for the nether creatures. A few well-placed tosses and elbow jabs later, Liz and Hagatha found themselves standing right in front of the elevator. The doors were a shiny black, protruding from the wall like a half barrel. Liz stared at their reflections, which separated into whorls of body parts in the dark curved metal.

A rushing sound issued from the elevator shaft, growing louder and louder until it sounded like a freight train. When the elevator came to a halt on their floor and the doors opened, a gust of wind escaped; so strong it blew Liz's hair back. She pressed down her skirt to keep it from blowing around her head. Souls and demons stumbled out. Even the nether creatures were discombobulated, but the souls were obviously the worse for wear. One moaning woman fell at their feet and Hagatha's cloven foot nudged her out of the way. Another soul was vomiting. Liz's stomach churned in sympathy.

"C'mon." Hagatha shoved Liz into the elevator. "This will get us up to the top lickety-split. We'll hit Witches Brew Liquor Store and then head back to your place to get your stuff and pick up the car."

"How does this elevator work, exactly?" Liz had nervously read the signs plastered on the wall beside the elevator doors while they waited: *Enter at your own risk. Do not walk close to open windows for one hour after taking elevator. Do not walk close to open stairwells for two hours after taking elevator. Do not eat for at least six hours after taking elevator. Anubis Mall, Anubis Mall Shops, and Anubis Mall management are not responsible for visions or hallucinations which may occur during, after, or before riding the Vortex Elevator (some riders may experience time anomalies).*

"It's sort of got a whirlwind under it," Hagatha said, frowning. "I don't know exactly. Does it matter?"

The elevator lurched once and then sped upwards so quickly that Liz fell to the floor. A whirring noise became a shriek as the elevator clanged and banged like a washer on a bad spin cycle. For a few moments, Liz saw dark spinning walls reflecting what seemed a crowd of millions, though it was only her reflection and those of Hagatha and the other passengers; the images picked up speed then melted together into a black mist where Liz found herself alone and stumbling forward. It was as if she'd left the elevator behind. This must be one of the hallucinations the sign had warned about.

She felt someone next to her and grabbed on for dear life. She realized she was kneeling, gripping a large hand. She felt the warmth of a wool sweater and smelled the light scent of woodsy aftershave. Brian. She could barely see him through the mist. He was bent over a black desert of lava sand and pointing at something tiny and green with his free hand. "What's this?"

Liz held onto Brian and tried to steady herself. "A hallucination? According to the sign, I don't think I'm really here."

Brian pointed frantically again, waving away the mist with his hand. "Hallucination or not, what's that and how did it get here?"

Liz hunkered down and squinted. "It's the pointed end of a lily bulb. Someone must have planted it."

"Sweet Lucifer," Brian sighed, shaking his head. "You can't plant lilies in Hell. The roots are too deep." The plant, which was growing larger by the minute, had now sprouted a luminescent white flower that was getting taller and wider. Within seconds it was almost up to Brian's neck.

"Lily bulbs don't have deep roots," Liz argued. The flower suddenly grew taller than Brian and began roaring. "It can't do that!" she yelled. "It's just a flower!"

The black mist parted. Liz blinked and found her chin in Hagatha's claw. The she-devil's face spun around her, one in a kaleidoscope of sickening images until it came to rest.

"I'm not a flower," Hagatha said drily. "Good thing for you, I know this elevator discombobulates people."

"Are we dead?" Liz managed to whisper.

"*You* are. That's how you got here, remember?" Hagatha dragged Liz over to a bench. "Sit there with your eyes closed. Store's right here. Don't move for a few minutes. I'm pretty sure they carry elevator antidote in the liquor store. I'll toss it on the card."

Liz couldn't have moved if she'd wanted to. She kept her eyes shut as tightly as possible to keep the refracted, spinning images at bay. Her back was against a wall, and the solid surface seemed to be whirling in circles as well. She could hear shoppers' voices but couldn't make out words. Only cawing and barking. She felt a foot strike her left leg, which was hanging off the bench. Her stomach did a cartwheel and she sat up just long enough to barf on someone's shoes.

The person cursed. The words bounced away. She didn't have the energy to attend to anything except her somersaulting stomach and a headache like a lightning storm bashing the inside of her skull. There was a flash inside her head every few seconds; hallucinations pulsed with every bolt. *Flash.* Liz was in a knot of small men, running with clubs, swatting one another. *Flash.* She was bent over a hole in the ground in a desert. *Flash.* Brian was there. At the next flash, a large shadowy hand pushed through the ashy dirt and grabbed the front of Liz's shirt. Brian yanked her backwards. *Flash.* The shadow grabbed Liz's skirt and tugged her towards the hole in the ground. She found herself screaming, eyes open.

Hagatha leaned over Liz. "Quit hollering for a sec." The demon poured some tasteless liquid onto Liz's tongue.

A slow wave of apathy moved from tongue to brain and her screams abruptly subsided.

"You did okay for a soul. Only barfed once and not on me. Not a drop on yourself either. I'm impressed."

Liz tried to stand up and failed spectacularly to do so, collapsing back onto the bench in a heap. Hagatha pulled her up and shook her by the shoulders.

"Let's get that stuff through the old system," she said. "Feel better?"

Tentatively, Liz took a step. It was like walking through Jell-O. After a fashion, she found herself ambulatory again. "The bar is low, but I think so."

"It's good stuff," Hagatha said. "Oughta be, considering what I paid for it. We can take the stairs to the roof. We're on the top floor."

In addition to her Nether Leather bag, Hagatha carried two large brown bags imprinted with a witch's hat topped with a glittery spider.

"Had to get all this stuff wrapped so it won't break on the taxi ride," she said, patting the bags. "Picked up a few necessary things besides the Old Nick's."

When they reached the roof, Edgar was standing next to the cage, eyes closed, snoring slightly. Liz felt she *ought* to be terrified, but the elevator antidote was liquid ennui. She couldn't generate any panic. She wondered if she could talk Hagatha out of the remainder of the antidote. It would come in so handy at the office.

Hagatha rapped on the cage "Wake up, bird. We've got a lot to accomplish, and now that I'm appropriately attired, there's a leather steering wheel I need to wrap my sweet claws around."

Edgar snorted himself awake, spread his wings, and hopped up to the top of the cage with a sigh. "Where to?" he yawned.

NINETEEN

Packing with Dennis

LIZ FORGOT THAT DENNIS HAD BARFED BY THE DOOR that morning and, of course, immediately stepped in it when they arrived at the apartment. Hagatha swung through the door right behind Liz, pushing her. Liz slid sideways on the vomit, doing a one-footed dance across the floor, and fell on the couch. She sighed and grabbed a tissue to wipe the bottom of her shoe.

Dennis laughed. Then he whined, "Why are you home so early? You didn't get fired, did you? I only want to torment you at night, not all day too. Besides, you get paid more than souls with an infernal pension; I eat better than the other nether animals. Why is admin security here? Did you get fired? You got fired, didn't you?" He stopped his rapid-fire questions, hissed once for good measure, then pulled his tail around and licked the end while he waited for an answer.

Liz ignored him. Hagatha stalked around the apartment, picking up various items: a candle, the remote, a vase. She turned each item over, glaring as if it had personally offended her, and then put it back in the wrong place.

"Nothing I want here," she said. "Where's the kitchen?"

"Right through that door." Liz grabbed her new suitcase and headed towards her room to pack. Dennis blocked her way.

"Why do you have a suitcase?" Dennis fretted. "Are you leaving me? Where are you going? Who will feed me?" He stamped his paw.

"I'm going on a trip." She couldn't quite bring herself to tell Dennis he was coming too. "Who fed you before?" she asked. "Didn't you take care of yourself? Can you please scoot out of my way?"

"No!" He stood resolutely between Liz and the bedroom door. "I was assigned to torment you. The last six souls that lived here were only temporary. I invested a lot of time in figuring out how to bother you and I don't think it's fair of you to leave me now. You're my eternally designated torment-ee. It's hard work; I shouldn't have to start over. Anyway, you'll miss me if you leave, I bet." His tail swung wildly, knocking a small potted plant off the side table next to the couch.

"Hardly." Liz picked up the plant and pushed past him into her room. Dennis followed, rubbing on her leg and drooling.

"You can't go! I forbid it! I want to watch TV while you bring me rotten fish. I shouldn't have to fend for myself," he sniveled. "Where are you going? When will you be back?"

"For Hell's sake, Brian says you're going too," Hagatha shouted. "Liz is just teasing you. Probably because you're an asshole." Loud banging noises came from the vicinity of the kitchen as the demoness rifled through the pantry and refrigerator. "You don't have to fend for yourself, you big baby. There's a huge stack of dented tuna cans over here in the pantry. Put 'em in a bag. We're leaving in, like, ten minutes." She appeared in the bedroom doorway with a bag of stale chips and tore through the plastic with her teeth. She poured the entire bag of snacks straight down her throat.

"Where's the rest of the beer?" Hagatha inquired. "Got all I could find out of the fridge. We can take what I don't drink right now."

"That's all I have." Liz folded clothes and packed her suitcase.

"Pathetic," Hagatha snorted. "Anyhoo, since I have the magic credit card, we can stop outside Perdition City at the Pandemonium Discount Liquor Emporium. Even with someone else's money, I wasn't going to pay what they were asking for Affliction Ale at Witches' Brew. It was ridiculous." She flung herself on the couch, where she opened yet another bag of chips.

"What if I don't want to go?" Dennis asked, ignoring Hagatha. "I took a car ride once. I got constipated. I like watching TV. I don't want you to go, and I don't want to go either."

"Nobody's asking you. Now pack your shit, little guy, and quit bothering us," Hagatha growled. She opened a beer, tossed it back and then opened another one. "Hey! Hurry up with the packing, kid. I'm anxious to get my ass in the driver's seat. Wait 'til you see that baby."

Dennis continued mewling from the doorway. "But I've got a bunch of stuff recorded and I'm compiling the worst of the Hannity show for you, Liz."

Liz stopped throwing things in her suitcase for a second and slammed the door. Maybe the outskirts of Hell wouldn't be that bad. Maybe they could find a way to "lose" Dennis.

When Liz reemerged, suitcase bulging, Dennis was standing next to the couch, a petulant expression pasted on his little whiskered face. Next to him, a bag full of canned tuna leaned against the couch. He drooled on one of his paws and wiped his tiny left horn with the spit, something he did when he was anxious.

"How am I supposed to poop on a road trip when I usually do that in your underwear drawer?" He folded his small green arms across his chest and frowned.

"I'm sure you'll manage," Liz said cheerfully. "Or else you'll explode. Where's Hagatha?" She closed the living room window and latched it.

"She went downstairs. Someone brought the car." Dennis thrust the bag at her. "Carry this tuna. It's too heavy." He kicked at the plastic sack, stuffed to overflowing with dented cans of tuna; his claws tore a hole in the bag, rendering it immediately unusable. Liz sighed and went to the kitchen for another bag—a fruitless search, but she did find some tape instead, and began to patch up the hole.

Dennis ran back into the bedroom and grabbed a couple of Liz's pillows and her quilt, all covered with moss green hair, like everything else in the apartment. He wrapped the pillows in the quilt and dragged the bundle behind him over the ashy, dirty floor, which stayed ashy and dirty no matter how often Liz swept.

She pulled up the handle on her suitcase and hefted Dennis's bag of tuna. "Fine," she said. "Can we go now?"

On the way down the stairs, he got under her feet about six times, wrapped the ends of the quilt around her ankle once, and scratched her for not moving fast enough. Finally, they landed at the bottom in one piece.

TWENTY

A Road Trip Through Hell

A TALL, WISPY, PALE-GRAY DEMON WITH A SINGLE HORN in the middle of its forehead was walking around the car with Hagatha, attempting to explain its features, continually referring to a small, royal blue book with a flaming wheel stamped on the cover in gold and red. The cover of the book matched the demon's blazer.

"This, madame," the demon said, pointing to a scarlet button next to the steering wheel, "is the Frenzy Drive. We recommend using it only a small percentage of driving time, as it will damage the car to use it more than two hours or so a day. It can be of great use while crossing such terrain as the Plains of Infinite Boredom. Judiciously used, the Frenzy Drive should allow you to finish your trip in weeks instead of years. If you abuse it, however, you may find yourself sitting in a sand bank in a nest of inferno ants while you await roadside assistance, so if I were you—"

"Which you're not," Hagatha interjected with a toothy grin.

"Which indeed I am not," the demon agreed. "Still, if I were you, I'd use the Frenzy Drive with care. Not that I doubt your sagacity in the least, but there's an emergency flare button in the glove box, just in case."

Hagatha stooped to admire her new leather jacket in the side mirror. "Whatever," she said. "If there's one thing I can do, it's drive. Toss the manual in the glove box and give me the keys."

The demon sighed and handed her the keys. "We've gone over the use policy, and you will note the car has no flaws or dents at this time. Are you certain you don't want the insurance?"

Hagatha flashed the Black Hole Card at him. "Pretty sure this is all the insurance I need," she said. The demon raised one eyebrow slightly, conveying polite yet nuanced disdain. She ignored it. "Trust me, I'm a great driver. No reason not to save Brian a little money when I can."

"Be sure to drive well out of the city before using the Frenzy Drive," the demon said. "There are signs that denote the start of Frenzy Zones. It will be better for all of us if the car comes back in one piece, don't you agree?"

Hagatha nodded. "Sure thing," she said. "I look like a rules-follower, don't I?"

The demon gave her a tight smile and handed her a clipboard. "Please sign here, madame. And initial here, and here."

Hagatha laughed as she scratched out her name on the form. "You'll get your car back," she said. Then added under her breath, "Probably." She pushed the clipboard back at the demon.

"Thanks. You can scuttle off now if you like. Go on! Shoo!"

The gray demon made a quick bow, slid the clipboard into a nice leather briefcase, and walked off towards the nearest taxi station.

Hagatha clicked the key fob. The heavy lid of the trunk raised itself slowly, opening to cavernous depths, lit by a snaking tube of tiny scarlet light bulbs.

"Throw your crap back there. Let's hit the road."

Liz pushed aside an assortment of liquor bottles, what little beer Hagatha had appropriated from the apartment kitchen, several bags of spicy chips she'd taken from the pantry, and a lacquered black picnic basket with a shiny scarlet serpent for a handle. She set her suitcase and Dennis's tuna inside, although the demon insisted on keeping the blanket and pillow with him so he could nap while they traveled.

Hagatha ran her claw-like finger gently over the hood. "See the basket? Did you know the car rental company packs those for you? The bog eel caviar in and of itself is worth almost what we paid to rent the car. So, it's kind of a bargain—if you do the math right."

She slid into the driver's seat and motioned for them to hurry.

"I guess you should ride up here with me, Dennis," Liz said, knowing he would do the opposite of anything suggested to him. "So, I can keep an eye on you."

"Screw that," Dennis said. "I'm going to take up the whole back seat and nap."

Liz sighed with relief as she slid onto the smooth black leather of the seat. No drool and rancid breath, for a few miles at least. She hoped he made good on his promise to sleep, though she doubted it.

The long, sleek car was a flat black that consumed light. Skull-shaped headlights gave the front a menacing look, while a thick blood-red streak ran from the front fenders down the door panels, ending at the taillights in a spray of glittering crimson. Gray smoke hissed and boiled out the tailpipe.

"I haven't seen anyone driving this sort of thing," Liz said. "I thought everything here was craptastic."

"Of course, you haven't seen this kind of car," Hagatha snorted. "You only commute from your neighborhood to the Admin Building and back again. No one with this kind of ride hangs out in our part of town. The top brass keep this stuff to themselves. There are some straight up decadent apartments on the far side of Perdition City and some killer Goth mansions in central Dis. Satan and his pals like things nice, you know? You gotta be at least D-12 to make the kind of dough to even be *invited* to those places. That's my goal. I'm gonna buy a camera and snap a few pics of myself in this baby. Might as well move up the food chain. Socially speaking."

Hagatha flipped down the mirror over the steering wheel and turned up the lapels on her new leather jacket. She pulled the pair of scarlet and chrome cat-eyed sunglasses out of the Nether Leather shopping bag and slid them onto her face. She grinned widely.

"Getting to use the Black Hole card almost makes up for having to make this trip with you. Almost. Probably won't come close to making up for having to take this trip with him." She jerked her thumb at Dennis. He shrugged and blew a snot bubble from his nose, then smeared it on the quilt. Liz ignored him. The car rumbled and purred like a giant cat as Hagatha gave Liz a big, scary smile, winked over her glasses, and put her hand on the gear shift.

"Let's go!" she hollered and threw the car forward. Before Liz could settle in her seat, they were tearing through the streets, scattering lost souls and demons like wind catching leaves. Liz groped for a seat belt. There was none. She gripped the sides of the seat.

Hagatha pointed above the door on the passenger side, where a silver handle was attached to the doorframe. "Grab the 'oh shit' handle if you need to, and let me assure you, you will need to."

They sped through the streets of Perdition City while Liz pictured herself spending the next couple centuries with poorly attached limbs, perhaps missing a nose, or trying to live with a giant sliver of glass lodged in her eye. Dennis stood against the back of Liz's seat laughing, screeching for Hagatha to go faster.

Demons jumped out of the way, cursing, shaking their fists. One elderly soul barely managed to leap out of the way only to disappear into an open grate, and a soul in a disheveled suit slid across the hood of the massive car as Hagatha yanked the car to a halt for a brief second at a stop sign.

"Unholy Hell!" Hagatha yelled out the window at him. "Don't scratch this thing. I didn't get the insurance."

Dennis giggled madly from the back seat.

As they flew out of town, a group of five tottering skeletons coming out of a Dr. Bones Pharmacy crossed the road. Hagatha did not slow. Two of them avoided the carnage; three were too slow and exploded in a blizzard of clinking ivory when the beastly car tore through. Liz turned and saw one of the lucky skeletons holding up his bony digitus medius while the other intact skeleton gathered bones from the road to puzzle back together. Liz didn't know whether these bony creatures had once been souls and this was their appointed punishment or whether they, like the demons, were created to horrify the damned. They were so fragile that they came off as more pitiful than frightening, constantly falling apart and putting themselves back together again.

Liz asked Hagatha, "So what's the purpose of the skeletons? They don't seem capable of punishing anyone. Are they just atmospheric?"

"Satan only knows," Hagatha said. "I don't try to make sense of stuff. They're fun to plow through with a car. I know that. Nobody tells you. Nobody asks. Best not to care."

"Questioning anything around this place is totally pointless," Liz sighed.

"I question why you can't pick up enough fish heads for me," Dennis leaned over the seat. "And why you don't like Full House." He hummed the theme song, completely off-key.

"Do *you* actually like it?" Liz turned to ask him. "I thought you were just watching it to torment me."

He shrugged. "Are those different things?"

Dennis informed Liz he might eventually want to sit in the front passenger seat with her if he felt like getting a better view of the scenery, but Hagatha explained to him how much easier it would be to fling him out the window from that position; in response, he curled up and pouted. To Liz's surprise he soon fell asleep, snoring away in porcine gurgles.

The tallest buildings gave way to square dark apartment buildings, tumbled down houses, jumbles of shops, and even a few factories. For a time, there was still plenty of traffic. Large trucks trailing dust and ashes thundered past them towards the city, while cars, buses and taxis blared and honked. Liz gazed out the passenger window to avoid having to watch the inevitable head-on smashup, but Hagatha was right—she was a good driver. Apparently, she rented and raced cars with some other demon pals on weekends. As promised, just as they reached the edge of the city, she pulled in at the Pandemonium Liquor Emporium to make sure she filled up every available inch of the enormous trunk with alcohol.

Eventually, the buildings and crowds of Perdition City gave way to a forest of tall black trees clinging desperately to sparse tufts of decaying leaves. Giant crows like Edgar preened themselves on thick dark limbs, accompanied by a few huge vultures, inky shadows against the glowing sky. Souls dressed in black could infrequently be seen skulking through the forest in the distance. None came close to the car.

"What is this place?" Liz was glad she hadn't been assigned to this spare and melancholy spot.

"The Bitter Wood," Hagatha said. "Gotta watch out for the trees. They're super irritable and covered in toxic thorns. I hike here sometimes. You hardly ever see souls. They mostly live in holes in dead trees or caves. Pretty skittish bunch. Especially when *I'm* hiking."

"I occasionally see a few souls who live here in line," Liz said. "Usually after altercations with the crows or the trees."

As they headed into the more monotonous Ashy Plains, Dennis woke up. "Are we there yet? I'm starving," he whined.

Liz snapped, "Of course, we're not there yet."

"I'm gonna have to stop soon." He began licking himself, with loud wet smacks of his tongue. Swallowing a large tuft of green fur, he began coughing and gagging with vigor.

"Listen, you little turd," Hagatha turned, scowling. "If you barf in this car—"

"We should probably pull over." Liz sighed. "When he's got a hairball, he's gonna barf. There's no stopping him."

"For Satan's sake. He better not do this all the time." Hagatha turned back to the road. "Does he do this all the time?"

Liz shrugged.

"I could use a snack anyway," the demon said, "So you're lucky, little dude. I won't have to toss you out of a moving car."

"I think I might have to poop too," Dennis moaned, rubbing his tummy. Hagatha pulled up to the pump at a Volcano Mart so she could fill the tank, while Liz went in to use the restroom and pick up snacks.

"This is going to take a while. It has a huge tank," Hagatha called. "Get me some HotDamn Chili Chips. And some Ghoulios if they've got 'em."

"More tuna and some rat's milk," Dennis screeched as he got out to do his business in the parking lot.

"Get away from the car, you little hellion! No, farther away than that!"

Hagatha kept yelling as Liz walked towards the small, tired mini-mart. Before this, she'd never deviated from the familiar places in Perdition City. She went from the apartment to the office and back again, with rare forays to the terrible, crowded mall or a tiny, dank, and exorbitantly priced market on her way home, never more than a block from her apartment towards the city limits.

No longer endless dirty concrete, the ground was hard packed with sooty ash. The Volcano Mart was dingy, the barred windows streaked with shadows. Tiny fuchsia and banana-colored lizards scuttled through the ashes. The sky was a dirty, opaque coral, pressing down like the roof of a low cave. To the west, a cloudy overhang wavered and flickered from deep smoky red to bright, crackling yellow—the Lake of Fire, still far ahead, reflecting off the smoky sky. The air hovered like an electric blanket crushing beads of sweat out of every pore. It was certainly hotter here than in Perdition City.

The huge, awkward buildings Liz was used to had given way to a series of flat, sad strip malls, aluminum sided buildings, and occasional mobile homes or campers baking in the heat of the ash fields. Liz had never seen a muggy day with a quivering coral sky that didn't end in an ash storm. She shivered. As bad as ash storms could be in the city, she dreaded to think what they might be like out here. Knowing that she would continue to exist, no matter what physical injury might befall her, was not a comfort.

Just the week before, a woman belching clouds of ash had come through the complaint line. She'd been caught out in a terrible ash storm almost three years before. Liz did not like the idea of belching ash for eternity, nor did she care to think about the other areas of her nether body, which might be invaded by soot and cinders. She thought of a funny comment to make to Brian and felt a pang of longing shoot through her chest. Just when she'd found her bright spot in Hell, she'd been sent to the barren wilderness. She realized she was still standing in the parking lot and hurried in to get snacks before Hagatha left her on the side of the road with Dennis.

When she returned, Hagatha was watching Dennis straining to poop in a small square of thick ash.

"I have a hard time going when your underwear isn't involved," he said. "Can you pass me some?"

The demoness rolled her eyes. "Shit or get off the pavement. We need to get on the road."

"That wasn't enough," Dennis whined, when he returned to the back seat. "There's more in there and I feel uncomfortable."

"You'll have to hold it." Hagatha slammed her door shut. "We're not stopping again until I get hungry or thirsty."

The pathetic strip of dingy, gray shopping centers continued, slithering down the sides of the black road. Someone had attempted to paint a few buildings in bright, cheerful colors like yellow or red, but those were so smeared with ash and dust that the original shade could only peep through in thin slivers. Dreary walls and windows looked as if someone had attempted to clean them; those buildings seemed more pathetic than the ones whose inhabitants had simply given in to entropy.

There was a Taco Hell a few miles down from the Volcano Mart. Dennis begged to stop there. He said it would loosen up his digestive system. Hagatha told him she preferred it tight.

They whizzed past a tattoo parlor with a bent sign out front which said *Tattoos while you wait! Or leave the appendage here and return for it.* A heavily tattooed arm hung from a bar in the window. Across the road, there was a dress shop with a series of bland, brown dresses veiled by the dusty glass storefront. A little farther along, a bored demon, presumably the proprietor, stood in front of a shoe store, picking his teeth. The line of sad, empty, ash-covered stores seemed endless. Occasionally, a melancholy soul dressed in some drab outfit walked out of a store, head down, moving towards a bus stop or dirty diner.

"This is a terrible assignment." Liz pressed her nose against the car window.

"Yeah. Glad I don't work out here," Hagatha curled her lip and sped up, spraying ashy dust over a demon grocer, who shook his fist as the car zipped past.

"How far are we from the motel?" she asked.

"Not far," Hagatha grinned. "And it's time for the best part!"

"What's that?" She was immediately distrustful of a happy Hagatha.

"The Frenzy Drive. Boy, are you gonna hate it!" Hagatha cackled. "Let's stop and have a snack first and give you some elevator antidote."

TWENTY-ONE

Dennis Is Surprised

THEY PULLED ONTO THE SIDE OF THE ROAD. THE DARK ash plains, which had stretched out flat to the far horizon, now showed a rough outline of mountains traced in red in the distance. The air was drier and hotter.

Hagatha pointed nonchalantly at the smear of scarlet on the horizon. "Lake of Fire." She retrieved the snake-handled basket from the cavernous trunk. A large quilt, made of various reptile skins, was rolled up next to the basket.

"Whew!" Hagatha said. "I never thought I'd see something with Black Mountain Firesnake skin on it." She rubbed a section of the quilt, which was covered in dark scales, flipping them over; the backside of the scales was a venomous red. She pointed to a glittering pale gray patch.

"Ice Lizard," she said, touching it lightly. "I almost hate to put my ass on it. Well, that's what it's here for. So, I'm going to."

She spread out the picnic quilt on the ash-covered roadside and they sat down to eat.

"I wouldn't overdo it on the snacks," she told Liz. "Trust me. The next couple hours are gonna be fun. Probably, only for me."

Liz took her word for it and stopped at only a few crackers with bog eel caviar and geyser water.

"Pretty sure you won't like the Frenzy Drive," Hagatha repeated when they got into the car. "I mean it's no Vortex Elevator, but souls find it unpleasant. It's okay, though. There's more elevator antidote in the glove box. Just put a tiny bit on the tip of your tongue and you might even sleep through most of it."

Liz ran her fingers along the glove box trying to figure out how to open it until Hagatha impatiently leaned over and pushed a hidden button.

"Thanks!" Liz said, pulling the tiny bottle out. The bottle was black with a tiny silver dropper that screwed in the top. A tiny image of a cyclone whirled on the label.

The demoness glared, "I'm just doing it because I don't want to listen to you whine," she said. "I'm not trying to be nice."

"I only thanked you because it annoys you," Liz retorted, dropping a bit of antidote on her tongue.

"Fine. Just don't want you to get the wrong idea." She waited until Liz put the bottle back and then pulled the car forward, craning her neck as she searched for the Frenzy Zone. She pointed and whooped when a sign appeared in the distance—a large green sign with a flaming "F" in the middle.

"Gotta speed into it," Hagatha shouted over the roar of the engine. "Hold onto your hat! Probably even your ears!" Her cheeks spread back over her teeth and she looked like the big, bad wolf from the fairytale.

"Whoop! Whoop!" The demoness punched the gas. The car flew forward with feral velocity. Black ash spun up from the tires in waves of sparks that pinged against the windows. Liz caught her breath and grabbed the Oh Shit handle for dear life.

"See you on the other side of Hell!" Hagatha shouted as she pushed the Frenzy Drive button with her claw. The car hovered a few feet above black ashy plains, between the ground and flashing red and yellow clouds, then exploded forward. Everything blurred together into a long bright line. Liz's head slammed backwards into the headrest, and she heard Dennis yell, "Yee-haw!"

Liz heard a loud scream and covered her ears before she realized the sound was emanating from her own throat. Just as she was reaching the apex of panic, the antidote took hold; apathy spread through her body. She looked through the windshield with disinterest. Somewhere her brain was telling her that she certainly ought to be afraid, but the pleasant cloud of ennui afforded by the antidote was too comforting to fight. The scene whirred around the car. At first, it appeared they were submerged in a red liquid, as though the car had plunged directly into the lake of fire. They could see nothing of the former landscape.

"How do you know where you're going?" she asked Hagatha over the rushing noise of the Frenzy Drive, her tone mildly interested. "I mean, how do you avoid hitting anything?"

"Frenzy Drive is only allowed out here where there's pretty much nothing to hit," Hagatha shouted. The windshield showed nothing except the dim blur of rushing colors and shapes. She nodded to what seemed like a radar screen in the center of the dash. "I'm steering the car using this," she said. "You set your coordinates and then it's kind of like a video game. You do your part and hope for the best."

The red liquid around the car began to grow darker and darker until the car was surrounded by a deep shadow. At first Liz could make nothing of it. Eventually, she realized the large cloud of darkness was a teeming lake of smaller shadows. Liz felt that she ought to be disturbed but she let the elevator antidote comfort her into unconsciousness.

When she woke, the Frenzy Drive was off. "Where are we?" she yawned.

The dark cloud was gone; she could barely remember it. It must have been a dream. She glanced in the back seat and noted with satisfaction that Dennis was still sleeping.

"Closing in on the motel," Hagatha said. "This would have taken us weeks, but we're only a couple hours out now."

Liz pressed her face against the window. To her right, instead of flat plains of ash, she could see an enormous range of dark mountains incessantly pouring out plumes of orange and yellow smoke; the fog rolled like syrup down the sides of the hills and onto the road. The car lights cut through the haze easily. Occasionally one of the mountains would belch out a plume of fire and hot red lava poured down the side. Liz gave a little yelp of fear when a thin stream of lava crossed the road. Hagatha laughed.

"These tires are impervious to lava," she said. "Fire Diamond Coating."

To their left the ashy plains had given way to fields of what appeared to be glittering red rocks. On closer reflection, the rocks appeared to be moving.

"What are those?" Liz asked, "Some sort of animal?"

"Nope. Fire-flowers. They grow red berries that are as hard as rocks. Takes a stone giant to pound the juice out of them. Makes a nice wine. Costs an arm and a leg though. We have some in the back. And some fire-flower cider too."

"Why do they look like they're moving?" Liz asked, squinting at the landscape.

"They're covered in tiny spiders," Hagatha said. "Spiders that spit tiny drops of slime right into your eyes. I hear it's really painful." Hagatha slowed the car down and pointed. A group of souls holding baskets came into view, moving through the fields, gathering bright red berries, tossing them into the baskets. Some were swatting themselves in the face and rubbing their eyes. Others moved slowly and carefully. Liz was appalled to see that all of them were covered in tiny swarming clouds of spiders.

Hagatha laughed. "You can tell the newbies. They're still trying to get the spiders off and rub the slime out of their eyes. The souls who've been here a century or more have given up. I hear the spiders crawl right up their noses and into their ears. They say you get used to it and either it doesn't really hurt anymore, or you can't be bothered to care. I've never seen them before. Pretty cool, huh?" The demoness sped up and the car whirled past the fields. The afternoon was growing dull, the clouds changing color from putty to charcoal. As twilight set in, the light was turning orange, a nightmare version of sunset as the Lake of Fire reflected and boiled against the evening clouds.

"We'll head south of the Lava Beaches and Abyss," Hagatha said. "The roads are trash either way, but the temperatures to the North are super cold, and I'm not a fan. The Ice Mountains formed north of the Lake of Fire, because the fire sucks away all the hot air."

"That doesn't seem right. Scientifically speaking," Liz said.

Hagatha gave her the side eye. "And you know so much about Hell, right?"

"Phooey," Dennis appeared over the back seat, yawning and rubbing his eyes. "I've always wanted to see the Lake of Fire and the Lava Falls by the Abyss."

Liz shivered. She would be glad if she never had to go anywhere near the Abyss. She thought of the brochures back in the office—blissful souls leaping into immutable nothing.

"You'll see plenty," Hagatha told him. "Tomorrow, we'll pass by the beaches and over a tributary to the Flaming River. You'll see as much of the Lake of Fire as any reasonable creature wants to. Did you know that the Lake of Fire burns souls' retinas out the first time they see it up close? Takes them a couple of decades to regrow eyes and get vision back. If you have special sunglasses, you can look at it from the road."

"What else will we see?" Dennis leaned over the seat, drooling, and clapped his paws together in excitement.

"Well, the Lucretia Bridge is just a little farther south, beyond the Weeping Jungle. There's a Frenzy Zone between here and there. We fill out our report, then we'll swing through the southern desert and go up to the Craggy Mountain Outpost. Right now, we're about an hour out from the motel."

The wind had picked up and was flinging bits of ash onto the windshield. The roadside was now littered with lumpy volcanic rocks, which varied from the size of softballs to the size of elephants. Liz hadn't seen any souls or creatures for some time. A few greenish brown cactuses grew among—and, oddly, through—the rocks.

"What's this place called?" Liz asked.

"The Rock Barrens," Hagatha said. "Only things out here are a few lizards and some stone giants. Not many souls. You'll see a few now and again. Not often. Stone giants are lazy assholes. They're worthless as tormentors. The only soul residences around are out closer to the Lake of Fire or at the edges of the Fireflower Fields."

"I've certainly never had any souls from the Rock Barrens in the Help Line," Liz said.

Hagatha shrugged. "They'd have to walk a long way from the Barrens to the bus. If a soul does get assigned out here, chances are they aren't the complaining kind. They're probably the "hide-all-day-from-rock-giants" kind. By the way, I could use a drink. Somebody give me the thermos. Anything left in there?"

Dennis picked up the thermos, unscrewed the lid and turned it over. A single drop fell out and he caught it with his forked scarlet tongue.

"Nada," he said. "What's in the trunk?"

"Loads of discount beer, some Old Nick, two bottles of blood burgundy, fire-flower cider, odds and ends," Hagatha counted on her claws. "It's gonna be a long trip. Fuck it, I guess we can spare a bottle or two."

She swung the car off the road onto a narrow pullout of black sand, then exited the vehicle and stretched out her tail. The smell of smoke had been gradually increasing as they drove. A cloud of thick vapor blew into the car's open door.

Liz coughed. Dennis laughed.

"I'm getting out," he said. "Gonna try to poop. The Frenzy Drive loosened me up. Wanna give me a pair of your underwear or a pair of shoes from the suitcase?"

"Just get out and go without them," Liz snapped. "It'll give you something to look forward to when we get home."

"Fine," he whined. "If I can't poop, I'm going to be very flatulent though. Just so you know."

Hagatha opened the trunk. "How's that different from any other time, you stinky little creep? You always reek." She rifled through bags of food she'd lifted from Liz's kitchen. "I know I put some Krakatoa chips back here. I bet they'll be great with eel caviar."

Liz didn't want to get out of the car and into the smoky air, but she soon realized that the air inside was just as bad now that the doors were open. Besides, her calf was beginning to cramp. She stepped out onto the sooty ground between the mounds of rocks. Her feet sank slightly into the warm black sand. Everything around her was the same charcoal gray, except for the green-brown cacti that dotted the roadside. The sky was beginning to fill with darker clouds and the orange light was growing dim. It was a bleak scene.

"I wonder if there's much difference between this place and the Plains of Infinite Boredom?" she asked herself, addressing no one in particular. Dennis, who had followed her, answered.

"The Plains of Infinite Boredom don't have dust or color or anything, just gray. Far as you can see. Even the demons are gray. That's what I've heard anyway.

"Never been there. Don't care to go. Don't really even want to be here," he said. "I wanna be home where I feel comfortable pooping."

"No wonder we get so many people in the complaint line from the Plains of Infinite Boredom," Liz said. "They seldom have real complaints. I guess they just want something to do."

"I hear you go blind if you stay there long enough without leaving," Dennis said. "They just want somewhere to go."

He pranced along on his hard little back claws, holding his tail over one arm and rubbing his tummy. Then he bent forward into a cat stretch, moaning.

"Maybe you should eat some fiber," Liz said. "Lettuce or something."

He turned and gave her the stink eye. "Shut up." He walked behind a shriveled gray green cactus. "Could I have a little privacy? Please?"

"I'm not looking at you, Dennis," Liz said. "I try to avoid that whenever I can."

She heard him grunting and turned to go back to the car to avoid the smell. But before she'd taken two steps, she heard him yelp, "Help! Oh, Sweet Satan! What's happening?"

Liz spun and ran to the place where she'd last seen him. When she reached him, he was clinging to the cactus, which was now leaning over a small dark hole about three feet in diameter. The ashy ground was flowing into the darkness like sand in an hourglass; some of the smaller rocks were rolling into it. Dennis was clinging to the cactus with both paws, trying to scrabble back up to the desert. His body extended downwards, tail disappearing into the gap. Liz was afraid to move too close to the hole for fear it might crumble even more.

She grabbed a broken piece of cactus from the ground.

"Ouch," she yelped, realizing that even the dried-up ridges were still sharp. Nevertheless, she extended it to Dennis, who managed to grab hold with one paw and his tail. She yanked the bit of cactus so hard that it flung Dennis up and away from danger. He landed behind her. For a moment Liz was mesmerized by the liquid darkness of the hole, oozing downwards, stretching into nothing. There was a whoosh; the sad little cactus that Dennis had been clinging to lurched into the opening. Gone. The hole expanded briefly, there was a burping noise, then the pit seemed to stabilize.

Uncertain how long it would remain stable, she ran towards the car. Dennis was way ahead of her.

"What in the name of all that's Unholy was that?" Liz panted as she reached the car. Dennis was pounding on the door with both paws and tail. Hagatha was waiting inside with a couple of open bottles of fireflower cider. Annoyed, she wasn't moving to open the door for Dennis.

"Quit banging on the door, you little bastard," the demoness said. "Then I'll open it."

Dennis retreated, whining. Hagatha clicked open the door locks and the two passengers vaulted into the car.

Hagatha was ripping open a bag of chips, calmly watching the two of them. Dennis pulled the quilt around himself.

"Lucifer's great aunty," Hagatha said. "What's up with you two goobers?"

"Just fire up the car and go," Dennis said. "I almost had to spend the rest of my eternity in a sinkhole."

Hagatha raised an eyebrow. "If only."

"I think he's right, for once," Liz said. "We should probably get out of here. A sinkhole opened about twenty-five feet off the road. There might be others."

Hagatha handed Liz the bag of chips and started the engine. "Hold these," she frowned. "What do you mean, a sinkhole?"

"Right where I was trying to poop," Dennis said. "I peed on this ugly little cactus and before I knew it, there was a hole, and I was sliding into it. Liz found a branch and pulled me out."

"Are those common around here?" Liz asked. "Sinkholes, I mean?"

"Never heard of any in this area," Hagatha said. "I worked the Bogs before I got my transfer to Perdition City. We had more trouble with waterspouts. They *could* be common out here, far as I know. You guys seem fine to me. Don't be such babies."

They sped through the thickening twilight of Hell. Sinkholes might be common, but Liz didn't want to spend the rest of eternity at the bottom of one. She sighed and for a few blessed minutes, Dennis didn't say anything and stayed huddled in his quilt. Eventually, though—he poked Liz on the arm with one of his sharp little claws.

"Hey! Why did you do that?" he asked.

"Do what?" Liz said.

"Keep me from falling down the hole," he said.

"Yeah," Hagatha chimed in. "Why *did* you do that? It could just be me and you on this trip now. It would be so peaceful. He has to come with you but there's nothing that says he couldn't meet with an accident." She shook her head.

"Yeah," Dennis said. "There's nothing that says I couldn't meet with an accident. What gives?"

Liz wasn't exactly sure why she'd saved Dennis. Probably a holdover from her time in the Upper World. Still, she didn't want Hagatha to see it as a sign of weakness.

"I was afraid they would replace you with one of those horrible little dragons like the one that Ellie has. She can't keep curtains and coughs up black phlegm all the time from being around him," Liz said.

"Can't blame you, really," Dennis said with a shrug. "Dragons suck balls. They're too stupid to torment people with anything other than what basically amounts to really, really bad breath. No skill in it."

"Whatever," Hagatha said. "At least we would have been rid of him for now. You work in the office; you could arrange it so your paperwork for a new companion was unexpectedly delayed. Bureaucracy, you know." She reached across the seat and tapped Liz on the forehead with her claw.

"Think, Liz!" she said. "Think smarter next time."

Dennis settled back to lick himself. Perhaps they *would* have a few minutes of peace and quiet.

Instead, Dennis began to wail, "My tail, my tail! My beautiful, horrible tail."

He was standing on the back seat holding his tail in front of him with one of his claws, staring at it. The forked, deep-green arrow tip was gone.

Hagatha stared at Dennis. "Satan's balls on toast," she said. "I've never seen anything like that." She slowed the car for a moment, looking at the stub end of Dennis's tail. If Hagatha was worried, Liz was worried. And now Dennis was howling at the top of his lungs. Liz wanted to determine why Hagatha seemed so freaked out, but the first order of business was to stop Dennis caterwauling so they could think.

"Waaaaaaaaa!" Dennis took a deep breath, "Meowaaaaaaa!" He held his tail in front of him and wailed for all he was worth. He blubbered and slobbered, tears mixing with drool.

"Calm down, Dennis," Liz said. "Howling isn't helping anything." She tried handing him a Kleenex. He knocked it out of her hand.

"Quit shrieking, you little asshole!" Hagatha yelled, reaching back to smack him. The car veered to the left.

"Don't make me pull over," she hollered. "You'll be sorry!"

"Meowaaaaa! How will I ever scare you again without my beautiful tail?" Dennis howled.

"I wasn't that scared of you before," Liz tried to reassure him over the noise. "Mostly annoyed. And I've always been more scared of your poop than your tail."

Dennis finally stopped yelling. "Really?" He sniffed a mucus bubble back into his nose. "You're not just saying that to make me feel better?"

"Really," Liz said. "It's dreadful. Traumatic, even. And the vomit, too. And the terrible television." She caught some of the snot with a wadded-up handful of tissue. Then she needed someplace to put it. Hagatha groaned and threw the snot rags out of the window where they blew behind the car and disappeared into the night.

Liz's reassurances had settled Dennis at least a little, and he subsided into quiet, slimy sobs.

For a few moments, Hagatha furrowed her brow and glared through the windshield as Dennis slowly quit sniffling. "I've never seen that happen before. An appendage just . . . vanish. You?"

"No," Liz shook her head. "I've never been out of Perdition City, though."

"Ever hear of it?" Hagatha asked. "You work the complaint line."

"No, I mean, I've seen people who fell in holes or through sewer grates; they come out broken, but not like that. It's like the end of his tail just disappeared." Liz felt a chill move up her spine. "I've certainly never seen a *demon* with an injury like that."

The purple headlamps picked out a path on the dark, compact ashes that made up the road. The tires made a whooshing sound as the car sped forward. Taller mountains burned red, closer than ever.

"Hmm," Hagatha said. "You gonna call Brian? When we get to the motel?"

"Yeah," Liz said. "He wanted me to check in when we got there. I'll ask. See if he's ever heard of such a thing."

Hagatha didn't say much else on the way to the motel. Liz noticed her occasionally turning to the back seat to frown at Dennis. Liz was forcibly reminded of why she'd been sent to the wilds in the first place. Brian had played it down. Maybe something weird really was going on in Hell.

TWENTY-TWO

Smokin' Joe's

THE ASH STORM LIZ HAD WORRIED ABOUT EARLIER THAT day was kicking in for real when they pulled into the parking lot of the motel. The wind was high, full of ash and acorn-sized hot embers. Smoldering trash skittered ahead of the storm.

A flashing neon sign by the roadside depicted a red demon bending over with his forked tail pointing towards the motel, the words "Smokin' Joe's" in eerie yellow underneath. The word "Vacancy" flickered in orange on a flashing arrow. The motel was a long, flat-topped building with rooms arranged in a V-shape, bending towards the road from the central lobby. A metal awning stretched from the door over the circular driveway. Hagatha pulled up to the front.

"We're the only ones here," she said. "Practically, anyway." A couple red demons were sitting on the hood of a beat-up orange car toward the edge of the parking lot. They took one look at Hagatha and loped behind the motel lickety-split.

She threw back her head and laughed. "They know trouble when they see it."

Liz kept her head down as she ran under the awning and into the lobby. Dennis followed, dragging the quilt behind him through the cinders. At reception, a demon was leaning on the desk, pipe hanging casually from his lip. He seemed similar to the demons who worked the Lake of Fire. But he was a deeper shade of scarlet, taller than most of them, with an athletic build and shining goatee. His horns and cloven feet were ebony, long tail curved into a sleek burnished arrowhead. He wore a cobalt velvet smoking jacket with black silk lapels and a pair of silk trousers. He was undeniably elegant—an odd choice to run a motel in the middle of nowhere.

Not only was the demon at reception tastefully attired, the lobby didn't have quite the same air of decrepitude as the rest of Hell. There was a worn-but-clean red rug with a raven and skull pattern on the dark tile floor. All but one of the light bulbs in the iron chandelier glowed weakly and the front desk looked as though someone had polished it in the last decade. At the back of the lobby a saloon door swung under a neon sign in the shape of a red goblet, offering the promise of refreshment.

"Welcome to Smokin' Joe's. I assume you're the reserved party from Perdition City Administration?" he said. "Brian called earlier."

"That's us," Liz announced. "I'm Liz and this is Hagatha and Dennis. Are you the manager?"

"The same." He smiled. "Call me Joe. Excuse me, sir?" He peered over the desk at the little demon dragging his blanket.

Dennis perked up. "Who, me?"

"Yes. If you could refrain from catching the motel on fire that would be very much appreciated."

Liz ran over and stomped on a glowing ember that was sizzling a small hole in Dennis' quilt. "Roll that up."

"Bar open?" Hagatha said, clearly in no mood for introductions.

"Certainly," Joe said. "Perhaps you'd like to check in first? I assume you would prefer a bed to sleeping in the bar?"

Hagatha slapped the card on the counter. "Maybe. We'll see how the night goes. Do you need the card, or did Brian already pay?"

"You're all paid up for three rooms," Joe said.

"Liz can give you the info you need. I will be in the bar 'perusing your selection'," Hagatha mimicked his posh accent.

"I'll be in in a few moments, and I can get you whatever you like," he said. "I'm the sole employee at the moment. You'd almost think *I'm* the one being punished." He winked at Liz.

"Hey, why do we need three rooms?" Dennis said. "I'm staying with Liz, right? I don't want to sleep alone! I want to go to bed now! I want you to come with me!"

"Think how nice it will be if you have some peace and quiet to figure out which TV shows I'll hate the most," Liz said. "I'll even give you a pair of my underwear to help with the constipation. And I'll bring you a beer."

He narrowed his eyes. "Two pairs. And tuck me in. With the remote and some tuna."

"Fine," Liz sighed. She turned to Joe. "Mind if I call Brian and let him know we made it?"

"Phone's on the desk," Joe waved at the office. "I'd best get back to the bar before your friend or some of our other guests starts helping themselves."

Dennis demanded his tribute of tuna and underpants and forced Liz to figure out how to work the remote before he crawled into bed with his stinky quilt. Afterwards, Liz hurried to the office to ring Brian. Joe had a surprisingly tidy workspace—dark wood shelves free of dust and a nicely polished desk with a dark snakeskin top. She picked up the old black rotary phone and dialed.

Brian picked up immediately. "How are things?" he asked. "I assume you're okay and you made it to Joe's? Please tell me the car is in one piece."

"We're all okay. Hagatha's a surprisingly good driver. Car's come through without a scratch so far," Liz said. "Oh, and thanks for getting Dennis his own room."

"Yeah," Brian said. "I thought I could stretch the rules that far. Joe's not a stickler. How's the schedule, do you think?"

"Hagatha says we can make it out to the bridge by tomorrow or the next day," Liz said. "Although she said to tell you she's sleeping in tomorrow. It'll apparently take a week or even more to get out to the Craggy Mountains, even using the Frenzy Drive."

"Yeah, I know," Brian said. "Absolutely no need to hurry back. Maybe we can get the meeting with Satan out of the way, and you never even have to see him. That'd be a *huge* relief. Sam seems to think he's got Satan dead to rights, and therefore he'll behave properly. I'll believe it when I see it."

"I hope Sam's team makes it," Liz said. "And Satan respects them as much as Sam thinks he will."

"I'm trying not to think about it too much," Brian sighed. "I don't have time. Between meeting with Ellie and Sam, to say nothing of getting ready for Satan, I don't have a lot of time to freak out. That's good, I guess."

"I'm sorry things are crazy. I feel like I abandoned you when you needed me most," Liz rolled the phone cord up and wrapped it around her hand, as if it provided some sort of intimate contact with Brian.

"Absolutely not," he reassured her. "Honestly, someone really did need to write those reports and I can't bear the thought of Satan doing something awful to you. I'd end up getting both of us thrown to the bog eels if he threatened you. I feel better knowing you're safely out of his way."

"Yeah," she sighed. "But I miss you."

"I miss you too, Liz," he said. "I hope you get back soon." He paused. "Then I hope we can get you out of here. To a better place."

Liz would be damned if she lost him, she thought. Or un-damned? She spent a few minutes updating him about the trip and when she couldn't put it off any longer, she asked, "Can I ask you a weird question?

Are there a lot of sinkholes out this way?" She gave a quick explanation of what had happened to Dennis.

"Not that I know of," Brian said. "There are some sinkholes around Hell, but I've never heard of losing a body part in one. I mean they're just holes, with bottoms. You might get hurt or lost falling into one, but that's the end of it. You said his tail is missing?"

"Yeah," Liz said. "The little arrow tip is completely gone. It's weird."

"It is," Brian said. "Especially for demons. They're nearly impervious to injury. As far as I know, the Abyss is the only place they avoid out of caution. Has it grown back yet? In the rare instance a demon does get injured, the damage repairs itself almost immediately."

"Nope. Still gone when I tucked him in."

"That's bizarre," Brian said. "Do you think it has anything to do with the reports we've gotten? Water disappearing? Demons disappearing? Now tails?"

"I don't know. It's pretty scary if that's the case."

"Ask Josephus."

"Who?"

"Joe, I mean. The guy who runs the motel. He might have some ideas. He's been around for a while. Longer than I have. Maybe he's heard of sinkholes around there? Anyway, I have to get off the phone now." He sighed. "I have a meeting with Sam and Ellie to discuss how to present this information to Satan. Sam wants to do a Power Point that goes line by line through the contracts and Ellie wants something more focused. The situation is getting tense. Plus, Satan and Mammon are calling me every twenty minutes from the Upper World with more requests for things they need in their hotel rooms or instructions for the catering staff after they arrive. Anyway, call me with updates—especially anything else that seems weird. Take care of yourself. I'd feel awful if I sent you out there to protect you and something bad happened."

"We're okay for now; I don't want to add to your stress. Sorry," Liz said. "I'll let you get to your meeting," It was so nice to hear Brian's voice; she couldn't quite bring herself to say goodbye.

"Call again tomorrow when you stop for the night? So, I know you're safe," Brian suggested. "Listen—be careful."

"You too," Liz smiled. "I think you're in more danger than I am with Satan coming in for a meeting."

"Maybe," Brian snorted. "Probably. See you soon."

She heard the click on the other end. She sat still in the leather desk chair for a moment holding the phone before she tenderly returned it to its cradle. She suddenly felt the distances of Hell stretching between them and was forced to wipe her eye with the corner of her blouse.

She yelped when she realized she'd rubbed a cinder into the corner of her eyelid and had to grope around the desk until she managed to find a box of Kleenex to get it out. Not willing to sit and wallow, she headed to the bar. Even Hagatha's company was preferable to thinking about how far she was from Brian. She'd finally made a little corner of Hell comfortable for herself and now here she was, on the edge of nowhere.

TWENTY-THREE

Nothing Is Wrong

LIZ USUALLY DRANK HER WARMISH BEER AT HOME OR AT Ellie's. Demons were not safe drinking companions and while there were plenty of bars that were off limits to souls, none were off limits to demons. The bar at Smokin' Joe's, however, was nearly empty and with Hagatha there, she wasn't worried.

When Liz walked in, the she-devil was sitting on a bar stool with a large glass of yellow liquid, which threw off sparks like tiny fireworks. Hagatha tossed the liquid down her throat. She belched glitter and pointed.

"That one on top," she demanded.

"Top shelf, top dollar," Joe said. Hagatha took the card from her pocket, waved it at Joe and pointed at the bottle again. He raised an eyebrow. And complied.

A few other demons sat at the far end of the bar, two fire-engine red demons Liz instantly recognized as Lake of Fire workers, accompanied by a short purple demon—adorned with antennae instead of horns and dark beetle wings—in a tight cocktail dress. They tossed back smoky, seething green shots and laughed loudly. Two lost souls sat in a round, faded leather booth in the back corner; both quietly nursed glasses of amber liquid as they watched the red candle on their table burn itself into a puddle of wax. One had on a red flannel shirt and jeans, the other a business suit, a slovenly tie knotted halfway down his chest. His jacket was threadbare and missing a button.

For Hell, the bar wasn't bad. Dark marble counter tops were scarred and yet clean. The mirrored wall behind the cash register displayed bottles, vials, flagons, and decanters from toxic blue to deep crimson, some bubbling with smoke or luminescent liquid. There were open cabinets below that displayed more liquor.

"I'm surprised to see souls here," Liz said, perching on a barstool. "They don't usually travel. I certainly wouldn't if it wasn't for my job."

Joe was washing a shot glass. "They aren't exactly guests. They're stuck here for eternity. This is their assignment," he said. "I haven't qualified for a tormentorship for quite some time, for reasons I don't want to go into. Their paperwork was lost in the shuffle and thusly they weren't redistributed when I took over the bar. Meet Bob and Dan," The two men waved from the back of the bar, then went back to watching the candle melt.

Joe put down the now clean glass and reached behind the bar for an elegant, stemmed wine glass.

"I take you for a wine kinda girl," he said, pouring a thin blood colored liquid into Liz's glass. "So let me ask, what exactly is a lost soul like you doing in a place like this? Brian didn't give me the full scoop." He smiled flirtatiously.

"Don't get too excited," Hagatha said. "She's with me. And my job is to keep her safe." She stood up and showed all her teeth, towering over the bar. Then she plopped wearily back onto her barstool. "And I get a bonus if I bring her back intact. So don't try my patience."

He laughed. "I'm not interested in torture, romantic intrigues, or any combination of the two. It's too tiring at my stage of eternity. A couple eons in this place will drain the romance right out of a demon."

Hagatha shrugged. "Whatever. Just doing my job."

"I don't doubt that you're very good at it," the proprietor said. "She'll be safe enough here tonight. I don't have the energy for nonsense.

I just hang out and pour drinks. One for the customer, two for me." Proving his point, he poured himself a large goblet of wine, twice the size of the one he'd given Liz.

"What the fuck D level do you have to be to get stuck here?" Hagatha asked.

"I'm D-12. I requested this gig an eon or so ago. Sort of." Joe seemed amused by the question.

Hagatha swished down a sludgy black gulp of liquor and squinted at him, "Don't believe you. I clawed my way up to D-9," she said. "I have a plum job in Perdition City."

"I'm happy for you," he laughed. "The only reason I'm *still* D-12 is because I agreed to come here. There were, shall we say, issues."

"You screwed up a D-12 job?" Hagatha shook her head. "I'd give my right eye and best pitchfork to be a D-12. Where?"

"The Abyss." He picked up his wine glass and stared into its depths. "I administrated the annihilation of souls—eternally watched them become nothing."

"Sounds cool to me. I hear there's brutally good pay." She licked her lips.

Joe shrugged and smiled again. "To each their own desires, forever and ever." He lifted his goblet.

All the demons, including Hagatha, lifted their glasses and repeated the phrase.

Since she'd arrived in Hell, Liz had never had alcohol anything more than insipid. She'd had to drink twice as much as usual to even approach a buzz. The wine that Joe served her was warm and bright, immediately intoxicating. She closed her eyes, imagined she was drinking melted rubies. "This is luscious! What is it?"

The wine had to be like the car they were driving—reserved for demons far up the hierarchy.

"Fire-flower wine—an eon old," Joe said. "On the house. It's not like you'll be able to drink more than one or two anyway. It packs a wallop."

Only a few sips in, Liz had to agree. The heat of the fire-flowers spread through her body, vaporizing her anxiety. Hagatha was also enjoying the wares. She'd ordered a second round of black liquor after slamming the first, which arrived in a strange glass bottle, each edge as sharp as a scythe. It was extremely dangerous, though it was no match for Hagatha's rugged claws. Surprisingly, she was slurring her words a little. She was tipsy enough to offer shots of the second bottle to the souls in the back booth, then the demons at the end of the bar. Bob and Dan bravely took Hagatha up on the offer and slipped deeper into their cushioned seats with each sip.

Joe chuckled at the pair as they slid downward, then turned back to Liz. "Souls don't need tormentors," he said matter-of-factly. "They torment themselves so nicely. Those two are eternally balanced between tragically drunk and hungover. Why do they need anyone to oversee their pain?"

The demons at the end of the bar loudly called for more shots and Joe obliged them before turning back to Liz. "Brian didn't have much time to talk when he called to make reservations. Just said you had to make some reports in anticipation of a visit by the big guy. What kind of investigation are you guys carrying out?"

Liz explained the situation she was being sent to investigate, carefully leaving out the information she and Ellie had discovered about The Mountain Group, and then, as instructed by Brian, told him what had happened to Dennis. Joe slowly sipped wine as she talked.

When Liz reached the part of the story where Dennis realized he had lost the end of his tail, Joe put his goblet down. He leaned forward, both hands on the bar.

"Disappeared, eh?" he asked.

"Yeah, totally gone," Liz said. "Brian thinks it should already be growing back. It's not. At least not as far as I can tell."

Joe rubbed his goatee. "There are some sinkholes around here. Usually, they drop ten to fifteen feet before you hit lava. Never heard of anything vanishing like that." He picked up his wine again and stared into it as though he might find the answer there, then swished it and took a sip. "Just the tip of his tail?"

"Yeah," Liz said. "He's awfully whiny about it."

"Can't blame the little guy," Joe said. "A tail is a demon's pride and joy. Hmm. A missing tail, water and bog eels missing from the Toxahatchee, and some demons missing out west." He tapped the bar with his long, elegant fingers while he ruminated.

"Why? Do you think they're all related? Eels dig all the time and Zenebrius didn't say anything about a sinkhole. He said "a nothing." Which makes absolutely no sense."

"Maybe. Due to my experience at the Abyss I'm wondering—" Joe didn't finish the sentence. He started cleaning the bar top. "I think I'm going to call it early tonight. Not enough customers to stay open." He turned to Hagatha. "What's your theory?"

"Don't know. Didn't see it. Can't worry about it right now," Hagatha said. "For one thing, I'm wasted." She left the bar, made her way to the booth in back, pulled Bob out by his neck, slid into the seat next to Dan, then pulled Bob back in next to her. She sat with an arm around each of the startled men. "You guys should be having more fun. How about some more of the good stuff?"

The demons at the end of the bar were taking in the discussion with interest. Abruptly, Joe turned to them and said, "You guys ready to settle? That shift is going to come awfully early in the morning."

"Kicking us out early, Joe?" one of the red demons asked.

"More or less," he said cheerfully.

"All the same to me," the purple demon said and stood up, yawning. She put down some money and sauntered out of the bar, blowing one last kiss before she swung through the door.

"Listen, I'm a paying customer," one red demon said. He lifted his middle finger and growled. "You can't kick me out early."

Hagatha stood up from the booth, nearly knocking Bob over, snarled and showed her teeth. The demon's companion threw some Hell Coin on the counter and poked his buddy in the ribs.

"No problem, Joe," he said. "C'mon, Azarath. I can never get you up in the morning anyway. Won't hurt you to turn in early for once."

"See you again next week, guys," Joe said, chuckling. "Don't lose him on the way home, Ulrich."

Ulrich led his befuddled companion out of the bar and the doors swung closed behind them.

"Bring us another bottle, barkeep!" Hagatha yelled.

Joe raised an eyebrow. He carried another bottle of the black liquor to the table without comment before returning to the bar. He and Liz sat quietly sipping wine for a few minutes, watching the drunken group. After Hagatha poured the souls a few more sips, Dan was face down on the table; Bob had slipped under the booth and was snoring on the floor. The demoness was running her fingers through the deep melted wax, which she used to make designs on the table and in Dan's hair.

"Demons always think they can hold their liquor," Joe shook his head. "And the She-devils are stout drinkers. I have the good stuff though. Feel free to finish your wine while I close shop."

He started taking liquor bottles from the shelves and locking them in the granite cabinets with iron doors underneath. One particularly noxious green bottle of liquid oozed a thin stream of greenish tears from the side; he stopped and scratched something that looked like runes on the metal cabinet door with chalk. "Gotta hex this one. You don't want a bottle of Fermented Swamp Frog Bile on the loose at night. Don't ask."

"I definitely don't want to know," Liz said. She was glad Joe had only offered her wine.

"Got your room keys?" Joe called to the group at the back table. "Closing time."

Hagatha's brows came together; she thumped the table with her glass, breaking it. "Ish too early." She glared.

"Sorry," Joe said. "Last call."

Hagatha pointed to the black cut-glass bottle. "Another bottle of thish for me and my friends." She pointed to the empty spaces beside her. Her "friends" were nowhere to be seen. A pair of dusty boots and a pair of dress shoes with a hole in the leather sole protruded from under the table.

"Jush for me then," Hagatha amended. Joe shook his head and pulled down a brownish bottle from the shelf. He walked over and plopped the bottle and another glass on the table.

"You have to drive tomorrow," he said. "Another bottle of Arachsinth and you'll be here a week or two. That swamp spider liquor is no joke."

Hagatha hissed, swept her companion's glasses from the table and attempted to rise from her seat. She realized quickly that it wasn't going to happen, so she shrugged, took the brown bottle, bit off the top, and started gulping the liquid, which smelled like a mixture of mud and rotten fruit.

"Dump Slide is a sweet thick liqueur made from berries that grow on the banks of the Bog of Despair. Good for sleep," Joe wiped his hands on the bar towel. "Helps you wake up without much of a hangover. She should be fine to drive by morning."

He grabbed a packet of blast nuts and an amber bottle of beer. "Haven't even paused for a bite this evening," he said. "What with all the excitement. Want some?"

Liz shook her head. Blast nuts had shells so hard that the nuts could only be extracted with powerful explosives. The nuts themselves were almost as hard. They'd been the cause of her only trip to the dentist since she'd arrived in Hell.

Liz headed to her hotel room, relishing a moment of happiness that she wasn't going to have to sleep with Dennis, followed by a short and unexpected pang of guilt. The little guy had lost the tip of his tail and while intensely annoying, his grief was real. Liz wished for the thousandth time that she possessed some of Hagatha's ruthlessness. She put the thought out of her head. She'd given him her underwear and tucked him in. Surely, she had earned one night of peace.

She'd expected the room to be awful, and it was. Well, it slightly exceeded expectations. It had a functional—if sulfurous—bathroom and two blankets with only a couple of cigarette holes between them. She fell asleep gratefully, the aftereffects of the wine lulling her into a deeper and more pleasant slumber than she'd had since she'd arrived in Hell.

She dreamed that she was wandering through the night with Brian, hand-in-hand. At first the scene was idyllic. She and dream-Brian walked through the fire-flower fields; he'd just plucked a bud for her when she tripped over a root and fell to the ground. As she spit out ashy soil, she saw a tiny dark hole in the floor of Hell. Fascinated, she touched the opening with her forefinger. The hole expanded, instantaneously turning into wide, gnawing shadow. She struggled to move away. Dream-Brian grabbed her hand, attempting to drag her from the growing pit. Too late. The sinkhole gaped enormous. Inescapable. She was sliding, dragging

Brian with her. Her screamed died in the air. No sound squeaked from her lungs.

The pit swallowed her left foot. She saw and felt it disappear. The darkness was devouring her.

The next moment, Liz found herself lying in the hotel bed, heart pounding. She lay under the blankets shivering. She forced herself to sit up and flip on the bedside lamp. "You're still here. Get hold of yourself," she said aloud. Still, she slowly moved the blanket from her feet then wiggled them to be completely certain. She'd fallen asleep to the sound of an ash storm blowing past. Now the quiet outside was eerie. Silence hovered, thick and suffocating. Nothing.

What could be wrong with nothing? Liz thought. Then she remembered the tip of Dennis's tail. And Jozz. And the missing bog eels. She took stock of herself and the room, cataloguing. All there. She had both her feet. She was stressing over *nothing. Nothing.*

"For hell's sake, stop saying that word," she admonished herself, her whisper immediately smothered in dense quiet.

Silence lapped against the window. It was as though everything outside this little room had ceased to exist—as though the silence was swallowing everything into itself.

She tried to calm her breathing, get out of the bed, go to the window. The storm was over; that was all. If she looked out, she'd see the red outlines of Cauldron Mountain. Liz forced herself to rise, shivering in her cheap nylon pajamas. As she approached the window and reached for the curtain, she held her breath. She couldn't hear her feet on the carpet, or the buzzing of the decrepit air conditioner. She let out her breath and realized to her horror she couldn't hear that either. The silence from outside seeped into her room, smothering all sound. She tapped her finger on the windowpane. *Nothing.* She stood still, heart pounding for an eternal second; then, as if from a distance, she heard the air coming back on, the sound of her breath, the ticking of the bedside clock again. The cloud of silence had moved past.

It still took every ounce of courage she had to pull back the blind covering the window. Was Hell still there? She breathed her heart back into rhythm when she saw the red glow of Cauldron Mountain, the source of the Lava Falls, looming over the motel.

Just as she dropped the blind, a loud bang startled her. She leapt away from the window and tripped over the bed. "Satan's Granny! Ouch." The noise was coming from the door.

"Who is it? What do you want?" The sound of her own voice still seemed weak and muffled.

"Open up. Don't make me claw my way in there."

Liz opened the door and there was Dennis, wide-eyed and panting, holding his tail in his hand. "Had a nightmare. I dreamed I was falling into another sinkhole. Only this time there were shadow monsters chasing me into it and everything was quiet. I hate quiet." Dennis ran past her, jumped on the bed, and burrowed under the pillow.

"Fine," Liz made a face. Secretly, she was glad of the company.

Dennis poked his head out from the pillow. "I don't know why you made me come. Great Lucifer only knows what kind of monsters live in this hell-forsaken place," He grabbed a second pillow and smashed it to make it comfortable. One of his claws caught on the fabric, ripping it; crow feathers leaked out.

She took the top pillow and climbed back into bed. "My bed, my rules. I get at least one pillow. Do you think I can protect you from scary stuff? Is that why you want in here?"

"No, I think I can convince any horrible monster that breaks in to eat you first," he said. He snuggled up next to her, pulling the blanket under his chin and up to his nose. "I'm your little tormentor, and I'm staying with you."

Liz turned out the light and they both lay there for a few minutes. She didn't push him away. The sound of his raspy breathing was vaguely comforting. Dennis pushed himself against her under the covers until she felt his heart pounding. Then he started vibrating.

"Are you purring?" Liz asked.

Dennis sat up and scowled. "I can't sleep. Where's the remote?" The rumbling abruptly stopped. The little demon still sat next to her as closely as possible. "Anyway, of course, I'm not purring. Don't be ridiculous."

Liz turned the lamp back on. Dennis sat beside her for a minute and slowly eased himself into her lap, as if he thought she wouldn't notice. Liz let him stay. She didn't even complain when he chose the show he wanted to watch, a Hell-a-thon funding a home for broken skeletons. They remained together, Dennis curled in her lap, until the limp orange light of dawn leaked around the curtains, diminishing Liz's fear of oblivion.

"Don't leave me here," Dennis whined, when Liz told him she was going to get him some tuna. "I'm still kinda scared."

"It's daylight. We have to get moving," Liz said. "We just had some bad dreams. I'll bring you some tuna, then I'm going to eat breakfast and find Hagatha. You can come with me or stay here."

"I guess I'll stay here under the blankets," he said. "They're going to have the skeleton skull choir on. You know, the ones who've lost all the bones except the skulls."

"Are they any good?" Liz asked.

"Of course not," Dennis said. "But somebody always drops one and it rolls around shrieking." He giggled with anticipation.

When Liz got to the bar, Joe was already there, bent over unlocking one of the liquor cabinets. Upon walking in, Liz heard a strange sound, like a buzzing chainsaw.

"What's that horrible noise?" she asked. Joe pointed towards the corner booth. Hagatha was curled up, possum tail wrapped around an empty brown bottle, glass in her hand. Her snores rattled the windows.

"We'll let her sleep a little longer," he said. "That stuff I gave her last night will have her up and functioning in another hour or so. Coffee?" He pointed to a table set with a yellowed, but clean, cloth. A tarnished silver coffee service sat in the middle. "I've already set it out. Breakfast, too."

"Thanks," Liz said. She walked to the table and filled a mug with hot liquid that smelled more like coffee than anything she'd had in Hell so far. There were a few Danishes on a battered tray. She put one on a plate.

"How did you sleep?" Joe asked as she seated herself at the bar where his own cup of coffee sat steaming. He sipped his coffee and pulled up a stool on the other side of the bar top.

"Great for half the night. Then I had a bad dream about falling into a sinkhole. Dennis had a nightmare too, and, of course, he insisted on sleeping with me." She wrinkled her nose.

"It's hard to get back to sleep after a nightmare sometimes." Joe frowned. "Too bad you couldn't take full advantage of a night away from Dennis."

"It was super weird." Liz shook a sugar packet into her coffee, "After the nightmare, I couldn't sleep because things seemed too quiet. When I was in the Upper World, we used to have a saying—the silence is deafening—and that's what I heard. Way too quiet outside. Like a solid . . .

nothing. Sorry. That probably makes no sense." She took a bite out of her Danish and raised her eyebrows in surprise. "Huh. This isn't awful."

"Can you repeat that?" Joe asked sharply.

"This Danish," Liz said, a little louder. "It's not awful."

"No, before that," Joe shook his head. "The thing about the quiet." He moved his coffee aside as if it was distracting him.

"After I woke up from my nightmare, it was unsettlingly quiet," Liz said. "Like I'd gone deaf. Maybe it was because I'm used to Dennis snoring, or because the ash storm was over when I woke up."

"Like a big blanket of nothing?" Joe asked.

"Yeah," Liz nodded. "Exactly. So quiet I thought Hell was gone. I even got up to look out the window, just to be sure." She turned her coffee cup nervously in her hand. "Everything seems fine this morning, though, right?"

Joe didn't respond for a few moments. He rubbed his goatee. "I've had that same experience. Back when I worked at the Abyss."

"What does it mean?"

"Unfortunately," Joe said. "It means we might be fucked."

TWENTY-FOUR

The Night Serpents

FROZEN, LIZ SAT AT THE BAR, HALF-EATEN DANISH ON her plate momentarily forgotten. Her fingers still entwined the handle of the coffee cup. "What do you mean, fucked?" The morning was not starting out as well as she'd hoped.

Joe set his coffee cup down. "Do you know what happens at the Abyss and exactly who—or what—Satan is working with out there?"

"The Nulentian Group," Liz said. "Is that who you're talking about?"

"You've seen the contracts?" He raised an eyebrow. "We can have that discussion in a few minutes. For now, yes, I'm talking about the Nulentian Group. Does the word *nihilidi* mean anything to you? It can be roughly translated as *night serpent*."

Liz's stomach dropped. "I'm sure I'm going to regret asking. What's a night serpent?"

"The night serpents are the entities behind the Nulentian Group. When a soul falls to the bottom of the Abyss, they don't just disappear. They're consumed by night serpents," Joe shuddered. "Soul essence is very hard to destroy. That's where the night serpents come in. The *nihilidi* are a manifestation of darkness that can devour souls—eating is the best metaphor to understand the process, although it's not a perfect one. Once they've eaten a soul, they excrete *nothing*."

"Is that even possible?" Liz's brain wanted very much to reject the idea. "When I first arrived, Hagatha told me there were scraps of souls whirling around the edge of the Abyss. She never mentioned night serpents."

"There are remains, yeah," Joe said. "The same way that there's something left in the litter box after Dennis eats tuna."

"Actually, Dennis's poop ends up in my underwear drawer," Liz replied without thinking.

"Too much information," Joe said. "Back to the point. That blanket of silence. The sinkhole you told me about."

"Wait, what does the silence last night have to do with these creatures?" Liz asked. She was afraid she already knew the answer.

"Out at the Abyss, we communicated with the *nihilidi*. It wasn't an easy process." Joe drained his coffee cup. "Buckle in. You'll need context first."

"You just told me we're fucked. And now—there's backstory?" Liz asked. "Seriously?"

"You're not going to understand why I'm concerned if you don't let me finish," Joe frowned at her. "May I finish?"

Liz shrugged her acquiescence and began to pick at her Danish again.

"There's a cavern underneath the facilities at the Abyss, many miles underground. It leads to the home of the *nihilidi*. Perhaps the bottom of the Abyss itself. The *nihilidi* manifest in the cavern with the help of certain ritual objects that allow them to manipulate the substance of Hell and make their requests or concerns known. Anyway, before they manifested, there was a blanket of . . . nothing. A heavy smothering silence. Just as you described."

"Wait, they've never left the Abyss before, right?" Liz argued. "There are surely lots of ways to explain everything that's happened besides blaming the night serpents. I mean, Brian says Zenebrius is drunk a lot; bog eels tunnel." She absently shook a couple more packets of sugar into her coffee to give her hands something to do. "Is it possible you're reading too much into a few minutes of silence?" She tried the coffee, wincing at the sickly-sweet taste.

Joe shook his head, "Think about it. The sinkholes, the 'nothing' Zenebrius was trying to tell Brian about, disappearing water in the Toxahatchee. Sounds like it could be *nihilidi*. Close to the Abyss, before you even reach Obliteration Ring—the jumping off point to nonexistence—there are breaches in eternity. Sinkholes—*nothings*—that bubble up here and there. Some souls fall into these and disappear before they reach the pit itself. The "nothing" at the Outpost sounds very much like one of those gaps." Joe leaned over the counter. "Besides, how do you explain Dennis's tail?"

The bar was silent, other than the sound of Hagatha's muffled snoring from underneath the back booth.

"So, what kind of things did these creatures want to talk about? When they manifested in the cavern?" Liz asked. She swirled her now undrinkable coffee. "If it *is* them, what do they want? You still haven't gotten to the part where we're fucked or why. What do night serpents with an eternity of souls to eat have to be angry about?"

"It was always about one thing. Consuming souls. Their language sometimes felt . . . menacing," Joe explained.

"Such as?" Liz prompted him.

"They used the phrase, 'we eat to manifest.' They implied that Hell's existence depended on it. The Abyss is the destruction of souls. And the lifeblood of Hell. It's them. I promise."

"That would be crummy," Liz said. "If it's true." She hadn't given up on finding alternative, less terrifying, explanations.

Joe went on, "I don't understand the immediate problem. There are still souls falling into the Abyss. It's never enough, according to them.

Although the meal service hasn't noticeably slowed. Something must have triggered them."

Liz opened her mouth to argue, but a horrible epiphany wormed its way up her spine. She twisted her napkin. "The Mountain Group sent a representative. About the trains. Would the night serpents be pissed if they knew there was a very slight chance Hell was going to shut down?"

"Well, well, well," Joe shook his head. "Some of us told Satan that letting the railroads run down would come back to bite him in the ass. Part of the reason why I'm here now." Joe waved his hand around his little fiefdom. "The big guy doesn't like to be told things he doesn't want to hear."

"So?" Liz pressed. "Do you think they could know? It's too big a coincidence that the rep just got here and now the night serpents are on the warpath. Sink holes forming in places no one has seen them before."

Joe abruptly stood up from his stool behind the bar and began to pace. "It would explain a lot. I'm not sure how, but they do seem to know things. They knew the trains quit running before anyone told them. They knew when we started getting a larger influx of souls before we told them."

"Maybe they're worried their buffet is coming to an end," Liz suggested.

"Maybe," Joe said. "If Satan doesn't hold up his end of the bargain, provide them with food, they reserve the right to eat Hell itself. It's in the contract. Once they tasted their first souls, they were insatiable. My working theory is that it's an addiction. Like a drug for them."

"If they eat Hell, though, they'll be eating souls that don't want to be eaten—and that will void their contract, right?" Liz asked. "I mean they did sign a contract with Satan. I've seen it, along with the grant paperwork. Even though I didn't understand what kind of entities were behind the Nulentian Realty Group."

"The only reason they've abided by the contract all this time is because they get an eternal supply of souls. They knew The Mountain Group would yank the contract if they ate unwilling souls. If they're soul junkies, maybe they don't have a lot to lose. *If* this is their last hit—maybe they don't care what comes next. It's just . . . I can't think of any reason they would be wandering around opening sinkholes if they aren't trying to get our attention. I hope it's not too late."

"Why don't they just talk to staff at the Abyss? If that's what they've always done before, why not now?" Liz asked.

"Because Satan replaced us with a bunch of idiots. I was fired, along with most of management, when Satan moved permanently to the Upper World. The last thing Satan had us communicate to the *nihilidi* was that he had another plan that would encourage more souls to jump into the Abyss. Who knows what the new staff at the Abyss is communicating, or if they're communicating at all? All I know is if the *nihilidi* are out and about and creating sinkholes in Hell, it isn't because they're happy."

Liz was quiet for a moment, trying to wrap her mind around the idea of becoming nothing. If she'd thought about it in the Upper World, the idea of nonexistence might have felt like calm or quiet. Eternal rest. Now that she was here in Hell, the concept was more real—imminent. It didn't feel restful at all. Nonexistence had a mouth, a horrendous, gnawing cavity full of teeth and acid, jaws that left just enough of a soul to scream gibberish into eternity and turned the rest of it into . . . nothing . . . which was . . . what, exactly?

Her brain halted, no longer attempting to work through the philosophy of non-existence. Instead, it occurred to her that she hadn't hit bottom in the way she'd thought. Instead of nothing left to lose, she had everything to lose. In a rush, the memory of Brian's wool sweater came to her. Brian gone and no one to remember his sweater or her cheek against it—a total gut punch.

They were both quiet for a few minutes, trying to think over the sound of Hagatha's rough snoring. She had rolled out from under the table, no longer muffled by the cloth.

Joe broke the silence. "I think I might have an idea. Something we can do if it is the *nihilidi*."

"You think there's a chance it's not?" Liz perked up.

"No," Joe admitted. "Not really." He drained the rest of his coffee, poured another cup and swallowed it in one gulp. "I know the former communications director of the Abyss, a demon named Melchior. I used to be his boss. He knows more about them than anyone else. Maybe he could contact them, buy time while we figure out what to do. If The Mountain Group rep says they want to get Hell working again, we'll let the *nihilidi* know their supply will keep coming. They won't like the idea of rehab, since it might cut down on the number of jumpers, but they'll have to compromise on something if they want souls. There's only one problem."

"Actually, I imagine that there are lots of problems," Liz sighed. "Because that's the way my afterlife is going. What's the specific problem you're thinking of?"

"Melchior has been banned from the facilities at the Abyss," Joe tapped his finger on the counter. "So have I."

"I wonder if Brian can give him clearance before Satan arrives."

Joe shook his head. "It's the one area where Brian doesn't have a lot of control. He can get into the facility, maybe even get some of you guys in. That said, I doubt he can get Melchior and I inside. I don't want to get into it too much. Satan created some of his own demons when he found out that those of us who came here with him weren't totally on board with every harebrained scheme. Unfortunately, Melchior and I were in the latter group; we had questions. That's why I got transferred here. And why Melchior got banished to the swamps on this side of the Bogs of Despair."

"In that case, I'm out of ideas," Liz said. The Lake of Fire glowed orange out the back window, more oppressive than ever.

"When does Satan arrive from the Upper World?" Joe chewed on his lower lip, thinking.

"Five days. Brian says he rarely comes when he says he will and mostly he's late."

"Sounds about right. Let's call Brian this morning," he said. "Whatever we do, it better get done before Satan arrives. The big guy will muck it up; maybe fire Brian—who certainly can't help us from the Western Wilds. I have a couple things to take care of out behind the hotel, and I'm going to check for sinkholes."

He pointed to the end of the counter where there were a few bottles of wine. "You can take those. On the house. Finish breakfast and get packed. I think your mission just got a little more urgent. Don't worry about Hagatha, though. I'll wake her—you don't want to spend the next century missing a limb. Get Dennis moving, then meet me in the lobby."

Joe pushed through the door and Liz watched it swing shut behind him. She hastily swallowed her coffee and shoved the rest of the pastry into her mouth, although it now tasted of anxiety. She felt sudden fatigue—for one second, the idea of becoming nothing almost seemed a relief, but the thought of Brian—sweater, bow tie, and tortoise shell glasses—shook her back to reality.

Twenty minutes later, she was packed and waiting in the lobby with a very grumpy Dennis and all their belongings. She'd decided not to tell him what she and Joe had discussed just yet. She couldn't imagine the news that monsters were on the loose and eating Hell would improve his attitude. Liz sat on the pleather couch in front of the motel window, watching wheels of smoke weed roll by. The fiery puffs were the size and shape of tumbleweeds, and they left trails of sparks and a thick gray vapor in their wake. The daytime sky was yellow orange; thick charcoal clouds billowed in the west. A noisy wind slapped cinders against the window. *Ping. Pop. Ping.* Sound was a relief after the silence of the night before.

Pain stung her hand. "Ouch! Don't bite, Dennis!" She slapped at his nose, wincing.

"Why did you make me come out here to sit?" he whined, kicking his legs against the seat. "They were just going to show the footage of how a pathetic old skelly got knocked apart."

"Joe told me to get packed," she said. "Hagatha will be up and ready to go in a few minutes and she won't want to wait on us."

"If she wants us to be out here waiting, where is she?" Dennis complained, his voice rising to a shrill, unpleasant pitch. "Meowrrr . . . "

Liz tried to shush him. He was obviously working himself up for a good old howl, when Liz found the remote under a stack of magazines and shoved it at him. He turned the TV on and started flicking through the channels until he found his Skelethon.

"Liz. Office," Joe directed, as he came through the front doors, holding a strange piece of black plastic in his hand. He sounded a little breathless. When Liz followed him inside, he closed the door. "Walked the back parking lot where we take deliveries. At the back corner, there's a sinkhole. Tiny. Only ten inches in diameter or so. I grabbed a crate from the back of the hotel and stuck the corner in. This is what's left."

He set the plastic cube on his desk. One corner was gone. It didn't look as though it had been cut or melted. It was simply gone, as if it had never been part of the crate.

"Will the sinkhole get bigger?" Liz choked out.

"Truthfully, I don't know," he said. "Nor do we know where else in Hell they might be opening. It's not a good sign; I know that. Let's call Brian."

It was a few minutes before nine a.m. and they caught Brian in the office before opening. On speaker phone, Joe and Liz tried to tell their story as succinctly as possible.

"I was just going to call you," Brian said. "Zenebrius called yesterday. Had his guys drive a Hell Rover out to inspect the 'nothing.' Lost the Hell Rover in the hole. Fortunately, the demons abandoned the vehicle before they went down with it."

"It's getting bigger then?" Joe asked.

Brian sighed. "No hard facts, but they think it's expanding. The floating islands of garbage on the Toxahatchee are washing into the sinkhole on the bank there. Got a call from the Bridge Captain. If he noticed it, that's a bad sign."

"I think we need to get Melchior to the ritual room somehow. He needs to talk to them," Joe said. "That's all I can think to do. Satan banned us from the facilities."

"Do you have the authority to get them in, Brian?" Liz asked, leaning over the speaker, trying to keep her voice from shaking. She missed Brian, her job, her old life, her warm sweater, lunches at Dante's. It occurred to her, as anything does in retrospect, that it wasn't a bad existence—and she wanted to keep existing it.

"No," Brian said, his voice glum. "I'm barely allowed in the facilities. It's the one place I can't hire or fire anyone or streamline protocol—not under my own authority. I only go there to deliver messages from Satan. Usually, to take some poor demon to task for a minor infraction or fire them at the big guy's direction."

"There has to be some way," Joe said. "Maybe Melchior can think of something. First things first, we need to see if he's willing to help. That will be my action item. You talk to the rep from The Mountain Group. If the *nihilidi* wanted to, they could have eaten Hell nine times over by now. These sinkholes . . . I don't know. Maybe they're trying to get our attention."

Liz could picture Brian on the other end of the line, posture slumped, running one hand through his hair, pushing his glasses up and down with the other. She could hear his deep, slow breaths. "I don't know what else to do, so why not?" he said. "It should be fun trying to save Hell at the same time I'm planning a conference for Satan. We'll save Hell from the night serpents and then someone will give Satan a thin towel and he'll torch the place himself."

Joe chuckled. "I would say this place isn't worth saving, except we don't exactly have anywhere else to go."

"Fair point," Brian said. "Get to Melchior, then call me back. We'll see what we can come up with. I thought things were bad enough as they were. I really, really did. I guess they weren't." He paused. "They never are." His deep sigh fizzled through the phone. Liz wished she was there to give him a hug.

"Be careful, Liz," Brian said. "I mean, I need you back in the office. And Hagatha, too."

"Okay." The sole word was all she could manage without betraying her feelings.

After Joe hung up, he contemplated Liz. "The manager of Hell seems to find you useful. Souls are typically more replaceable than that."

Liz felt a blush spread over her cheeks and down her neck. "It's a good job. I do what I can to keep it."

Joe shrugged. "Probably you're a damn sight better than a demon would be. Back in my day though, the souls that came our way were the worst of the worst. Seems like we're getting a better class of soul these days. Don't understand it. Anyway, we need to get going." He ushered Liz back into the lobby where Dennis was pointing at the TV and howling with laughter. Liz started folding up the quilt he'd left on the floor.

"I'm going to wake Hagatha," Joe winked. "Wish me luck."

Hagatha was in a dour mood, to say the least. When Joe had plied her with coffee and a dozen Danishes or so, she finally allowed herself to be coaxed into the lobby.

"Have you heard? We have another passenger," she grumbled. "Joe's coming. Satan's balls! What am I, a bus driver? Something about talking to night serpents. Sounds terrible, doesn't it? I think I'd rather bring Satan room service." She paused for a second. "Nah. I probably wouldn't."

"Hold on a second," Joe went into the office and emerged a few minutes later with a pair of sunglasses, a black trench coat, and an elegant emerald scarf, which he wrapped around his neck. "Can you load everything up, Hagatha? I'm going to rouse our other guests. They've been here so long I'm sure they can handle themselves and keep the place from burning down while I'm gone. Of course, it may not matter, so there's that."

Bob and Dan hadn't had the benefit of the Arachsinth antidote, and so they stumbled into the lobby gray, disheveled, and very, very confused, although they looked better than Liz would have expected. She suspected they'd both spent most of eternity with a hangover and were quite used to it by now. Joe took them behind the desk and showed them where to find everything.

"If I were you guys," he told them, "I'd lock these doors and turn off the sign. We take deliveries every third decade, but there are none scheduled and plenty of supplies in the cooler. Eat and drink what you want."

Bob and Dan nodded.

"Behind the hotel, there's a sinkhole, about ten inches in diameter. Check it several times a day without getting too close. If it gets much bigger, get in my car—keys are in the register drawer—and drive. My best guess is that you should drive towards Perdition City, where you got off the train. Otherwise hold tight unless I call."

The group made its way out to the car and Liz realized to her annoyance that she would have to sit in the back seat of the car with Dennis. As soon as they got in, he made his quilt into a bed and put his head in her lap. "Be my pillow," he ordered. She took a corner of the quilt and pulled it over her skirt to shield it from drool. He immediately yanked it back.

Joe, riding shotgun, was busy poring over the maps. "As I said, we're going to see my friend Melchior. Brian has agreed we should talk to the *nihilidi* if possible." To Hagatha he said, "We'll head southwest towards the Bogs of Despair. After we pass Cauldron Mountain and the Shadow fields there's a Frenzy Zone. Melchior's tormentorship is on the other side of that."

"Uh-huh," Hagatha said, sliding on her sunglasses. "You got any aspirin?"

Liz dug through her purse and leaned forward with the bottle of painkillers. "How many?"

Hagatha took the bottle and swallowed it whole. "Peachy to start the day with a hangover and news of monsters from the Abyss."

Dennis jumped up and stuck his nose over the seat. "Monsters? What monsters?" He pulled up his tail to lick it and then appeared to remember the tip was gone. "Meowahh! Isn't it bad enough that my beautiful tail is gone? And now there are monsters?"

Hagatha jerked her thumb at Joe. "Ask the guy who decided to wake me up to that happy news. I don't know the details either."

As the car pulled away, Joe explained about the *nihilidi*.

"So? Some souls want to become nonexistent turds . . . nothing-shit or whatever," Hagatha said. "And the snake thingies are hungry. What's the problem? Seems like it works out great for everyone involved."

"Do they like to eat small demons?" Dennis nervously spat on his paw and rubbed his horn. "I expect I'm 'specially delicious."

"They especially like to eat souls," Joe said. "But they *will* eat whatever falls into their realm. And I'm very much afraid that they might eat everything including Hell itself, if they think they're going to lose their favorite food. The best-case scenario for what's happening now is that they are simply showing their power. Letting us know that they *can* eat Hell, turn it into nothing. The worst-case scenario is something we won't consider today."

Liz felt wobbly. She should have known that as soon as she started to enjoy her death the tiniest little bit, that would be taken from her too.

"We're going to see the former communications director of the Abyss," Joe said. "Melchior. To see if he'll help us contact the *nihilidi*."

"Where are we going now?" Dennis asked. "Will there be lunch? If I'm going to be eaten into nothing, I want lunch first."

TWENTY-FIVE

Passing the Abyss

"SO, WE'RE GOING TO TALK TO GIANT, HUNGRY BEINGS of darkness, are we?" Hagatha asked. "That's the plan, is it? Ask them pretty please not to eat us?" She sighed. "What a fucking Monday."

"It's not Monday," Dennis corrected her, bouncing up and leaning over the front seat.

"It's an expression, doofus," Hagatha said. She swatted at him from the front, and he hid under his quilt on Liz's lap. "By the way, you guys might want to look out the window to your right. We're passing the Lava Falls close enough that you can see it. Who knows, maybe for the last time from the sound of things. So, grab an eyeful."

"Here, put these on." Joe handed Liz his sunglasses. "It won't hurt my vision, but it might damage yours."

Liz slid the glasses on and cautiously glanced out the car window. Cauldron Mountain was the largest volcano in the central hot spot of Hell. She had to crane her neck to take it all in, repeatedly pushing Dennis's head aside since he was standing in her lap, trying to take in the sight too. Cauldron Mountain was a festering pimple grown enormous on the face of Hell, bubbling up in warty knots to form a rough cone that ended in a cloud of yellow orange vapors. Toxic fog writhed below the peak. Ropes of red-hot lava roiled down the knobby face of the volcano, oozing into a river at its base. Steam issued from fissures between crimson rivulets, forming ghostly swirls. Each swirl formed a wailing face for a few seconds before evaporating.

"Those look like ghosts," Liz remarked. Near the bottom of the mountain, close to the road, a vaporous phantom formed and rushed towards the car. Liz flinched, braced for impact, but the phantom broke apart before making contact.

"Steam wraiths," Joe said. "They appear suddenly and burn whatever is in their path, shrieking like kettle whistles. Unpleasant. Easy to avoid. They can only materialize for a few seconds at a time."

They passed the base of the mountain and the landscape opened. "Look ahead," Hagatha said, "and you'll see Magma Beach and the Lake of Fire. On the far side, the Lava Falls drop liquid fire into the Abyss."

They peered out at a black beach dotted with round, thatched huts, roofs on fire or smoldering. Smoke weed tumbled into the lake and back out again, covered in flames. Souls lounged in metal lawn chairs—some roasted hot dogs on the flaming weeds as they careened past. A smattering of souls swam in the burning waves or paddled in the red surf. A soul in a partially burned Hawaiian shirt and cargo shorts waved aggressively as they passed, as though he were trying to flag them down, not greet them.

"Wow," Liz said. "I guess I should be more grateful for my damp little office. I can't believe souls are swimming in that."

"Souls can get used to almost any level of horror—especially if they think other souls are suffering too," Joe said. "Particularly the hotheads that get sent to the Lake of Fire. I tried to tell Satan that punishment wasn't a good stand-in for rehab. It just exacerbates the issues. And here we all are." Joe seemed resigned.

"What about the Abyss?" Dennis wiped his horn with a trembling paw. "Do we have to pass by it? Will there be monsters? Will they eat us?"

"The shadow fields are as close as we get. Hopefully, we won't be eaten. I can't guarantee anything."

As they left the lava beach area, dark fields hove in view. Huge yellow signs with bright red lettering yelled out a warning every twenty yards: DANGER! ABYSS! Dennis crawled back under the quilt.

Liz squinted at the shadow fields. The darkness that hovered beyond the DANGER signs had no form; it was merely a vacillating gray-black expanse. She couldn't determine whether the place was full of dark plants, clouds, or an absence that her mind couldn't comprehend, a nothing her brain desperately needed to fill with something. Anything.

"That's the outskirts of the Abyss?" Liz asked. "How could you work there and not lose your way?" She averted her gaze. Her eyes were fatigued from trying to make out phantom forms. She rubbed her eyelids with her fingers.

"The shadow fields are the penumbra of the *nihilidi*, so to speak. The area is functional in that souls lose their way once they wander in," Joe said. "Stumbling into the Abyss makes them fair game. We tried to be as good with the signage around the edges as possible so that the souls who enter the fields are either zombie souls—so morally bereft that they are hollow when they arrive in Hell, their choice to be nothing already made in the Upper World, often the famous and the powerful, dictators and the like—or souls who *choose* nonexistence. A specially constructed road leads to the facilities. The building is close to Amnesia Falls, where the River Nepenthe drops its waters of forgetfulness. Demons remain within the confines of the compound to remain safe from the effects. It's as unpleasant a place as the universe has to offer. Even from a theoretically safe distance."

No one said anything for a few moments. Liz noticed that Hagatha didn't reiterate how stupid Joe was to quit his D-12 job after they passed those strange, unquiet fields.

"There's a small bottle in the glove box," the demoness said. "Give it to Liz. We don't need her barfing in the car. We should be getting close to the Frenzy Zone, right? What coordinates do we put in?"

Liz blocked out the rest of the conversation and put a small drop of elevator antidote on her tongue. She put the rest of the bottle in her purse. It might come in handy if one was being eaten and excreted by night worms. It might make the experience less . . . less . . . her brain fuzzed out as she struggled for an adjective. *Noticeable.* The word popped into her head as she fell asleep. It might make being devoured less noticeable. It wasn't much comfort, but it was all she had.

TWENTY-SIX

The Road to Heaven

WHEN LIZ WOKE, SWAMPY GREEN LIGHT FLICKERED outside the car. At first, she thought the elevator antidote had broken her brain. Since she'd been in Hell the light—day or night—had been some version of red, yellow, or orange. Here the light was dim, pulsing blue then green. As she surfaced into consciousness, Liz grasped that they'd already passed through the Frenzy Zone. Hagatha was driving down a road lined with tenebrous green-black shapes, the vehicle swimming through a thick downpour. Balls of acid-green swamp gas and flashes of blue lightning illuminated the road.

The shapes were willows, but instead of fine-toothed drifting branches, fronds of seaweed blades swayed around their trunks. As they drove, the swamp willows reached slimy, wet arms toward the car imploringly. This was unfortunate because at the speed Hagatha was driving, the branches broke against the car. Every time this happened the tree in question would quiver and begin keening, a high-pitched sorrowful sound that almost exactly summed up how Liz felt. Then the broken tree's neighbors would join in. By the time the car sped through, the entire forest was wailing a unified dirge.

Dennis was in Liz's lap with the quilt wrapped around his head. He howled, "Make it stop. It's hurting my ears."

Joe turned around, frowning. "Hagatha is driving as fast as she can."

"Shut up, Dennis," Hagatha said. "You're only making it worse. I'm trying to get out of this devil-forsaken place as fast as I can. Before a sinkhole opens in the road." She sped up as if to make her point, taking out several sea-weedy branches in the process. The keening increased and Liz put her hands over her ears. Before long, they left the arboreal lamentation behind. The road fell away into a swampy plain with shorter scrub-trees, leaves clinging desperately close to the branches, as if they feared falling onto the damp ugly soil. Browned ferns, saw-like clumps of grass, and brackish puddles in the undergrowth muddied the ground as far as the eye could see. Giant brown nettle flies with horns and bat wings circled the muddy ground and taunted a few pony-sized, sad-eyed frogs watching the car scoot past.

"We're on the eastern side of the bridge from the Bog of Despair," Joe said. "Should be coming up on Melchior's place shortly."

"Smells like Beelzebub's stinky farts," Dennis said, holding his nose.

Liz was wondering what they could possibly find to help them here in the middle of this damp, odious patch of Hell when Hagatha swung the car into a dirty parking lot of packed mud.

"Think the ground will swallow up the car?" Hagatha asked Joe. "Looks like they've dredged up this property from swamp mud."

Joe got out and stamped the ground with his hoof a few times. "It's wet, but I think it will hold. We shouldn't be here too long anyway. Either Melchior can help us, or he can't. Besides, he parks here." Next to the fence sat a sleek three wheeled motorcycle the size of a young elephant. Every part of it was black except for the purple headlamp and a thin line of purple trim on the leather seats. Everyone else slid out of the car.

"Your friend must be a big dude." Hagatha whistled admiringly. "Bigger than me."

"He's a minotaur."

Liz inspected the fence as the group walked alongside it. To put it kindly, the fence was made of found objects. To put it truthfully, it was made of trash; old tree branches, stacks of empty bottles, cardboard, a tire, all twined or nailed together haphazardly. It reminded Liz of a fort built by elementary school children.

Dennis's short legs were no match for the others. He grabbed Liz's skirt, nearly pulling it down. "Carry me," he demanded. "I can't walk that fast."

"Oh, for Hell's sake," Liz complained. She reached down and picked him up anyway.

"What is this place?" she asked as she and Dennis caught up to the others.

Hagatha and Joe were waiting by an entrance gate, made from the rusty grill of a bus, held closed by a bit of metal wire.

"It's Melchior's tormentorship," Joe said. "I got sent to the hotel and he was reassigned here."

"I think you got the better end of that deal," Hagatha remarked. "Are we supposed to bang on this thing?"

A trash can lid hung from a twisted tree branch close to the fence— on the ground next to it was an old metal post. A sign nearby read "Ring Gong for Entrance."

"Seemingly," Joe said. Hagatha picked up the post and bashed the trash can lid several times. It made a godawful racket so exactly unharmonious that it almost seemed to mean something. Probably that they should all get back in the car and drive away.

"Ow, my ears!" Dennis howled.

"Stop shrieking!" Liz tried to lower Dennis, but he clung tightly to her arm with his claws and refused to be pried off.

When no one appeared within a few seconds, Hagatha bashed the trash can lid a couple more times. "Whadda ya think? Want me to tear the gate off?"

Joe peered through a hole in the fence. "Someone is coming."

Shortly thereafter, the gate creaked open slowly. A pathetically thin soul, clad in what appeared to be a dirty bed sheet, stood behind the door and gave a low bow. He was nearly bald, as pale and clammy as spoiled milk. A pair of black glasses held together by scotch tape perched on his nose. The lenses were grimy; he had to look over them to see his visitors. A fine film of greenish mud covered his sandaled feet, a twist of seaweed willow wrapped into a sort of crown around his head.

"Welcome to Heaven's waiting room. The antechamber in a manner of speaking," he said nervously. "A few of us have come here, with Saint Peter, to wait for the return of . . . " he paused, " . . . Him. You know."

Liz gasped. "You think this is Heaven? This?"

"Oh, fuck," Hagatha said, "we do not have time for this kind of nonsense."

"Saint Peter, eh?" Joe asked. "Would he be about this tall?" He raised Hagatha's arm above her head.

"Hey!" she snarled and snapped her arm back.

"Covered in short hair? A couple of fine horns in the front of his head?" Joe went on.

The sad little man bristled. "He is quite tall, as a matter of fact." He glared at them for a moment and then sighed. "Do come in. Please shake the mud and dust of the other place from your shoes as you enter. We do our best to prevent contamination."

They stepped deeper inside. Liz could see that there was no point in trying to scrape mud from the bottom of her tennis shoes. They were on a path covered in gravel, but the small rocks sunk into the mud at every step.

"Follow me." The little man walked a few steps behind the fence, waving them on after him. "Visitors must remain on the path." Quietly, he added, "I doubt you'll be here long anyway."

"Wow. This place." Hagatha hissed. She lifted her tail in disgust.

"It's gross," Dennis said to Liz in a stage whisper. The small man turned and glared. Frowning, Joe stepped through the mud without comment.

Just inside the fence of castoff garbage were two warped tires transformed into planters. A poisonous looking green plant with three leaves sprouted from one, while the other contained a tall, pointy plant—some sort of succulent, if Liz had to guess—with one arm growing out from the middle and sagging towards the ground like a sad pornographic appendage.

"Kinda sexy for Heaven," Dennis whispered to Liz, and she couldn't help giggle—at least until their guide frowned. Not wanting to appear impolite, she pretended she was coughing.

"Enjoy the lovely gardens on your way in," the man said.

As they trailed along behind their host, they observed the "gardens." There were cracked plastic totes with rotting tumbleweeds inside, an old toilet with a Hades fly trap that was leaning over the edge, slapping at gravels, insects, or passersby. There was a discarded motorcycle helmet with sword grass growing right through it. A dented metal trash can held a giant ochre herb of some kind, stretching out flat arms with balls of teeth on the end. It too cast about for food, nearly nipping off the feet of the poor little soul when he veered too close.

At one point the man swept his arms out over the scattered trash and plants, nearly losing the dirty sheet in which he was dressed. "Our entry gardens are spectacular this time of eternity," he said. "You really should see them at daybreak."

"Sorry we missed it," Hagatha said. "It's just too bad."

"Interesting," Joe said, as the man pointed out a were-beast skull overflowing with a blood red fungus.

Their guide stopped to point out a black thorn-covered vine creeping up a pile of broken rocks and didn't show signs of moving again. A compliment was evidently required. "Great," Hagatha said.

"Heavenly," murmured Liz.

"Too much," Dennis whispered, slapping Liz's ear. "Even that bozo will think "heavenly" is over the top."

Beside the path the ground was an ooze of mud. Here and there, mounds of trash had been piled up as though purposefully, though what that purpose might be none of them could have guessed until the little man proudly pointed out the "sculptures."

"Don't see anything like this in Hell," Hagatha said nodding at a stack of broken bowls, pots, and bottles topped by some kind of rusty faucet.

The man's cheeks reddened. "Of course not! Certainly, there's no comparison between the very edge of Heaven and the 'other place.'" He used air quotes and his voice dropped to a whisper when he referenced Hell.

As they went farther into the encampment, they saw small huts made of found objects and the limbs of black iron trees, impervious to nails. The souls had twined the sides of their homes together with string, old wire, bindweed, and poison ivy vines.

As Liz and her friends made their way down the garbage path, souls appeared and whispered to each other behind their hands. Most were dressed in sheets, too. The mens' linens came to their knees, knotted over one shoulder, while the womens' attire fell to their ankles, with sleeves made of pillowcases.

The little man smiled at the souls. "Back to your work, folks!" he said. "As always, we'll see what Saint Peter says about our visitors."

The women stared.

"Dressed like tarts, the two females are," one of them said in a stage whisper. Two women next to her smirked.

"They shouldn't be here!" an old lady called out, "I can tell by looking at 'em."

"You know the rules," the little man said, "Saint Peter says everyone who rings the gong must be brought before him."

From behind them, Liz heard someone say, "I thought St. Peter was supposed to be at the gate."

The little man turned around. "What was that?"

No one spoke.

"Go back to your work," he snapped. "You know the rules. You lot, come along. You must be presented to Saint Peter."

At last, the diminutive male soul led the four of them through two splintery telephone poles, which leaned into each other like inebriated lovers. They had been dug into the mud like columns, and over time the beefy posts had lost their footing in the muck and sought solace and stability in each other's embrace. Liz assumed the poles were meant to be a grand entrance to something because as the group turned off the path of muddy stones, they stepped onto a walkway that was somewhat better constructed. This path was made of flat broken stones and tiles laid on black plastic sheeting, leading to a huge hut made of trash stacked up to about six feet high. Above that, an arched wall of thorn branches rose fifteen feet in the air. Where the thorn walls came together, willow branches had been woven through to create a poor roof. Light trickled in from broken windows that had been worked into the twiggy walls. Swamp gas lamps formed a path leading to a dais made of lava rock. On the dais, a huge empty chair—fashioned from an old bus seat and raised on concrete blocks—stood in pride of place. Perhaps the same bus that had sacrificed itself for the front gate had also graciously gifted the seat.

"I shall fetch Saint Peter," their guide said. "You must wait there." He pointed to some bent folding chairs to the lower left of the dais and scurried away.

"What the actual fuck?" Hagatha asked Joe. "Please remind me why we've come to this swamp asylum."

"I have no idea what's going on," Joe said, with a tight smile. "But I bet I'm familiar with old Saint Peter." He tapped his hoof impatiently on the makeshift floor and twitched his tail.

In just a few minutes, the small man was back. "Please rise," he said, before realizing no one had sat as per his instructions. Frowning, he whipped out a long, bent piece of metal that bore a vague resemblance to a trumpet, and blew a rusty, wheezing sneeze. Then he bowed low to the ground. "All hail Saint Peter!" He looked over his shoulder and hissed, "Bow, you heathens."

From the back of the pavilion, clad in several white sheets fastened together with duct tape, strode an extremely large demon, a good couple of feet taller than Hagatha. He had the head of a bull and large muscular arms covered in fine chocolate-brown hair. In a regal tone, he bellowed, "You may rise. Oh, never mind, you're already standing."

"Saint Peter, here are supplicants who have rung the gong. I bring them before you. May their names be found in the book of life." The small soul seemed dubious about this likelihood.

The minotaur seated itself on the giant chair. "Thanks, Norbert. At ease."

Joe rubbed his temples. "What's going on here, Melchior?"

"Wanna stay here in heaven?" The minotaur gave them a sheepish grin. He seemed entirely surprised to see Joe standing in front of him with this odd assortment of guests.

"Sell us." Hagatha raised an eyebrow.

"Oh dear," Norbert retorted. "I wouldn't talk that way to Saint Peter if I was you."

"Settle down, Norbert," Melchior derided the little man. "Run and get me a sandwich if you don't mind. In fact, bring a stack. A whole platter of them."

Norbert bowed his head slightly. "As you wish, Excellency. Are you sure you don't want me to wait so I can escort them out?"

"Shoo!" 'Saint Peter' hollered. "Sandwiches!" He thumped the side of his bus seat and stomped his foot.

Norbert skittered off. Joe rubbed his goatee and said, "What's all this?"

"Yeah," Hagatha said. "Satan's balls on toast. What a scam!"

The giant bull demon laughed. "Not my idea. I just went along with it. It's chill. I don't spend a lot of time tormenting them and they do stuff for me whenever I tell them to, or I tell them I'll kick them out of Heaven. I'm always having them build odds and ends, fetch me things. It's not a bad life, you know, being Saint Peter. I tell them I've got meetings with God, crap like that. Sometimes I go away for a week or so, have a little peace and quiet. When I can stand to have them around, they wait on me hand and foot. The best part is that while I'm gone, they torment each other. Always accusing each other of *this*, not being worthy of Heaven *that*. I've convinced them that this is only Heaven's lobby, and I might not let them in 'real' Heaven when the judgment day happens. Does it blow? Sure. I mean, after losing the job down at the Abyss, I gotta make do, you know?"

"Aww, I can see how it sucks to be you, gatekeeper to Paradise," Hagatha scoffed.

"Is that weird little guy bringing all of us a sandwich?" Dennis asked, still clinging to Liz's shoulder. "I'm super-duper hungry."

Before Melchior could respond, Norbert returned with a stack of sandwiches. Melchior lifted the moldy bread on the top sandwich. "NOT ENOUGH MUSTARD!" he roared.

Norbert's lower lip quivered. "I'm sorry, your Excellency! I shall repair it," he bowed with his hand out to take the platter back.

"Nah," said Saint Peter/Melchior. "I mean, it's fine. Just could be better. Now scoot, I want to interrogate these potential heavenly citizens. Check the book of life and whatnot. You leave it here?"

"Yes, sire," Norbert said, bowing and backing out of the room. "'Tis on the table by your chair. I believe you set your beer bottle upon it last night." Norbert pointed at a folding table holding a wire bound composition book topped with an empty beer bottle and a lone cheese puff. Norbert frowned at the sight. He caught himself and simpered again.

Just before he left the pavilion, he made a final bow, pointed at Liz, and said, "The length of that one's skirt does not seem very pious, sire. And sire, the other young woman is not even wearing pants!"

"OUT!" his boss roared. "I have perfectly good eyesight. I'll call for you when I need you." After the little man left, Melchior stretched out on his throne, contented. "What's up, Joe? Good to see you. I'm assuming you're not here on a whim. Especially since the big guy was pretty specific about us never leaving our new posts."

"I think the *nihilidi* are on the move," Joe said. "Sinkholes like the ones in the shadow fields have been spotted in various places around Hell."

"Fuckety! What do you think has them riled?"

As briefly as possible, Joe outlined the situation.

"They're worried they're not gonna get their favorite food anymore. That's gotta be it," Melchior shook his head. "The more they ate the hungrier they got. It was weird like . . . like . . . "

"An addiction?" Joe finished the minotaur's sentence.

"You guys really think it's them?" Hagatha asked. "I mean, there are holes all around Hell. Are we getting hysterical for nothing?"

Joe turned to Dennis. "Show St. Peter your tail, kid."

"No." Dennis whined. "It's embarrassing." He hid against Liz and wrapped his tail around her back.

"For Hell's sakes," Hagatha reached around Liz and grabbed Dennis's tail, showing Melchior the missing tip.

"Just disappeared?" Melchior asked, coming over to inspect it.

"Yup," Hagatha said, "he fell in a hole and came back with a missing tip." She let the tail drop. "Never grew back."

"That's the *nihilidi*, alright." Melchior inspected the tail, ignoring Dennis's low growls. "I'd bet on it. They disappeared so much inventory in the comms room. We had an area set up where they manifested." Melchior shrugged. "Sometimes they would touch an object and a piece of it would disappear, just like Dennis's tail. Had to replace cables, mics, goblets for the dragon tears, the amphoras of frog venom. They played hell on our supplies."

Everyone was quiet for a moment, then Dennis tugged on Liz's ear. "I think things are going really bad. Put me down. I wanna get some sandwiches while I still exist."

"Everyone grab a sandwich," Melchior offered. "There's beer in the cooler behind the throne. Heaven's best." He winked.

"Sounds to me like we have a big old mess on our claws." Hagatha grabbed a beer and tossed it down, grabbed a couple more, and threw one to Liz. "Don't know what we can do about it." She slugged another beer. "Go back to the bar, hole up, and polish off the liquor while this thing falls apart or resolves itself? Or is that just me?"

She plopped into a folding chair. Dennis leaned into the cooler, grabbed a beer, and popped the top off with his claw.

Liz gingerly reached out and took a sandwich from the plate. It didn't look too awful, considering some of the things she'd seen in Hell. She picked off some mold and washed it down with a swig of beer. Melchior was right, definitely needed more mustard.

"What do you propose we do?" Melchior asked, studying Joe. "Is there anything we *can* do?"

"If the grant gets pulled," Hagatha interjected, "couldn't Satan just keep Hell going without The Mountain Group? I mean couldn't he just use the money from the night serpents to run Hell?"

Melchior bellowed with bitter laughter. "The Mountain Group owns the patent on souls; they'd never allow it. They're going to ask for their money back if they pull the grant, and they're going to have questions about the real estate contract. Lots of questions. They might sue for more than the funds they've contributed. I don't know if they've ever lost a lawsuit." Melchior rubbed his chin. "The second problem is, of course, Satan."

"The Big Guy is entirely unlikely to use any money that doesn't have strings attached to run Hell," Joe said. "That's been the point the last few centuries of budget cuts. Make people here miserable and more of them will jump into the Abyss. He gets paid more and spends less money. I hear he's got some stuff going on in the Upper World. Who knows? He might just cut his losses. Besides, it's not clear to me that he's making money from the *nihilidi*. It appears they are allowing him to lease the property for free as long as souls keep coming."

"If The Mountain Group is so scary, won't that keep the night serpents from eating the souls? I mean, aren't they worried about being dragged into the lawsuit?" Liz asked.

"The Mountain Group's grant had nothing to do with the *nihilidi*," Joe said. "It does not bind them. They had their own contract with Satan. They own this plot of real estate. I guess they can do whatever they want with it. What if Hell's grant disappears while all the souls are still here? And what about us? If there is an evacuation, you think The Mountain Group is going to evacuate *us*?" All the demons looked at Liz.

"I don't think—" Liz started to answer, then shook her head. "I don't know. One representative from The Mountain Group showed up to resolve this issue. Just one. The Mountain Group is powerful, but I'm not sure they're taking Satan's mismanagement seriously. When it comes to auditors, caseworkers and the like, they don't seem well-managed themselves. For all I know, their C-Suite barely knows we exist."

"Exactly." Joe threw up his hands. "If The Mountain Group decided to shut down Hell, then the *nihilidi* might not wait for an evacuation to take place—if there is one. Their contract doesn't bind them in that regard. Anything that goes into the Abyss belongs to them in a practical, gustatory sense—whether we legally belong in their stomachs won't matter."

"Still leaves the question of what in the name of Hell we're going to *do* about it." Hagatha grabbed another sandwich. "If we do manage to talk to them, they don't sound overly reasonable. Although they're probably more reasonable than Satan if it comes down to it."

"She's got a point," Melchior said. "Communicating with them is mostly just them saying they, 'need to eat to manifest.'"

Hagatha chewed a mouthful of bread. She winced. "Ugh, I found the mustard. That little dork put it all on this one sandwich. How do you talk to them?"

"Spells and rituals must be performed; there's a special room to which the creatures have to be summoned so they can interact with the materials of Hell, blah, blah, blah," Melchior said. "I can't explain it, but I can do it."

"Melchior has the deepest voice in Hell. He's one of the few demons who can speak in their octave," Joe said.

"Not everyone can speak their language either. Took me over a century to learn it and write the translation grimoire," Melchior informed them, pride booming through his deep baritone. "So, we contact them. What then?"

"Maybe all we *have* to do is buy time. The Mountain Group probably won't shut down Hell. Seems to me that the best thing for everyone, including Satan, is to get the trains running again. We get them to chill while we get things back to normal." Joe realized the sandwiches were going quickly and grabbed one.

"Back to Hell's status quo," Melchior snorted. "Say we get the auditor from The Mountain Group down there to talk to the creatures. He says all is well. Hell's buffet stays open. No problem. Right?"

Joe scratched his goatee. "Yeah. Tell the *nihilidi* things will go on like normal. It might work."

"Doesn't Satan talk to them?" Liz asked. "Won't he know what you're up to?"

"Satan never liked to talk to them or The Mountain Group," Joe said. "He avoided it when he could. I don't know how often the new staff at the Abyss communicate with them."

"Or if they do at all," Melchior chewed, huge jaws working to grind the sandwich down. "Could be one reason the *nihilidi* are on the warpath. The last message that I was instructed to convey—before Joe and I got sacked—was that Satan was going to go to the Upper World for a while. Said to tell them he had a plan. More souls would jump. That kind of bullshit. Said it might be a while before we contacted them. There's nothing that says how often we have to communicate in the contract. Maybe they aren't communicating and that's the problem."

"Does it matter much if Satan knows or doesn't know?" Hagatha interjected. "We don't have much choice." She shrugged and noticed

Dennis reaching out a claw to hook another sandwich. She wrapped her tail around him and set him aside. "Beat it, puss."

"You said you and Melchior aren't allowed back on the premises, right?" Liz addressed Joe. "That seems to be the elephant in the room."

"What elephant?" Dennis peered under Melchior's chair, fluffing up to make himself appear more threatening.

"It's an expression," Liz said. The demons all stared at her. "Uh. An expression that only makes sense in the Upper World, apparently."

"You're right about the issue, at any rate—even if I don't understand where the elephants come in," Joe responded. "We can't waltz in through the front door. Satan put our pictures in the lobby saying we are persona non grata. No problem getting Brian and the rep into the facilities, at least. We can give them directions to the comms room. How do we get in?" He stamped his hoof, his tail twitching in exasperation. "Maybe Hagatha could find some way to take out some of the security and we—"

"Whoa!" Hagatha interrupted. "Who's this 'we'? I don't want any kind of dealings with demon-eating night serpents. I would like to be one of the last demons to get eaten if it comes to that. New life goal. Just came up with it."

"Don't worry. I have that covered," Melchior laughed. "I know a back way in. Used to party with a succubus out at Rust Canyon on the weekends. We'd hang out with a bottle of Arachsinth, you know what that stuff can do to you. Anyhoo, we ended up crawling through miles of tunnels, found some Hellocybin mushrooms, and after a few months of chasing a psychedelic spider apparition we emerged in the ritual room. And the great thing is, Rust Canyon isn't far from here."

"Wait, was that the time you took vacation and came back six months late?" Joe asked.

"Nah," Melchior said. "I really don't want to talk about that time." He looked off into the distance, an air of melancholy suffusing his huge, cow-like features.

"Doesn't matter," Joe said. "The big problem is whether a new comms team will be waiting for us when we get there. How will they feel about us showing up? And can you find your route in again? Could we all get in that way?"

The giant demon shrugged. "Dude, I'm a minotaur. Labyrinths are my thing. We got fired because Satan wanted *less* interaction with the *nihilidi*. Their constant whining was bringing him down. According to scuttlebutt, he boarded up the cavern and depends on some unreliable medium in the Upper World to get in touch with them—if he does at all. The path we're taking will be tough even for demons. If we can get the auditor in through the front door, I think we do that. Plus, it might be good to suss out what's going on at the Abyss if we can."

"Well, there's no eternity like the present," Joe said. "If we're going to do this, better sooner than later."

"Does this mean we cancel our trip to the Toxahatchee and Craggy Mountains?" Hagatha asked.

"Let's call Admin and figure this out." Melchior walked to the back of the pavilion, tossed aside some boxes and trash bags and uncovered a bent metal desk. He pulled a drawer open and plopped an ancient speaker phone on the battered top.

With Brian on speaker, everyone—except Dennis, who wandered back to sneak as much lunch and beer as possible—gathered around the phone. Brian listened to the plan; Liz could picture him running his fingers through his hair until the cowlick over his forehead was standing straight up, could feel his anxiety crackling over the line.

"Here's the thing," Melchior told Brian, "Satan didn't want just anyone knowing who he was leasing the property from, so he hid the entrance to the comms room. Most of the staff doesn't know where it is—probably none of them if Satan is using a medium to contact them as we suspect—and you don't want to explain things and cause a panic. What you need is a pretext, so they think what you're doing doesn't concern them."

"Okay. They're not interested in things that *do* concern them. Like their jobs. What do we do when we get there?"

"There's a broom closet in the back of the men's restroom. Obviously, the staff will avoid that in case someone asks them to sweep. Open it. There's another door at the back of the closet. The sign says plumbing supplies. That's the door to the staircase that leads down into the cavern slash comms room."

"Won't someone notice if we just disappear after we get there?" Brian asked.

"Nah," Melchior said. "Tell them you're there to oversee some plumbing repairs and clean up because Satan will be inspecting. They'll leave you alone for sure. Bring some official- looking paperwork. The new staff was created to look the other way."

"This all sounds ludicrous," Brian said. "I guess we have to do it." He paused. "Are you certain this is the work of the *nihilidi*? If we contact them and upset them for nothing . . . " he trailed off. "Besides, I'm supposed to be getting everything ready for Satan. I can only imagine how pissed he'll be if things aren't perfect, then he finds out I've buggered off to meet with creatures I'm not even supposed to know about."

"Positive," Melchior said. "These sinkholes aren't due to shoddy construction. They're disappearing holes. Like the ones around the shadow fields. Satan should be glad you're saving his ass."

"I guarantee he won't be," Brian said.

"On the bright side," Hagatha said, "he won't be happy no matter what you do. He never is."

"True, although it doesn't make me feel any better." Brian sighed. "When will this meeting take place?"

"I figure Joe and I can be there and set up in two days' time," Melchior said.

"So, that's three days before Satan's current ETA," Brian sounded defeated. "I'll have to rent another car with a Frenzy Drive to get there and back. I really hope you guys are right."

"We are," Melchior rumbled.

"Get Gadreel to drive you," Hagatha shouted. "He's a pretty damn good driver. Also does this mean I'm off the hook for the trip to the bridge and Outpost 989?"

Brian was silent for a few seconds. "Well . . . how long would it take you to get to the Toxahatchee?"

"I can get there today," Hagatha said. "We were supposed to head out there and then stay at the Dreary Inn tonight after the inspection."

"Go ahead. Make a last-ditch effort to see what's really going on."

"Fine," Hagatha said. "At least it puts me out of the reach of the worms. For now."

After Brian hung up, Melchior proclaimed, "We have a plan. Let's get started."

"One question." Hagatha opened another beer, evidently unconcerned about being impaired for the trip. "How will you get out to Rust Canyon that fast without a Frenzy Drive?"

Melchior's grin broadened. "You see that cycle out front? It's got a NOS system. Better than a Frenzy Drive. Another reason why you guys can't follow our route."

"Lucifer's granny!" Hagatha whistled. "Noxious Oxide?"

"Yep. I'm not supposed to leave this place, but sometimes you gotta get away from these self-righteous assholes. I take a few bike trips around the swamps, up into the mountains where no one will care to report me. There's a harpy up at Rust Canyon that'll give your horns a real good twist."

"Is she the one that hung out with that incubus I used to date?" Joe asked. "Remember Llewellyn? The guy who supervised the lava harvesters on the north side of Cauldron Mountain—the one with the sexy scarlet forelock that curved over one eye? He was something else," Joe got lost in memories, his eyes misty and distant. "Are you talking about his friend, Harpy Shebat?"

"Yeah."

"Sheesh, she'd twist up more than your horns," Joe made a face. "She terrified me."

"Oh, me too," Melchior nodded. He smirked."Me too."

"Guys, can we get away from your sex lives for a minute?" Hagatha asked. "You know, before Hell collapses?"

Melchior shook free of his memories. "Give us two days to get back to the ritual room. You guys check on the bridge. You'll see I'm right."

"Are you sure it'll only take you a few days to find the cavern?" Liz asked Melchior. "I thought you said last time it took a couple months."

He waved away her concern. "I wasn't looking for it, though. I was otherwise occupied." He smiled dreamily again. "I'm a minotaur. If I've got a talent, it's mapping skills."

"So, I guess the gang splits up," Liz said.

"What kind of nonsense is that?" Hagatha asked her.

"Never mind," Liz said. "Just some cartoon I used to watch in the Upper World." The demons all stared at her blankly.

"So," Liz needed to change the subject. "What, exactly, is this place? And why do those people think it's heaven when it's clearly not?"

"Got me," Melchior threw up his hands. "It obviously doesn't meet a single metric of what they think of as Heaven. Satan knows I'm almost exactly unlike the entity they call Saint Peter. In fact, come with me." He rose and took them to the far end of the pavilion. "Look."

A row of taped pictures lined the wall. The pictures had been crudely painted or inked on scrap wood, paper, or poster board. Melchior pointed at a bent-up poster board with "Saint Peter" marked in sharpie at the top. In colored pencil, someone had drawn a picture of a man with a yellow beard dressed in a bed sheet standing behind a gate. A halo had been crudely drawn around St. Peter's head and he was holding something that might have been a scepter or possibly a hammer. Melchior pointed at the picture and then waved his hand up and down himself.

"See any resemblance?" he asked. "I sure don't." He then showed them some pictures of Heaven; green, rolling land dotted with poorly drawn flowers. And one picture titled "God" that showed an angry man with a gray beard, also arrayed in a bedsheet.

"They really can't believe they're in Hell, so they fabricate their own reality," Melchior said. "Total denial. They pretend all this garbage is beautiful and they're very pious, even though they fight and scrap with each other the minute I take my eyes off them. It's truly amazing what souls can talk themselves into." He looked at Liz. "Uh, no offense."

"None taken," she said, shrugging. "I feel pretty much the same about souls after working with them all day."

"Sheesh," Hagatha said. "What a bunch of dorks!"

"What are you going to tell the souls about leaving?" Joe asked. "Hopefully, we talk to the *nihilidi* and everything goes back to semi-normal. We start rehab again when the trains start running, like Hell was meant to operate. No point in telling these souls any of that yet."

"These goobers have their own narrative," Melchior said. "Nothing I say or do will change the story they're telling themselves. I gotta kick you guys out, though. They like the fanfare. Who knows? This may be their last time. I mean—there's not much I can do for them except give them one last bit of fun. I'll tell them you guys are so terrible that I have to escort you into Hell myself to prevent shenanigans."

"Whatever. Let's get on the road," Hagatha belched and patted her stomach. "Heaven has shit for beer."

The giant bull cupped his hands to his mouth. "Norbert!" he bellowed. "Where have you wandered off to, you little sneak?"

Norbert came scuttling in, seeming eager. "Yes, your Excellency?" he asked, eagerly searching the faces of the heavenly applicants for signs of distress.

Melchior pointed towards the four of them dramatically. "They have been found wanting and must be cast into the eternal flames!"

"I thought as much sire," Norbert's pale weasel face lit up. "I will prepare the shame parade."

"Do you pretend to know the ways of the Lord?" Melchior roared.

Norbert hung his head. "No, sire."

"Good. Get them ready," Melchior waved a hand. "Go on. Get your ass in gear."

Norbert picked up his sad trumpet from behind the folding table where the book of life sat. Then he ran through the door calling, "Four for the flames of Hell! Gather your instruments!"

"A parade of shame?" Liz asked.

"Keeps them happy," the minotaur said. "And amuses me. Just play along. Try to look a little sad. Maybe hang your heads. Don't worry, I've convinced them that they can't touch the "sinners." I tell them *vengeance is the Lord's* or some rot. Really, it's to keep them from getting pulled apart. Most of our visitors are demons. If they *do* get injured, they refuse to go to off-site to visit an emergency clinic to help patch them up until they can heal, and it's tough for them to wait on me while they're re-growing hands and feet."

"Sure thing." Hagatha rolled her eyes.

"Let's go." Melchior led them out of the pavilion and back to the path. As they approached the row of huts, they saw a band of souls waiting. Some had gongs made of pot lids, some had plastic bottles with the ends cut off, a few had kazoos and a couple were holding badly made recorders; the latter two instruments were quite prevalent in Hell. Norbert proudly held up his bent trumpet and waited for the sinners to get in place. When Melchior nodded, Norbert blew three sharp, squeaking blasts.

"Let the parade begin!" he shouted, hopping up and down.

Melchior raised his hand and dropped his voice to a low sonorous bass. "These sinners have been found wanting. They must be banished to the flames of Hell!"

"Hell! Hell! Hell!" the crowd chanted. "Go to Hell!"

Two of the women picked up rocks as Liz and Hagatha made their way down the path.

"Guys! No rocks. What have we talked about?" Melchior put his hands on his hips and shook his head.

One woman dropped her rock immediately, the other stood gripping her stone hard in her hand for a moment. She had gray hair piled up on her head, her lined, elderly face twisted with anger. She glared at Melchior.

"Dolores," he sighed. "C'mon. I don't want to have this talk again. Vengeance is the Lord's and whatnot."

Dolores frowned deeply and flexed her fingers around the dark, ashen rock. Everyone in the parade waited, carefully watching her and Melchior. Finally, she dropped it. *Hmmm . . . Liz thought . . . Dolores. This woman seems familiar . . .*

"Elizabeth Rose," the old lady said as she took her stubborn eyes from Melchior's and looked at Liz. "I should have known. Now you're going to end up in Hell just like I said you would. Ha. Sometimes an aunt knows."

Liz stared back. "Hey, Aunt Dolores." She wasn't sure whether to laugh or cry. She remembered the time Dolores had told her father the whole family was going to hell for missing Christmas mass, and she briefly considered telling Dolores the state of things, but she could hardly do that with Melchior and Hagatha standing there. "Guess you were right. I'm happy for you. Glad you made it to heaven." She'd often wondered if she would eventually come across someone she knew in Hell. And here was her sainted—in her own mind—Aunt Dolores. A stunning turn of events. At any rate, she knew now that religion didn't have a thing to do with getting a ticket to the good place. She'd never known anyone more religious than her aunt.

Dolores said, "I warned you about those skirts. That one doesn't even reach your kneecaps."

"Yep," Liz said. "Probably the skirt."

Dolores gave Hagatha a glance, "And what did I tell you about the kind of whoring women you were hanging around with? This is what comes of not going to church regularly. And this tart—she's not even wearing pants."

Hagatha made a strangled sound.

Aunt Dolores stood, shaking her head at them for a long moment before she turned to Norbert. "Well, get on with it, the Devil will be glad to have them, no doubt."

Norbert blew into his trumpet, which gasped out a sad little wheeze. The rest of the "saints" started banging on their pots and lids or blowing through their bottles and kazoos. Melchior pointed at the gate and Liz and the demons walked towards it, followed by the noisy crowd. At the gate, they turned back one last time to gaze upon the crowd. Melchior gave them a wink over the rumbling mob while Aunt Dolores shook her fist.

Melchior raised his voice to address the crowd. "As you can clearly see, these guys are particularly evil. Total sinners. I'm going to escort them straight to the devil myself. Be back shortly. You guys behave. Norbert, keep Dolores and Barbara apart. I don't want to come back and find anyone missing a hand or an eye again."

After Norbert tied the grill of the bus back in place, Joe shook hands with Hagatha and Liz. "Good luck." He gathered his things from the back of Hagatha's car. "Hopefully, we'll see each other again this afterlife."

Melchior laughed his booming laugh and said "Let's save Hell! What else have we got to do?!" He swung himself onto his giant cycle. Joe swung up behind him. The bike's tires spun and flung mud before it leapt forward.

"Watch this," Hagatha pointed at Melchior as he reached the straightaway. "The NOS is about to kick in."

As the cycle reached the road, there was a puff of green smoke; the vehicle stretched into a long blur—then vanished.

Hagatha whistled. "Damn. Noxious Oxide is impressive." She thumbed at the car. "Hop in, guys. Might as well get some more driving in myself while I still exist."

Dennis crawled into the front seat and started to settle in. Hagatha grabbed him by the scruff and tossed him over onto his quilt. He started to caterwaul but when he saw the she-devil's deep frown, he wrapped himself in his quilt and pouted instead.

"So, that old bat knew you, eh?" Hagatha asked as she slid into the seat and started arranging the mirrors.

"Yeah," Liz said. "That was my Aunt Dolores. She taught my Sunday School class."

"She was a hag," Hagatha said. "And I bet Sunday School was boring as crap."

Liz had to agree.

TWENTY-SEVEN

The City of Dis

"SHOULD ONLY TAKE US THREE HOURS OR SO TO GET TO the bridge," Hagatha said as they got in the car. "No Frenzy Drive. The bridge is on a main thoroughfare. When we get out of the backwoods and onto the main road, we will be on the biggest truck route in all of Hell—right through the City of Dis. Food and supplies come in from the Netherworld then get shipped out to the bogs and the wilds, bog eel caviar goes the other way. *Everything* goes across that bridge and through distribution centers in Dis. If something happens to the bridge, Hell will be tied in knots. The merchants in Dis—biggest grifters in the Afterlife—would go monkey shit. That's why Brian has to send someone if anything goes wrong. Of course, now that we know about the night serpents . . . " She shrugged. "This might all be totally pointless. Might not be anything we can do about it."

Liz was almost sorry they didn't have to go through a Frenzy Zone—not because she enjoyed it, but because there was no excuse now to take the elevator antidote. It was all for the best, probably. She should save as much of it as possible to take before she tipped into oblivion. Before being eaten. She shivered and placed her hand on her purse; she'd guard that bottle like gold. She hoped she'd be back in Perdition City with Brian when it all went down. Maybe they could polish off the antidote together.

The muddy lane through the swamp on the way back to the main road was muckier and nastier than the wetlands they'd already come through. The car ran on a thin strip of mud so close to the swamp on either side that the vehicle felt like a water bug skimming on a lake.

The rain hammered harder than Liz had ever seen before. When the deluge hit, it was like driving under a lake, especially when small frogs and bug-eyed fish began falling from the sky, slapping the windshield. Liz tried to keep her eyes closed as she held onto the Oh Shit handle. On at least two occasions she was forced to open them as the car slid sideways on the muddy road; brown water swirled underneath the car, threatening to submerge them. Once, she saw a school of imp-headed piranha licking their lips. Another time she saw a bog eel staring back at her with hopeful, egg-shaped eyes, evidently wondering whether lunch might be about to slide into the bog, delivered in a metal box. Both times, Hagatha straightened out the car and kept them on the thin spit of road threading through the marsh.

"Fucking mud is worse than lava," Hagatha swore a few minutes later as she steered them around a puddle so deep there was a small shark fin circling in the brown depths. "Slurry sharks. They bite the tires and hubcaps. Doubt they could puncture these, but they could scratch things up. Those posh demons who rented us this car would not be amused."

The rainfall of fish and toads fascinated Dennis. "Wish I was home," he said. "I'd get my broom after them." He tried to open the window to catch one. A simultaneous scream from Liz and Hagatha halted the action, so he went back to pouting.

At last, signs of civilization emerged. At the edge of the swamp were a few huts made of mud and thatched with swamp willow. Glum souls huddled in doorways. Thin clouds of smoke rolled from the center of some huts, where quickly fizzling fires had been attempted. Damned sat on the edges of banks, feet in the muddy, swirling waters. After a while, the huts receded, and they began to pass gas stations and stores. Finally, the road merged with a much larger highway. Enormous black semis pulling multiple trailers zoomed past them. One truck pulling five trailers at warp speed began to jackknife just as they passed it, kinking up like a psychotic snake. Hagatha zoomed around the flailing vehicle, driving under one of the trailers as it flew above their heads. She zipped in front of the chaos just before the truck turned upside down and slid off the road, taking several other vehicles with it.

The demoness looked in the rearview mirror at the carnage. "Unholy crapoly, I'm a good driver."

The traffic was so bad and Hagatha was driving so fast that Liz was starting to wonder if she might have a drop of the elevator antidote after all when the city of Dis heaved into view. The moody, mirthless skyline glowered against the brown sky, smeared with tar-colored pillars of smog billowing from smokestacks. The streets were packed with long black cars and limos. Liz counted more luxury cars on one street than she'd seen during her entire time in Perdition City.

The windows of these posh rides were uniformly tinted; passengers were mere shadows behind the glass. Occasionally a chauffeur leaned out, waving a fist, and shouting at pedestrians or other drivers. These sleek cars were juxtaposed with monstrous trucks, ramshackle taxis, and jalopies. Pedicabs either lazily looped in front of trucks and cars or skittered and darted through the traffic-packed streets, the former operated by apathetic demons, the latter by terrified souls. The whole aspect of Dis and all its inhabitants was busy and brown. Everyone seemed to have a destination they needed to arrive at instantly, except for the pedicab demons. The place was suffused with a somber air that made Perdition City seem almost frivolous by comparison.

"Lotta money here," Hagatha said. "Mammon has a house up on a ridge overlooking Dis. It's her city." They passed a fence strangely draped with cardboard and plastic, and it took a moment for Liz to understand that these were makeshift shelters with homeless souls underneath. The shelters couldn't have kept off the constant drip of rain. "Well, more money for some, less for others," Hagatha said.

Liz felt a pang of guilt. They had a terrible time providing housing for souls assigned to Dis. Brian was always trying to work through a dizzying array of regulations and housing policies—worse than any other region of Hell—and Admin was constantly at war with the housing imps in Dis. Now she could see the result of their failure, and it wasn't pretty.

The rain slowed to a thin drizzle as they closed on the bridge. "I think we're gonna have to park on this block and walk over to the river," Hagatha said, craning her neck. "They gouge you like crazy on parking near the river. All the good spots are like three-minute only. They don't put up signs. It's a sheer money grab. We don't want to get booted or towed, because I don't have time for the beatings I would have to give out. Come on. There should be a ladder up to the Bridge tower at the corner of Mangrove and Marsh, about two blocks from here. We'll talk to the bridge keepers and see what they know."

Liz got out of the car on trembling legs, went to the trunk, and pulled her rain slicker out of her suitcase.

"Hey!" Dennis fretted. "What am I going to wear? I'm gonna get wet!"

"You don't need a raincoat, Dennis," Liz said. "You won't melt. You're definitely not made of sugar."

He frowned and jumped into her arms, unbuttoned her slicker and crawled under it close to her chest. "You can carry me. I'm not purring, by the way. That's just a light growling that I do when I'm annoyed."

Liz sighed. "Whatever." If he was smelly, he was also warm, so at least she had that going for her.

"You're gonna be impressed by the size of this sucker," Hagatha said of the bridge. "Took six Rock Giants to carry the stones for the footers. Each footer is about the height of the Admin Building. The bridge tower is made of a huge piece of lava that broke off Cauldron Mountain. The bridge itself is twenty lanes wide, and five miles long. Can't see the other side of it from here."

"That does sound like Hell," Liz shivered. "I mean, driving across it."

"Yeah, it requires some skill," Hagatha laughed. "There are souls who are assigned to live underneath it too; they pick up trash and dodge river eels. They get eaten and passed through the eels' digestive systems once every couple weeks. It's not good for hygiene."

"Tell me about it," Liz wrinkled her nose. "They come through the line sometimes." She immediately felt guilty. You could smell souls who'd been through the intestines of river eels for blocks. The lobby smelled like them for days if not weeks after they'd come through, always made worse by Sheena, the receptionist, and her trusty spray can of Lava Flower air freshener. Liz tried to shake the mingling scents of lava flower, rotting seaweed, and eel poop from her memory and concentrate on following Hagatha.

Dis wasn't like Perdition City, crowded with new souls wandering to and fro, or demons in town on holiday. The citizens of Dis walked purposefully and quickly, most with sour expressions, as though everyone in the city was ten minutes late for a root canal.

"Bring your clipboard?" Hagatha asked as they approached the bridge. "To fill out the report?"

Liz nodded. Hagatha led them onto a street next to the Toxahatchee River. The broad river flowed brown and green; huge bundles of garbage the size of small islands vied with tugboats, tankers, and barges; the latter packed with so many shipping containers that Liz couldn't imagine how they stayed afloat.

"Water's definitely down," Hagatha pointed to the islands of garbage. "Trash is piling up instead of sweeping downstream."

The enormous iron and stone bridge hulked in front of them. Liz craned her neck to see it. A torrent of traffic gushed across the bridge. Hagatha pointed out the pedestrian and pedicab lanes on the sides; twice, a pedestrian or pedicab flew from the bridge and landed with a splash in the water and garbage mixture below. Dennis had settled himself inside Liz's rain slicker, so his head was poking out over the zipper. Compared to the river, he didn't smell so bad. She was holding his bottom with one hand and digging in her purse for a pen so she would be ready to fill out the report with the other when she slammed into Hagatha's back.

"What in the infernal Hades is going on?" the demoness yelled.

Liz peeked around Hagatha's broad figure at a knot of people in front of her, right next to the pedestrian entrance of the bridge.

Two tall, warty demons, one poison-green and one mud-brown, in black caps and uniforms, were standing in front of a short, squat demon with a massive beard. The shorter demon sported a pirate captain's hat and a snazzy red jacket with gold epaulets. The pirate demon was bright scarlet—Liz wasn't certain if that was the usual color of his skin or the color of his outsized emotion. Other demons, some in suits and ties, and even a few tattered, homeless souls had gathered around to solemnly watch the argument, no doubt hopeful that it would tip into physical violence and thus break up the monotonous day with entertainment.

"Posting warnings to the seafarers and river rats be your job, be it not?" the pirate demon was screaming. "What're you lot good for then?"

The green demon shrugged. "These things happen, dude. We reported it to Perdition City Admin. If you're a fisherman, you should know it's fucking dangerous on the river. That's why I *personally* have a job on the bridge tower instead of working on the river. That's for low-class chumps like you." It waved its hand over the muddy water, and stared coolly down at the pirate demon, now so angry he was dancing with rage.

"Besides, none of the other boat captains lost their vessels. Maybe you're just crap at navigating. Ever think of that, little pirate guy?"

"I barely missed going down with me boat! Coulda lost a hundred demons, and they wouldn't be able to tell you the tale from the bottom o' that gash. A whopping hole in the bank ought to at least have a sign, you blighted overgrown toads," the shorter demon shrieked. "Bridge tenders, my fanny! You lot are no doubt up in your tower the live-long day swilling down the liquor. Likely entertaining yourselves with incubi and succubi and harpies and sirens and—"

A well-dressed harpy watching the scene unfold gasped and swung her structured black bag with fat brass clasps at the pirate's head, knocking him backward. He rolled around on the cement howling. The green frog demon kicked at him half-heartedly and then turned to go. The brown bridge keeper leaned down and plucked the hat from the old pirate demon's head, nodded, and placed it atop his own hat. He gave the screaming, flailing pirate one last glance, squinted, then thrust out his long tongue, snatched a beetle from the demon's beard and then turned on his heel.

"We gotta get back to the tower, dude," the bright green demon said, as they walked away. "The boss said to take care of the problem and I'm gonna call this one solved."

The crowd began to disperse. Hagatha waited until the bearded demon rolled himself up off the road.

"Tarnation," he said, dusting off his pants. "Never saw a city with more worthless employees."

"What's up, old guy?" Hagatha asked.

"Lost my fishing dinghy in a sinkhole on the bank. Got pushed in by a floating pile of trash." His face had relaxed into a pasty, apricot color. He fingered his dull gray beard, pulled out a few beetles, then popped them into his mouth, making a loud, crunching sound. "At least they left me part of me lunch. Hell's sake!"

"What do you mean?" Hagatha asked. "How did you lose your dinghy?"

"Got pushed towards the bank by a giant floating mound of garbage. I was runnin' aground when I seen a sinkhole on the bank. First thing I knows, the old girl is slipping into the gap. I'da been down there too if she hadn't a tipped up sudden like and flipped hersel'. Satan knows how. I was thrown clear. Came so close to sliding into the hole, I could feel me old tail a'hangin' over the edge. Managed to scramble up the bank. Stupid eels tunneling again. That lot's supposed to post warnin's and fill holes. What's the use of 'em? And what's to become of old Beetle Beard now?" He slapped his chest dramatically.

"I expect you'll head back to Perdition City for a new boat or re-assignment," Hagatha frowned. "Where's the hole?"

"Quarter mile downstream from the tower. They shoulda seed it easy," the bearded demon said, pointing. "Ye can get a good gander from yon pier. Shoulda been able to spot it from the tower, they should. That lot should pay the cost of a new boat." Beetle Beard started to adjust his hat and then realized it was missing. He cursed.

"Good luck with that, dude," Hagatha said. "This is Dis."

"Bunch of fuckin' assholes," he grumbled as he walked away.

Hagatha punched Liz in the arm.

"Ouch," she yelped. "Why did you do that?"

"Check it out!" Hagatha pointed at the bearded demon's tail. The arrow tip was gone.

"Unholy smokes!" Dennis grabbed his own tail and surveyed the missing end. "He's just like me."

"Alright, c'mon." Hagatha announced. "I wanna see this for myself."

"Aren't we supposed to go see the bridge tenders? Up in the tower?" Liz asked.

"Nah. Beetle Beard was right. They're worthless. Let's go look at the hole."

"I don't wanna go anywhere near it," Dennis whined. "How do we keep from falling in?"

"We'll see when we get there," Hagatha said. "Don't bug me and maybe I won't throw you in."

"What if we fall in?" Dennis curled into a ball, trembling. "What if it's getting bigger and bigger and it swallows up the city and—"

"If that happens, we're just screwed. Too big a problem to even worry about," Hagatha shrugged. "That hasn't happened yet. It may be just another eel hole. Or maybe the nothing snakes are trying to send us a message. Trying to get us to notice them. Frickin' drama queens. On the other hand, if they wanted to tear down Hell, they could have done it by now."

They made their way towards the sinkhole. Liz tried to keep up with Hagatha's long strides.

"Don't get too close" Dennis commanded from his perch inside her rain slicker. "Let Hagatha check it out first."

Liz slowed her pace. He had a point. She followed behind Hagatha carefully bringing herself to the she-devil's side on the edge of the river. The sinkhole was bigger than the hole Dennis had fallen into. Standing on the corner of the pier and Marsh Avenue, they could see a dark gap in the rocky brown shoreline about twenty yards away. A couple large boulders sat next to it on the land side, shielding the hole so it was hard to see from above the river. Most of the demons and souls on the street ignored the rupture in reality, as did the boats and tugs that sailed by, though water and trash constantly washed up the bank, into the hole— and disappeared.

A demon in a fishing cap stood with his line over the water, placidly staring out with vacant eyes. Hagatha walked up to him, grabbed the pole, and said, "Be right back."

"Hey!" the demon howled. "I'll sue!"

"Whatever." She took the fishing pole, which had been baited with a wriggling foot-long Hell worm, then cast the line towards the hole. Her aim was perfect. She reeled the line back in and displayed the bait; now it was only half a worm.

"Another sinkhole just like the one that ate Dennis's tail," she said flatly.

They stood on the pier for a moment more, watching trash disappear into the hole. The hole undulated and expanded toward the river side. One of the boulders on its border shook and fell in.

The fisher demon ran up and yanked the pole out of Hagatha's hand. "You owe me," he began, but Hagatha snarled, and he thought the better of it. He retrieved his tackle and wandered away.

An island of garbage the size of a barge came floating by. A small ripple of water pushed it towards the hole. The trash rolled over itself and into the hole, cups, empty jugs, an old chair, a bent bicycle, and an old mattress. Everything was swallowed.

"Another eight feet and that sinkhole will meet the river's edge," Hagatha said.

"What do we do?" Liz asked, panic rising.

"How about we get the fuck out of here?" Dennis suggested from her rain slicker. "The sooner the better." He dug in his claws.

"For once, I have to agree with the little asshole." Hagatha conceded.

"Should we warn someone?" Liz asked.

Hagatha shrugged. "What would they do about it? They can't fix it. There's only one thing anyone can do about it, and that's talk to the monsters eating Hell. We don't have time to fuck around with a bunch of assholes who will find every reason not to believe us anyway. Trust me, Dis wouldn't shut down if the night serpents were eating the mayor on toast in front of the entire city. It wouldn't be good for the bottom line."

"Should we evacuate near the bridge?" Liz asked, still mesmerized by the sinkhole.

Hagatha laughed. "If you think I'm going to be responsible for stopping the entire economy of Hell, you've got another thought coming. Let Brian figure this out. That's his job. Right now, we beat it before we end up at the bottom of a hole."

She put her claw on Liz's shoulder, whirling her around. Then the demoness tromped back in the direction of the car.

"Where do we go now?" Liz puffed from behind.

"To the Abyss," Hagatha said. "On the way we're going back to Smokin' Joe's where we are going to eat and drink anything and everything lying around."

"I thought you said we were staying away from the demon-eating monsters," Dennis said. "Why are we going there?"

"I've changed my mind. I want to know exactly what's happening, when it's happening, and what my chances are. And the only way to do that is to go where the plans are being made," Hagatha said.

"I don't want to go to the Abyss!" Dennis howled, his fur standing on end. "I'm scared. What if I lose more than my beautiful tail?"

"If someone doesn't solve this problem, you'll lose your ass in a sinkhole and so will the rest of us. I want to have a say in how this goes down. Back to the car, nitwits." Hagatha strode grimly back to where they'd parked, Liz now racing to keep up. Dennis was nipping at her in his panic. She didn't have any breath left to tell him to stop.

When they arrived a dumpy meter demon was standing by the car with a pen in its mouth and a ticket book in one hand. It was scratching its rear end with the other. As they approached, it took the pen from its mouth and started writing out their ticket.

"This is a no parking zone from," it checked its watch, then droned, "Three-thirty PM to eight-fifteen AM except on Plague Day, Bureaucracy Day, Insurance Adjustor Awareness Day, or any other approved holidays when there is no parking unless you have a permit for—"

It stopped, finding itself swinging upside down, held in Hagatha's powerful tail. She glared. "There are no signs posted."

"That's not my problem," the meter demon protested. "Putting up signs is not my job and according to Edict 437.9JB-678, penalties accrued by illegal activities as determined by the Bureau of Traffic Retribution cannot be ameliorated by failure of the City Planner Signage Unit to fulfill their duties by posting—"

Hagatha shook the demon until its pudgy jowls shook like Jell-O and its teeth rattled. Hell Coin and ink pens fell from its pockets. Still holding the little demon aloft with her tail, Hagatha reached down, grabbed the ticket book out of the demon's hands, then threw it down a storm drain.

"Get fucked," she barked as she dropped the demon back onto the pavement. "Let's go." She motioned to Liz and Dennis.

The meter demon was at a loss without its ticket book. As it bent down, glaring into the storm drain, Liz heard it mumble, "It's a class D offense to disregard a ticketing officer according to Edict 899.11I IL-007, and a class H offense to purposefully destroy a ticket, and immobilizing and inverting a ticketing officer is punishable by . . . "

Not wishing to be left behind, Liz jumped into the passenger seat and slammed the door. Dennis, seeing Hagatha wasn't in the mood for shenanigans, climbed out of Liz's raincoat, and scrambled into the back seat. Hagatha got in, put her sunglasses on and started the car.

"Fucking Dis," she said. "I hate this place."

TWENTY-EIGHT
The Plan

HAGATHA WAS IN A HURRY, MERGING BACK ONTO THE highway as they left Dis gave Liz nightmare fuel for the rest of her afterlife. The on-ramps to the highway were shaped like corkscrews. Fast moving trucks, slow-moving taxis, luxury cars with cursing demon drivers, an old jalopy full of skeletons, and even a clown car full of jester and buffoon demons competed with them to reach the top and merge.

As they raced up the curves to enter the crowded lanes of traffic, Hagatha said, "Gotta beat these trucks. Hold onto your butts."

Liz let out a gasp of relief when they made it onto the highway intact. But there was no time to relax as they whizzed between trucks, dodged sports cars, and watched the clown car collide with the skeleton jalopy, which exploded in a cloud of confetti and bones in the rearview mirror. They zipped past regal limos as long as football fields—zoomed past pedicabs. On the plus side, Liz thought, the trip back through the swamps, dodging slurry sharks and mournful willows would be a piece of cake after the horror of the highway in Dis.

When they arrived back at Smokin' Joe's, Hagatha didn't have much trouble convincing Bob and Dan to open the doors; their previous experience drinking with her had left them admiring and fearful in equal parts.

She stomped into the lobby ahead of Liz and Dennis, headed for the bar. "I'm going to drink. A lot. I'm staying away from the Arachsinth tonight though, and so is everyone else. I'm saving that for when Hell comes apart. Oh, and you should call Brian. See when he's gonna get here. Tell him I'm going to the meeting." She swung through the saloon door, Bob and Dan close on her heels.

Liz found keys behind the desk and carried Dennis back to his room. "I'm not purring. I'm doing that low growl thing again," Dennis said as she set him down and opened a can of tuna. "Just so you know."

"Yeah," Liz said, "I know." She plucked a piece of ash from his ear, patting him a little, and his "low growl" increased.

Liz settled into Joe's comfortable leather desk chair. When she called Brian, she was surprised to hear a female voice answering the phone.

"How the hell are things, Lizzie?"

When Liz didn't respond immediately, the voice said, "It's me, Ellie. Hello? Are you there?"

"Sorry, I thought I dialed the wrong number for a second." Why did Ellie get to be with Brian while she was here in this desolate wasteland? Sam's voice in the background caused another wave—this time relief and embarrassment. Of course, they were planning the meeting with Satan. Brian had sent her here for her own good. Still the little sting of jealousy surprised her.

"I've been helping out here in the office," Ellie said. "The school shut down. Remember Pudding-for-Brains? Our janitor? He fell asleep with a cigarette on his break—started a fire in a wastebasket, then flooded the first floor trying to put out the fire. It's going to take a month to get the mud and imp piranhas out of the classrooms. So, Sam and I have been working here in the office every day. We're helping and planning at the same time."

"I'm glad you're helping," Liz said. "I hate to think how long the line is getting."

"Well," Ellie said cheerfully, "maybe that's the least of our worries."

"If it's not one thing, it's being eaten by monsters," Liz said. "I was nervous about the meeting with Satan. Now I have something bigger to worry about."

"I'm not that worried," Ellie reassured her. "I don't see The Mountain Group getting too excited about closing this place down. Sam can barely get his boss on the phone for five minutes. All she wants is for the problem to go away so she doesn't have to tell her boss, who in turn doesn't want to tell his boss, and so on. Sounds like they just want to get the trains running and rehab facilities opened again. It should be a win for everyone—including the creatures of the Abyss."

"I hope so." Liz had her doubts.

"By the way, I'm staying here to help run the office. I'll see you when you get back. Please hurry so I can take the rest of the school renovation time as a vacation. Brian's bringing Theo along. He'll explain the plan when he gets there."

"Hagatha says to tell Brian she's going with us."

The sound of the phone was muffled for a moment. Then Ellie came back on the line. "Brian says he expected you and Hagatha both to go with him. Wait at Joe's. Be ready to go . . . " the phone was muffled again for a moment. "By eight-thirty am tomorrow, he says. He'll pick you up on the way to the Abyss. I gotta get back to work. I don't think he has time to come to the phone right now."

"Bye," Liz mumbled. She realized how much she'd been counting on talking to Brian. She sighed and headed for the bar. Maybe Hagatha had the right idea.

After a night of tossing and turning, dreaming that she was nibbled apart slowly by imp piranhas, Liz woke far too early and sat up in bed.

The clock read five-fifty a.m. Dennis, who'd had another nightmare and demanded to sleep with Liz again, was still snoring. She got out of bed, careful not to wake him, and tiptoed to the window. Cauldron Mountain was clearly visible. She wondered about the sinkhole Joe had found behind the hotel. How big was it now? An unpleasant fantasy suddenly obtruded—a sinkhole opening in the road to the Abyss. Her breathing grew shallow and ragged as she pictured herself and Brian sliding into nothing.

She jerked the curtains shut and closed her eyes. Giving up on going back to sleep, she showered, dressed, and found some magazines on the nightstand. She tried to amuse herself for a while with funny stories about bog eels and plumbing in *Demon's Digest;* when she couldn't concentrate on those, she flipped through *Bog Living* glancing at pictures of swamp houses made over with willow rugs and turtle shell lamps. Perhaps she needed company.

Hagatha was already sitting at the bar with a giant mug of steaming coffee when Liz ventured out of her room in search of breakfast. Bob and Dan were up as well, in their usual booth quietly drinking coffee, staring out the window at the back parking lot. The demoness waved her hand across a plate of croissants.

"Croissant? There's a bowl of boiled wart-goose eggs too," Hagatha slid a bowl of large green eggs with lumpy shells down the counter toward Liz. "Eat up. Who knows how many more breakfasts you'll have."

"Thanks. Did you make the coffee?" Liz eyed the carafe suspiciously.

"Yep. Might want to add some cream and sugar. Gadreel says my coffee is so strong it grew hair on his—"

Liz put up a hand. "Please. It's too early for me to think about where Gadreel has hair."

"Went out and looked at the sinkhole Joe found," Hagatha said casually. "Twice the size as before. Hope our little conversation with the night worms works. I like my existence. I mean it could be better. But eternity was improving for me. And now? This B.S.," She slammed down the coffee mug. "We better get this fixed, is all I know."

She was silent for a moment, her possum tail twitching irritably. "It's seven forty-five," she said. "They're going to be here at eight-thirty, right? You ready? And is the brat coming?"

"As ready as I'll ever be. And yeah, I suppose I'll bring Dennis." She ate breakfast hurriedly and took a boiled egg back to Dennis. That plus the tuna meant he'd be flatulent and have hellish breath, but she didn't want to listen to him whine about being hungry. According to Joe and Melchior, it was a long clamber down the stairs to the cavern, so she packed a knapsack with snacks.

Liz thought briefly about asking Dennis if he wanted to stay in his room at the hotel and wait for her, but she remembered him slipping into the sinkhole, flailing, and shrieking and ultimately decided against it. Somehow, along the way, she'd developed an unfortunate soft spot for the little jerk.

Liz returned to the room and extracted him from the warm blankets, despite his protests.

"I was watching *Eaten by Bog Eels*," he complained. "Then I was going to watch some old episodes of *Dr. Odd*. You know that quack from the Upper World? I used to save his shows for you. He scored a show with Hell TV when he got down here. He tells souls to do stupid shenanigans like drink spider egg and frog venom milkshakes when they're feeling down and stuff." His voice dropped conspiratorially. "It's really because Pazu's Potions sponsor his show. All their potions are crap. Total waste of Hell Coin. But the side effects are hilarious!"

"Interesting," Liz said, tonelessly. "You can watch that stuff later." She set him on the desk chair with his tuna and allowed him to finish his show while she packed.

"Make sure you're ready to go in a few minutes," she told him. "I think we'll come back by the hotel to get our things later. You can take your quilt in the car with you. Here's a wart goose egg too. We have a long day ahead of us and I don't want to listen to you whine about being hungry the whole time."

Dennis slurped his tuna without responding, so Liz went to wait for Brian and the others in the lobby. She stared out at the orange, ashy day without really seeing it. In her mind's eye, she and Brian slid into sinkhole after sinkhole. She tried bringing herself back to the present. The night serpents loved soul essence; they couldn't get that if they destroyed Hell. Ellie said that Sam and his management didn't want to shut down Hell. There was only one way this could end! She would stay with Brian, take trips to the Netherworld or to the mountain. Maybe he'd go with her.

Every time she built up a cozy future in her mind, however, the image melted and became a dark, slavering gap in existence.

"No," she whispered—as if vocalizing thoughts was a spell of hope. "Things will be better after today. *They will be.*"

Fortunately for Liz's sanity, Gadreel pulled into the parking lot at eight twenty-three. The extra seven minutes of waiting until half past might have found her curled in the fetal position sobbing with anxiety. Gadreel slid the long gray SUV under the portico. Sam and Theo crawled out of the back, Sam clearly worse for wear and Theo hoisting his pants. Brian unfolded from the passenger seat. There were bags under his eyes and his bow tie was slightly crooked. Liz hurried out to greet them.

"Liz!" Theo saluted her in his booming, friendly voice, "Long time, no see. Don't suppose there's any breakfast floating around?"

"What a fucking drive! Where's the coffee?" Gadreel chimed in as soon as he got out of the driver's seat. The big blue demon pulled his shoulders back, rubbed the back of his neck, then tugged at his loincloth. "*That* wedged its way somewhere uncomfortable."

"Coffee and food inside, at the bar," Liz said.

"Fine." Gadreel stomped toward breakfast, Theo at his heels.

"Restroom?" Sam had turned a shade of green. "Turns out I don't care for Frenzy Drive."

"Right off the lobby," Liz said as Sam stumbled inside.

Liz wondered if she could risk a hug.

"I am so glad to see you," was all she could come up with. *Lame*, she thought.

Brian seemed nervous too. Then, for just an instant, she found herself engulfed in his big wool sweater, her cheek smushed to his chest, so briefly that she almost wondered if she'd imagined it.

"Everyone ready to go?" he asked. "It's going to be quite a day."

"I think so. Come get breakfast. How are you holding up?"

"As well as can be expected." He followed her to the bar. "Simultaneously planning a conference for the big guy while also sneaking away to another meeting where I will attempt to save his ass, for which I will receive exactly zero gratitude. Could be worse, though. I feel calmer than I would have thought about having him throw things at my head, since my other choice is being eaten by creatures of darkness and excreted as nothing. Nothing like a bigger calamity to put a smaller calamity into perspective."

"Glad you're so cheerful. Is Ellie alone at the office?" She led him into the bar and poured coffee while he peeled a boiled egg.

"Believe it or not, I got Gla'ap from the hotel to take time off and come over," Brian said, as he shook shrieking pepper onto his egg. "She's good at paperwork and if Satan calls, she's as good as anyone at giving him the runaround. Comes from dealing with hotel guests and flying monkeys all day, I guess."

"I hope you put up the breakables." Liz thoughght of her paperweight back at the office—a tiny globe with the skyline of Perdition City. When she shook it, a shower of tiny bats flew around the little glass sphere. She felt a momentary stab of heartbreak at the thought of tiny Perdition City breaking.

"I brought your sweater," he was saying. "It's in the SUV. I put your vase and bat globe in a file drawer, and I let Sheena borrow your dragon heater to keep Gla'ap from breaking it. Don't know if you'll get that back. Sheena's always complaining about the damp and cold."

"I suspect I will have to fight Sheena for the heater. Thanks for remembering the sweater. Joe says the cavern will be cold. You think things are going to go smoothly at the Abyss facilities?" She watched his face carefully as she chattered at him, noting his furrowed brow, his tight jaw.

"I'm going to tell the crew at the Abyss that Satan is coming in town for a meeting and there are bog eels in some of the plumbing systems. Theo, our plumber is going to do "some work on the bathrooms." You and Sam are there to fill out reports. If there's two things demons hate, it's plumbing and paperwork. I don't think they'll question it. It feels like a plan that might work . . . so it prob-ably won't."

"A wise man once told me to keep my expectations low." Liz sipped her coffee.

"Aha! I *have* taught you something," Brian chuckled. "Now, let's hope Gla'ap doesn't destroy the office so if Hell still exists, I'll have something to go back to. If we can explain to the *nihilidi* there will still be souls who jump into the Abyss—without mentioning rehab starting again, maybe things go back to normal."

"I hope they've at least stopped with the sinkholes by the time Satan arrives." Liz worried.

"No doubt he'll blame me if not. Last night a sinkhole appeared in the back parking lot of Admin. It's only a foot in diameter, but I dropped my pen in and it totally disappeared. I've had emails from all around Hell. Some reported sinkholes have grown. The sinkhole behind the Last Outpost is twice the size, according to the latest from Zenebrius. I've evacuated the demons from the Outpost to a cave a couple miles away for the time being. If we convince the night serpents to stop destroying Hell, then I can go back to stressing over Satan. I can't even allow myself to *think* how pissed he's going to be when The Mountain Group tell him the trains have to run again."

"Yeah," Liz nodded. "I want to go back to worrying about our old set of problems—problems we can actually solve. The rehab thing is going to be a pain, but if we work together, we'll manage it."

Brian's lips thinned into a straight line. "I wish I didn't have to bring you with me to the Abyss. I don't know if anywhere in Hell is safe right now. And if—I mean I think it's an off chance—what if we just rile them up and . . . the worst happens. I just want us to be—"

"Together?" Liz asked.

"Yeah." Brian smiled, although it didn't quite reach his eyes. "That."

Hagatha was not excited about leaving "her" car behind. Brian reminded her they could probably only get one car in under his authorization, in any case.

"Besides," he told her, "if this doesn't go well, you won't be needing it anymore."

Hagatha's tail swished from side to side. She glared at Brian. He was obviously right.

Reluctantly, she left the keys with Bob and Dan. "If we're not back in a couple days, you guys might as well jump in the car and have a good time," Hagatha said. "Everything will be over pretty soon after that. I grabbed some bottles of Arachsinth for me and Gadreel. I left one for you, so if things go south, start drinking. You'll never feel it when you turn into nothing. Trust me."

Bob and Dan exchanged worried glances. Bob gingerly took the keys. "Errr . . . thanks."

As they walked out to the car, Liz cast a longing glance back at Smokin' Joe's. She could no longer convince herself of the rationality of their plans. It sounded like the plot of a *Three Stooges* episode—*Larry, Moe, and Curly Save Hell.*

Before Brian could get into the passenger seat, Hagatha jumped in.

"I call shotgun," she announced. "I need the legroom." She put on her sunglasses and scooted her seat backwards. Liz took the seat behind Hagatha with Dennis curled in her lap under his quilt; Theo and Sam climbed into the very back seat. Brian got in behind Gadreel, next to Liz and Dennis, folding himself awkwardly.

Hagatha turned on the radio. The sounds of loud whooping barks layered over gut-drums and shriektars roared. "Might as well enjoy some good old-fashioned muck metal on the way out. Hey, this sounds like the Sewer Monkeys!"

Dennis pulled the quilt over his ears. Liz wished she could join him.

They drove past Cauldron Mountain and the beach again, toward the Abyss, although this time they weren't just passing through. By the time they passed the shadow fields full of DANGER! ABYSS! signs, Liz's stomach was in knots. At a fork in the road, Gadreel turned right, following a sign that read: ABYSS FACILITIES. AUTHORIZED PERSONNEL ONLY. The darkness increased. They could see only a few feet off the road. Everything else was swirling shadow.

A sluggish green light barely illuminated a gate house that blocked the road before them. Hagatha quit singing/howling along with the

SuccuGrrrls and turned off the radio. Gadreel slowed the car to speak to the guard. The gatehouse was empty. A large rolling gate stood in front of them, blocking the road to the facilities. Gadreel and Hagatha got out of the SUV and inspected it in the headlights. After a few moments, they pushed it and it rolled.

Gadreel got back in and shrugged. "Unlocked."

"What in Hell?" Brian said. "Unlocked?"

Silence fell as they moved forward. Dennis poked his head out of the quilt, then nervously started spitting on his paw and rubbing his horn until Liz covered him again. She could feel his body shaking.

As they drove towards the parking garage, the lights of the SUV picked out dark road, nothing more. Weak streetlights flickered on the shoulder. The feeble green light they cast was little better than nothing.

The ride from the gate to the facilities went on forever. And somehow, took no time at all. Eternity stretched like a rubber band in the darkness. Liz put her hand on Brian's, twining her fingers through his. She closed her eyes. A moment outside of time: sitting next to Brian; fingers twined; faint scent of wool and aftershave; their combined warmth; Dennis's "low growl." Forever—then the car slowed.

They had entered a parking garage, like the guard shack, unattended.

"This is the most highly secured facility in Hell," Brian said. "Last time I was here, there were two demons here at the entrance of the parking garage and two more security guards by the elevators. They checked IDs at every door."

Gadreel parked as close as possible to the elevator tower. He opened the hatch and gave Liz a couple bottles of swamp water, some flashlights and batteries. The weight of it all in her bag along with Dennis's snacks was like lead. Brian gently took her knapsack and carried it for her. The backpack appeared comically small on his back.

Liz had to pry the quilt from Dennis's claws. "We'll fall down the stairs if we drag this quilt with us."

He crawled into her sweater, whimpering, too scared to whine.

Gadreel pushed the elevator button; they stood waiting. Sam cleared his throat repeatedly.

"Think the elevator is working?" Theo asked.

"If it is working, it's taking its sweet time," Hagatha punched the elevator button again.

"Think that'll make it come quicker?" Gadreel asked. "Button's lit up."

"I need to punch *something*." Hagatha glared at him.

The elevator doors finally opened; a purple demon with stooped shoulders and two small yellow horns stepped out, beady eyes and pig-like snout just visible over the top of the cardboard box it carried.

"No point. We're closed." He attempted to scoot past them. Gadreel grabbed the back of his shirt and spun him to face Brian.

"Closed?" Brian asked. "What are you talking about?"

"Don't know. Going home. Boss says don't come back." The demon tried to wrench free; Gadreel's grip tightened.

"Uh, Brethorn," Brian said, leaning forward to check the demon's name tag.

"Name's not Brethorn. It's Bargflop. Lost my name tag last week. Borrowed this one." The demon tried to leave again, but Hagatha wrapped her tail around one of his ankles.

"Bargflop then," Brian rolled his eyes. "What do you mean closing? We're here for an inspection. Satan himself is coming in a few days."

Bargflop pushed against Gadreel's arm. "Satan? Whadda you mean? Satan's the one that told us to shut down."

The group exchanged glances. Hagatha lifted the demon off the floor, dangling him in mid-air. The cardboard box slipped to the floor, contents spilling everywhere. "You'd better explain. Pronto."

"It's not my fault," he protested. "All I know is that yesterday, Grog—our Administrator—said Satan called. He's shutting the place down. Closing it, forever."

Hagatha shook him hard. "Spill the beans, Porky. I'm not playing around."

Bargflop squealed. "I don't know. I don't know. I just came back to clear out my desk."

Hagatha leaned over, poking through the contents of the box. "You came back for a stapler, three sticks of gum, some cough drops, a used tissue and what's this?" She pulled out a couple of half-used tar pencils.

Bargflop wriggled. "I thought there might still be some Ghoulios and Little Devil snack cakes in the break room. It's hard to get that stuff out here."

"Anyone else still here?" Brian asked.

"Boss was in the control room," the demon admitted. "He's getting ready to leave, too. If you wanna talk to him, you better hurry."

Hagatha dropped him unceremoniously on the concrete parking lot. He scuttled out of sight, leaving his beloved possessions behind. Moving forward the group entered the elevator.

"This is super fucking weird," Gadreel said as the doors slid shut.

"Maybe Satan went back and reworked his deal with the creatures when he found out my boss was coming," Sam said eagerly. "Maybe he's taking the idea of rehab more seriously now that he knows we're inspecting him."

"Yeah," Hagatha snorted. "No way."

Brian's hand pressed against Liz's. She wrapped her pinky around his.

The elevator opened on a dingy lobby with a drop-down ceiling, no windows, and a couple dirty plastic chairs to their right. To their left was a tall reception counter in front of an expanse of wall, which was lined with metal doors. Sticky elevator floors gave way to gluey lobby floors.

"If I remember correctly, the first door is the administrator's office; the second is the control room." Brian lifted his foot and stared at his sole. "Is there gum on this floor or is it just really dirty?"

"I think it's made of gum." Liz's shoe made a *squick*. "What do they do in the control room? They can't *control* the Abyss, can they?"

"No, no. It's more like security. They monitor the perimeter of the Abyss," Brian said. "They watch video feeds to make sure fences are still up, signs are placed, that no one is accidentally wandering into the shadow fields, stuff like that. If there's a problem, they use hover suits, so they don't accidentally fall into a sinkhole. Honestly, I've only been out here a couple times since I've been manager. Usually, to deliver angry messages from Satan or pick up sealed paperwork that I forward to him in the Upper World. I've never even met this administrator. Satan goes through a lot of them."

The lack of windows and low polystyrene drop ceiling gave the office a claustrophobic ambiance. Voices bounced and fell flat. Fluorescent lights buzzed disagreeably. Dennis stuck his nose out of Liz's sweater and sniffed.

"There's nothing here," he said. "I don't smell lizards, rats, bugs. *Nada*. I don't like it."

Theo and Gadreel simultaneously leaned over the long reception counter to see if anyone was hiding behind it. Upon finding no one, Brian rang a little black bell shaped like a bat. They waited for a few moments, feeling rather silly.

"Should we just go?" Theo asked. "I mean, why not, if no one's here?"

"Might as well," Hagatha said. She turned to walk away when the second door on the wall, the one labeled CONTROL ROOM, opened. A snot-colored demon in a mis-buttoned white dress shirt and fat red tie slithered out with a cardboard box full of wires, cables, and microphones. He was a Limax demon, whose body ended in a slug-like tail instead of legs, which explained the gluey floors.

"Hey! Where are you going with those?" Hagatha barked.

"Yeah," Gadreel leaned forward over the desk. "Are those things actually yours?"

The short demon put down the box on the counter. "Might as well be. This place is shutting down. Never opening again, so I've been told."

"Satan told you that?" Brian asked.

"Yeah," the slug demon narrowed his eyes. "How'd you know?"

"Guy downstairs told us," Gadreel said.

"Listen," the administrator said. "I'm gonna have to ask you all to leave. Satan was very clear that I was to be the last one out of this place. So beat it." He puffed himself up, so his bulk moved into his chest. Unfortunately, this defense mechanism resulted in a rather thin bottom half; he couldn't hold the pose for long without swaying. He let out his breath and settled back into a slug shape.

"What do you mean?" Brian asked. "Why?"

"Satan said something about a new job. I didn't pay much attention. All I remember is he said, 'don't let Brian know.' You know, that prick who runs Admin in Perdition City?" He shrugged. "Never even met the guy."

He stopped and squinted at them. Liz was afraid that at any moment he would realize who they were. The thought, knocking politely on the outside of the slug's skull, evidently wasn't welcomed. He started taping up his cardboard box, using the last of a roll of sticky tape, tossed the empty plastic tape dispenser onto the floor and began to ooze away.

"Satan's giving you a new job?" Hagatha called after him. "As what?"

"No," the slug turned, "*he* has a new job. As a hedge fudge manager or something."

"You mean hedge fund?" Liz prompted him. "Like in the Upper World?"

"Don't know. Don't care," the slug shrugged. "Anyway, he said something about how the Abyss shutting down would upset mountain people or something. And that this Brian guy might kick up a fuss. Prick's a freak for rules, apparently." He clutched the box close to his chest. "Who are you, again?"

"The closing crew, obviously," Hagatha lied.

"Satan said I'm supposed to be the last one here," the slug stared at them. "If you're the closing crew, how come you're asking all this stuff? Didn't Satan call and tell you he's going to fudge hedges?"

"He just meant the last of the Abyss staff," Hagatha said, sounding confident. "We've got to shut down the plumbing and stuff." She pointed at Theo, in his uniform, looking the part. "Satan told us to come and ask you this stuff to be sure that you were doing what he said. You know how suspicious he is. Wanted us to make sure you heard him when he told you not to talk to that prick, Brian." She shot a glance at Brian, grinning widely.

"Yeah," Brian sighed. "Not that anyone ever tells *him* anything. The poor sap is always out of the loop."

"He's pretty dumb, that Brian guy," Dennis piped up over Liz's sweater. She smacked him in the head.

The slug stared at them for a few minutes. "Whatever. I have everything I want. I assume you can see yourselves out."

As he left, he said, "There's a sinkhole behind the elevators in the parking garage. Don't leave your car there. It got twice as wide yesterday as it was before." He flipped off the light switch next to the elevator. The doors opened and swallowed him.

Unsettled by the darkness, Liz took the flashlights out of her purse and handed one to Sam and one to Brian. She tried to hand one to Hagatha too, but the demoness brushed her off.

"Demons see fine in the dark. One of our many, many advantages over souls. Never have seen why soul essence was any kind of big deal." Hagatha lifted an eyebrow at Sam, who looked away.

"The big guy is shutting down the Abyss, and he's worried I'll make trouble," Brian said. "I'm not sure I like our chances. He knows something we don't."

No one said anything, then Hagatha piped up, "The supply closet with the hidden staircase is at the end of the hall. We might as well see this through, since we're here, unless someone else has a better idea."

"Wait a second," Gadreel spoke up. "Should we leave the car in the garage? I mean if the sinkhole expands, what will happen to the SUV? Will we be able to get out of here?"

Liz realized she hadn't thought past the moment. Since she'd learned about the night serpents, she'd been mourning her afterlife. Somewhere in the back of her brain, she knew things would never be the same. This was proof.

"What do you propose?" Brian asked.

"That I go back to the parking garage, keep an eye on things. Park the SUV as far away from the sinkhole as possible and be prepared to move it."

"Is this just a ploy to abandon us in the bowels of Hell as it turns to poop?" Hagatha glared at him.

"I'm just going to move the car. I'll still be there. If things don't go well, won't matter anyway," Gadreel shrugged.

Brian nodded. "Makes sense. Take Theo with you. In case you need someone to help open the gate or something."

"I don't think we need my ruse anymore," Theo said. "No one here to stop us."

"I should contact my boss again," Sam said. "Let her know what's happening. Sounds like the Abyss has a line that dials out if they could contact Satan. If they hear this, they'll send someone."

"There are no phone lines left," Hagatha pointed at the blank, clean areas around the floors where the ghosts of stolen wire showed in the dust. "They've taken every inch of cable."

"I don't think we have any option. We just have to keep going," Brian said.

The door to the control room stood open. The walls were completely bare; not a screen, cable, or electric cord to be seen. They walked down the long corridor towards the men's room as described by Joe. It was lit by more buzzing fluorescents and painted internal organ pink-beige, making Liz feel slightly nauseated. At the end of the hallway there was a sign that said "restrooms." They walked into the men's. Sure enough, at the back was a closet labeled PLUMBING SUPPLIES.

"Here we go." Brian pulled open the banged-up metal door.

The staircase was just where Melchior and Joe had told them it would be. Once the door was opened, a stone staircase dropped steeply before them. Dry, hard steps curved into darkness, still and cold with a ghostly scent of dry rot or dust. Faint, achromatic lights sporadically illuminated the wall. Still, it was impossible to see beyond the first few steps. They stepped into the hole, lowering themselves into the unknown.

"Is there a handrail?" Sam asked, groping around in the dark, as they began their descent. "There should be a handrail. You know, in the Netherworld, they have regulations about that sort of thing."

"How long have you been here?" Hagatha asked him. "There aren't any fucking handrails. C'mon, let's go. Anyone have an idea how many steps we're talking about?"

"Nope," Brian said. "A lot. That's all I know."

"Let me have that," Dennis said and grabbed for Liz's flashlight. "I want to see." He managed to pop a button off her sweater; it plinked down the stone staircase for a very long time before the sound was swallowed by silence.

"Demons can see in the dark, asshole. You're a demon, remember?" Hagatha told Dennis. "Sounds like this staircase goes on forever. Great." She stomped down, her tail twitching dangerously behind her.

Sam let her move forward for a few seconds before following. "Have I mentioned that I hate my job?" he asked no one in particular.

Hagatha's voice bounced up from the staircase below. "Quit complaining and let's go get eaten like dummies. I figure that's how this will end. I was hoping to get back to the car so I could drink the Arachsinth on my way out. Whatever."

Liz followed Sam, and Brian brought up the rear.

"I feel like we're crawling into the ass of Hell," Dennis complained into Liz's ear. He had climbed onto her back and was holding her ponytail like a handle.

"Ouch! Dennis! Don't pull so hard!" Liz complained.

She was thankful for the flashlight. The going was slow and treacherous. Bits of the staircase had broken over eternity; there were dry pebbles lining some of the steps. Liz slipped once and Dennis yanked her ponytail hard. "Don't fall!"

Brian steadied her with his hand on her shoulder and they continued downwards. At some point, Liz started to lose track of her place in time, every step like every step before. Claustrophobia washed over her. It wasn't about the place; she was trapped in the moment. Only the dark stairs existed. Step, step, step. Down, down, down. Stumbling and having Dennis pull her hair were her only reminders of time, and she began to almost welcome them.

It came as a shock when she bumped into Sam, who'd stopped abruptly in front of her. Brian's hand tightened on her shoulder.

Dennis broke the spell. "Open the door!"

"Back up, everyone," Hagatha commanded.

They all retreated up the stairs and Hagatha fell backwards, tail coiling under her like a spring. She launched herself into the wooden door at the bottom of the stairs hooves-first, and it splintered into dust.

"I thought I smelled dry rot," Sam said.

Liz didn't want to move forward into the cavern, but Brian steered her gently from behind. The cave yawned in front of them. After drilling down the staircase like a worm into the earth, she suddenly felt very exposed. The emptiness stretched as far as she could see towards the ceiling above them until it was swallowed in darkness. There was a wall in front of them and a wall to their left. If Liz had to guess, she would have said that the distance to either of those walls was about twice the length of the Admin Office. But when she glanced to the right, it was the same as looking up. She could see for some distance towards that edge of the cavern, where the floor sloped away. Darkness yawned. Her stomach twisted. The tunnel to the Abyss.

The cave was quieter than she would have expected, their voices slightly muffled instead of echoing off the stone. Like Dennis in the lobby, she noticed a peculiar lack of smell. The only thing that stood out about the cave was the cold.

It had been getting chillier as they descended, but not uncomfortably so. Now she shivered.

Joe and Melchior were waiting for them. The two demons were sitting on an old couch that had been placed against the left side of the cave. Joe was wearing his trench coat, elegant green scarf wrapped around his neck, smoking a long, delicate cigarette. Melchior was leaning back on the couch, his eyes nearly closed. The couch tipped towards Melchior's end so that Joe had to cling to the opposite arm of the couch with his free hand.

Melchior rose when he saw them and the couch bumped down, bouncing Joe up and onto his feet in one sudden movement.

"Took you long enough," the minotaur bellowed. "We got here in no time flat."

"And it's a wonder we aren't flat ourselves," Joe remarked, dryly. "We had an interaction with a dragon annoyed out of a nap by the motorcycle. We narrowly missed being stomped."

"You're here, aren't you?" Melchior shrugged.

"Just. It's all lava under the bridge now. I guess we might as well get started, eh?" He tamped out the cigarette under his hoof.

"Do we have to?" Dennis whined. Liz tried to put him down. He clung to her until Brian peeled the little demon from her back and set him on the floor. He wormed around her legs and clung to her skirt.

Opposite the door, there was a large metal cabinet on the wall, half again as tall as Melchior and twice as wide. Inside was a variety of objects, old jars, and plastic totes.

"I would have thought the ritual room would be more . . . I don't know. Ornate? Ritualistic?" Sam offered.

Joe and Melchior laughed. "Satan doesn't waste money on anything he's not using himself," Joe said. "Or that no one is going to see."

"So, what happens now?" Sam asked. His hands were shaking.

"We start the ritual," Melchior said. "The night serpents show up; we talk. I'm the intermediary. I translate. You reassure them. We're gonna get the trains running; they should quit stomping around Hell leaving sinkholes as footprints. Do *not* mention the possibility that there may be fewer souls."

"Verbatim," Hagatha glared at Sam. "Got it? We want things back to normal."

"Of course." Sam shrank into his overcoat and shoved his hands in the pockets. Liz copied him, thrusting her hands deep into the pockets of her thick sweater. She was glad she was wearing her knit tights.

Melchior took a four-foot folding table out of the cabinet and handed it to Joe, who unfolded it, attempting to put the legs in place. It collapsed; Joe cursed, refolded it and unfolded it again several times before he got the legs to stabilize. He carried the table close to the boundary of darkness on the right side of the cave. Like someone lighting a fuse and scurrying away, he didn't linger long in that area.

"Kinda tacky, isn't it?" Liz whispered to Brian. "Maybe the night serpents feel disrespected."

"Here's the swamp frog venom," Melchior threw a green plastic bottle and a couple jars of multicolored powder to Joe, who set them on the folding table. Melchior then grabbed a stack of five-gallon metal buckets; Joe placed six of them just beyond the folding table.

Melchior took an enormous burlap bag of briquettes from the cabinet and poured them into the buckets. To these he added potions, small ritual objects and charms from a black trunk.

He then dragged a beat-up wooden podium to the front of the plastic table. The last item from the cabinet was a hidebound grimoire from a small trunk. The book struggled and flapped as he carried it to the podium, wrestled it in place, then strapped it down. He set up a mic. He gave his audience a thumbs up.

"All systems go," he bellowed.

Liz touched Brian's pinky with hers. Dennis's claws bit into her tights.

Melchior walked back to the cabinet and retrieved a long metal tube with a yellow plastic handle.

"What in Satan's name is that?" Dennis hissed.

"Hush, Dennis," Liz whispered. "I don't know."

It was a lighter. Melchior stopped at each bucket, leaned over, and lit the contents. For a moment, nothing happened. Then thick smoke, the consistency of whipped cream, foamed up from each of the buckets. Instead of rolling through the cavern, the smoke climbed straight up, layering on top of itself. The vapor rose until it formed a panel across the top of all the buckets, a thick oily screen.

"What's happening?" Brian asked Joe.

"This screen will allow the beings to manifest," he whispered. "You'll see images—presumably not their true forms—forms they wish us to see and interact with. And then Melchior will speak with them."

Sam shied away. Even Hagatha shifted backwards. "Should be any minute now." Joe fidgeted with his scarf, wrapping and re-wrapping it, lit another cigarette, and then stomped it out under his hoof. "Once the screen is up, Melchior will call them. If they wish to speak with us, they'll ring a bell."

As the smoke rose higher and higher, Melchior stood, arms folded, tapping his hoof on the cavern floor. He checked his watch a few times. At the right time, he poured powder and green liquid into a few of the buckets. Walking over to a tube in the wall, he bellowed into it in an octave so low, Liz could feel the ground of the cavern shaking beneath her feet.

Deep underground a bell answered, the sound reverberating through the cave until all of them were covering their ears. When the ringing ceased, Liz found that, like the others, she was moaning. Not from pain, from a yawning hopeless chasm in her soul. They looked at each other sheepishly as their lamentations ceased.

"That was too weird," Dennis said. He climbed straight up Liz's leg and settled on her hip like a toddler. She wrapped one arm around him. Brian pressed in on her other side.

The cold grew deeper. Goosebumps rose on Liz's arms. A wave of sorrow poured from the tunnel—threatening to drown her in pitiless grief. The sound of the bell had hollowed her out. Deep down, a spark of life desired existence, but she couldn't reach it.

Melchior bellowed into the tube again. Now it was numbingly cold. The enormous screen was midnight-dark. Darker shapes formed against it—or behind it? Shadows on shadow. Squinting hurt her eyes; she blinked.

One shape took form in the center, a twisting tube of darker darkness. Two other swirling funnel shapes appeared on either side. Melchior bellowed something into the speaking tube. They replied. When they "spoke," Liz felt as if sound and air were being extracted from the room. When she was a child, Liz had been unable to whistle unless she drew air in, instead of pushing it out. She had the impression that the *nihilidi* were doing something similar.

"I have reassured them that none of the souls that are here have come to be eaten," Melchior bellowed at the night worms again.

This time though when he heard their response, Melchior seemed confused. "I don't understand," he said. "You don't speak the language of Hell." He scooted the podium with the mic closer to the screen and turned it, so it was facing the creatures.

"They say they want to address you directly," he told the others. "I don't understand. But . . . here goes."

The creatures writhed on screen. A deep guttural noise bounced around the cave, similar to the suction noise they'd produced before. They twisted around each other, the middle creature larger than the others when they separated again. "Ummm . . . Hey. Hello?" The voice was deep, gargling, but it formed words they could hear. "Can everyone hear us okay? Hello?"

"Hello?" Liz whispered to Joe. "They want to say hello?"

He shook his head, obviously as confused as Melchior at this turn of events.

"You've learned the language of souls and demons?" Melchior inquired. "How is that possible?"

"Well," the middle figure said. "We think it's all the eating. Most likely."

Melchior glanced from the creatures to the mic. He even bent down and picked up the cable and stared at it as if it might be responsible for this odd turn of events.

"Oh, you don't really need that thing," the middle creature spoke.

"Certainly not," said the creature on its left.

"Not at all," said the *nihilidi* on the right. "We can hear you just fine. And we sense that you hear us clearly."

"I can't make heads or tails of this," Sam said. He was shivering so hard his teeth were clacking. "Can we please tell them what we've come to tell them and go somewhere with blankets and cocoa?"

The creatures writhed around each other for a moment and reformed. "We've eaten many souls. We have become. We have learned. We speak and hear and feel and tell jokes. That sort of thing."

"I learned a joke," the creature on the left said. "Shall I tell it?"

"Maybe not right now." Hagatha's tail was switching. "We have some things we really need to talk about."

"Oh." The creature seemed to deflate a little.

"There are holes opening in Hell," Melchior said. "Like the ones in the shadow fields. Are you going abroad, away from the Abyss? Are these holes your doing?"

The creatures hissed for a moment among themselves. The creature in the center of the screen spoke. "Sort of?"

The other two creatures at his side writhed in agreement. "A bit?" the one on the right said.

"Not how you think," said the creature on the left.

"Great," Hagatha stage-whispered at the others. "This is going great. Fantastic plan, guys."

"Why have you left the Abyss and the Shadow Fields?" Melchior asked them.

"Look," the middle one said. "I mean, we ate a lot of souls. And we're full. We quit."

"Totally," said the creature on the left.

"I think I'm actually bloated," said the creature on the right.

"Quitting?" Melchior asked them. "Then why are you making sinkholes all around Hell?"

The creatures wiggled, contorting themselves into a single sphere, then separating again.

"The thing is," the middle one said. "We're not *making* them. We're just not *not* making them."

"For sure," said the right one.

"Correctamundo," said the left one.

"If we don't *not* make sinkholes they appear," the middle creature said. "If we don't eat the burdens of souls, their sadness expands, creating gaps. But we are full. We can not *not* make holes. We can not *not* undo Hell anymore. Our penance is done. And our becoming has begun."

"Oh, a rhyme! Done and begun," said the one on the left. "Delightful."

"What the fuck? What penance? What is this not knotting that you're talking about?" Hagatha moved towards the creatures. Joe put out his arm and held her back. "This is total fucking nonsense." She stopped with her arms folded.

"We're here to tell you that we want you to quit making the holes," Melchior said. "Or, I guess, we want you to quit not *not* making the holes. Or something. The upshot is, we need Hell to continue existing. We live here. We've got someone here who wants to talk to you." Then he whispered at Sam, "Now!"

Hagatha pushed the small man forward.

"I'm from The Mountain Group," Sam said. His teeth chattered. "We're going to get the trains running again. Of course, it will be a rehab situation so there might be fewer—" Hagatha whipped her tail around him, wrapping the end around his mouth.

"Remain positive," she hissed, before letting him speak again.

"Like I was saying, there will still be souls to eat if that's what you're angry about."

The creatures moved in and out of each other. And then, they became three equal parts.

"Angry?" the middle creature exclaimed. "For goodness' sake, we're not angry." The shadows bumped up and down the screen for a moment. "We are full. We can eat no more. It was decreed we should consume souls and their despair until we learned and became. We have done so."

"Satiated," said the figure on the left. "Weary."

"We were made manifest by the Eldress of the Mountain. Do you know her, mountain man? The price for our existence was to eat souls.

We had to manifest a *where*—if you will—in order to do so," the middle shadow spoke.

"A *place*," said the creature on the right. "Not a *where*."

"Sorry," said the middle creature. "A place. We manifested Hell. We eat the burdens of souls before the burdens consume them. This was not desire. This was necessity. To become. The Eldress spoke this at our manifestation."

Hagatha shook Sam. "What is it saying? Who is the Eldress of The Mountain?"

"She's so far above my level that I don't even know anyone who reports to anyone who reports to anyone who reports to her. She's almost a myth." Sam tried to explain.

"We are tired and full. We have become," said the middle creature.

"Stuffed," said the creature on the right. "Now we must spend ten eons dreaming. It has been decreed."

A deep buzzing sound like air being expelled from a balloon rattled around the cave.

"Did one of them just fart?" Dennis whispered to Liz.

"Hush, Dennis."

The middle shadow writhed for a moment. "We must . . . "

A heavy silence fell, like the blanket of silence outside Liz's window at the hotel. For a moment, she thought that this was the end . . . her existence would stop at the end of an unfinished sentence.

But then the creatures finished with, "Nap. We must nap."

"What does that have to do with anything?" Hagatha piped up. "Take a fucking nap, then. Quit talking in riddles. We don't want to end up in the bottom of the Abyss being excreted into nothing because you guys over-ate and fell asleep."

"Satan's granny!" Dennis whined. "She's going to get us eaten for sure."

"We don't want to harm you," the *nihilidi* said. "We must sleep. We have fulfilled our purpose. Now we dream. All we have swallowed will be dreamt. From dream—manifestation. All will be manifest."

"Wait," Brian said. "Please, listen. We don't want to quit existing. If Hell crumbles into nothing, we'll go with it." Brian threw up his hands. "What will we do? What will become of us?"

The shadows paused to think. "We mean no harm. But while we sleep, we cannot *not* make holes."

They huddled, separated and then the left one said, brightly, "You should leave Hell."

"Yes," the one on the right agreed. "Best to leave now."

"Do we have time to do that?" Brian asked. "How are we going to get souls out if Hell is crumbling?"

"Satan knew our punishment was ending," the middle one said, "you should have left already. Eternity becomes time without us. Eternity sleeps with us."

"Well, Satan didn't mention it to *us*," Hagatha retorted. "Leaves us in a bit of a tight spot, don't you think?"

The creatures wriggled amongst themselves, thinking it through.

"We will give you thirteen days," the middle creature said. "Please leave during that time. We're very sleepy."

"Do you know how time works?" Brian asked. "We have a hell of a lot of souls and demons to get out of here."

Before he could finish, the central night worm said, "We have eaten the knowledge of time. We ate time before we ate souls. We understand time."

It yawned.

The left creature said, "And now it's *time* to sleep. Do you see what I did there?"

"Will we be able to evacuate *everyone*?" Brian demanded. "I need more to go on. Help us out here."

The shadows combined themselves for some time. The central shadow would stand out and, Liz felt, start to speak and then it would reform with the other shadows, picking their brains. At last, the central shadow said, "We will wrap a bubble of eternity around thirteen days. It will be thin." It paused.

"It's really going to be crappy," the creature on the right said. "We didn't know we needed to do it. I mean it's going to be totally last minute."

"We will do our best," the creature on the left said. "We are very tired."

"And bloated," the creature on the right reminded it. There was another sound of escaping air. "Excuse me."

The middle creature said, "It's really all we can do, guys." Another yawn.

Liz and the others waited for further instructions. After a few seconds, the middle creature said, "Ummm . . . maybe you guys should get started."

The pillars of smoke forming the screen collapsed suddenly. The group found themselves in the dark cavern blinking at each other in disbelief.

For a moment no one said anything. Finally, the minotaur huffed out a breath. "Fuckety."

"That's it, then," Brian said.

Liz rubbed her temples. "What was all that crap about time and eternity? I thought Hell was supposed to be forever. Thirteen days is nowhere near long enough to evacuate Hell."

"Only the Mountain is forever," Sam said. "Everything else is just eternity-adjacent. I don't know much about how these creatures formed

Hell. The Netherworld, for instance, was built on the Plains of Infinity. It's not so much eternal as simply . . . endless. I took a class on it to get my portals cert."

Hagatha switched her tail. "Does any of it mean anything? As far as I'm concerned, it's all hell-bat poop and balderdash. Hell is going down and we're going with it. That's the message in a blast nutshell."

TWENTY-NINE

An Unexpected Guest

SMOKIN' JOES WAS THE CLOSEST PLACE TO REGROUP, SO after they found the SUV, they headed back to the hotel. Melchior, who wouldn't fit in the SUV, followed on his motorcycle.

"I'm gonna end things driving around, drinking Arachsinth," Hagatha announced as she flopped into the passenger seat.

"The first thing you can do is drive some of us to Perdition City," Brian corrected. "Gadreel and Theo are going to drop us at the hotel, then drive out to the Lake of Fire to put them on alert. I suspect that the areas closest to the Abyss will start to crumble first."

"Why should I?" Hagatha asked. "What's in it for me other than wasting the last few days of existence I have left?"

"I'm not convinced that we aren't going to get out," Brian said. "While we're still here, there's still a chance. Besides, we need the best driver to get us back to Perdition City fast. That's you, isn't it?"

Hagatha turned on the radio without answering. She didn't say anything for a few minutes, just drummed her clawed fingers on the dash.

She turned to Brian. "I'm loading up on liquor in case I have to return to my original plan. I'll give this stupid idea a chance. I'm going to be anger-driving—just so you're prepared."

Liz groped around her purse for the bottle of elevator antidote. She'd be needing it.

On the return to the hotel, the trip down and back up the endless stone staircase and the emotional drama took their toll. Liz fell asleep, head on Brian's shoulder. Dennis curled against her, snoring. When they reached the parking lot of Smokin' Joe's, she woke abruptly when Brian jolted.

Dennis stretched and growled. "Be still, I'm sleeping," he said.

"Shit," Brian cursed. "Shit, shit, shit."

Liz rubbed her eyes and peered out the window. In the parking lot, a long, ruby red stretch limousine sprawled. Decorative yellow flames moved and flickered up and down the sides of the car as though it was on fire.

"The dimension jumper," Hagatha pointed at the car. "Only one in Hell. Maybe the universe. It's how they get back and forth from the Upper World."

"There goes what's left of our afterlife," Gadreel noted as they slid into a parking spot. He put the SUV in park and stared out the window at the elongated car.

Hagatha unbuckled herself but stayed in her seat. She let out a low whistle. "Lucifer's granny."

"Well, things just got worse," Joe sighed. "Wouldn't have thought that was possible. The big guy is here, and I can't say I feel like it's going to help anything."

"You and me both," Brian said.

"I thought he'd abandoned us for the Upper World." Liz was suddenly very awake. She shivered even though the hot wind blew bright sparks across the parking lot.

Brian rubbed his face with both hands. "We're screwed."

Melchior slid into the parking lot on his bike and waited while the passengers clambered out of the SUV.

Gadreel didn't even bother to get out. "Climb up in the passenger seat, Theo. We don't want any part of this conversation. We gotta put the area near the Abyss on alert." When everyone else piled out, Gadreel gave them a wave, rolled up his window, and beat it out of theparking lot.

When they reached the lobby, Bob was at the front desk rummaging through drawers, his tie askew and his suit jacket buttoned wrong. "Our towels aren't good enough for them. Dan's in the bar trying to serve them drinks. Do we have a key to open the vending machine? Satan and Mammon want Diet Cokes to go. They've already finished the soda from the fountain. I can't get the register open."

They heard *whoops* from the bar and someone yelping.

"Dan in there?" Joe asked. Bob nodded. Joe reached behind the desk, opened the cash register and dug out some quarters. "Get the Diet Cokes; leave them on the front desk. Make yourself scarce otherwise."

They walked into the bar where Dan was trying to pour beer from a tap with one hand and slap flames from the back of his jeans with the other.

A short, sleek man with dark hair and hard, dark eyes was sitting at the bar. He was wearing a short-sleeved black shirt and tight dark-wash jeans. He was slender and well-muscled. He snickered as Dan ran around slapping his jeans. "That will teach you to move faster," he said.

Next to the short man was a tall, beefy, broad-shouldered man with a crewcut, in a black t-shirt that said "Born to Raise Hell" on the back, a studded leather belt, and elaborate cowboy boots. A black cowboy hat sat on the bar in front of him. He had a power lifter's build—all thick muscles and ropey veins. A guy who enjoyed bar fights because he didn't lose them.

The short man pointed his finger at Dan's feet; fire shot from it. Dan hopped up and down. The big man guffawed. "That's funny, Luc. Do it again!"

"Don't be such a toddler, Bubba," Luc said. "Let the man put out the flames before I hit him again. He's the only one who can serve us right now."

"Afternoon, Luc," Joe addressed the short man. "In human form, I see. Ashamed of your horns? So nice to see you again."

"Too bad I can't say the same for you," Luc returned. Bubba laughed again. He apparently liked Luc's joke so well he slapped the smaller man's back, sending him forward and causing his drink to spill.

"Geeze, Bubba," Luc said. "It wasn't even that funny. Settle down, would you? You made me spill my beer and now this nice gentleman is going to have to get me another one or get his pants flamed again." Liz had often heard Brian talk about Lucifer and Beelzebub, had sometimes even heard them yelling over the phone, but she'd had no reference for what they looked like up until now. She was not reassured.

In the back booth, where Hagatha had drunk with Dan and Bob the last time they were there, sat a tall man, quite handsome, slim and elegant, a wave of honey blond hair brushed back from his face. He wore a sleek black suit, a red and blue paisley scarf wrapped around his neck, tied in a knot that suggested he'd worked very hard to make it appear "carefree."

"Do come in, my ragtag band of heroes. Off trying to save Hell, were you?" He sat next to a platinum blond woman with the most precisely edged bob Liz had ever seen. She wore a white skirt-suit, her slim legs ended in extremely tall white stiletto pumps and her too-perfect lips were very, very red. Every feature of her body—from her legs to her silky hair to her bee-stung lips—looked like she'd chosen them by flipping through a Vogue magazine. Satan tried to put his arm around the woman as he spoke. She brushed him off. She had a sheet from the hotel draped across the seat behind her. It appeared yellow next to her immaculate suit.

"Darling, these seats are disgusting, and you've been touching them. You'll dirty my suit," she frowned lightly at Satan, then deeply at the group gathered in front of her.

"You said you hated that suit; you said you wanted a new one. For Hell's sake you had the designer tortured," Satan folded his arms and pouted.

"It's the suit I'm wearing right now though, isn't it, darling?" she asked softly. She booped his nose lightly. "Behave."

She turned to the group. "So, you've heard the bad news I take it? We decided to come early. And leave early." Her scarlet lips parted in a cool smile. "As you might imagine under the circumstances."

"Nice to see you too, Em," Melchior stamped his hoof. A small stream of smoke plumed from his nostrils.

"Only her friends call her that," Satan hissed, standing up and sliding out of the booth. "And you proved a time long ago that you didn't fall in that category." He thrust his shoulders forward and balled his fists.

Mammon stood up and slid next to him. She made a noise that Liz could only think of as a purr, and lightly touched her red nails to Satan's suit. "Calm down, love. You need to save your energy for me. I'm going to need a drink and a little something else after we get back to Vegas. After all, these people have important things on their minds," She allowed her eyes to rake up and down the length of Satan's body. "Maybe we can get that chubby show girl you're so enamored with to come up to the room."

Satan glared at Mammon. "She's muscular. Not chubby."

"Have it your way, love. It's all the same to me if you like them buxom. I can make sacrifices."

"Gross," Hagatha gagged. "I need eye bleach for my brain."

Mammon smirked. "You won't need anything soon, Possum. At least not here in Hell. Maybe you can ask shorty there if his company is going to give demons refugee status too. If you can even get everyone out in time."

"You knew Hell was closing down?" Brian asked. "And decided not to mention it? Why are you here?"

"Would you believe just to say goodbye?" Satan smiled. He dropped his defensive posture and strutted over to the bar. "We haven't known long. Just longer than you."

"I thought you might be here to help with the evacuation." Brian stared at Satan over the top of his glasses, the muscles in his jaw working.

Mammon pursed her lips and made a sympathetic clicking sound. Satan and Luc laughed; Bubba joined when he realized the others were laughing.

"It was mostly to get the last three bottles of Old Krampus Bourbon in the known universe," Satan responded. "We had a little business to take care of in Perdition City, so I figured I'd come out and pick up the bourbon. One of the few things I'll miss about Hell. Probably the only thing."

He looked sad for a second, then perked up. "Actually, I won't miss it because I'm taking it with me. Anyway, I feel confident that you and the squirt there," he nodded towards Sam, "can handle the evacuation."

"You're not staying to help?" Sam asked. "I think The Mountain Group would expect more from—"

Satan cut him off with the wave of a hand. "I'm starting a new job as a hedge fund manager tomorrow, and there's nothing in the contract that says I have to give notice."

"The contract states explicitly that you do!" Sam gasped, obviously shocked at this flagrant violation of rules.

"We're also introducing our own cryptocurrency," Mammon added. "So, we don't have time for any of this drivel." She dismissively waved her hand around the room, taking in the assembled demons, Liz, and Sam. "Regardless of the contract."

"For pity's sake," Sam addressed Satan, "you're not an employee. You're the founder of a nonprofit entity responsible for a massive quantity of souls. Soul essence is one of the most precious substances in the universe. You certainly can't just quit on a dime. Even giving two weeks' notice would be unacceptable! I mean according to the contract—"

"You're boring me, squirt. And I'm not giving two weeks. I'm barely giving two minutes. I'm having a shot of vodka, then I'm leaving,'" Satan walked to the bar and slapped his hand on the counter. "Barkeep, shot of that Gray Goblin Vodka from the top shelf. Then we need to be on our way."

"Indeed, we do," Mammon said. "I have a hair appointment. And then an afternoon of relaxation in the penthouse." She slapped Satan's butt playfully. "These trips are so wearing. A gimlet, barkeeper." She nodded at Dan. "Gray Goblin if that's the best you have."

Dan hurriedly climbed the bar ladder to get the vodka, nervously glancing around.

"Wait a minute. You've already been to Perdition City?" Brian said. "What kind of business did you take care of?"

"Odds and ends," Satan smiled. "Odds and ends."

Luc laughed. "Barkeep! Fill her up!" He tapped his beer mug and Bubba pounded his mug on the counter too. Dan poured a shot for Satan, mixed the gimlet, and then scurried around to pour the beer.

"Odds and ends?" Brian persisted. He ran his hands through his hair and pushed his glasses back up his nose.

Liz was frankly glad Satan was leaving. It was obvious he would be more of a hindrance than a help, but she could see Brian was worried about his boss's "business."

"Are you questioning me?" Satan's brows knitted together. A gentle cloud of steam rose from his head. He flushed red. "You're ruining my complexion. You know you can't upset me." His hand gripped the shot glass as if considering throwing it. Without thinking, Liz stepped in front of Brian, who placed his hands protectively on her shoulders.

"You know the dude hates to be questioned," Luc swigged his beer.

"Yeah," Bubba said. "Hates it." He drained his glass, slammed it on the table and pointed at it. Dan quickly refilled it.

"Well, well, well," Satan smiled at Liz. "I see you've been dilly-dallying with the souls, Brian my boy." He shook his head. "I wouldn't think you had it in you. I certainly didn't add that to the mix when I made you. Have you been experimenting on yourself?" He looked from Liz to Brian and back again. "I could feed you both to a bog eel and wait to see what came out the other end, but you know, I don't have that kind of time. Maybe I could just run over you both in the parking lot." He pointed to his shot glass again. Dan refilled it.

Mammon put her hand on Satan's arm but addressed Brian, "Please don't play with the piranha, Brian. Neither you nor your little sweetheart are cut out to handle it. He's had a rough day. We just needed some paperwork from the office safe. That's all. For hell's sake, you of all people should know not to question him. And fraternizing with the souls." She shook her finger lightly at Brian. "Naughty."

"It makes me so angry when they question me," Satan complained. He emptied his shot glass again. "I wouldn't care about the sex. However, it reduces productivity, and I didn't give permission." For a moment he said nothing, his face slowly turning purple. He tapped his foot on the barroom floor as he contemplated what to do. Mammon stroked his arm lightly with her finger and made clucking sounds.

"We really do have to get going, sweetie," she said.

Satan didn't respond for a moment. He kept his hand wrapped around the shot glass. At last, he said, "Well, you won't be having sexy time with the souls much longer. I'd love to stick around and see how this all plays out. Just wait and see what happens when . . . "

Mammon patted his sleeve. "Darling, we've talked about this. We need to be on our way."

Satan narrowed his eyes at Brian. "Fine. Let The Mountain Group take all the souls . . . and the demons that I personally made . . . and then there's you. A creature patched together from angst and spare parts, specially to manage Hell. Remember, you have certain "ingredients" that none of the others have. We've been over that, right?"

Liz felt Brian's hand grip hers so tightly that it hurt. His face went pale. He didn't utter a word.

"If I were you, I'd take your little girlfriend and get a room and get in all the shagging you can while you still exist, instead of worrying so much about everyone else." Satan tilted his head like a puzzled dog, staring at Brian. "You know how this is going to go down, surely. But if The Mountain Group ever catches up with me, it will help my case if you save some of them. You do you. C'mon, guys." He swept his shot glass from the bar onto the floor and the shards scattered across the tile.

"So, we're just fucked, and you couldn't give a hoot?" Hagatha's tail was switching.

"Now, now," Mammon said. "Who knows what might happen? You *might* make it out. At any rate, I'm certainly not going to worry about it."

"You don't have to," Hagatha said. "You're leaving. Remember?"

"Oh yes. I forgot," Mammon smiled. "That does put another spin on it."

"Now wait just a minute," Sam said. "You have an obligation to the souls and to all these demons you created as well. You must understand that the spare parts you used were from one of The Mountain Group's warehouses—illegally sourced according to our records—and therefore they were made with the byproducts of soul essence. In fact, these by-products in themselves are now protected under the Phanerozoic Soul Conservation Act that was passed at the very beginning of this eon. My boss says, you're required by law to work with us to help get everyone out of here safely if possible. When The Mountain Group finds out about this dereliction of duty, I'm sure they'll start legal proceedings. They *will* expect to be paid back; there will be civil and criminal charges. However, if you stay here and try to help us with the evacuations, they may go easier on you." Sam stopped, out of breath.

Satan stared at Sam as though he was contemplating a toad that had just started discussing its life insurance policy. Mammon was clearly amused. Even Melchior and Joe shook their heads at his speech. Sam obviously didn't know who he was dealing with.

"Good try little guy," Hagatha didn't sound hopeful. "I mean, I admire your gumption. Totally pointless. Good try, though."

Dennis climbed onto Liz's shoulder. "If we're depending on that guy, we're truly fucked," he whispered.

Satan chuckled. "The Mountain Group lost control of the Upper World a long time ago. Good luck extraditing us. I've set up my headquarters in Vegas and I'm planning to dominate the place. The whole Upper World will be mine sooner or later. Secondly, no one will know anything about it. Because I doubt that—" He stopped abruptly as Mammon shushed him. "Whatever. Besides, Mammon had our lawyer call your boss to see what The Mountain Group has on us." Satan put his arm around Mammon.

She brushed him away lightly, saying, "Darling, my suit," as she patted his arm in consolation. "Your boss let the cat out of the bag," she said sweetly. "It turns out that you've been a little lax in checking up on our operation. High caseload, not enough staff. Government work is so trying, isn't it? So even if they could extradite us, which seems quite unlikely, they've been in violation of various clauses of the contract themselves. It may not be much, but it should keep the whole thing tied up in court for eons."

Liz felt Brian's hand tighten on hers.

"What are you saying?" Sam asked.

"I'm saying that I don't think we need to be worried about *our* future," Mammon replied.

Luc raised his glass and sucked down the remainder of his beer. "And we certainly aren't worried about yours."

"Of course, you shouldn't be anxious on our behalf! You have enough hassle, what with the evacuations and all," Mammon smiled sweetly. "I would say *au revoir*, but I'm pretty sure we'll never see you again."

She linked her arm through Satan's, and they turned to walk out of the bar followed by Luc and Bubba, who slammed down the rest of his beer and sent his glass spinning across the bar just as Satan had done. He giggled gleefully when it broke.

As they reached the door, Satan turned to Mammon. "Can I tell them one thing, though? You know what I mean."

Mammon rolled her eyes. "If you must."

Satan grinned. "One of the best parts of this whole thing is the joke we played on some of the souls."

"What's that?" Brian asked.

"Recently, we bribed two of the ticket agents at Netherworld station to change some of the tickets, hoping that souls who expected to be in Heaven might despair when they got here and cast themselves into the Abyss. While the percentages weren't what they could be, it kept those horrible worms off our backs for a bit." Satan nodded at Liz. "I just thought you might be consoled by the knowledge that you were most likely never meant to be here in the first place." He smirked, and the group turned and left.

Liz gasped. "What a fucking asshole." They heard the hotel doors slam shut and glass breaking. She somehow knew that Bubba had kicked them in without even seeing it happen.

"I knew it. I knew a person like you didn't belong here." Brian released her hand, stumbled to the back of the room and collapsed in the booth. "I'm sorry, Liz. I'm so, so sorry."

Liz scooted in next to him. Tears brimmed in his eyes. His large hand covered hers on the tabletop.

"Of course, you didn't know." She forgot her fear for a moment. "It wasn't your fault." She wondered who else hadn't been meant to end up here. The universe, the whole thing had been a cheat all along. Assholes could not only ruin your life, they could ruin your afterlife. What was the fucking point? She rubbed the top of Brian's hand, unsure who should be comforting whom.

Joe slid into the booth across from them. "I realize your world is coming apart and whatnot," he said. But we don't have time for self-pity right now." Despite his words, his voice was kind.

"What's the point of any of it," Liz gasped, feeling the sobs start to bubble. "If they can do this to us . . . forever?" Maybe being nothing *was* the best way out.

"I don't know," Joe said. "At least you're still asking the question. Maybe if we get out of here, we can figure out the answer. If we don't, we'll never find out."

Hagatha punched the nearest table. "We don't have time for you to contemplate the meaning of life, the universe and everything right now, Liz. I for one am going to try to get out of here now—just to piss off Satan, if nothing else."

Liz felt a sharp pain in her leg. "Ouch!" she said.

Dennis crawled out from under the table. "You can't give up. We need to get out of here and I need someone to give me tuna on the train. I'm afraid to go by myself. You have to quit being selfish." He bit her hand as he crawled into her lap.

"They're right. I have to get you out of here," Brian said. "Time to go." He squeezed Liz's hand and gave her a weak smile.

"Gross," Hagatha rolled her eyes. "You two are disgusting."

Joe smiled at Liz. Dennis was sitting in her lap, nervously washing his ear with his paw. Hagatha glaring, and maybe a little concerned. Melchior handed her a shot of Gray Goblin and Sam handed her a cocktail napkin. Brian's warm sweater brushed against her arm.

Liz stood up, feeling like a general addressing an army dwarfed by the opposition. "Well, in that case, we'd better get back to Perdition City and see what we can do."

THIRTY

The Beginning of the End

JOE SLID INTO THE BACKSEAT OF THE CAR NEXT TO LIZ, while Sam sat on the other side of her. There was no way Brian would fit in the back of the car the way he had in the SUV, so he was riding shotgun alongside Hagatha.

"Sorry to crowd you guys," Joe said. "I couldn't face another trip on the Hell Cycle. I'd like to make it to annihilation day intact. So, Sam, how will your bosses handle what has unfortunately become the worst-case scenario?"

"I requested refugee status for everyone, including the demons, who should gain status under the Phanerozoic Conservation Act. I'll call my boss as soon as we get back to Perdition City, make sure we're approved, ask for personnel. TMG will start negotiating with the Netherworld about accepting refugees and how to take care of them." Sam's confident words wobbled with nerves.

"Doesn't matter to me," Dennis popped his head out from under the quilt on Liz's lap. "I'm going to fight and scratch my way to the Netherworld with as much tuna as I can carry and hope for the best. And when I get there, they'll never catch me to send me back." He made kung fu motions with his paws and crawled back under the quilt.

For a few miles, Hagatha didn't say anything. "What a fucking waste of time!" she exploded—with irritation that had evidently been building for a while. "Satan and crew, I mean. Why even bother to show up?"

"Old Krampus Bourbon is good, but not that good." Brian stared out the window as they passed the fireflower fields. "When did they find out and why did they come *here*? Did they understand right from the start that the *nihilidi* weren't eating souls because they *liked* them?"

"Maybe that story about the medium in the Upper World was right," Joe said. "Maybe the *nihilidi* contacted him through the psychic?"

"It doesn't matter now," Brian sighed. "We just have to get back to Perdition City and worry about getting you all out."

"Maybe you could even spare a few seconds of worry about getting yourself out of here," Liz reached forward and patted him on the hand.

"Ow, you're crushing me," Dennis muttered from under the quilt, and scratched her arm.

When they got back to the office, it was late; souls in the complaint line had already been sprayed with tranquilizers. They lay in piles on the floor, unconscious. In fact, souls stretched out snoozing on each other for blocks before they arrived at the Admin Building.

"Must have been a lot of souls acting like hellions for them to spray tranqs this far down the line," Hagatha remarked.

When they walked into the lobby, the demons on nighttime security detail had pulled out some folding chairs and were sitting in a corner playing cards.

"Lazy assholes," the demoness sneered as they walked into the lobby. She went to the registration desk, dug around underneath until she came up with some Hell Coin. The demons often shook souls in line until coins fell from their pockets; these were then used for the vending machines.

Liz and Hagatha went to buy snacks; Sam went into the office to call his boss, Brian in tow. The rest of the crew headed for the break room where Ellie had promised there was coffee. Liz got Bat Bite crackers—tiny peppery black crackers that wriggled a little when you ate them—a Spurt Soda, and a bag of rat tails for Dennis. Hagatha wanted the last bag of dried Skink Livers, but it clung stubbornly to the spiral arm that held it in the machine. The demoness was in the middle of tipping the machine upside down when Brian came out of the office.

"Liz," he said, "Hagatha! Can you guys come in here for a second?" His voice was oddly strangled.

Liz left Dennis happily munching his rat tails and followed Brian. Inside the office, Sam was sitting in Brian's chair appearing forlorn, chin in his hands.

"What's up with the squirt?" Hagatha said as she ripped open the bag of Skink Livers with her teeth.

"The call won't go through," Brian answered.

"Why not?" Liz felt a sense of growing dread in her stomach.

"The line out isn't working," Brian said. "I think Satan destroyed our communications systems. We can dial inside Hell. Calls out have been blocked."

Sam shook his head. "The logistics meeting I was supposed to have with my boss isn't going to happen. We needed to plan. We needed permission! Do you have any *idea* how many souls will be disembarking the train in the Netherworld? And demons? That aren't even officially included yet? We need funds and camps. We can load the train with everyone who wants to leave Hell and head back . . . to what? I don't know the answer. And I have no way to find out." He shivered in his coat.

Brian opened the door to the inner office where he'd retrieved the Black Hole credit card. The safe was open and empty, lying on its side. On the ground next to it was an envelope. Brian picked it up, squinted at the handwriting, and opened it. He took out the handwritten note and read through it, then immediately stuffed it in his sweater pocket.

"What's that?" Liz asked. "From Satan?"

Brian's hand went to the pocket. "Yes. Not very helpful. More or less a final insult."

Liz bit her lip. "He's such a jerk."

"Yeah, quite the asshole. Oh well, it's not like I didn't expect it." He stared above Liz's head at the skull phone for a moment.

"You okay?" Liz asked.

"Yeah, dude. Wake up!" Hagatha snapped her fingers at him. "No time for daydreaming."

He took a long, deep breath, then gave Liz a quick hug. "I'll feel a lot better when I get you out of here."

She hugged him back. "When *we* get out of here."

"Eww," Hagatha winced. "Stop."

Ellie, Joe, and Melchior walked in, laden with coffees. Ellie handed one to Brian, Joe handed one to Sam. "Gla'ap went back to the hotel to get some rest before the evacuation," she said. "What's up with you guys? It's like you died and went to Hell."

She looked into the back office and saw the empty safe. "Oh, that? Doesn't matter," she said. "I have copies. Sam and I are taking them on the train. Just in case The Mountain Group ever decides to pursue legal proceedings. Is he that stupid? Does he think we don't have copies?"

"It's not that he's stupid, he's a narcissist," Brian said. "He just plows through the afterlife doing whatever he wants and so far, he seems to have gotten away with it. He'll just declare the copies fake and get some vampire lawyer to spend eons contesting them in court before the real trial even starts. Besides, I would bet that there were a lot worse things in that safe. I get the feeling he's got stuff on entities from the Netherworld to halfway up the Mountain. It was the blackmail he was after." His hand went to his pocket again. He was touching the note inside. "He has a lot of power over a lot of creatures—souls, people, demons, gods, demi-gods."

"Let's talk about practical stuff, When do we start evacuations? How did Sam's call go?" Joe interrupted Brian's ruminations on Satan.

"The line out has been disabled," Brian said. "Sam can't get in touch with his boss."

"Is there any chance we can fix it?" Ellie's eyes were wide.

Joe let out a whistle and shook his head. "If there's one thing Satan knows how to do it's destroy things. After lying, it's his biggest talent. I'd guess fixing it is out of the question." He sat on Brian's desk and stared glumly into his murky coffee.

"I'll have someone try, anyway," Brian said. "Melchior, I think Jezreel is on night shift. Grab him and see what you two can do on that front. Maybe we can get the lines working again. The rest of us start evacuating, loading the train. There's not much else we *can* do."

"Since the line over the chasm was apparently destroyed at some point," Sam said. "The only thing we can do is get everyone back through the tunnel to the Netherworld."

"How can we fit all the souls on one train?" Liz leaned down to pick up Dennis, who had wandered in with a now-empty bag of rat tails.

"The train is equipped with an *almost* infinite capacitator," Brian explained. "That's how it can carry so many souls into Hell every day. Hell is much easier to administrate if we deal with the infinite as a series of weeks, days, years. That said, the train should theoretically be able to carry at least as many souls out as it's carried in, even in one 'day.'"

"You'll have demons too," Hagatha pointed out. "There's lots of us."

"We may be pushing our limits," Brian shrugged. "The thing is, I'm not sure how we round everyone up in thirteen days. Finding everyone and getting them on the train is the difficult part. Then there's the puzzle of what happens when we get to the Netherworld. I don't know." Brian leaned back against the wall and sighed. He lifted the shade at the complaint window, surveyed the sleeping crowd. There were so many, even in the lobby.

"Well," Liz said, "there's not much we *can* do except start putting souls on the train and hope for the best, is there?"

"What if we just put *us* on the train. I mean if we can't get everyone on the train, we can't." Dennis shook his empty bag at Liz. "Can I have more Hell Coin? I'm still hungry."

Hagatha ran her fingers along her whiskers. "The little doofus has a point."

Sam spluttered, "But the contract. It says—"

"Unholy fucking bat poop! Who cares about the contract?!" Hagatha said. "The contract is worthless at this point. Especially because I bet it says nothing about demons in the first place. I don't give fuck all about your contract."

"Has anyone noticed how slowly this day is going?" Joe gazed at the clock. "It's the same day as the day we talked to the creatures. You drove to the Abyss; you walked down those infernal stairs, which took a day in itself. We talked to the creatures, then we returned to the hotel and talked with Satan, then we drove back here, and the day's still not done."

"Yeah," Ellie said. "This afternoon has seemed eternal. We processed so many more souls today than I've ever seen."

"So what?" Hagatha growled. "All the days around here are super fucking long. Except for the weekend. I've heard rumors that Satan speeds up the clock on weekends."

"Maybe that's what they meant about the bubble of eternity!" Joe said. "They're stretching the days we have left. Maybe we *can* pull this thing off."

"It'd still be easier to just get on the train and say forget it." Hagatha's tail lashed.

"We're not going to do that," Brian said. "My job is to take care of the souls and that's what I'm going to do."

"We really don't know how long we have—just that we have longer than we thought," Joe pointed out.

"Let's quit talking about it and get started," Ellie raised her voice. "I'll make some more coffee. I brought some Ghoulios and Little Devil cakes. Once everybody gets some sugar and caffeine in their systems, this will seem doable."

"We have lists of every neighborhood in the housing records," Liz said. "We can start sending out the word for people to come and get on the train. Maybe if these days stretch long enough, we can get everyone out."

"Fine," Hagatha snorted. "However. If we don't have everyone on the train when that clock speeds up, all bets are off."

Sam stood up. "We still don't know what will happen when we get there. Do you think I can approve dropping the entire population of Hell at the Netherworld station in a single trainload? I mean, I thought my career was going nowhere before, but now I'm going to be the guy who oversaw the worst refugee crisis in the history of the afterlife?" He wrapped his arms around himself and hunched his shoulders, swaying back and forth. "I must make this phone call. It must be documented, or—"

"Or you'll get a demerit?" Ellie asked. "I taught school for years, and I can tell you it's far better to ask for forgiveness than permission. We don't have a choice. Drink your coffee, grab a snack, and get hold of yourself."

Sam continued rocking himself. "All I ever wanted was a nice little job in an office. All I got was a cubicle, a dead fern and too much work. So much work. I'm going to be responsible for dumping—I don't know—billions of souls into the Netherworld? I don't. I can't . . . " He was unraveling, fast.

Hagatha's tail shot out from the other side of the office and wrapped around him. Yanking him across the room, she lifted him to eye level. "You *can* help oversee this debacle and you will. I do not give the slightest shit about your career and neither do these other fine demons. This may not be your fault exactly, but you're in charge; you are going to pull yourself together and do it. You're going to help us load the train. You're going to get on the train. You're going to lie your ass off or be charming or whatever it takes when we get to the Netherworld Station. We're going. The souls are going. The difference between hero and zero is self-confidence. It's entirely up to you." She set him down and searched for Ellie. "Now where in the hell is this coffee I keep hearing about?"

Brian pulled out his notebook. "My sentiments exactly. Let's make a list."

The hated database allowed them to organize the exodus, at least to a certain extent. Hell was to be evacuated region by region, neighborhood by neighborhood. Gadreel and Theo had returned from the Lake of Fire region, where they confirmed new sinkholes were opening, and old sinkholes expanding. Hell was beginning to crumble.

Strangely, demons—created to expect the worst—seemed to thrive as the crisis heated up. Hagatha told them, "Expect this to go badly and maybe it will be better than you think."

While Liz and Ellie organized evacuees from Perdition City, Hagatha and Gadreel supervised a team of demons to spread the word in farther reaches. Demons who could fly or had access to transportation were sent out to announce the evacuation and report back as areas were cleared. Joe organized demons to call every transportation company in Hell to make sure every area was served. Sam kept track of the number of souls and demons, their needs and as much information as he could gather about who was being evacuated. They would need the information on the other side. Gla'ap rallied her staff to help provide necessities at the train station. Theo and the station staff loaded the train. Souls that could help were assigned jobs; elderly, weak, or injured souls were loaded onto the train first. Demons without practical skills, like the academics from Ellie's school were also loaded onto the train—mostly to get them out of the way.

The first group of souls to be moved to the train station were the souls from the complaint line. Hagatha's advice about lowered expectations came in handy. First, they realized that the souls would have to be given a stimulant to wake them up. This was unexpected and confusing. They all shuffled uneasily back into the line formation, staring out at the still dark sky, murmuring amongst themselves.

At the outset, Brian tried to stay positive. He entered the lobby, tried getting the crowd's attention. One of the gargoyles flew overhead and shouted down, "Shut the fuck up or you're out of the line!"

The line simmered to a low boil. "I need everyone to remain calm," Brian said. "We are closing down the line because we're all going to the train station." He smiled, trying to alleviate any concern. This did not work.

There was a collective gasp, followed by boos and hisses. Someone threw a shoe. The gargoyle flew over and kicked a soul on the head. "I said shut up!" it shrieked.

"I need the person in the very front of the line to follow our security succubus. Everyone follow right behind the person in front of them." Brian waved towards the security succubus.

As always, some souls were compliant and began shuffling around to get in line as requested. A good number of souls immediately began complaining and cursing.

"Why?" yelled a soul with bushy hair and a beard. "I won't go anywhere if you don't tell me why."

A soul in a torn t-shirt, combat boots, and jeans yelled, "Don't go! They're trying to send us to the Abyss," then turned and ran for the lobby doors, accidentally kicking another soul on his way out.

The soul who had been kicked, kicked back, hit another soul, causing a chain reaction. Pandemonium reigned. Some souls attempted to comply but couldn't find the line in the confusion. Some souls kicked, bit their neighbors, or shrieked while a few tried to escape as security battled them.

Hagatha, who had been in the office giving orders to the demons she'd chosen for her team, walked into the lobby. Her tail whipped; her teeth showed. "Enough," she barked out.

Silence fell. Everyone in line knew Hagatha. Even if they hadn't been in the lobby yet. Hagatha made it a point to walk down the line outside the Admin Building "introducing" herself on her way back to the demon dorms each night and quite a few belligerent souls had already tasted her wrath.

"Hell is fucking closing. You either get on the train or you fall into the Abyss. I don't have time to explain. I don't give a shit if you believe me or understand. You're going to get in line and follow that succubus right over there—raise your hand, Eileen. You'll follow her right to the station where you will either be given a job to do before the train leaves or be seated. I do not give a flying rat's ass how you feel about it. If you want to go to your next stop in the afterlife without some of your appendages, come at me." The souls stared at her. The soul standing in front of the complaint window with sticky frogs clinging to its long hair turned and followed Eileen. The rest of the line trailed behind her.

Hagatha yelled at the detail assigned to move the line, "Go outside. Follow them to the station." She turned to Brian. "Once you get souls moving in a line, they'll follow the one in front of them. Souls, man. Pathetic." She shook her head.

Liz was printing lists of names, neighborhood by neighborhood to check off at the train station when Melchior and Jezreel returned.

"Bad news," the minotaur boomed. "The interconnection comms facility to the Netherworld and Upper World is done for, lines melted, equipment smashed beyond recognition."

"Luc and Bubba, I bet," Jezreel said. "Assholes."

Brian shook his head. "I guess we're winging it."

Liz saw his hand go back to the letter in his sweater pocket. She hadn't had a moment to ask him about the letter or its contents. She couldn't help wondering why he would keep the memento, if it was, as he had termed it, the final insult from Satan. She wanted desperately to get him alone to ask him about it.

Evacuees began to pour into Perdition City. The capacitor on the train being only *nearly* infinite, inhabitants of Hell were to bring absolutely nothing with them. Before putting them on the train, the demons shook souls whose pockets were filled with Hell Coin, trying to convince them that it would be worthless where they were going. Some souls had bags of takeout from the diner or foods that would spoil. This was taken from them before they boarded the train, although they were allowed to have it at the station. Canned food and preserved food was confiscated. It would be loaded onto the train—if there was room—so the refugees would have something to eat when they arrived in the Netherworld. Although the demons still harassed souls and occasionally took their food, they also often encouraged the souls to eat it themselves.

Liz noticed a strange camaraderie sprouting. Demons began whisper campaigns about what a jerk Satan was. They had new respect for Brian, who won them passage on the train. Some were initially suspicious, but when they saw fellow demons boarding, were reassured. All the demons who knew Hagatha were certain she'd never let souls on the train if she wasn't going herself. Bit by bit, they talked themselves into supporting the mission.

At first the days stretched so that it seemed they'd never end. Liz was surprised that every time she checked the clock the minute hand and second hand were in the same place. They really were in some strange bubble of eternity. But as each day passed, time sped up a little. She and Brian worked frantically. He wanted to make sure that every soul had an opportunity to leave Hell. They had bare seconds alone. When she caught his eye, he smiled at her. When their hands touched over paperwork, he sometimes gripped her fingers for a second. Occasionally, she cleared her throat and started to ask him about the letter. Inevitably, someone would barge in or there would be a fire to put out.

When she worried over how exhausted he appeared he would repeat, "Getting you out of here makes all this worth it." Sometimes as she worked, she was enveloped by a quick, sweatered hug, and a kiss on the top of the head. These moments made it possible for her to continue the breakneck pace.

A few souls flatly refused to go. Sam said that was the nature of souls. They could not be forced to get on the train. Liz worried about her Aunt Delores and all the souls in "Heaven." Melchior had told them to travel to the nearest bus station, but he had not heard from any of them since and no one had seen them arrive at the train station.

"Of course, it's so busy that they could already be on the train," Joe reassured Liz and Melchior. "You never know."

Bob and Dan had driven Joe's car to the city, which had taken some time as Joe's car did not have a Frenzy Drive or NOS. Once they arrived, they both worked at the station on Theo's team. In their own quiet way, they helped feed and seat passengers, rumpled and hungover the entire time. When the mall and its employees evacuated, the clerk from Nether Leather showed up at the station while Hagatha was there discussing the evacuations with one of her team members.

The clerk walked up to Hagatha and smiled, "Recognize this lipstick? You bought it for me."

Hagatha's tail switched. She grinned. "I have good taste."

"The leather jacket is great on you," the clerk said as she flipped her hair and looked up at Hagatha.

"Save me a seat on the train," Hagatha said.

"I'm not getting on yet. I'm here to help," the clerk told her. "And my name is Brendle."

"Well, Brendle. I think I can figure out how to put you to work," Hagatha said. "Maybe the rest of my eternity won't be quite as sucky as I think."

"I expect it won't," Brendle smiled.

Loading the train was a trial in itself. Souls tried carrying on suitcases full of shoes, clothing, bags of dirty laundry. One strange bug-eyed man had a collection of bones and limbs he'd picked up on the street. He sobbed when the demons found the last small, detached and gangrenous toe in his pocket, but they stuffed him on the train anyway, toeless. Souls tried to take books, desk lamps, rolled up string, used tape, old, stained rugs. Loading each car left a huge pile of garbage on the platform, which the Erratus had to move before they could load another.

The worst part of it, Liz thought, was not knowing how long they had. The bubble of eternity encasing Hell was wearing thin. Time pressed against them; they grew steadily more exhausted, chests tight, legs like jelly. Liz was so tired that the thought of eternal nonexistence started to sound like a vacation. She struggled on.

One day, the band of demons sent to the far Western Wilds returned with a group of souls and bad news. Hell was crumbling at its edges. The rocky, mountainous area was an avalanche of gravel. Mountains had crumbled into dust; the dust was fading into nothing.

THIRTY-ONE

The Middle of the End

ETERNITY WAS NO LONGER ON THEIR SIDE, IF IT EVER had been. They worked round the clock, taking only minutes at a time to rest. Demons had no time to torment or argue with souls; they were working with Brian better than they ever had. The strange camaraderie in Hell grew stronger. Souls wandered in from every edge of Hell—telling stories of crumbling ground, of lava pits going cold, an encroaching nothing. Some souls could not be accounted for. There wasn't much anyone could do. The team worked harder. Every soul, even the fragments, every beetle and winged rat they could find was gathered and put on the train.

They kept ticking off souls from the database, more with every movement of the great clock of bone that hung over the station house. One day, just when they thought they were making headway, Belial, the former administrator of the Lake of Fire, now leading the brigade to pluck burning souls out of it and bring them to the train, came back with a truckload of souls and an extraordinary announcement.

"The lake of fire is out cold," he said flatly. He dumped out some souls whose charred skin was no longer smoking. "Feel this guy." He thumbed at a large man wearing the remains of a blackened suit.

Brian reached out, touched the man's sleeve. "Clammy."

Arabella—the fallen angel collecting soul fragments from the edge of the Abyss—also returned.

"Lava Falls no longer falls," she said. "River Nepenthe is dry, the Abyss crumbling sand. It has ceased releasing soul fragments." In her long thin fingers, she held a squirming black bag. "These are the last."

Brian checked his list. "Still a few souls to get on the train. Who knows . . . maybe we can do it. I'd like to at least accomplish my last task."

The train station pulsed with energy. Liz and Ellie stood by the doors of the train cars marking the registry of souls. Hagatha sent out final scouts. Theo lifted elderly souls onto the train. Brian was a blur of action.

Liz worked through a fog of fatigue, forcing herself to put one foot in front of the other. She moved back and forth from station to office as more and more action now centered on loading the train. All she could think about was settling into a train seat and putting her head on Brian's woolen shoulder. It kept her moving.

She was going back to the office to let Brian know that the entire City of Dis had been crossed off the evacuation list, when she saw his sweater hanging over the chair, the crinkled note sticking out of the pocket. In the days since they'd returned to Perdition City, she'd noticed him touching it. Patting his pocket. Rereading it, frowning.

Sam had just left the office for a final trip to the men's room. He told her Brian had gone to evacuate the housing imps who'd been helping coordinate the exodus. She never knew what possessed her—and she was overwhelmed with guilt at the mere thought. She reached into the pocket and pulled out the note.

It read:

BRIAN,

Goodbye and good riddance. Remember that I mixed you with darkness from that pit of monsters. You felt it when you talked to them, didn't you? You know what that means. I needed a manager who would stay in fucking Hell. Remember that time you tried to get out through the tunnel, and it collapsed? Hilarious if it hadn't cost so much to repair. You're just like the worms. Well. You sort of are one. Keep trying to exist—you'll tear the place down. Mammon is asking why I'm writing this. I don't know.

I guess I hate you. You were my worst mistake. You were supposed to make things easy, never ask questions. I totally got your recipe wrong. Also, I guess I needed to make you feel bad one more time before the end. My therapist says you can't let these things fester.

Not really yours,

SATAN

Liz shoved the note back into his pocket. She tried to make sure it was sticking out just as it had been before. What did it mean? Very little, she suspected—just another cruelty. But the line about Brian's existence; he'd told her before that he couldn't exist outside Hell. Liz didn't have time to puzzle it out. It was like the time she bit the inside of her mouth and then kept biting it every time she ate; a sore spot she couldn't attend to, growing ever more painful and raw. When she could, she smiled at Brian, pressed his hand, gave him a quick hug. He smiled back, and she saw his hand going to his pocket.

As they were dashing to the station together, she said, "Brian, you know how we've talked about you being—real?"

"Yeah." He shifted a box onto his other hip.

"You said you really liked me even though you weren't made to like people, right?" Liz tried to shift the bag of snacks for the train that was cutting into her left arm. Brian reached down and took it from her. "That means that you're more than what you were made to be, right?" She was nervous that he would know she'd read his letter.

"I suppose so," he said. "I believe that whenever I'm hanging out with you, anyway."

They walked on in silence for a few minutes pushing alongside the steady stream of evacuees that were also heading for the station. It reminded Liz of that first crazy day when she'd followed Brian to Admin.

"Well, Satan was very rude to you at Joe's," Liz said. "I think he's trying to make you believe things that aren't true. I'm just saying he's a liar and you should remember that."

"He's the worst kind of liar," Brian said. "The worst liar is the one who sometimes tells the truth. Because you never know when they're lying."

Liz stopped for a second—a small herd of rat demons ran under her feet towards the station. Brian paused beside her.

"I just want you to know that one of the things that's getting me through all this is thinking about hanging out with you on the other side. I mean, in addition to sexy time that Satan was so rude about, I just like being with you. I'm not trying to pressure you into an eternity of anything. I'm just saying that you're one of the best friends I've ever had. I just want that to keep being true."

"Liz," Brian leaned over the top of his boxes and kissed her head. "You will always be the best friend I ever had in this eternity or any other one they can throw at me."

"Promise?" Liz asked.

"Cross my heart, if I have one," Brian smiled.

THIRTY-TWO

The Actual End

THE MORNING DAWNED—THE LAST DAY. EVERYONE knew it. The clock was moving at a breakneck speed. Liz was nervous. They had been as successful as they could have hoped—and yet there were still souls lined up to get on the train. They met up at the Admin Building for the last time. Stygian darkness loomed on the horizon.

"I think we can do it," Brian stood in the office, surveying the last stack of checklists. "Should be able to get everyone on the train today if we push. Everyone, grab what's left of the coffee. Let's get to the station."

Everyone turned to go. "Joe," Brian said. "Can you stay behind for a second?"

Liz turned and stopped, puzzled. Brian smiled at her and waved her out of the office. "Go on, I'll catch up."

She turned to go. When she glanced back, she saw Brian take the letter out of his sweater pocket and hand it to Joe.

When Liz reached the station, they were still loading souls. Panic was increasing. The always insipid light of Hell was fading rapidly. Instead of yellow and orange the western sky was black. Oblivion encroached. What bland light there was hovered over Perdition City. Visible sky grew smaller, an ever-tightening circle. The ground had rumbled occasionally as the edges of Hell crumbled into dust. The tremors were almost constant. There was more pushing and shoving as souls and demons recognized the same thing. Still, things were more orderly than anyone could have expected.

Hagatha was moving souls with her tail while Brendle marked checklists. Liz nervously watched for Brian and Joe. They arrived about ten minutes after everyone else. She waved at Joe; he didn't wave back. She had no time to think about it. Brian ran back and forth to the office, even checked the bathrooms in the station to make sure no fearful souls had tried to take refuge there.

A group of exhausted gargoyles flew in and settled in front of the train to report that the arctic regions had melted, then dissolved into nothing. A flock of imps announced the Bitter Forest was no more.

The team kept moving passengers over the roar of destruction that closed in on Perdition City. By lunchtime the ground beneath the platform had begun to noticeably quiver. Behind the Admin Building, there was nothing, just flat blackness. Hagatha carried a small man and his pet demon lizard. Brendle had a ghost demon in a jar.

"That's all for me. There can't be any more out there and if there are . . . well, good luck to them," Hagatha said.

Brendle groaned. "I've done all I can do." Hagatha reached down and rubbed Brendle's neck.

All the souls who had come or been brought to the station had at last been loaded. They were down to staff and miscellaneous souls that had either been in hiding or didn't understand the order. Edgar, the huge black crow who had been Liz and Hagatha's taxi driver, swooped in and landed on a broken light post.

"It has reached the city," he intoned wearily. "If there are any other souls, I cannot find them. They have surely become one with the nothing."

The platform shivered as he flew up to the train and ducked inside the car. Around them, the station buildings creaked. Somewhere close by, close enough to make Liz jump, a window cracked like a gunshot.

The last of Hell's citizens now stood on the platform.

"All aboard," Sam said. "Ladies first." He helped Ellie onto the train and then offered his arm to Hagatha.

She rolled her eyes. "I've got this, dude," she said, and leapt onto the train, sweeping Brendle up behind her on the train, then Sam.

"This is it. The first and last train out of Hell," Brian said. Behind him, a tall black tower from across the city fell with a great crash. The ground shook again.

"Do we have everyone?" Liz asked.

"Everyone that wanted to take the chance, surely."

The train sat trembling on the tracks, puffing steam as the last of Hell's citizens clambered aboard.

Liz said, "I'm scared. The rest of eternity is waiting out there. If we make it."

"Yes, time to go," Brian agreed. He pointed at Gadreel, Jezreel and a couple of the blue demons who were left standing on the tracks. "C'mon, people!"

He called to the clusters of demons huddled on the red banks that led the train tracks out of Hell. The hillside was beginning to tremble. "Get on top of the train!" he called out. "Ride this one out! It's time!"

In some confusion, they clustered on the top of the overstuffed train cars and scrambled to dig claws into the windows on the side. A red rock rolled from the top of one of the banks and landed next to the train. Liz scurried up the steps of the caboose.

Brian climbed up on the back of the caboose next to her and handed her a carrier with Dennis inside. The little demon had become so frantic the day before that Liz had repurposed a small cage to keep him from scratching her arms off on the train.

Brian took Liz's hand for just a brief second and leaned forward and gave her a kiss. "Thanks!" he whispered. "I love you. You made me real. Even if it was just for a little while. Remember me. You know you'll always be my best friend. And the love of my eternity."

"I love you, too." Liz gripped his hand hard. He loved her. It had always been love. The memories came rushing back. Brian pushing obnoxious souls out the window; Brian secretly trading lunches with her and taking the moldy sandwich or the impermeable soup. Stolen kisses, his hand touching hers, her cheek pressed into his warm, sweatered chest. Love. Solid and real. Bigger than her whole existence. Nothing could part them.

The ground quivered under the train and the whistle blew. Liz kept her grip on Brian's hand, and he smiled, but then he pulled his hand away and stepped off the edge of the caboose and back onto the platform.

"Brian, what are you doing? Take my hand!" Liz reached out for him; he leaned forward and touched her hand one last time, a fleeting brush of fingers—nothing more.

He shook his head. "I love you, Liz, but I was made for Hell. I can't go. You have to get to safety, and I'll be—" his words were drowned out by the train whistle and the reverberating sound of falling buildings on the far side of the city.

The train started to huff and tremble forward, and Liz reached back again, flailed, gripping his fingers in hers. Rocks rained down on the top and bounced up to the caboose platform.

Dennis wailed, "Ow! Get inside the train you idiot! Ow! Help, I'm being pelted with rocks!"

Liz ignored him. "Brian, please! Give me your hand," she urged, leaned forward, trying to take his hand entirely in hers. His fingers slipped away. The train began to move in earnest.

"Brian!" Liz screamed. Her voice fell flat into the swirling dust, drowning in the noise of Hell's destruction.

She felt Joe's arms around her. He was pulling her backwards. "He can't leave. He was made for Hell. If he tries to leave, the tunnel will collapse around him and take the train with it."

"No!" Liz screamed. "No, that's not fair!" She was clambering onto the back of the caboose trying to reach him when she felt Hagatha's powerful tail wrap around her waist.

The last thing Liz saw of Hell was Brian standing alone on the oscillating platform. Behind him the main office swayed, almost gracefully for something so squat and ugly, then collapsed. Brian still stood waving while Hell collapsed around him. He appeared calm and efficient in his bow tie. She saw him take off his glasses and wipe his eyes, then he wiped the tortoiseshell spectacles on his button-down shirt. The thick dust of Hell's collapse obscured him from her view.

SOMEWHERE, A TRAIN IS PUFFING ALONG THE TRACKS, just this side of eternity. No one knows exactly where it's going. Now it moves through a dark tunnel; the riders sleep. Now it stops in a quaint village; passengers disembark and eat at one of the inns along the way. Most return to the train; some remain. Sometimes new passengers join the train.

The train stops in a sleepy golden meadow. A tall creature with a tail and a mohawk and a smaller, curvy creature in a tight red dress get off the train. Between them they carry a basket. A young woman follows them with a large cat. Together they make their way to the center of the field. The two holding the basket bend down and open the lid. Dark, bat-like creatures flutter out of the basket and into the air. At first, the heavy golden air pushes the bat-creatures to the ground; they flail and jerk. After a few moments in the sun the tattered creatures rise, and the sky fills with colored butterflies and birds. For the first time since she left her former home as a refugee, the young woman laughs. A beautiful gold and green bird settles on the cat's head and gently pecks at his nose. The woman picks up the cat and they watch birds and butterflies rise and fly until the last one is a speck in the distance. After a moment of silence, they hear the whistle blow, return to the train. It moves into the distance.

Toward a mountain town.

ACKNOWLEDGEMENTS

I simply could not have written this book without the help and guidance of my publishers, Shanna McNair and Scott Wolven, who worked on every aspect of the story from development through publication. It would be hard to find better companions to help a person get through Hell.

A special thanks to Jeffrey Ford both for his foreword and for his guidance in workshopping the story and shaping my writing style.

I would also like to thank a variety of friends and editors who read the book in various stages:

Scott Branks del Llano, Lindz McLeod, Josh Brandon, and Blake Carpenter. Thanks also to Ben Turner, a terrific copy editor whose detailed examination of the book was incredible.

And finally, I don't want to forget all the preachers who preached long and hard about Hell in the churches of my childhood. While we might not agree on the theology of hell, I owe them the stories and trauma that formed the narrative of this book.

ABOUT THE AUTHOR

Julie Price Carpenter graduated from Tennessee Wesleyan with a BA in English Literature, and an MA in Professional Writing from University of Memphis.

She is the author of the Linked Short Story Collection, *Things Get Weird in Whistlestop*, which was the President's Book Award winner for the Florida Authors and Publishers Association for 2019. Julie is a Pushcart nominee for "Letter to Essie" in *The New Guard VII*. She published "Camping with Barbie and Ken" in *The New Guard X* and has published four stories online on Fiction on the Web.

As a former evangelical, and therefore an expert on Hell, she cohosts the podcast "Perdition City Station". Along with her cats, she administrates the Sacred Chickens blog, which publishes original fiction and poetry, book reviews and blog posts on various subjects.